SF   Forward. Robert L.
FORWARD Timemaster

88049492

TIMEMASTER

TIMEMASTER

Dr. Robert L. Forward

A TOM DOHERTY ASSOCIATES BOOK
NEW YORK

TIMEMASTER

Copyright © 1992 by Robert L. Forward

A Tor Book
Published by Tom Doherty Associates, Inc.
49 West 24th Street
New York, N.Y. 10010

Tor ® is a registered trademark of Tom Doherty Associates, Inc.

Library of Congress Cataloging-in-Publication Data

Forward. Robert L.
        Timemaster / Robert L. Forward.
            p.   cm.
        "A Tom Doherty Associaties book."
        ISBN 0-312-85214-2
        I. Title.
    PS3556.0754T55   1992
    813'.54—dc20
                                    92-3276
                                    CIP

First edition: May 1992

Printed in the United States of America

0 9 8 7 6 5 4 3 2 1

DEDICATION

To the original Timemaster, Albert Einstein—who taught us our first grappling-holds on that slippery and relentless foe of us all . . . Father Time.

ACKNOWLEDGMENTS

A hard science fiction novel draws upon many sources of factual information. That information has been laboriously gathered or deduced, and then published, by many researchers, scientific, engineering, and literary, scattered over decades of time. A few of the specific publications that I used the most in writing this novel are listed in the bibliography.

In addition, there are many people who gave me novel ideas, valuable insight, or factual information that contributed significantly (sometimes by showing me it *couldn't* be done that way) to my fictitious story of a universe in which time machines could exist. When the story follows the reader's personal version of the "known scientific facts," the people I acknowledge below can take most of the credit. When the science unrolled in the story begins to raise doubts in the reader's mind, then it is my responsibility. Either: (1) I made a mistake in my interpretation of the science, (2) my interpretation of the "known scientific facts" does not agree with the reader's interpretation, or (3) I followed the Final Law of Storytelling—

"Never let the facts get in the way of a good story."

With this understanding, I would like to acknowledge the help of the following people: Paul Birch, David Garfinkle, Todd B. Hawley, Hans P. Moravec, Michael S. Morris, Gerald D. Nordley, Paul A. Penzo, Kip S. Thorne, and Matt Visser. I also want to thank David Hartwell for his extensive and helpful editorial comments.

➢   ➢   ➢

There exist semieducated but obstinate people who have raised the concept of strict local causality to godhead, and attempt to use such words as "obviously" and "it only makes sense that . . ." in an attempt to "prove" that their version of causality cannot be violated, and that *any* sort of time machine is logically impossible. From my reading of the scientific literature, they are wrong. If I receive a letter from this sort of person complaining about the "impossibility" of the time machines in this novel, I will throw the letter in the nearest wastebasket . . . *unless* the letter is accompanied by a reprint of a scientific paper published in *Physical Review* (or any other reputable, refereed scientific journal), written by the person writing the letter, which *proves* that the paper "Cauchy Problem in Spacetimes with Closed Timelike Curves" by Friedman, Morris, Novikov, Echeverria, Klinkhammer, Thorne, and Yurtsever, is erroneous.

CONTENTS

TIMEMASTER

1 ➢➢

Silver Threads up in the Sky

THE music from Holst's *The Planets* filled the interior of the cavernous Rolls-Royce Silver Shadow parked at the very end of the road at Cape May on the southern tip of New Jersey. The young couple in the front seat were sitting slightly apart from each other, holding hands and looking up at the bright full moon rising in the east.

The young man, Randy Hunter, was very small in stature, but had the muscular build of a weight lifter. His wavy chestnut-brown hair was tied back in a "Paul Revere" by a pearlidescent ribbon, while his expensive, custom-robotailored evening suit sported a matching pearlidescent throat choker. A graded set of large pearls climbed up his right ear, and from his left earlobe dangled the world-famous Venus's Tear. The young woman, Rose Cortez, was small and dark-complexioned, with short ringlets of dark-brown hair, deep brown eyes, and a full-bodied figure with a wasp waist. Like all women in 2036, her face was devoid of makeup and jewelry.

Just above the moon was a slender silver thread. Together they watched as the thread, seemingly keeping time with the majestic music, rotated slowly in its lunar orbit like a brilliantly illuminated spoke on an otherwise invisible, gigantic Ferris wheel rolling along the lunar surface.

"Watching the moon rise is sure a lot more interesting than it used to be a few years ago," said Rose.

"Wait until my Rotovator Division gets the next two Lunavators installed in their oblique orbits," replied Randy. "Then one of them should always be visible in the sunlight, even during a new moon."

One end of the silver thread touched down at the north pole of the moon, then lifted off again.

Another thirty thousand for the income side of the Reinhold Astroengineering Company ledgers, Randy thought in satisfaction. *Not much, but in twenty-eight minutes the other end will touch down and I'll get another thirty thousand. A little here . . . a little there . . . it all adds up.*

Passing slowly by one side of the moon was another silver thread in a low Earth orbit. This thread was one terminal of the cable catapult system for transportation to and from the asteroid belt. The thread had two beads strung on it—a small bead at one end and a much larger one just short of the other end. The smaller bead started to move along the thread at high acceleration. It went faster and faster, passed through the large bead, and shot off the end of the thread out into space. When the crew in the high-speed bead reached the other cable catapult out in the asteroid belt, the process would be repeated in the reverse direction.

"Another of my prospecting crews off to the asteroid belt," Randy murmured to himself. "I wonder what they'll find out there next?"

Randy's cuff computer chirped a warning. He silenced the alarm with a brusque "I hear you." Releasing Rose's hand, he reached over to the car stereo controls. The digital bits of music that trickled from the petarom cartridge of classical music ceased their flow, and the quadraphonic speakers in the car switched to the sounds of a crowd at a racetrack. Rose looked slightly annoyed.

"I've got Silver Sailor entered in the feature race at Santa Anita in California," Randy explained quickly, then listened attentively as the announcer went through the lineup for the race.

➤   ➤   ➤

Far out in the asteroid belt, two Reinhold Astroengineering Company prospectors left their spacecraft and used their jetpacks to investigate a strange find. The identification patches on the backs of their fluorescent-red outeralls identified them as Jim Meriweather and Bob Pilcher.

"There it is, Bob," Jim said, pointing. "On the other side of that nickel-iron knob."

"Holy spaghetti!" Bob exclaimed. As the two moved closer, they could see a giant ball of silver threads floating motionless in the windless emptiness of space. It was a good ten meters in diameter and made of thousands of long, thin, shining threads coming from a compact center. "I've heard of metallic whisker clumps forming in space before, but none with whiskers this long. Must be some sort of rare ultrapure nickel-iron ore. I'll get a video of it." Bob activated the camera in his chestpack and scanned the scene. "Reminds me of a toy I used to have as a kid—I think it was called a Koosh-Ball."

"I'll jet over and get a sample," said Jim, taking out his prospector's tool and a collection bag. His jets fired and he moved closer to the strange mineral formation. Suddenly the sphere of threads grew larger and fanned out toward the approaching figure.

"Watch out, Jim!" called Bob. "It's coming after you!"

"Migod!" exclaimed Jim. "The damn thing is alive!" His fingers danced desperately across his chestpack, and his jets fired in an attempt to reverse his motion toward the silvery creature. The exhaust from the jets excited the creature into more violent action. The threads reached for him with a twirling motion, as if they were feeding on the exhaust plumes. One of the threads struck Jim on the arm.

"Ow!" Jim called out in pain. "It got me!"

The contact must have been painful to the creature, too, for it immediately drew back and shrank in size, leaving behind a two-meter segment of severed thread rotating slowly in space.

"What happened, Jim?" said Bob as he jetted to the rescue.

"One of those damn silver threads sliced open my arm!" Jim growled between clenched teeth, his right tightsuited hand holding his left forearm. Between his fingers oozed bubbles of frothy blood.

"Is your suit tourniquet working?" Bob asked.

"I think so, but I'm beginning to feel woozy," Jim replied.

Bob looked over at the strange creature that had attacked Jim. It was now only two meters across, and still shrinking in size, but its form was still just that of a ball made of thousands of silvery threads. The only difference now was that the threads were much shorter. There was no evidence of any "body" underneath all the silvery "hair."

"The threads from the creature are pulling back," said Bob, grabbing Jim by his backpack. He activated his chestpack jets to take them both back to their ship parked nearby. "Let's get you to a medic."

"While we're on the way in, you should transmit your video to Philippe," said Jim.

"You're right," replied Bob. "Boss-man Randy is going to flip when Philippe tells him what we've found."

➤   ➤   ➤

"Silver Sailor won!" yelled Randy excitedly as he switched the car stereo back to music. "I knew he would be a contender. Now I'm *definitely* going to ride him in the Belmont Stakes this June."

"I wish you wouldn't do that," said Rose, a concerned note in her voice. "You could get hurt like you did last year. You're too important to your company to take chances like that."

"It's *my* company. I have no stockholders to be concerned about. If I get hurt and my company suffers, the only one who loses money is me, so I can do what I like," Randy snapped.

"What about your employees?" reminded Rose. "What about me? Don't you care about *us*?"

Randy slid across the seat, took Rose in his arms, and gave her a kiss. She responded coolly.

"I've *got* to do it," pleaded Randy. "What's the use of having the best horses in the world if you don't ride them?" He shook his head in disgust. "I don't understand those corpulent hippos who collect horses like they do corporations . . . and have the nerve to call themselves horsemen." He paused and smiled to himself. "When I'm sitting up on my winner, they sure look small standing down there beside their also-rans!"

"You certainly are competitive, aren't you?" said Rose, cocking her head to one side to look at him.

"You bet, baby," said Randy. "I intend to be the biggest and the bestest in everything." His face took on a wry look. "Zap that. Biggest I'll never be. But bestest I *will* be. I'll *be* the best and *have* the best." He drew her close for another kiss. "I'm off to a good start," he murmured in her ear. "I've got the best woman in the universe for a girlfriend. How about becoming the best wife in the universe?" He kissed her long and hard.

"You know the answer to that one," she said, as their lips finally parted. "I'm not ready to commit myself yet. When I get married, I intend to stay married, have some children, and see that they're raised properly." She paused as she considered her next sentence. "You'd be a hard man to live with, Randy. Your wishes come first—and always will. I'm not sure I want to subject myself and my children to your life-style, grandiose though it may be."

"Grandiose," Randy mused. "That's a good word for it. I have the ability and wherewithal to do anything I want to do . . . except be an artist," he added.

"You're getting much better now that you've switched from charcoal to oils," said Rose.

"I never did understand why artists do charcoal sketches," said Randy. "To me, it's just another way to get your hands dirty. I had to scrub my hands for twenty minutes after every class before I got all the black out of my pores. I prefer oils—much cleaner."

"Most artists get grubbier using oils than charcoal," said Rose. "But not *you*. After each session, out goes the whole palette, and you start with a fresh one the next session. Same with the brushes. Change colors, change brushes. Haven't you heard of brush cleaner?"

"Messy," said Randy with a grimace. "Besides, all it costs is money—and I've got lots of that. Enough to do anything I want to do."

There was a long pause. Rose's face turned serious.

"What *do* you want to do?" she asked.

"Marry *you*!" said Randy quickly, reaching for her again.

"Not that," said Rose, pushing him away with an annoyed frown. "What do you *really* want to do with your life?"

Randy leaned back and thoughtfully considered her question. He had asked himself that many times and had come up with an answer—four answers. Now he was considering them once again before he bared this very private part of his soul to this woman. A woman he loved almost as much as he loved himself.

"I want four things," he said finally. "I want to be the best horseman in the world. I want to be the richest and most important man in the solar system. I want to explore the stars. And . . . I want to live forever." He paused, then added, "But marrying *you* comes first."

Rose wasn't listening. Her heart had sunk lower and lower as she heard Randy reel off his list of dreams. There wasn't much room for her in them. If she wanted this man, she would have to take whatever she could get, whenever his drives and ambitions gave him a few moments' respite.

"You don't dream small, Harold Randolph Hunter," she said. "But I don't doubt you are going to achieve those goals . . . at least most of them."

"Then you're going to marry me?" said Randy brightly, sitting up.

"Not so fast!" said Rose, her face raised haughtily. "I'm just as hard to get as those other goals of yours. You have a lot of work ahead of you, young man."

"Always bringing in that two-year age difference," said Randy. He stopped abruptly as a thought came to him. "I've got a way to fix *that*. I'll simply build a relativistic interstellar spacecraft and send you on a round-trip journey to Alpha Centauri. When you come back you'll be *younger* than me."

"You aren't getting me in any cramped, dreary, interstellar tin can, Mr. Buck Rogers Hunter," replied Rose.

"We shall see . . . we shall see," said Randy thoughtfully.

"Here comes your Terravator," said Rose, pointing toward the north. Another silver thread, thicker than the others in the sky, loomed larger and larger over the horizon. As the Terravator rose, the tip of it rotated downward toward the Earth. It was still in the process of construction, since it had to be much longer and more massive than the silver thread now rotating around the Moon. They continued to watch as the Terravator pole-vaulted its way majestically toward the south to the strains of the "Saturn" movement.

"The resort hotel on the Terravator is almost finished," said Randy. "I ought to go up and check out the penthouse apartment. Want to come along?"

"Remember what I promised my mother when I left home," reminded Rose.

"You can have a separate bedroom on some other floor of the hotel."

"Separate *roofs* is what she said," said Rose. "I'm sorry . . . no."

"Maybe for our honeymoon," said Randy eagerly, reaching for her again.

"I haven't said yes yet," Rose reminded him in a muffled voice. But within the next half hour she did say "Yes" *and* had picked a date for the wedding.

As the hour grew later the winds faded, and the fog bank that had been waiting offshore rolled in on them. They soon were shielded from peering eyes in neighboring cars by their own private grey hemisphere, subtly lit from above by the bright full moon.

A number of minutes passed in silence. Since Randy didn't seem to be engaged in conversation, his cuff-comp chirped quietly from inside his sleeve.

"Mmmm," said Randy, to shut it up. The cuff-comp obediently went quiet.

"You really liked that kiss?" asked Rose as they finally broke apart.

"I like them all!" said Randy, leaning toward her again.

"Then why did you go 'mmmm' at *that* one?" asked Rose. "What did I do that was different?"

"I was just telling my cuff-comp to be quiet," said Randy.

"Oh . . ." said Rose, slightly disappointed. Randy leaned over to kiss her again. She turned away, asking pointedly, "Aren't you going to answer it?"

"Naw," said Randy. "Probably some business. But you're the most important item on my agenda tonight."

Rose, like most modern people, had an instinctive reaction that a chirping telephone took precedence over anything else. She sat up.

"Answer it!" she said. "It might be something important."

The magic of the moment broken, Randy pushed up his sleeve and pulled down the cuff-comp. "You're probably right," he said. "It's not supposed to page me outside working hours." He punched the icons and an electrofax flashed into view. It was from Reinhold security.

Urgent encrypted message from Hygiea mining base in outer asteroid belt.

"Get me security," said Randy to the cuff-comp, and instantly the face of the uniformed guard at the security post at the mansion was on the screen. She obviously had been waiting for him to return the page.

"You called about the message, Mr. Hunter?" said the guard.

"Yes," said Randy. "Any clues as to why it was urgent? All I have at Hygiea is a small base to support the prospector ships."

"I don't have any idea, Mr. Hunter," said the guard. "Except it was marked 'Eyes Only.'"

Randy looked perturbed. Whatever the message was, it wasn't anything ordinary. Major new ore findings, serious personnel problems, even major accidents, should all go to the manager of the Space Operations Division, with only a copy for him. Besides, the boss of Hygiea Base, Philippe Laurin, was a calm space veteran who didn't get excited over trivia.

"I'm putting my cuff-comp into scramble mode," said Randy. "Send it over."

"Right away, sir!" said the guard, her face lighting up. She switched off the screen. Randy punched the icons on the screen to set the cuff-comp so it could receive the scrambled message. Within a second, the screen said *Ready*. Randy lifted his head as he tried to recall a semi-nonsense phrase that he and Philippe had memorized together long ago before Philippe had left to take his new post. Translating the phrase into numbers, he punched in the long string. The cuff-comp flickered for a second as it decrypted the message. The message flashed on the screen.

Found alien life-form. Only one example so far. No accompanying artifacts. Will send video shortly. More as I learn more.

Randy's mind whirled as he tried to imagine what Philippe had found. Unfortunately, he would have to wait to find out, for it would take a fairly long time to transmit a video in scramble mode all the way from the asteroid belt. He cleared the screen and had the cuff-comp erase and wipe both versions of the message as well as his password from its memory. You couldn't be too careful, what with all the sophisticated industrial-espionage techniques that existed today. Reinhold Astroengineering Company, being the leader, was always being monitored by those companies less capable and less scrupulous.

"What did it say?" asked Rose.

"The fewer people who know, the better," said Randy, not really paying attention to her as his mind raced furiously over the various possibilities.

"Don't you trust me?" said Rose, pouting.

"No," said Randy, unthinkingly, his mind still whirling. Then, suddenly realizing what he had said, he pushed the cuff-comp back up his sleeve and slid across the seat to try to thaw out his stiffly frozen Rose. It didn't work. With a resigned sigh, he slid back to the driver's seat, activated the custom button that raised the seat upward and forward, and recklessly drove the Silver Shadow at high speed out to the major interstate heading north, gravel flying from his Michelin diamond-belted radials.

He finally got Rose back in his arms about halfway down the turnpike as the Rolls's computer wafted them rapidly along the autopilot lane back to her apartment in Princeton. She didn't find out what was in the message, however.

➤   ➤   ➤

The next day Randy went to the secure room in the security office on his large estate, and looked at the video that had been decoded during the night. He would have preferred to talk to Philippe directly, but the round-trip delay time to Hygiea was almost an hour.

"It is truly amazing, Mr. Hunter," said Philippe's video image. Philippe Laurin was an older man with a pudgy face, a classic Gallic nose, a bald dome, and a mustache so massive it merged with his bushy sideburns. He had school 'rings in both earlobes, one from the French Space Academy.

The video image switched to a chestpack camera showing what looked like a nest of thousands of fine silver threads. The threads sprouted from a tiny spherical region at the center and spread out many meters in all directions. As the space-suited figure with the name "Jim Meriweather" on the back approached the object, the threads suddenly became alive and started to grow longer.

"Jim Meriweather and Bob Pilcher found the 'Silverhair' feeding on an asteroid. When Jim got too close, the threads started to reach for him. He tried to get away by using his suit jets, but that was a mistake. He ran into one of the threads and it nearly cut his arm off. The automatic tourniquet mode of the electrolastic in his tightsuit activated, and kept him under pressure and prevented excessive loss of blood. Fortunately, Bob was right there and got him back to the medic in a hurry. He'll be all right once the cut heals. The cut, however, went all the way through one bone in his left forearm. Bob reports, however, that the Silverhair's thread suffered worse than Jim's arm."

The video picture switched to a close-up of a single silvery thread rotating slowly in space.

"The thread that touched Jim was severed by the contact, as if a section of it had evaporated," continued Philippe. "What is most strange is, when the engineers later took a close look at Jim's tightsuit, they found the material had not been cut. The weave in the fabric didn't match up, indicating there was a thin section missing, as if it had evaporated. Our first guess was that the creature was made of antimatter, and the thread had annihilated its way through Jim's arm, but that would have released a lot of energy and hard radiation. Both Jim and Bob saw nothing, and the radiation monitors on their suits show nothing unusual happening at that time."

The video picture switched back to Philippe's face.

"That's all I have for now, but I have a crew on the way out to learn more," he said. The screen went blank.

Randy had a million questions to ask, but the one-hour communications time delay made two-way conversation impossible.

⮞   ⮞   ⮞

"I've got to get out there in a hurry," said Randy, extremely agitated. He glared at the three faces his cuff-comp had brought together in a conference call.

In the center of his screen was the image of Anthony Guiliano, manager of the Cable Transportation Group. Tony was looking his usual dapper self, his Paul Revere held in a subdued ribbon in red-and-grey silk plaid, a matching throat choker, and engineering school 'rings glittering in each ear—MIT on the left, Cal Tech on the right, and a Tau Beta Pi tucked discreetly away under the upper-left earshell.

"I'm sorry, Mr. Hunter," Tony said nervously to the annoyed image of his youthful boss. "The best our asteroid cable-catapult transportation system can do is eighty-five days. Hygiea is in the outer part of the asteroid belt, and on the opposite side of the Sun to boot."

"Eighty-five days!" exploded Randy. "That's almost three months!"

Flanking Tony's image on the right was "Bull" Richardson, manager of the Cable Catapult Division in Tony's group. Bull was seven feet tall and built like a bull. He had a permanent case of severe psoriasis that resisted all attempts to treat it. Bull had stuck with the now unfashionable skinhead look of a few decades ago. The red patches on his shaven skull looked bad, but not as bad as a Paul Revere full of huge flakes of dandruff.

Bull's image replied. "I can cut a little off the time by cutting the payload in the capsule and increasing the acceleration of the cable catapult to five gees," he said, nervously scratching the back of his neck. The red patches on his head were reacting to the stress he was under.

"How much time?" demanded Randy.

"I can get you there in sixty days," said Bull.

Randy snorted impatiently. "Not good enough! This could be the most important discovery of the century—maybe even the millennium. I want to be there and get things under my control before the word leaks out and every Tom, Dick, and Oscar is demanding I turn it over 'for the common good of all mankind.' Don't we have a longer cable?"

To the left of Tony was the image of Mary Lewis, manager of Tony's Rotovator Division, and Bull's wife. Mary's greying hair, instead of being in a proper, feminine short bob, was long and pulled back in a mannish Paul Revere. She even had school 'rings in her ears, just like a man. Her only concession to femininity was the flowery pattern on her hair ribbon and throat cloth. Randy noticed that the pink flowers and green leaves were in the Reinhold company colors.

"Sorry, sir," said Mary, the perky nose on her image twitching under her large glasses as she thought. "I'd be glad to turn over all the cable we've been making for the Mars rotovator, but by the time Bull's division could turn it into a cable catapult, you'd be there using the existing system."

"Can we push the gee limit higher?" asked Randy.

"Well . . . yes . . ." admitted Bull. "We have small express pods we use to send emergency cargo. We can accelerate those at ten times the normal three-gee launch acceleration and get them up to three hundred kilometers a second."

"How soon would *that* get me there?" asked Randy.

Bull, his fingers too large to operate a cuff-comp, pulled an hp pseudocray out of his shirt pocket, and did a short calculation. "Three weeks," he said. "But those capsules accelerate at *thirty* gees! You'd be squashed flat!"

Randy paused for a while as he thought. "I've read about deep-sea divers who survived at high pressures by breathing an oxygen-carrying liquid," he said. "If I floated in a tank of that, I could handle thirty gees easily."

Tony, Mary, and Bull each thought for a while; then all three nodded, although reluctantly.

"If I were you, I'd check with some medical and diving experts first," said Tony. "It could be hard on your lungs."

"You do that for me," said Randy. "Meanwhile, Bull can fix up an express capsule with an acceleration tank in it." He started to turn off his cuff-comp, then looked at them in the screen again.

"Oh! Bull?" he said.

"Sir?" replied Bull, turning back to the screen.

"Make sure the zero-gee toilet is the latest design." Randy paused. "And put in *two* of them."

"Yessir!" said Bull.

➤   ➤   ➤

That night, Randy had a visitor at his mansion in the Princeton Enclave. Alan Davidson found Randy out in the observatory that Randy had inherited from his father. Alan slipped through the observatory door into pitch-black darkness. As his eyes adjusted, he finally could make out the diminutive figure of Randy looking through the eyepiece of the custom-made telescope.

Randy was looking at the Boötes Void—a gigantic bubble of emptiness outlined by glowing clusters of galaxies.

Megalight-years of nothing . . . Randy thought to himself as he gazed at the dark portion of the sky. For some reason, there was nothing there in that region of the universe . . . and no one knew why.

Randy shifted the telescope slightly and a dense cluster of galaxies swam into view. He stepped down from the makeshift wooden platform on top of the steps, laboriously moved it over, and stepped up again in order to look into the eyepiece more comfortably.

He found a moderately bright guide star, centered it in the cross hairs, and pushed the button that started the automatic tracking and supernova detection routine on the computer. A mirror responded by tilting in front of the eyepiece, blocking his view. The light from the telescope was now going to an imaging array many times more sensitive than photographic film or the human eye. The digital data streaming from the electronic camera would be compared with a digital map of the heavens stored in the memory of the computer. With luck, Randy would detect another extragalactic supernova—or perhaps a comet. He already had one each to his credit, and he was only twenty-four. But then, he didn't sleep much . . . bad dreams, practically every night, since both his parents had died in the crash of his mother's corporate jet. He kept himself from dreaming by coming out to use his dad's telescope whenever there was a chance the sky would be clear.

Randy finally turned to speak to the tall, dark figure waiting patiently against the dark wall of the observatory dome.

"It's all set," he said. "You wanted to see me?"

"I come here both as a friend and as the Sequence Bank trust officer for the Reinhold Trust," said Alan. "I have something serious to discuss with you, and I hope you will listen to me."

"I always do," said Randy. "You're one of the few people I can always rely on. That was why I insisted that you be the trust officer when I took over the company. You were a good friend of Mom and Dad's, and all my life you never treated me as a kid, no matter what age I was. Even now, when most people look at this tiny body I'm stuck with, they immediately assume I'm immature. They don't actually start spouting baby talk at me, but they might as well, from the way they treat me."

"You have always earned my respect, Randolph," said Alan seriously. "Starting with your first lemonade stand at six. You bought your own lemons and sugar at the store instead of getting them from the cook, and you adjusted the selling price of your lemonade to maximize your profits from your market niche."

"I had a corner on the rich bastards going to Enclave school," said Randy with a chuckle. "Soaked them for five dollars a glass." He paused, and an unseen smile spread over his face. "It never occurred to me at the time that I ought to have paid Mom for the use of the car and chauffeur to go get my supplies at the Enclave grocery store."

"Your parents and I were amused by that," said Alan. "But your mother was very understanding. Rich children take a lot of things for granted, like chauffeur-driven cars, but you did less than most. What really impressed us all was that you *saved* most of your profits. I had to bend the rules a bit at Sequence Bank to get you a combined savings and checking account at your age. But you did well with it."

"Sure did," said Randy. "Started my own mail-order software business at thirteen. I didn't realize it at the time, but I got a lot of help from Mom and Dad. When they upgraded their own personal computers, their hand-me-downs were always *just* what I needed for the next phase of my business. At the time I thought I was just lucky."

"I couldn't comment on that," said Alan diffidently.

"You don't have to, Mr. Davidson," said Randy, smiling sadly to himself in the darkness. He continued. "Because of their help, my software business brought almost fifty thousand when I sold it after Reinhold Astroengineering Company was dumped on me at sixteen."

"That demonstration of business ability was one of the reasons the courts decided to let you have control of the company at eighteen, instead of making you wait until you were twenty-one," said Alan. "The last person to do that was Howard Hughes, and he was given control of his father's business when he was nineteen."

"I know," Randy replied. "I've read his biography a number of times. Most people only remember Hughes as an eccentric, secretive billionaire who died without a will. They don't remember that in his younger years he was the greatest aviator in the world, who almost single-handedly demonstrated that worldwide intercontinental air travel was not only safe, but profitable. I want to do the same for the solar system."

The dome was silent as they both looked up through the chill air at the dark starry skies.

"It should be coming over soon," said Randy. "I'll have to blank out the 'scope, or the detector array will be overloaded." He flipped aside the deflecting mirror inside the telescope and waited, looking up out of the slit in the dome.

Alan Davidson looked thoughtfully at the small, dark outline of the young man bathed in starlight. Randy's tiny body was not that of a midget or dwarf, but more like that of a jockey—a perfect four-foot-eleven-inch replica of a normal man's body. Randy had inherited his build from his mother, Golda Reinhold, former president and CEO of Reinhold Astroengineering Company and sole trustee of Reinhold Trust, which owned the company. At board and trust meetings she had used a special chair that elevated her to table level after she had sat down.

Unlike his mother, who was of perfect proportions, Randy had a chunky muscularity to his chest and shoulders, for he religiously lifted weights and practiced karate exercises every morning. No one dared insult Harold Randolph Hunter. The rumors of what had happened to those snobs who did while he was attending the Princeton Enclave High School were enough deterrent now that he was a man.

"Goddamn industrial light polluter—I'll have to write a letter to the owner of the company and complain he's lousing up my supernova searches," muttered Randy.

An object brighter than the moon drifted past the edge of the slit in the dome. The glare almost hurt Alan's dark-adapted eyes.

"There it is! Mom's *tenth* asteroid hauler coming back from the belt!" said Randy proudly. "A thirty-kilometer circle of heavy-duty next-to-nothing bringing back a billion-dollar cargo.

"I'd better have a talk with the engineers," he continued thoughtfully as he critically watched the large lightsail pass overhead. "If the sail were a *perfect* mirror, then *none* of the sunlight would be deflected our way. We ought to work harder on surface finish and wrinkle control for the next models."

He paused and chuckled. "That way I'll get fewer crank letters about light pollution from that pesky amateur astronomer in the Princeton Enclave." His mood changed back to that of a concerned engineer-entrepreneur. "Besides, it's bound to improve the propulsion efficiency too. The faster we can make the round trip, the greater the profits."

There was a formal-sounding knock at the door to the dome. Randy flipped back the deflector mirror on the telescope and climbed down the steps.

"You can come in, James!" called Randy to the door. "Just don't turn on the lights. I've got the telescope open."

The door to the dome opened, showing the rolling hills of the Princeton Enclave, covered with snow and sparkling faintly in the starlight. In the doorway was a dark, rotund shape. Randy could have afforded a robotic butler, but James had been with the family since long before he was born.

"Good evening, Mr. Hunter and Mr. Davidson," said James. "Dinner is ready."

James led the way back up the long pathway to the distant mansion set on one of the large lots in the Princeton Enclave. Princeton Enclave was a walled-off city for the extremely rich. Like a number of other places built at the same time, it was constructed on farmland that had suddenly come on the market when a combination of plant genetic research, cheap power from solar-power satellites, and strict environmental laws had forced the farming industry off open land and into multilevel farmfactory buildings. Princeton Enclave even had its own private shopping center and an exclusive private school that took care of the Enclave's spoiled offspring, from toddlers to teenagers.

At dinner, Alan brought up Randy's proposed trip to the asteroid belt.

"I suppose it was Tony who warned you about my plan," said Randy.

"Not only Tony, but Bull and Mary too," said Alan. "They are all very concerned about your safety."

"Oh . . ."

"What you are proposing to do is very dangerous," said Alan. "There is no need for you to do it. You have competent engineers and scientists already out there in the asteroid belt who can do all the investigations that are needed and report the results back to you here on Earth."

"But I want to *be* there," said Randy firmly.

"But the company needs you here," said Alan. "The only reason banks are willing to give Reinhold Astroengineering Company the huge construction loans we have for the Lunavators and Terravator is that you, like your mother, seem to be able to pull off astroengineering miracles that pay off in the end. If something happens to you, nobody could replace you. The company would lose financial credibility, flounder, and die. The company *needs* you here to manage it."

"I don't want to *manage* the company, I want to *lead* it," said Randy. "Just like Howard Hughes led his company. He not only was the lead designer for nearly every project, he was the test pilot for the first flight of every new airplane his company built."

"And he nearly got killed when one of his airplanes crashed on its first flight," reminded Alan sternly.

"Actually, he crashed at least three airplanes," said Randy. "But he didn't die." His face took on a determined look. "I'm going."

"As the Sequence Bank trust officer for the Reinhold Trust, and good friend of you and your parents, I can't let you do it," said Alan firmly.

Randy's face grew even more determined. "For six years I have obediently taken your advice, Alan," he said. "And I appreciate your present concerns, for both me and my company. But I'm no longer a kid learning the business. I'm twenty-four years old and I know what I'm doing."

"But—" started Alan, but Randy interrupted him.

"I would like to remind *you* that *I* am the sole trustee of the Reinhold Trust that owns the Reinhold Astroengineering Company," Randy stated in a challenging tone. "You are merely the bank trust officer, whom *I* appointed. *I* am the boss of the trust *and* the company . . . and *I* say I'm going."

There was a long silence. Then Alan sighed. "Very well. I and the rest of the managers will do what we can to keep the company running while you are gone."

"I'll be just an electrofax away," replied Randy, trying to lighten things up with a big grin.

➤   ➤   ➤

It was only a few days later that Randy found himself in space, riding one of the silvery threads that he and Rose had observed not long ago. He was on the cable catapult that supplied transportation out to the asteroid belt. The cable was 170,000 kilometers long—thirteen times the diameter of Earth. Randy's capsule was at one end of the long cable, inside the linear motor that would catapult the capsule and him toward the asteroid belt. The power station was near the other end of the cable. Beyond the power station was a shorter section of cable used to decelerate the linear motor to a halt so it would be ready to capture an incoming payload.

The cable itself consisted of six cables in a hexagonal pattern five meters in diameter. Every forty meters there was an external brace structure that supported the six cables from the outside. The linear motor ran along the inside of the hexagonal track on six magnetically levitated rails that magnetically coupled to the superconducting film that covered each cable. The film also acted as a low-loss power line. The six superconducting wires formed a hexagonal transmission line that channeled the rf power that was generated at the main power station and pumped down the transmission line. The power was then absorbed and used by the linear motor, which was designed to be a perfect load for the impedance of the transmission line.

Randy, after purging himself and filling his empty gut with a fiber filler and antigas medicine, carefully scrubbed himself down and put on the high-gee pressurized tank suit.

Next came the contact lenses that would allow him to see the display console through the liquid that would surround him in the tank. Finally, the soft helmet with the hard faceplate that would allow only newly filtered fluid to get to the tender tissues in his lungs. He climbed into the tank and closed the door.

The worst part was the first inhalation of the thin, oxygen-loaded liquid. The membranes in his nose, mouth, and throat had been desensitized by the spray he had inhaled a few minutes ago, but his vivid imagination more than made up for the lack of actual feeling as his nose, throat, and lungs filled with fluid. He was drowning—but he must not panic.

Deep breath, he thought to himself. He watched the bubbles from the bottom of his lungs drift upward past his eyes, where they were scavenged by the exit hose on his helmet. *Deeper*, he admonished himself, and his chest muscles expanded even more, sucking the fluid deeper into the alveoli, where tiny air bubbles were displaced and sent outward as he exhaled.

After a few minutes, Randy was ready. He looked in the submerged videoscreen at the worried face of Bull. Bull's red patches of skin were now scarlet with stress.

"I wish you would call this off," said Bull. "I've done everything I can to make it safe, but I can't make any guarantees when we're pushing the margins so close . . ."

Unable to speak with his vocal cords full of fluid, Randy was reduced to typing out his reply.

YOU MAY FIRE WHEN READY, RICHARDSON.

The countdown proceeded smoothly as the long thread of the cable catapult slowly became aligned with the direction to Hygiea. At the proper instant, the acceleration started as the linear motor surrounding Randy's capsule absorbed the rf power pumped down the center of the cable. The acceleration rapidly grew stronger until it reached thirty gees. Despite the protection of the fluid surrounding and inside him, Randy was pushed heavily into the acceleration couch. The clock on the console ticked slowly down. He would have to endure thirty gees for sixteen full minutes to get up to speed. Normally Randy flew first class. This time he was going steerage.

Finally it was over. Randy was on his way out to the asteroid belt at three hundred kilometers per second—and the rest of the trip was in boring free-fall.

≻　　≻　　≻

Randy kept himself busy on his three-week journey to the asteroid belt by trying to run things over the laser link to Earth. What bothered him the most was the long time delay between messages. At first it was only seconds, but as he approached the orbit of Mars, the round-trip delay took good fractions of an hour and he would forget what he had been talking about when the person finally got around to answering his question. He soon gave up trying to run the company at a distance and let Alan Davidson take over. Instead, he spent his time talking with Philippe Laurin on Hygiea and watching the daily videos being taken as the crew on Hygiea tried to figure out exactly what they had found.

2 ➤➤

Silverhair!

"WE are learning more about the Silverhair each day," said Philippe's image over the tight laser communication link. The video image switched to a camera showing the alien creature with its thousands of fine silvery threads. Near the creature was a small, slender figure in fluorescent-red outeralls with the name "Siritha Chandresekhar" printed across the back. The figure was using its jetpack to sway back and forth in front of the creature, which responded by swaying its threads in synchronism.

"What is she doing so close!" exclaimed Randy. "That creature is dangerous. Look what it did to Jim Meriweather." There was a long pause as the message made its way across the millions of kilometers of space and back again.

"The Silverhair is not really dangerous," replied Philippe calmly. "It was hurt as much as Jim, and since then, it has been careful not to let any of its threads get too close to a human. It *is* curious about us, however. It seems to enjoy its dances with Siritha every day."

"Dances!" exclaimed Randy, not quite believing what he had heard.

Philippe, not yet hearing Randy's reply, continued. "Siritha is our medic. When she was taking premed at U.C. San Diego, she used to work summers at the San Diego Sea World. She's trying a number of her animal training tricks on the Silverhair and they're working. She has gotten it to respond to her motions as she 'dances' in front of it using her jets. She noticed the Silverhair became agitated when jet exhaust came near its threads, as if it were trying to collect as much of the exhaust gases as possible. She is now trying different 'baits' to see which one works best. Any questions?" He paused.

"What does it eat?" asked Randy, finally getting used to the long delays.

"Practically everything," replied Philippe some seconds later. "As long as it's in gaseous form. It actively avoids anything solid or liquid, as if it hurts to touch it, but it positively dotes on any kind of fine dust or gas. It especially likes iron—and there's plenty of that in the asteroid belt."

"Is that why it's there?" asked Randy. "Feeding on the nickel-iron asteroids?"

"Probably so," said Philippe. "We took a close look at the asteroid where we found the Silverhair. It had obviously been feeding on it for a long time, because there was a large, hollow, bowl-shaped depression in the surface of a nickel-iron knob. The surface of the depression was crisscrossed with fine scratches where the threads had somehow torn up the surface. Although it can eat solids, it much prefers its iron in a finely divided form. The engineers modified a plasma-cutter torch for Siritha so it emits plasmas of different metals. That's how they found it prefers iron."

A chime came from the control console in Randy's capsule.

"I'm a few hours away from landing," said Randy. "Got to go into my preconditioning routine for the deceleration tank."

"I'll have a lot more information for you when you arrive," said Philippe.

After purging himself (in the process making a mess of the backup zero-gee toilet), Randy got into his suit, climbed into the tank, and started the distasteful task of breathing the protective fluid. To keep his mind occupied, he thought about Rose, and the first time he had taken her to see the stables . . .

⮞　　⮞　　⮞

"I've never been to this part of your estate before," Rose said. "I didn't even know it was here."

"Mom bought one of the prime lots in the Princeton Enclave," replied Randy. "A one-by-five-mile plot right in the center, with one end adjoining the golf course. You haven't seen the half of it. Mom had a nature trail set up around that wooded hill over there. She and Dad took walks to the top, had lunch at the little fake castle there on the top, and walked back."

"Say," said Rose brightly, "that sounds like fun. Why don't you and I go on a picnic someday, Randy?"

"Nah!" said Randy, maneuvering his powerful Mercedes at high speeds over the narrow bridge. "I get enough exercise every morning in the gym." The car burst out of the forest onto a large, flat meadow area. There were a number of barns with adjacent office areas, a long row of stables, and, next to the forest they had just left, a long line of small duplex homes for the workers. The yard was busy, with six people, three yard robots, and five beautiful thoroughbred horses in evidence. In the background, on the other side of the exercise yards, was the curved railing of a racetrack. There was even an empty grandstand on the far side of the track.

"Here're my stables," said Randy, jumping out of the car and running around to open Rose's door.

"Looks more like a full-up racecourse to me," said Rose.

Randy looked around. "I guess you could call it that," he said. "The foreman once told me that except for the parking lots this place is as big as Belmont."

Randy took Rose over to a large, dark horse tied to a ring held by a life-sized statue of a jockey.

"Rose," said Randy, "I'd like you to meet Winter Winds and Willie Shoemaker, my hero." He stood in front of the statue and compared heights with his hand. "We're both the same height, four feet eleven inches. I only wish I could ride half as well as Willie did."

The thoroughbred whinnied and Rose rubbed its nose.

A big, burly black man with a bald head came over.

"Hi, Curly," said Randy. "Is Winter Winds ready?"

"Waiting for you to get your practice silks on and weigh in," said Curly. "I'm going to put extra weight on him so the other horses can give him a challenge."

"Good," said Randy, grinning. "We want him in good shape for the Belmont Stakes on the fifth of June. I've been able to clear my calendar for a few days before that. Pencil me in as jockey, with Billy Fraser as backup in case you don't think I've gotten into proper shape before the race."

"You're not going to ride in a real race, are you?" Rose asked with concern.

"Why not?" Randy replied nonchalantly. "I'm certainly built for it. Besides, as Howard Hughes once said when someone asked him why he test-piloted his own airplanes, 'Why should I pay someone else to have all the fun?' "

➤ ➤ ➤

It wasn't always fun. Riding thoroughbred horses and high-speed machines could sometimes turn out to be very uncomfortable. Winter Winds had taken a tumble at Belmont last year. Randy had broken an arm and Winter Winds had broken a foreleg. The vets had wanted to shoot the horse, but Randy wouldn't let them. He flew in the emergency team from the Veterinarian Prosthetics Center in Moscow, Idaho, and they pinned an external brace across the break. Winter Winds was now on Earth, at stud and having fun, while Randy was out in the asteroid belt, drowning and uncomfortable.

No, it wasn't always fun . . . but it sure *was* exciting. Shortly he would be hitting the end of the Hygiea cable catapult at three hundred kilometers a second. That would be like riding a needle being shot down a straw!

The distant sphere of Hygiea started to show on the screen of the submerged tank console. Stretching out from the south pole of Hygiea was a long cable, the shorter end pointing at Randy. As they drew closer, Randy could see the long linear motor module start accelerating toward the south-pole power station from its resting point at the end of the shorter portion of the cable. It accelerated at a hundred gees and in five minutes was matching the velocity of Randy's capsule.

Attitude jets flashed on Randy's capsule as it moved between two of the six cables that made up the catapult. The capsule took up a position just behind the rapidly moving hollow linear motor. Slowly the capsule inched its way into the hollow interior of the massive machine, riding the six nearly invisible cables. There was a ripple of *clanks* as the grapples brought the two machines together. For a few seconds, nothing happened as they continued on their way to the power station. The power-station building flashed by in the display, and the deceleration started as he moved onto the longer section of cable stretching out away from the inner solar system. Within a few seconds Randy was decelerating at thirty gees. He had experienced the acceleration before back in the solar system, and now knew the most comfortable position to take on the couch. The pressures from the high acceleration went on and on—the sixteen minutes seemed like an eternity—then it was over. He had come to a stop near the end of the cable.

"Are you OK, Mr. Hunter?" came the concerned voice of Philippe Laurin through Randy's headset. Unable to answer because of the liquid in his vocal cords, Randy typed out his answer on a keypad.

OK. NO FUN.

"We're going to bring your capsule back up the cable to the south-pole station," said Philippe. "It'll take about two hours, one hour accelerating and one hour decelerating, but it'll be at one gee this time. I'll sign off for now. You can call me when you get your voice back."

Good, thought Randy as he unstrapped himself and opened the door to the acceleration tank. *At least I'll have good footing while I cough my lungs out.* His uncomfortable bladder reminded him of something else. *I'd also better use the head while I'm still under one gee. Once I get on Hygiea, it'll be back to those damned zero-gee toilets again.*

➤   ➤   ➤

After changing from his tank suit to a jumpsuit, Randy passed through the airlock from the capsule to the power-station building for the cable catapult. There he had a light meal with Philippe, going over the business aspects of the mining operations on the asteroids around Hygiea.

"Production has slowed down since we found the Silverhair," apologized Philippe. "Jim Meriweather is still nursing his arm, and I have reassigned Bob Pilcher from prospecting duties to the job of backing up Siritha Chandresekhar and Kip Carlton as they try to learn more about the creature."

"Don't worry about a small loss in production," said Randy. "We're bound to learn something of more value studying the alien. Can I go see the Silverhair myself?"

"I was sure you'd want to do that," said Philippe. "So I had Bob bring the 'Silverhair Special' back to the base before you landed. They're ready to take you to see it."

The two floated down the sealed corridors tunneled through the rock of Hygiea to the spacecraft port. There, Randy put on the custom-made space suit a technician had brought over from his capsule. The inner vacuum-protection portion of the space suit was a one-piece woven electrolastic tightsuit. The technician had the relaxer voltage at maximum and the tightsuit looked like a floppy, oversized set of long johns with built-in booties and gloves. Randy stripped down, then adjusted the molded-plastic combination codpiece and antibind protector between his legs until it stayed there by suction.

"That's a pretty big codpiece for such a little guy," remarked the technician.

"It's only my calcium bones that are small," replied Randy nonchalantly.

The tech then helped him step through the large, diameter-relaxed neckband.

"Stand with your arms and legs straight out," said the tech. "Like the da Vinci drawing."

Randy spread his legs and arms and fingers out while the tech slowly lowered the relaxing voltage on the electrolastic. The suit tightened up on Randy.

"Set your fingers deep in the gloves," said the tech. Randy shoved his fingers together until the gloves were on tight, then reached down to smooth out some wrinkles in his crotch and under his armpit.

"Feel smooth?" asked the tech.

"Squeeze away," replied Randy.

The tech removed the relaxing voltage, and the electrolastic tightsuit squeezed on Randy's skin while the segmented neckband shrank and assembled itself into a hard collar with built-in seals and locking grooves for his helmet. Now, with his air pressure maintained by his skin, supported by the tightsuit, Randy put on the fluorescent-red Kevlar-armored protective outeralls, gauntlets to protect the back of his hands, black stiction boots, and the chestpack and backpack harness. He donned the plastiglass globe helmet, locked it in place in the tightsuit collar, and hooked the air-hose to the backpack. Finally he strapped his cuff-comp onto his wrist.

"Say! That's a terrific-looking cuff-computer," said the tech, admiring the sparkling gems set in the jet-black plastic clasp. Randy turned his wrist over so he too could see the clasp.

"It was a gift from my father for my fifteenth birthday," Randy said. "Terahertz parallel-processor optical chip, gigabyte of RAM, touch-screen display, ten-year battery, and continuous satellite linkage to Worldnet." He undid the clasp and handed the thin, flexible band over to the tech.

"That *is* some collection of stones," said the tech.

"All the major stars in the sky are represented by diamonds, graded in size and color to match the size and color of the stars," said Randy with pride. "Custom-made. It's the only one like it." The tech handed the cuff-comp back to Randy, who strapped it back on his wrist.

➤ ➤ ➤

Philippe suited up with Randy and they went through an airlock out to the surface of the tiny planetoid. After loping a short distance across the grey dust, they boarded a cramped prospector's flitter. Once inside, Philippe introduced Randy to the engineer-pilot Bob Pilcher, medic Siritha Chandresekhar, and materials scientist Kip Carlton. They were all stripped down to their tightsuits and boots, with their helmets, outeralls, and packs stowed in the locker next to the exit.

Siritha was tiny and thin, with dark-brown skin, lively dark-brown eyes, and black hair in short ringlets. She had a scarlet caste mark in the center of her forehead and two nose rings. One was from an engineering school Randy didn't recognize, and the other was the medic's caduceus. Randy's eyes skipped past Siritha's tightsuit-covered body and instead focused impolitely on the caste mark. The mark really bothered him. No self-respecting woman wore any makeup of any kind . . . but then again, a caste mark was not *really* makeup.

Siritha bore the long stare with a Mona Lisa smile. She knew exactly what was bothering her boss. She was far from religious, and would never have bothered with a caste mark if she were in India, but here she took advantage of the heritage that allowed her to apply that socially permissible but very provocative dab of bright red makeup to her face. She enjoyed the attention it brought her.

Bob Pilcher was a typical space pilot, with the rugged face of a video tough-guy, a brown Paul Revere tied back with a no-nonsense rubber band, and no jewelry on his face. His well-worn tightsuit had two circular smudges in the fabric, one on his left forearm and one on his back, spray patterns from micrometeorites that had been fragmented to harmless dust by the Kevlar armor of his outeralls. The smudges were only noticeable because Bob had painted large bull's-eyes around them.

Kip Carlton's curly black hair was cut into a pillbox flattop, while his chocolate-brown face was almost hidden by a full black beard and large, owlish sports-spectacles. His ears seemed covered with golden 'rings from various schools and professional societies.

After shaking hands all around, Randy said eagerly, "If you're ready, I'd like to go see the Silverhair."

"You four go have fun," said Philippe. "I've got to stay here and run a base." He put on his helmet and went back out the airlock.

Bob lifted the flitter on its jets and took off toward a distant rock still invisible out in the black void around them. After a short trip, they came to rest some distance from the small asteroid. Next to it, floating in space, was a small nest of waving silvery wires. It was the Silverhair.

"When we first found it, it was a lot bigger," said Bob. "It was almost as large as that asteroid it had been eating."

"Now that we've set up daily visits to it," said Siritha, "it has stopped eating the asteroid and just waits until we come to feed it. That indicates it has a reasonable amount of memory and intelligence, and can engage in long-range planning."

Bob helped Siritha don her outeralls, helmet, and pack harness that included a jetpack, and soon she was shooting off from the airlock toward the Silverhair. In one tiny gauntleted hand she held a plasma torch, powered by a battery module jury-rigged to the jetpack.

The minute Siritha started toward the Silverhair it seemed to grow. The threads grew longer and reached out in a large circular fan shape toward the tiny trainer, as if wanting to take her into their silver embrace. Siritha slowed slightly, but continued on, unafraid of the gigantic beast that was now almost twenty meters from tip to tip.

"It can obviously see you," said Randy through her suit links. "But I don't see any eyes."

"I believe the individual threads are sensitive to light," replied Siritha. "I have seen one twirl itself around a piece of trash that had come loose from my boot treads, as if it were 'looking' at it."

"It's that amazing growth in size we don't understand," said Kip. "We've been thinking it must have a dense core and it grows these long silver strings when it's feeding."

"I brought along a Forward Mass Analyzer on this trip so we can measure not only its mass, but its mass distribution," said Bob.

"Good idea," said Randy. "Do it."

Bob started tapping the control screen. "I'll set it for a large scan radius," he said, "to keep the sensing elements far away from those threads."

He switched on the intersuit radio and called to Siritha outside. "Come on back, skinny but beautiful. You may not weigh much, but you might louse up our mass measurement."

While Bob was talking, there was a rumbling from the rear of the spacecraft, and a launching arm reached out from a cargo pod and set a rotating package out into space next to them. Bob backed the spacecraft away in the general direction of Siritha. Once she was aboard, and the spacecraft was at a safe distance, he tapped his finger on the screen. A small jet started the package moving slowly toward the distant Silverhair, which was slowly contracting its large fan shape as it realized Siritha had left. The rotating package separated into six smaller packages connected together by long tethers to form a large spinning ring.

"Let's see," said Bob thoughtfully, punching data into the screen. "Got to put in the mass and position of the spacecraft so the computer can separate its gravity field from that of the Silverhair. Same for the asteroid. The mass analyzer can measure the asteroid shape and position accurately with its imager, but we'll leave its mass an unknown to be solved for." Randy and Kip came forward to look at the screen over Bob's shoulder, while Siritha watched with concern out the forward porthole as the mass analyzer came closer to the still-contracting Silverhair.

The rotating ring passed around the body of the Silverhair, the six gravity gradient sensors tracing out a spiral pattern in space. The pattern was repeated on Bob's console screen, and in the center, a three-dimensional map of the mass distribution of the Silverhair was building up.

"Basically a fan-shaped mass distribution, with most of the mass concentrated in a core somewhat off from the center," said Bob as the sensors continued their spiral pattern.

As the ring of sensors passed the Silverhair and the amplitude of the data started to decrease, the console beeped and a large red message appeared at the bottom of the display.

ANALYSIS ERROR!

"Hmmm," said Bob, reading the display. "The analysis program has given part of the Silverhair mass distribution a negative mass!"

"Must be something wrong with the program," said Kip disgustedly.

"The asteroid is totaling out at roughly sixty thousand tons, while the Silverhair has a net mass near zero. That's funny enough by itself, but the Silverhair seems to have a small, dense core off to one side, with a positive mass of four hundred and twenty-three tons, while the fan-shaped body structure that we see has a negative mass of minus four hundred and twenty-three tons," said Bob.

"Run the sensor package over the asteroid," Randy suggested. "If there's some bug in the program, it should give the asteroid a negative mass, too."

"Good idea, boss-man," said Bob, punching the console screen. The ring of six sensors sped up their rotation as they came together into a single package again. Bob jockeyed the package around until it was headed for the potato-shaped asteroid. The six sensors spread out into a ring again and passed slowly over the rock.

"Looks like a normal mass-distribution analysis," said Bob as he watched the data build up again on his display. "Most of the asteroid is dirt, except for that nickel-iron knob the Silverhair was feeding on."

"There's no error message this time," remarked Randy.

"Total mass for the asteroid is six thousand three hundred twenty-three tons . . . positive," said Bob.

"What was the estimate for the Silverhair this time?" asked Kip. Bob punched the screen and the data came up, but there was an error message attached to it.

"The mass estimates for objects outside the scanned region are subject to a lot of error," said Bob. "The Silverhair still nets out to near-zero mass, but now the central core is only plus one hundred ninety tons while the body is minus one hundred ninety tons."

"That's considerably less than the first measurement," said Randy.

"That's because it's been shrinking," Siritha said from the window.

"That doesn't make sense!" Kip blurted.

"Neither does negative matter," said Randy. "But there it is."

"Negative or not, matter has to be conserved," insisted Kip. "If the mass isn't here, then it has to go somewhere. Maybe it's evaporating into space and shrinking that way."

"I don't think so," said Siritha. "The Silverhair is always small when I come to dance with it, but then it grows very large when I feed it. It can't grow by 'un-evaporating.' I'll go out to dance with it again, and you can take another measurement after it gets bigger again." As she suited up, she took a petarom chip-cartridge out of her chestpack. "I'm tired of this music," she said to Bob. "Do you have any chips with waltzes?"

"You've got to be kidding, brown-eyes," Bob said. "All my audio chips are heavy-metal rock."

Siritha looked around at the others. "Anybody have any chips with music you can dance to?"

"Sorry . . . opera," said Kip.

"Language lessons," said Randy.

"Well, I guess I'm stuck with this," she said, putting the cartridge back in her chestpack.

"Wait, babe," said Bob, turning to the console. "I'm sure the ship's library files have what you want. You just go out there and I'll broadcast it to you."

"Great!" said Siritha, giving him a dazzling smile. She put on her helmet and headed for the airlock. "Find some nice slow waltzes. This jetpack has a pretty slow response speed."

"Waltz . . . slow . . ." muttered Bob as he punched at his console.

Soon Siritha was making her way with her jetpack toward the Silverhair, swaying slightly to and fro to the strains of the "Blue

Danube Waltz" being beamed in her direction by the ship's radio antenna. She watched the creature carefully as she approached. Then, sensing something different in its waving motion, she came to an abrupt halt and held herself perfectly still. Ahead of her, the Silverhair was growing in anticipation of her arrival, and as it grew, the silvery hairs were swaying gracefully in wide arcs that grew larger and larger. But even though she was now motionless, and supplying no dance cues to the Silverhair, its threads were waving in perfect time with the music coming by radio from the distant prospector spacecraft.

<<Me move me self up, and round, and round. Me move me self down, and round, and round. Me move me self here, and there, and here . . . >>

"Bob," Siritha called quietly over the intercom, her voice low so as not to overpower the music.

"What is it, beautiful?" Bob replied.

"Turn off the music for a few seconds, then turn it back on."

"Want me to find you some other tune?"

"No," said Siritha. "Just turn it off, then turn it on, but watch the Silverhair as you do it."

"OK," said Bob, interest peaking in his voice. He turned to Randy and Kip. "She says to watch the Silverhair." They looked out the port at the swaying flood of silver threads.

Bob turned off the music. Off in the distance, the coordinated swaying of the Silverhair soon became random, then stopped. Bob started the music again, and the swaying resumed, exactly in time to the music, although Siritha was still holding herself motionless.

"It's detecting the radio signals somehow!" exclaimed Randy in an excited voice. "Now we have a method of talking with it!"

"Try saying something to it over your radio link, Siritha," suggested Kip.

"I'd better feed it first," replied Siritha, starting toward the Silverhair once again. "It's expecting that. But I'll stop midmeal and try to teach it some words."

"I've got the mass analyzer on the way, curly-top," said Bob. "How much do you weigh? I want the mass analyzer program to ignore you . . . not that *I* ever would."

"Seventy-five kilos," replied Siritha. "With suit," she added. "Probably better add another twenty-five for the jetpack. Its tanks are pretty full."

The spiraling ring of mass detectors passed around Siritha and the feeding Silverhair as they danced together to the music.

"The error message is still coming up, Mr. Boss, sir," said Bob as he watched the screen. "But the program must be OK, because it shows three masses, one a positive ninety-six kilograms at Siritha's position, and at the Silverhair's position a dense core of a positive eight hundred and thirty tons surrounded by a fan-shaped blob massing a negative eight hundred and thirty tons."

"So the outer portion of the Silverhair's body *is* made of negative matter," said Kip in disbelief.

"And it seems to be able to change its mass at will," added Bob.

"Negative matter . . ." mused Randy. "I remember reading an article about negative matter years ago in *Astronomy* magazine." He looked back at Bob. "Does this ship have the standard reference library chips?"

"The Library of Congress, all the major universities of the world, the International Patent Registry, and every magazine that's ever gotten near a scanner," said Bob. "Never know when you might need to know something to bring you back alive."

"I'm going to look up something," said Randy, heading for the console in the engineering section.

"I could recommend a good magazine if you're randy, Randy," said Bob over his shoulder. "The text is in Chinese, but the pictures of the chink chicks are something else."

➤   ➤   ➤

"It's starting to slow its feeding," said Siritha. "Time for a language lesson. Turn off the music, Bob."

"Gotcha, sweetheart," said Bob, tapping his console screen. As the music died, the swaying stopped, and Siritha backed away from the now gigantic fan of fine, silvery tendrils.

"I Siritha," she said, pointing to herself. There was no reply.

"My wideband distress-call monitor showed some static," said Bob. "Try 'all channels' and see if you get anything."

Siritha's fingers flickered over her chestpack and changed her receiver settings. A loud hiss of static now filled her helmet, and she had to turn down the volume.

"Sir-i-tha," she said again, pointing to herself. There was a temporary increase in the level of static, but that was all.

"This is going to take a long time," said Siritha with a sigh. She pointed to herself again.

"Sir-i-tha," she said.

➤   ➤   ➤

"I've found it!" said Randy from the engineering console.

"What is it, top-man?" asked Bob.

"It was in an article on space warps," said Randy. "It described a new kind of space warp that didn't involve black holes. Basically, it's a wormhole or tunnel in space held open by force fields."

"What kind of force field?" asked Kip.

"Well, most of the support can come from electric or magnetic fields," said Randy. "But they're not adequate to hold open the throat of the wormhole where the contracting forces are the greatest. For that region you need something that has negative energy density." Randy paused for effect. "In other words, something that has negative mass!"

"And the Silverhair's body seems to have negative mass," said Kip.

"There's more," said Randy. "According to the article, if you pass a charge or a mass through the space warp, the electric or gravity fields get threaded through the wormhole throat. That means that if a negative mass passes through the wormhole, the input mouth develops a negative gravity field, while the output mouth develops a positive gravity field. That must be the positive mass near the center of the Silverhair that we can detect with the mass analyzer."

"So Silverlocks has a hole it can duck into," said Bob. "No wonder its mass can change. It's going somewhere else."

"I'm getting nowhere," called Siritha. "I'm coming in." She jetted away from the Silverhair and back toward the ship. Off in the distance, the tendrils of the Silverhair rippled randomly back and forth as it slowly shrank in size.

"Time to give the Silverhair a rest and let it digest its food," said Siritha. "And way past time for us to have some dinner and climb into our bedsacks. We have a busy day tomorrow."

➤   ➤   ➤

The following day, when Bob, Kip, Siritha, and Randy approached the point in space where the Silverhair waited, they could see a crew of people outside in space suits with various instruments. One of the crew was dancing with the Silverhair and feeding it from a plasma gun.

"That's Hiroshi Tanaka. He don't dance near as pretty as you, skinny-butt," said Bob, patting Siritha on her tightsuited rear. She slapped his hand away and headed for the outerall rack.

"I hope he hasn't fed it too much," said Siritha. "It won't pay attention to its language lessons if it's too full."

Bob carefully checked Siritha's suit indicators and jetpack, while Kip cycled the airlock. As Siritha moved away from the prospector ship, the radio waves carrying the "Blue Danube Waltz" drifted once again over the ether. Randy, Kip, and Bob watched as Siritha approached the Silverhair on the opposite side from where Hiroshi was dancing with it.

The portion of the Silverhair closest to Hiroshi had flattened out into a gigantic circular fan that waved slowly back and forth to feed on the iron atoms being emitted by the plasma generator Hiroshi was waving. The portion of the Silverhair closest to Siritha was in its normal spherical shape, looking like a silver dandelion gone to seed.

For a while, the Silverhair ignored the music and the approaching form of Siritha. She noticed the lack of response and added that fact to the other facts about the alien she had been collecting.

"Too busy feeding to notice either me or the music," she said to herself. "It must be so dumb it can't think of two things at the same time."

Slowly the portion of the Silverhair closest to Siritha started to wave in time to the waltz music. Gradually, more and more tendrils joined in the motion, and grew into a gigantic waving fan that reached out toward Siritha as she approached. Hiroshi, seeing that Siritha was coming to take over, started to back away. The tendrils on that side attempted to follow him, feeding on the iron atoms still coming from his plasma generator.

Through the radio static on the intersuit link, they could hear the alien-sounding melodic voice as it called out over the airwaves.

<Sir . . . > said the Silverhair, the portion closest to Siritha moving to meet her while the portion farthest away continued to follow the retreating Hiroshi.

<Sir . . . > the Silverhair said again.

"It's calling me!" squealed Siritha in delight as she was nearly enveloped by the approaching fan of silvery hairs.

"Ohmygosh, look!" exclaimed Randy, pointing to a growing segment of empty space between the two fans of silver tendrils. "The Silverhair has split in two!"

Randy turned to the pilot. "Bob," he said, "ask Hiroshi to look at the space between the two Silverhairs and report if he sees anything strange . . . but tell him not to get near. It might be dangerous."

"Hey, Hiroshi," called Bob into the intersuit radio link. "The boss-man wants you to look between those two hairy balls and report what you see . . . and that's not supposed to be a dirty joke. Keep well off, though. There might be a warp region between them."

Hiroshi's jetpack fired and he drifted around his Silverhair toward

Siritha and the other Silverhair. He pulled a rescue lanyard with a weighted hook out of his chestpack, tossed the "come-to-me" into the region between the two Silverhairs, and pulled it back through again with a jerk that formed loops of line that covered most of the region.

"Nothing strange happening," reported Hiroshi.

"Stay away anyway," said Randy. "We'll take a better look at it with instruments later." Bob watched the small, youthful face of his boss twitch as Randy's brain raced furiously.

"I need a pole," said Randy. "A long one."

"Fresh out of ten-foot poles," said Bob. "Planning on touching something? Don't forget the Silverhairs don't like being touched."

"I'm counting on that," said Randy. "I need something long and fairly stiff . . . I've got it! Do you have a tape measure?"

"There's a ten-meter one in the tool cabinet," said Kip, heading for the rear of the ship.

"Great!" said Randy. "Help me get suited up."

➤　　➤　　➤

A short while later, the diminutive figure of Siritha was joined by the even more diminutive figure of Randy. Kip, having delivered Randy to the vicinity of the Silverhair with his jetpack, pulled back. Randy pulled out the curved metal tape until it was a few meters long. With no gravity, it didn't bend, but stayed in a nearly straight line.

"Grab my feet and push me as close to the Silverhair as is safe," he said to Siritha. As she took his boots and pushed him slowly toward the fanned-out Silverhair, he spoke again over the intersuit radio link.

"Hiroshi and Kip!" he called. "Go to opposite sides of the other Silverhair and let me know if you see anything strange."

Siritha had steered her boss as close to the Silverhair as she dared. Randy fed the end of the tape measure slowly toward the alien. The silvery tendrils pulled away to avoid contact.

"Be careful, Mr. Hunter," Siritha cautioned. "We don't want to hurt the Silverhair."

"I'll go slowly," said Randy. "Got my thumb on the automatic rewind in case there's a problem."

Randy pushed the end of the tape deep into the hairy center of the Silverhair. The body of the Silverhair, avoiding contact, formed a deep cavity around the penetrating sliver of metal. Randy used his other hand to push out meter after meter of tape and feed it into the center of the giant alien.

"Something's happening!" said Kip with excitement. "Some of the threads are pulling apart. There's a hole developing . . . I can see the end of the tape measure coming out!"

"That's enough for now," said Randy, activating the automatic rewind but using his gloved fingers to keep the tape under smooth control. As soon as the end of the tape could be seen, Siritha activated her jets and pulled her boss well back from the Silverhair. Kip and Hiroshi jetted over to join them.

"How far apart would you say those two Silverhairs are?" asked Randy. "Twenty meters?"

"Thirty, at least," said Kip, gauging the distance.

"I agree," said Hiroshi.

Randy held up the tape measure. "Less than ten meters," he said, ". . . on the *inside*."

<Sir . . . > came the plaintive call from the nearer Silverhair.

"The poor thing is hungry after all that effort," said Siritha. "Turn on some music, Bob."

"I wonder if they like hard rock?" Bob muttered as he punched the icons on his control console. Out of the radio antenna came the opening bars of the latest hit offering by the Deadly Scum—a screechingly loud, descending glissando from a virtuoso guitarist overlying the hard driving beat of a master drummer. Bob blinked in shock at the result. The Silverhairs had disappeared!

"Where'd they go?!?" he exclaimed.

"Bob! You bonehead!" yelled Siritha. "You scared them away!" She jetted to where the nearer Silverhair had been.

"There's nothing here but a silver blob the size of a golf ball," she reported. "Wait! I see a single silver thread about two meters away from the blob. It's only a few centimeters long. There's something funny with one end of it. It looks like it's distorted."

"That's probably the entrance to the space warp," said Randy. "Stay well away from it. It may be strong enough to drag you in."

"The thread is wiggling," she reported. "Maybe we can coax it out. Turn on some music again—*waltz* music this time!"

"Yes, ma'am," said Bob contritely. Shortly, the soft music of the "Blue Danube Waltz" drifted out again over the airwaves. The single silver thread started to wave and grow longer; then more threads peeked out in all directions from the single point in space. Siritha danced with the Silverhair and soon it was the same size as before. Then she went over and coaxed the other Silverhair from its hole in space. There was no blob near this one.

The silver golf ball floated by itself, showing no signs of life despite the music and Siritha's dancing presence. The Silverhairs ignored it, and in fact seemed to move away as they grew so as to avoid contact with it. Siritha fed the Silverhair some more iron molecules from the plasma gun.

Kip was watching the performance thoughtfully. "Bob was right. What we see of the Silverhairs is only a small portion of the total animal. Most of their body must be hidden away in the wormhole, like an octopus backed into an amphora in a Mediterranean shipwreck. Only the feeding tentacles come outside, while the bulk of the body is somewhere else in space, reaching through the wormhole to this point in space where there's food."

Once the Silverhairs were back to normal size, Siritha waved good-bye to them and headed back toward the ship.

"It's been a long day," she said as she took off her helmet. "Let's head for Hygiea."

"I want to find out what that silver ball is!" said Randy.

"We really ought to be going back, boss," said Bob. "The zero-gee toilet in this tub doesn't always do what it's supposed to."

"Hmmm . . ." Randy considered his options. "I'll have Philippe come out with another crew."

3 >>

Return
to Rose

THE next day, Philippe gave Randy a briefing on what the engineers had found out about the silver ball the Silverhairs had generated. Jim Meriweather was there too, arm still in a cast. The three of them floated around a conference table, fingertips keeping them levitated at the same height in Hygiea's low gravity.

"The silver ball seems to be made of the same material as the Silverhair, but it's not alive and it doesn't seem to have any connection to a wormhole," reported Philippe. "It has a negative mass of about ten tons, which gives it an approximate density of a ton per cubic centimeter."

"Certainly not normal material," said Randy. "That's a much higher density than anything previously known."

"It also has a very high electrical charge," said Philippe.

"As it would have to . . ." said Jim Meriweather.

"What do you mean by that?" asked Randy, puzzled.

"Since this cast keeps me out of a tightsuit, I've been spending my time talking with some physics experts on Earth about the Silverhair," said Jim.

Randy looked perturbed. "I was trying to keep the Silverhair secret!" he said sternly. "Have you been blabbing about its existence to a bunch of academics? They can't keep secrets."

"I've only talked to Reinhold employees," Jim assured him. "And made them understand it was company-confidential," he added. "Everyone said the same thing—'Talk to Steve Wisneski.' So I did."

Randy knew Steve Wisneski well. He was a bright and brash theoretical Ph.D. at the Reinhold Research Laboratories. "What did Steve have to say?" he asked.

"'You're crazy. There's no such thing as negative matter.'"

"That's Steve, all right," said Randy. "Then what did he say?"

"After I gave him all the facts and showed him some video segments, he conceded that maybe negative matter could exist after all. What really convinced him was the description of my injury, where the cut edges looked like a thin sliver of material had been evaporated."

"Why is that?" asked Randy.

"Well, as Steve explains it, according to one theory, when negative matter touches normal matter, equal amounts vanish—nothing is left, not even energy. The process is called nullification. It's like the annihilation of matter by antimatter, but in the nullification process, since the normal matter has positive rest mass and the negmatter has negative rest mass, the net rest mass is zero, so zero energy is released. That's why we didn't notice any radiation when the Silverhair and I collided."

"What else did Steve have to say?" asked Randy.

"He told us to look for electric or magnetic fields around the Silverhair and the ball," said Jim. "Negative-matter particles repel each other gravitationally, so they would normally tend to spread far apart from each other. But since the negative-matter particles in the Silverhair and the ball are jammed together at high density, there must be some other force field involved that holds them together."

Philippe spoke up. "Hiroshi found a very strong positive electric field associated with both the ball and the Silverhair. It's as if the material were all made of particles with the same charge."

"Normally, particles of the same charge would repel each other and be pushed apart," said Jim. "But according to Steve, when you attempt to repel a negative-matter particle, it responds in a perverse manner and comes toward you."

"That explains one thing," said Randy. "Siritha noticed some static-cling effects of space dust on her helmet. But there was nothing large—no lightning bolts."

"Both the Silverhair and the ball rapidly develop a cloud of orbiting electrons around them," said Philippe. "They must attract the negative electrons from the plasma in space while repelling the positive ions.

The negative electric charge of the electron cloud cancels out the positive electric charge of the negative matter, unless, of course, you get inside the orbiting cloud of electrons and very close to the surface of the negative matter. Hiroshi got some good measurements of the electric field around the ball by enclosing it in a plastic container, sweeping up all the electrons near the ball with a grounded metallic plate, then making measurements inside the container while all the interfering electrons were forced to stay outside the container. We then did some experiments on the ball."

"What kind of experiments?" asked Randy, looking intently at Philippe.

"Since the ball is charged," Philippe answered, "it's easy to push it by charging up a metal plate placed near it. Of course, being negative matter, when you push it, it comes toward you."

"That can get dangerous," said Jim, holding up his cast. "If it gets too close, you get nullified."

"In the experiment Hiroshi did," Philippe went on, "he used a metal plate with a negative electric charge so it would attract the positive electric charge of the ball. The ball pulled away in the opposite direction, pulling the test apparatus, the power supply, and Hiroshi along with it. When Hiroshi saw what was happening, he quickly turned the field off. He then had to reverse the field and push on the ball for a while to bring it to a halt again."

"It was just as Steve predicted," said Jim in awe. "A true reactionless space drive."

"A space drive?" exclaimed Randy in amazement.

"That is correct," said Philippe, his voice deepening as his face turned deadly serious. "When that ball of negative matter was pulling Hiroshi and his test apparatus along, there was nothing going in the opposite direction. There was no reaction mass and no energy source involved, but they moved nevertheless. That means a large enough negative-matter ball electrostatically coupled to a positive-matter spacecraft can propel the spacecraft at any acceleration the crew can stand for as long as you want. Flight to the stars at near light speed is no longer a dream . . ."

When the enormity of the finding hit Randy, a broad smile spread across his face. *An interstellar space drive! He had dreamed of exploring the stars and now his dream could come true!* He leaned forward over the table, eyes on Philippe.

"What are the limitations?" he asked, knowing there must be some.

"The mass of the negative matter must be exactly equal and opposite to the positive mass of the spacecraft," said Philippe. "If it isn't, then the separation distance between the mass and the spacecraft will change with time. If it gets too close, you risk nullification. If it gets too far away, you risk losing it."

"You have to control the mass of one or the other, then," mused Randy. "Not easy." He thought some more. "Didn't you say the silver ball has a mass of ten tons?"

"Yes," said Philippe. "A *negative* ten tons."

"Then that one ball can drive a ten-ton spacecraft. Do you think you could arrange for a demonstration using one of the prospector flitters? They mass around ten tons."

"Perhaps," said Philippe, thinking. His finger rose to feel the mustache under his nose, then followed it across his face and up over his ear as he thought further about the idea. "Yes," he said finally.

"Do it!" said Randy. "I'm going to get some breakfast and then go back out to see the Silverhair. I wonder if Bob can get it to lay more of those silver eggs."

"Careful," warned Philippe. "Don't kill the goose . . ."

➤   ➤   ➤

A week later, Philippe took Randy to the hangar cavity on the other side of Hygiea.

"We've installed the negmatter drive in the hold," said Philippe, leading the way as he and Randy floated in through the cargo door in their space suits. "Right at the center-of-mass of the ship."

In the center of the cargo bay was a large, cubical metal box nearly twice as tall as Randy. Surrounding the box were some large power supplies. A technician was tying up some stray wires.

"Is the negmatter ball in there?" asked Randy.

"Ready to go," said Philippe. "All six high-voltage supplies are operating and pushing on the ball equally from all directions. In the control room is a three-axis maglev joyball just like the ones that are used in the drop capsules on the rotovators. You push the ball forward, the fore and aft power supplies change their voltages, the negmatter ball gets pushed in the backward direction, and it responds by moving in the forward direction, pushing the spacecraft ahead of it. If you want to go sideways or vertically, just move the ball in that direction and the power supplies for those axes will respond."

"How simple!" exclaimed Randy. "I'd like to try it out!"

"I'll call Bob Pilcher and have him come out from the base to pilot it for you," said Philippe.

"Call Bob out in case there's a problem," said Randy. "But I'm going to be the test pilot for this first run myself."

"But, Mr. Hunter . . ." Philippe began; then, seeing the determined look in his young boss's eyes, he stopped. After all, Randy was an accomplished airplane pilot and often flew the Reinhold company jet himself.

"Yes, sir, Mr. Hunter," he said.

➤   ➤   ➤

Bob and Randy entered the control room of the modified prospector's ship through the airlock and took off their outeralls. There was someone already there, sitting at the engineering console behind the flight deck.

"Mr. Fixit himself," said Bob, when he saw who it was. He floated toward the pilot seat.

"Good day, Mr. Hunter. I am Hiroshi Tanaka," said the small young man. He rose from his chair, but kept his toes hooked underneath the seat so he could push himself forward in free-fall to shake hands. "Dr. Laurin assigned me to be your engineer for this test flight."

"Do you know the negmatter drive system well?" asked Randy.

"I have some familiarity with it, Mr. Hunter," replied Hiroshi.

"Don't let sushi-breath feed you that humble stuff, top-boss," said Bob over his shoulder as he buckled himself in and checked out the console. "He designed, built, and tested it. He may be a lousy dancer, but he's the best engineer I've ever seen."

"Everything is ready for the test flight," said Hiroshi, as if he had not heard Bob.

With Bob buckled into the pilot seat with the standard spacecraft controls in front of him, his eyes glued to the acceleration indicators, and his hands ready to move if there were problems, Randy sat in the copilot seat and put his hand into the special negmatter controller box. His fingers closed gently around the silvery superconducting ball floating in the center of the box in its invisible net of magnetic fields.

"How many gees can it do?" asked Randy.

"I designed it for one gee," said Hiroshi. "But until we have established all the operational parameters, I have set the acceleration limiters to a tenth-gee."

"Good enough," said Randy. Carefully he pushed the silvery joyball forward a tiny amount and kept it there. Nothing seemed to happen.

"Two-hundredths of a gee," announced Bob Pilcher from the pilot seat. After a number of seconds he read, "One meter per second velocity and increasing."

"Good," said Randy. "The control motion was perceptible and the feedback push was detectable. I assume the response is logarithmic?"

"Yes," said Hiroshi.

"We're now at three meters per second," reported Bob.

"I'll want to try all three axes before taking off in earnest," said Randy, pulling the joyball directly backward to bring them to a rapid halt. For the next few minutes, the three were pulled this way and that in their seat belts as Randy got a feel for the controls. Finally, he was ready.

"Off we go!" said Randy. He pushed the silver joyball slowly forward until he hit the limits of the controls.

"One-tenth gee," Bob announced. Their velocity slowly built up over the minutes as they pulled away from Hygiea Base.

"Don't want to get out of sight of the base," said Randy, as he pulled the joyball to one side to bring them around in a large circle.

"We're going sideways!" he complained.

"With only one ball of negmatter, I was unable to obtain any torque control," said Hiroshi.

"I'll fix that," said Bob, firing some attitude rockets and turning the ship around so that it faced in the direction it was traveling. "You just do what you want with the drive controls, boy-boss, and granddaddy Bob will follow your every move and keep us lined up with the straight and narrow."

After Randy and Bob had completed a few more practice turns, a warning chime came from the engineering console in front of Hiroshi. Randy instinctively pulled back on the joyball until they were once again in free-fall.

"Is there a problem?" he asked apprehensively.

"The ball of negative matter is starting to drift away from the center of the drive control box," reported Hiroshi. "As Bob uses fuel to control our orientation, the mass of the spacecraft slowly decreases."

"Too bad we can't control the mass of the ship," said Randy.

"There is a way to do that," said Hiroshi. "But I didn't include that feature in this first design."

"In that case," said Randy, pushing forward on the controls again, "let's head for base and rework the drive. I want to go back to Earth in style!"

➤　　➤　　➤

A few weeks later, Randy reboarded the prospector ship. Philippe was with him, waiting for the airlock to cycle.

"Both Bob and Hiroshi were near the end of their tours," said Philippe. "So I have arranged for them to travel home with you."

"I can do it myself," said Randy, slightly annoyed at being patronized.

"Including fixing the negmatter drive if something goes wrong?" chided Philippe gently.

"You're right," admitted Randy.

"Hiroshi's new six-degree-of-freedom negmatter drive is pretty complicated," said Philippe. "It has linear drive and torque control in all three axes. For control of the ship's mass, the hull is covered with activated metal foam that absorbs and holds on to any gas or dust that strikes it. With a constant flow of positive matter coming in, we can afford to shoot propellant out from ion engines to provide mass trim and drag makeup."

"It's amazing how fast Hiroshi and the rest of your techs solved the engineering problems of coping with negmatter," said Randy.

"Since the negmatter is electrically charged, it turned out to be easy," said Philippe. "You use radio fields to make the balls vibrate. If you vibrate them at just the right frequency, you can make them break into two, three, or four pieces, or even spit out little droplets."

"Glop those small pieces together and you can make any-sized ball you want," said Randy. "I still think it's amazing. There's going to be a big bonus coming to everyone on the base."

"Make sure Hiroshi's is a large one."

"You make out the list, and I'll approve it," said Randy. "Minimum is a half-year's salary . . . No maximum."

The airlock door opened and Randy cycled through. Hiroshi and Bob were at their control consoles, waiting for him.

"Ready to go home, gentlemen?" asked Randy, sitting down in the copilot seat.

"All in readiness, sir," replied Hiroshi.

"Can't wait to see my honeys," Bob added.

Randy held the silver joyball between his fingers and slowly pushed it forward. The acceleration level rose to one gee and they were forced heavily into their seat backs. Suddenly Randy felt the joyball being pushed back.

"Not that way, jet-jockey!" hollered Bob.

Randy looked over to see that Bob had a copy of the negmatter controller in his armrest and was countermanding his control. Somewhat irritated, yet conceding that Bob might know more than he did about piloting spacecraft, Randy removed his hand from his control and let him take over. Bob rotated the silver joyball, and the negmatter torque drive rotated the ship until the top of the spacecraft was pointing at Earth. Then Bob lifted the joyball *up* in the controller and the acceleration started again, only this time directed downward toward the floor. Bob locked the control at one-gee acceleration, got heavily out of his seat, and clumped across the deck to the toilet.

"My first worry-free shit in nearly a year," he said as he closed the restroom door.

➤   ➤   ➤

One gee for two days is one AU, but Hygiea was unfortunately on the opposite side of the sun from the Earth. They had to take a dogleg around the Sun to keep from getting fried, so it took them a whole week to get home. During the deceleration period the bottom of the ship was facing the Earth so the control deck would be "down." Hiroshi rigged up a video camera held by one of the grapple arms so they could see where they were going.

"Seven days at one gee is certainly a lot more comfortable than sixteen minutes at thirty gees," said Randy as the Earth-Moon system started to fill the screen. They were coming at the Earth and Moon from the direction of the Sun, so both globes were fully illuminated. The polar Lunavator was just about to touch down at the lunar south pole. As he watched it, Randy recalled his first visit to the Moon, way back during the "tumble in" of the first Lunavator, nearly five years ago.

➤   ➤   ➤

His spaceship from Earth had docked him at the central hub of the newly built Reinhold Lunar Rotovator. After being shown around the Central Station a little, he was taken to the cable capsule that supplied transportation along the length of the Lunavator. Randy clumsily climbed his way into the capsule. Having left Earth for the first time only a week ago, he was still a little awkward in free-fall. The pilot turned, grabbed him by the arm, and held him until Randy got himself properly positioned in the seat and buckled up.

"Thanks, Captain Anderson," said Randy.

"Just call me Sue," said the pilot. "This hunk of junk is nothing more than a glorified cable car, so it isn't like I'm the pilot of anything—more like an elevator operator." She paused to shift her gum in her mouth. "Ready?"

"Yep," said Randy, peering eagerly out the windows fore and aft on the simple cylindrical vehicle. The cable car was situated in the center of a hexagonal array of six thin, diamond-fiber cables stretching off into the distance in both directions. The car reached out with six pairs of electromagnetic shoes to push against the six diamond cables plated with superconducting metal. The coating not only levitated the cable car, but brought electricity down from the central power station to power the car. At intervals the cables were cross-linked with diamond-cable strands that would take up the strain if any of the main cables happened to be cut by space debris. Through the open web of the diamond-cable lattice surrounding them, Randy could see the Moon filling the sky almost dead ahead of them.

"Up or down?" Sue asked.

"Take me to the end that will touch down on the Moon first," said Randy.

"That's up," said Sue. She swiveled in her chair until the Moon was at her back. She pushed some buttons and the car started moving down the tunnel of cables. As the acceleration built up, Randy's chair swiveled automatically toward the front and he lost his view of the masts and cylinders that made up the central station that surrounded the main cable at the middle of the long Lunar Rotovator.

"We're in no hurry, so I'll set the cruise speed at two kiloklicks," said Sue. Randy felt himself under Earth gravity again, but this time it was directed toward his back instead of his seat. After not quite a minute, the acceleration fell off and they were back in free-fall. The cross-connections between the six cables had blurred into invisibility.

"Two kiloklicks," repeated Randy, calculating. "That's two thousand kilometers an hour, isn't it?"

"Yep," said Sue, looking up from her paperback. She switched her wad of permachew to her cheek. "Faster than a speeding bullet," she continued proudly, then turned her attention back to her paperback while Randy swiveled back and forth, admiring the view. As their twenty-minute journey drew to a close, Randy could see the asteroid at the end of the cable grow in visibility. It was a carbonaceous chondrite, a portion of which had been used as the carbon supply for the diamond cable. There was a similar asteroid at the other end of the cable, and a few smaller ones set up at strategic intervals along the cable.

Sue parked her permachew under her armrest, tucked the paperback into a pocket in front of her, and brought the high-speed car to a halt at the small terminal station. Behind the station, like a granite knob lost from some national park, loomed the thirty-meter-wide asteroid, blocking half the view of the sky. It had been blasted into a hundred pieces, each piece wrapped in a diamond cable net, then reassembled again into a roughly spherical bag of rocks.

Sue, without being asked, efficiently unstrapped Randy, pushed her small boss unceremoniously out the hatch, climbed out after him, and disappeared down a corridor. Randy was met by the station supervisor, Bradley Harrowgate.

"I would have thought you would prefer to be at the control center in Central Station for the tumble-in, Mr. Hunter," said Bradley.

"Why?" said Randy. "All the action is out here."

"You are certainly correct about that," said Bradley, stroking his short, greying schoolmaster beard as he reevaluated his opinion of his eccentric young boss.

"When does tumble-in commence?" asked Randy eagerly.

"We've already started the first phases," said Bradley. "Your ride out through the cable will be the last one until the Rotovator is in place and the cable has stopped twanging."

"We've already started?" asked Randy with some puzzlement.

"You haven't been in space long enough to notice," said Bradley. "But to those who've been in free-fall for the past three months, it's obvious." He looked down at the floor and pointed at his feet. "See?" he said. "My feet are on the floor."

Suddenly Randy noticed that, indeed, instead of floating around, everyone in the room was oriented in the same direction, feet firmly on the floor in the low gravity.

"Although Central Station is in free-fall, we aren't," said Bradley. "Same with Terminal Station A at the other end."

"Of course . . . the tides from the Moon," said Randy.

"Right now it is mostly tides," said Bradley. "The asteroid at the other end is closer to the Moon than Central Station, so it is pulled harder by the Moon, and wants to speed on ahead, but the cable holds it back, creating artificial gravity there that's pointed toward the Moon. We, way out here, are further away from the Moon and so are pulled less, but the cable drags us along, creating an artificial gravity that points away from the Moon. Later, after we and our asteroids tumble in and the cable starts rotating, most of the artificial gravity on the terminal stations will be due to rotation, and pointed outward from Central Station."

An engineer who has been hovering in the background looked at the time on her cuff-comp, then spoke up softly.

"We'll be dropping off the first of the rock baskets soon, Dr. Harrowgate," she said.

"Good," said Bradley. "If you'll come this way, Mr. Hunter, we can see the first drop-off from this viewing port."

They gathered at a viewing port that gave them a good view of the pile of net-covered rocks "below" them.

"Now!" said the engineer, and almost instantly they all felt a slight increase in the pressure on the bottom of their feet.

"Something happened," said Randy quizzically. "but I don't *see* what caused it."

"The first basket of rocks was dropped from the backside of the asteroid," said Bradley. "It will take a few moments to come into view . . . There it is!" He pointed. "As the asteroids approach the Moon and the tides get stronger, the cable stretches. The asteroids weigh more than the cable can support, so we have to drop off more and more mass as we get closer to keep the cable from breaking. Each time we drop some of the mass off the ends of the cable, it has less weight pulling on it, so the cable shortens up slightly. If we do everything just right, however, the cable will end up in low orbit around the Moon, rotating at just the right speed to touch down on the lunar surface six times an orbit. Meanwhile, all the chunks of asteroid will be flying off into space or onto safe places on the moon, taking away the energy and angular momentum from our tumble-in that we want to get rid of."

As the hours passed in their headlong plunge to the Moon, the giant orb became larger and slowly moved off to one side. The long, curved arrow of the Rotovator now pointed to the horizon over the shadowed side of the Moon, spreading a spray of netted rocks out into space as it fell. The leading terminal station dipped down to within a few kilometers of the lunar north pole. Those on the station felt a strong increase in the artificial gravity pulling down on their feet as the stretched diamond cable pulled the station ponderously back as the remaining load of asteroidal rock was dumped into the middle of the rocket-booster safety range below. The same thing was happening to Randy and the others in the opposite terminal station.

"There they go!" said Bradley Harrowgate. "We're now in orbit and rotating." The acceleration on Randy's feet jumped; then a few moments later he could see the widening gap between the mountain of rock and the station. Randy turned to look at Bradley.

"Where's the landing capsule?" he asked. "I want to be in it and ready."

"The capsules are at the bottom floor down that circular staircase over there," said Bradley, pointing. "But there's plenty of time. The first touchdown is still twenty minutes away."

"Hold on to the railing!" said the engineer, looking at her cuff-comp. "Here comes the first of the twangs." As she spoke the room began to tilt, and soon Randy found himself almost hanging from the railing as the wall temporarily turned into a ceiling, then a few moments later into a floor, as the end of the giant cable whipped about violently from the residual forces left from their dramatic arrival at the Moon.

"That was pretty bad!" said Randy seriously.

"That's the worst it will get," the engineer assured him. "As the pulse moves along the cable we dissipate its energy by making it throw off the last few baskets of rocks spaced along its length. When it gets back here the next time, you won't even notice it."

"Now the cable has quieted down, it's safe to use the staircase," said Bradley, leading the way in the moderately strong artificial gravity produced by the rotation of the cable.

The circular staircase took them to the center of a circular room at the bottom of Terminal Station B. It looked like an airport loading area, with four numbered doors spaced around the periphery leading outward, and consoles between the staircase and the doors. The room was decorated in the pink-and-green Reinhold Astroengineering Company colors—leaf-green carpeted floors and walls, and pink doors with leaf-green lettering. A smiling young man in a leaf-green uniform with pink trim looked over at them from behind a computer terminal screen.

"Our first passenger!" he said brightly. "Welcome to Reinhold Rotovators–'We whisk you on your way.'"

As they approached the center console, the young man flicked his fingers expertly over the screen.

"No ticket needed for *you*, Mr. Hunter." He pushed sideways at an icon on the screen and a door to one side of them whooshed open. "Flight 101 is now boarding at Gate One," he said, pointing to the open door.

Two capsule attendants were waiting on the other side of the door. The capsule interior continued the green-and-pink color scheme, with leaf-green carpeted floors and wall, and leaf-green seats with pink headrests.

Bradley Harrowgate lead Randy to a seat, then waited while the capsule attendants made sure Randy was properly fastened in and the various seat buttons explained to him.

"I'd better go now," Bradley said. "Have a lot of things to clear up on the station so we'll be ready for paying customers."

"That's the right attitude," said Randy. "Meanwhile, I'll just take a little vacation trip to the Moon." As Bradley left, the pilot of the capsule came down a ladder from above and walked down the aisle.

"Welcome aboard the first drop of Flight 101, Mr. Hunter," said the pilot, extending his hand. "We leave in three minutes. Anything I can do for you?"

"This window seat is very nice," said Randy. "But I'd sure see a lot more from a jump seat. I've always wanted to see what it was like to fly a spacecraft."

"It would be an honor to have you, sir," said the pilot. "But once we start the drop, the passenger capsule and the cockpit capsule are separately sealed."

"Oh! Of course," said Randy, remembering. "After you put the passenger capsule down, you take right off again."

"Since you have a cuff-comp," said the pilot, noticing it peeking out of Randy's sleeve, "you can watch through our video monitor. It's on Channel 88."

"Great!" said Randy, shooting out the cuff-comp and switching it to television mode. The pilot went back up the ladder to the cockpit and sealed the door behind him.

Watching from the wide-angle video monitor camera behind the pilots, Randy could now see the control tower that hung below the boarding area at the bottom of the terminal station. Down below was the rapidly rising surface of the Moon, getting closer and closer as the long swing of the rotating diamond cable came down, bringing Terminal Station B with it.

"You are clear for drop," said a voice from the control tower.

"Clamps off," said the pilot, his left hand throwing a switch on the console while the fingers of his right hand held steady the silvery joyball in the controller box. There was a series of loud clanks that rattled through the hull overhead, and the capsule rocked slightly as its weight was picked up by eight thin diamond threads coming from the terminal station above. The pilot pushed down on the metal ball and they started their drop.

Down ahead of them was Lunaris. Outside the partially buried city, on the other side of the main road leading to the Boeing-Lockheed rocket terminal, was their destination, the Reinhold Rotovator terminal. It was still under construction, with two terminals completed and two others still under way. The pilot guided the capsule rapidly down, the cable reels singing as they let out the almost invisible diamond threads. As the pilot moved the shiny control ball back and forth, the slight variations in speed of the reels pulled the capsule from one side to another just as a stunt parachutist controls his descent by pulling on the canopy shrouds.

The timing was perfect. The passenger capsule for Flight 101 settled into the yellow rectangle designated for it, its reels now swallowing cable as fast as it fell from the sky. The pilot looked over his shoulder at the video monitor.

"Have a nice visit on the Moon, Mr. Hunter," he said. "I have to get my pickup capsule now."

The copilot also looked back and grinned. "Thank you for riding Reinhold Rotovators," she said. "We hope you will travel with us again soon."

The videoscreen blanked as the pilot cut the link. The cockpit capsule, reeling in cable even faster than before, swooped up and over to settle on an empty passenger capsule a short distance away. Randy peered out the window and looked up to see Terminal Station B dropping almost vertically down. It came to a halt about a half-kilometer above them, then started its elevatorlike rise back up into the sky, dragging the upgoing passenger capsule with it.

As long as the mass let down to the lunar surface equaled or exceeded the amount lifted, the rotovator could operate forever. The dropping of Randy's minuscule extra mass to the lunar surface would, in part, make up for the small amount of friction energy lost by the stretching of the diamond cable during the operation.

One of the flight attendants was talking over the capsule intercom. "We have arrived at Lunaris. The local time is ten-twelve Universal Time." Randy reset his cuff-comp.

"We thank you for traveling on Reinhold Rotovators," she continued. "We hope you will use our services on your next trip on or off the Moon. Don't forget—we also offer interlunar hops between Orientale, Backside, West Base, and Lunaris, as well as interplanetary journeys to Earth, and soon to all the planets and moons out to Saturn. For complete details, please contact your travel agent or ask your cuff-computer for the toll-free connection to Reinhold Rotovator reservations . . ."

➤ ➤ ➤

Randy's musings were interrupted by Hiroshi's voice. "There is a message coming in for you, sir. I'll switch it to your console screen."

"Uh-oh!" Randy said when he saw the angry face of Rose on the screen. They were still far out past the orbit of the Moon, so the time delay was many seconds.

"The wedding is in two days," said Rose sternly.

"Rose, honey," Randy said, "this Silverhair breakthrough is so important and has so many ramifications that I've *got* to stay on top of it! Let's postpone the wedding for a few weeks. Wait . . . it'll take at least a month to get things under control. Make it a month. OK?"

A number of seconds later, Randy saw Rose's visage become even sterner as his words finally got to her. "I am leaving my apartment to go to the home of my parents in California," she said. "If you want me back, you must come and get me. And if you're not at the church by two o'clock on Saturday . . . don't bother coming. I'll be gone." The screen went blank.

➤ ➤ ➤

Rose turned from the communicator screen and stared blankly at the rain pouring down on the Princeton countryside.

Randy could be the most exasperating person . . . Was she doing the right thing by marrying him?

She thought back to the time she had first met him. It was at his eighteenth birthday party, six years ago . . .

➤ ➤ ➤

There was a good crowd in the living room as Randy entered. Along one long wall was a banner saying "Happy 18th Birthday, Randy!" while along the other was a banner with the date "29 February 2030," although the party was really being held on Randy's "unbirthday"—Friday, March first—for there was no 29th of February in 2030.

Randy had looked magnificent in his new formal black tuxedo with a bright-red cummerbund, his wavy chestnut-brown hair tied back into a Paul Revere with a matching bright-red ribbon. A graded set of large rubies climbed up his right ear; the left ear was naked. Immediately, an impromptu rendition of "Happy Birthday to You" started up. Randy beamed, then turned to welcome some new guests the butler had escorted in.

When the song was through, someone started in on the almost-obligatory sequel. It was Oscar Barkham, who had lived "next door" to Randy since he was born. Of course, in the Princeton Enclave, next-door mansions could be anywhere from a tenth of a mile to ten miles apart, depending upon where they were placed on the large lots.

"Happy birthday we will say . . ." continued Oscar in a loud, carrying voice from his position next to the roaring fireplace in the long living room. "For you're four-and-and-half years old today . . ."

He hollered over at Randy across the room. "How does it feel being just a little four-year-old kid, Randy?"

"When *you* are a hundred years old and tottering off to your grave,

I'll just be reaching my prime!" retorted Randy, having coped with leap-year-baby jokes all his life.

When the new arrivals had slowed to a trickle, Randy came over to the champagne waterfall and got himself a glass of champagne from the android maid. As he turned away he almost bumped into Rose. She remembered that she had been wearing a provocative red party dress with a deeply scooped neck and a peekaboo overlapping flounce cut up one side that showed a lot of net-stockinged thigh when she moved.

"Hi, beautiful," Randy said with a smile. "I won't say that corny old line, 'Haven't I met you somewhere before?' because I haven't. I wouldn't have forgotten a lovely thing like *you*."

"Hi," she replied. "I'm Rose. Rosita Carmelita Cortez."

"Buenas tardes, Señorita Cortez," said Randy. "I am most honored you have graced my home with your most beautiful presence," he continued in well-accented Spanish.

She was impressed. This young man was apparently more than just a rich playboy. She began to take an interest in him.

"Your fluency in Spanish is most impressive, Señor Hunter," she replied. "You must have taken many years of classes to be able to speak so well."

"I picked up a number of languages when I was very young," said Randy. "My mother was setting up a number of subsidiaries in Europe and the newly formed Socialist Economic Bloc, and we spent almost all our time overseas. We would live two or three months in one country, then move to the next. In each place I would pick up the accent and basic vocabulary like a sponge. It helped that Mom could speak German and Dad knew Russian. Later, in school, I took some classes to polish up on the more important languages. But enough about me. Let's talk about you . . ."

"I came with Oscar Barkham," she replied. "We take Chem 102 together over at Princeton University."

"Say . . . Oscar has finally developed good taste," said Randy, looking her over discreetly.

"You have a very nice place here," she said, trying to change the subject by making polite conversation.

Randy took a quick look at Oscar. Oscar was still occupied over at the fireplace, his football-player bulk blocking the view of the large grandfather clock that had been an antique before Randy's grandfather was born.

"Would you like me to show you around?" Randy asked, taking her arm possessively.

"All right," she answered, then looked around at all the people. "But don't you have to take care of your guests?"

"That's what the butler and house staff are for," said Randy, leading her to the wide stairway that led upstairs from the large entry hallway. "Come on."

Upstairs Randy began the tour. "Now . . . this is the older part of the house. It was built before Granddad Reinhold died and left Reinhold Company to Mom to run." He opened a door and walked into a small room. They interrupted a small household robot in the process of cleaning the floor. It stopped and, skittering around them, went out the door and down the hallway.

"This was my room when I was a baby. It's still the way my mother left it when I was moved to a bigger room. I guess she was thinking that maybe I might have a younger brother or sister. But being president of a major company kept her too busy for that . . . or perhaps it was the difficulty she had with me."

"Difficulty?" Rose asked.

"I was born five weeks prematurely," said Randy. "I only weighed three pounds. It was a struggle keeping me alive. The doctors realized that with my mother's genes and the premature birth, I wouldn't grow very tall. They recommended growth-hormone therapy, but when Mom heard there was some cancer risk associated with the therapy, she vetoed the idea.

" 'Everybody has to have *something* wrong with them,' she said. 'So let him be short. He'll learn to live with it—like I did.' So I'm short, and I've learned to live with it . . . but it doesn't mean I like it."

Randy walked over to the ancient wooden-slatted crib and rubbed his hand over the teeth marks at the end.

"This was my crib. Dad told me it was handed down through his side of the family. It's over a hundred years old." He laughed. "It almost didn't make it past me!"

"What do you mean by that?"

"I nearly wrecked it," explained Randy. "As a kid, I always wanted to explore. Still do, as a matter of fact. I became quite an escape artist from this crib. First thing I learned to do was to unscrew the nuts and bolts, and get out to go exploring. Then my dad wired the nuts to the bolts. So I *chewed* my way out through the wooden slats."

He pulled up the far edge of the mattress and showed her a chewed slat, now repaired with a splint of hardwood and twisted wire.

"I pushed aside the upper part of the slat and crawled right out over the sharp spike at the bottom," Randy went on. He pulled down the red cummerbund and pulled up the front of his dress-suit dickey so she could see the long, jagged, ancient scar on his stomach. "They didn't know I'd escaped until they heard me crying from the front lawn. I'd fallen there from the veranda roof. They found a fresh-picked apple lying next to me."

"You could have been killed!" she said, looking out from the low dormer window at the apple-tree branch hanging over the veranda roof.

"Takes more than a fifteen-foot fall to faze me," said Randy proudly. He tucked in his shirtfront and, taking her by the arm, led her from the room. "Now, let me show you my latest crib—no bars on this one—and three meters in diameter . . ."

"Maybe we had better go back to the party," she said.

➤　　➤　　➤

Oscar and Randy soon got into a petty argument about Randy's taking Oscar's date upstairs to look around. According to what she had been told previously by some of the others at the party, the two had been bickering ever since they were kids. Oscar was two years older than Randy, and had dominated the younger and smaller man most of his life. The two disliked each other intensely, but had managed to stay civil most of the time, since their parents had been good friends.

Because of the argument, she and Oscar left the party early. The instant Oscar's chauffeur had closed the door on them, she turned to Oscar.

"I hope you realize that absolutely *nothing* happened between me and Randy," she said firmly. "All he was doing was showing me around the older sections of the mansion. We never even went anywhere *near* his bedroom—"

"I know that," said Oscar with a wave of his hand. "It's just that the cocky little twerp makes me jealous."

"You? Jealous?" she asked incredulously. "From what some people have told me, you're worth ten times what he is."

"The Barkhams are worth tens of billions," said Oscar supercil-iously. "While the Reinholds are in the penny-ante hundred-million-dollar class. What irks me is that my parents control the Barkham billions and all I get is an allowance, while that immature midget now controls all his."

"Your allowance must be pretty generous," she said dryly, sitting back comfortably in the plush seat of the limousine and looking around.

"More than I can spend," admitted Oscar. "I can have anything I want."

Just then a small white light blinked above an intercom speaker. Oscar reached forward and pushed a button.

"What is it, Maxwell?" he asked.

"We have cleared the Reinhold property," said the chauffeur. "Where do you wish to go, sir? Home?"

"No," said Oscar. "The night has only just started. Take us to Atlantic City and we'll party the night away there."

"Yes, sir," came the reply. Shortly after, the large limousine passed through the Enclave guard gate, swung onto the high-speed autopilot lane on the turnpike, and headed toward the ocean.

"It'll take us about an hour to get there," said Oscar. "But there's no reason we can't start our own little party now." He turned to look at her as he reached for the door of the refrigerator in front of him. "Would you like some champagne . . . or perhaps something stronger?"

"The night *has* just started," she replied. "I think I'll stick to a small glass of champagne."

Oscar pulled down a table between them, loaded it up with crystal goblets from a cabinet and a large plate of hors d'oeuvres from the refrigerator, and started working on the cork of the champagne bottle. The hors d'oeuvres tray was piled with delicacies. In the middle were three small jars of caviar, Beluga, Caspian Imperial, and Sevruga. Next to the caviar were four different kinds of bread and crackers to spread it on, along with three mother-of-pearl caviar dipping spoons and three crystal spreading knives. Surrounding the caviar were assorted canapés with delicious-looking bits of lobster, shrimp, ham, smoked salmon, and turkey peeking out from under slices of olives, partridge eggs, and cheese. At one end of the tray was a large assortment of dried fruit and nuts and at the other an equally large array of intricately cut fresh vegetable sticks and slices, glowingly fresh.

As she took her first bite of Beluga caviar on a small piece of toast, she began to like the idea of being rich. For a third-generation Latino from West L.A., she was keeping pretty good company. Oscar was not only a smart, blond, handsome football player, he was a billionaire. This was only her first date with him, but she was beginning to like him.

After a few sips of champagne, Oscar pulled out something from the inside breast pocket of his tuxedo. It was an old-fashioned silver cigarette case with the Barkham monogram on the cover.

"I've got something here to liven up this party," Oscar said.

She looked at the silver case with interest. It must have been an old family heirloom. For certain, it didn't contain cigarettes—almost no one smoked tobacco anymore. She had a suspicion what was inside, and looked expectantly as he started to open it. A couple of puffs of some high-quality Durango Gold might be just the thing to help while away the miles to Atlantic City.

Oscar opened the silver case, but instead of the marijuana "styx" that she had expected, the case contained a small plastic eyedrop bottle and a number of square Band-Aid plasters. Oscar tore open one of the plasters, screwed off the lid on the bottle, and squeezed out a few drops of clear liquid on the gauze patch in the center of the plaster. He looked up at her expectantly.

"Patch of ZED?" he asked.

She was horrified, but tried not to let it show. "No thanks!" she said in a slightly shaken voice. "I've got classes Monday."

"It's all over in a few wonderful hours," said Oscar enticingly. "No side effects and no flashbacks . . ." He held out the soaked patch to her. "Just put it on the inside of your wrist."

"No!" she had said more firmly. "Please . . . no."

"OK," said Oscar agreeably. "You don't know what you're missing." He held the patch carefully in his right hand while his left hand lifted his golden-blond ponytail.

When she saw the shaved bare patch at the base of his skull, she gasped. "You're not going to brainstem it, are you?" she whispered.

"The only way . . ." said Oscar as he pressed the patch onto the bare skin. Within less than a second an ecstatic smile spread over his face. His head and body went into slow motion, while his face and eyes flickered wildly at high speed. He looked her up and down, sniffed the air, and took long savoring bites of hors d'oeuvres and lingering sips of champagne.

"It's like the whole world has slowed down and brightened up," he finally said in a slow, deep, slurred voice. "It's like I'm living ten times faster than normal and sensing everything a hundred times better. What delicious caviar . . . what wonderful wine . . . You are so gorgeous . . . every hair . . . every pore . . . And the intoxicating way you smell . . ."

She became concerned as he looked her over lasciviously, but he wasn't making any advances and the table was still between them.

"You really ought to give that stuff up, Oscar," she said. "Whoever told you that ZED has no side effects is lying—especially if you brainstem it. I've been wondering what's wrong with you during chemistry lectures. Every once in a while your eyes start shifting back and forth and you're gone for the rest of the class."

He wasn't listening to her. "So delightfully beautiful you are . . ." he murmured, his eyes flickering over her body. He was behaving as if he were seeing her for the first time.

"It's like the whole world has slowed down and brightened up," he said, repeating himself. "It's like I am living ten times faster than normal. Like I controlled time. Yes . . . that's it . . . ZED makes me the master of time!"

➤   ➤   ➤

The following week, she found that her Chemistry 102 class had a new student—a late enrollee. Normally Randy took his college classes over the Princeton Extension Television Network. He had been too busy with his business and horses and astronomy to be bothered with commuting to classes. That is, until now.

Randy wasn't a typical student. When he wanted to take a course that interested him, he told the registrar and soon the teacher found the name of Harold Randolph Hunter on the class enrollment list. It helped that his father had been chairman of the Princeton University Physics and Astronomy Department at the time of his death, and the Space Engineering Department was housed in a large building with the name REINHOLD emblazoned on the frieze above the portico.

Besides Chem 102, Randy soon found himself in Spanish 422, Drawing 202, and Art Appreciation 102, all of them classes she was taking. She then found that somehow she and Randy were teamed together for the next experimental problem in the Chem 102 laboratory class. She had welcomed Randy's attention, for she had made it clear to Oscar after the Atlantic City ride that she wanted nothing to do with a ZED-head, even if he was a billionaire. It was in Chem 102 lab that Randy had first put his arms around her, right in class . . .

They were doing a solubility experiment. Randy took a tall beaker and filled it with hot water. He held the beaker while she carefully poured in the white chemical she had weighed out. It all dissolved after a little stirring.

"That's the other thing I could never understand about chemistry," she complained. "Look. We put all that sodium carbonate into the water and the water level hardly rose any. How come?"

"Well," said Randy, "let's suppose that you are a sodium carbonate molecule and I am a water molecule. You are sitting in that chair and I am sitting in this chair. We take up two chairs' worth of volume." He reached out his hand to her. "Now come over here and sit on my lap."

"What!?!" she said, drawing back and frowning.

"Come on," said Randy, a little impatiently. "I'm not trying to get fresh. I'm just doing a serious demonstration of an important fact of chemistry. Come on, now," he said, patting his knee. "Sit in my lap."

She came—not too reluctantly, she remembered—and perched on his lap, her feet still on the ground since Randy's small body didn't have much lap.

"There," he said, putting his arms around her. "Now the sodium carbonate molecule and the water molecule only occupy one chair's worth of volume because they like to snuggle up to each other. You *do* like to snuggle up, don't you?"

"I think this lesson is drifting away from chemistry," she retorted, turning to look at him with a wry smile but still sitting in his lap. Then a thought came to her and she looked off into the distance, murmuring, "With a twenty-to-one molar ratio, that means that for every Rose molecule there are twenty Randy molecules to snuggle up with. Sounds like fun . . ."

It obviously didn't sound like fun to Randy, for he leaned forward and tipped her off his lap. He probably didn't like the idea of sharing her with anyone, not even himself.

"Well," he said in a more serious tone, "I see you now understand the concept of solubility. Shall we get on with the experiment?"

➤   ➤   ➤

Over the following years, she had grown to like Randy very much. He cared for her too, and tried to show it in many ways, but he was so self-centered, and so devoted to his own pursuits, that he would sometimes neglect her for days, even weeks at a time. Without warning, he had rushed off to the asteroid belt and stayed there for months, only calling occasionally. Now he wanted to delay their wedding for a month!

She sighed. If she married Randy, it would be like being married to a sea captain—a few days or weeks of intense and loving courtship, followed by many months of neglect and loneliness. She was now resigned to expect no more than that from Randy after they were married. Besides, she couldn't help herself . . . she loved him.

4 ≫

Terravator

AFTER their joyful wedding, Randy and Rose spent their honeymoon at an exclusive resort that was literally out of this world—the "penthouse" suite of the Reinhold Spaceport Hotel. The hotel was one of the first things constructed out of the captured near-Earth carbonaceous chondrite asteroid that would ultimately become the Terravator. A flotilla of Golda Reinhold's AsterSails had been used to haul the forty-meter-wide, fifty-thousand-ton asteroid into its circular polar orbit.

For a whole month, Rose had Randy to herself. At the end of the month, Alan came to visit the newlyweds up on the still-under-construction Terravator.

"How do you like being in space?" Randy asked Alan as they walked together into Randy's penthouse apartment.

"I didn't particularly care for being in free-fall," replied Alan, "but this one-third gravity is very pleasant." They went to look out the large viewport in the center of the living room floor. Only the penthouse, the outer apartment of the multistoried hotel, had such a viewport.

The Earth was passing majestically beneath them as the hotel rotated around its pivot point to supply artificial gravity to the outer rooms. A rocketship floated past one of the view windows and they walked over to look at it. The ship was painted in the bright-pink and leaf-green colors of the Reinhold Company.

"Another shipload of tourists," said Randy.

"I still think it was a mistake for Reinhold Company to get into the hotel business," said Alan sternly. "We are in the transportation business, not the entertainment business."

"But the cash flow from the tourists helps pay for the workers who are turning the carbon in the asteroid into diamond cable," said Randy. He thought for a second, then nodded in agreement. "You're right, though. I'll sell the hotel part of the Terravator to Hilton-Helmsley as soon as the novelty wears off and the tourists start balking at the high room rates."

The Earth rose in another window and they turned to observe it. It was half sunlit and half dark, with the spotted glow of cities on the dark side lighting up as the sun set for them. The Terravator was in constant sunlight, for it had been placed in a nearly polar, sun-synchronous orbit that kept it constantly over the terminator line between the bright and dark halves of the blue-white marble that now filled the large window. After watching for a while, Randy turned to Alan.

"How has the effort gone to quash that subpoena from the House Subcommittee on Space Transportation?" asked Randy.

"The lawyers are having a difficult time," replied Alan. "They have been able to delay it somewhat, primarily because you're not on Earth at the present time, but they don't know how long they can keep it up. Chairman Barkham is threatening to have you cited for contempt of Congress."

"Well, I have nothing but contempt for Congress since they let that vacuum-head take his seat. I don't know what got into the voters in the Enclave district. If he flushed out of Princeton, he certainly doesn't have the brains to be a Congressman. His parents must have been tired of having him around the house and bought his way in."

"His campaign *was* well funded," admitted Alan.

"The Barkham billions strike again," said Randy with a sneer. "They probably bought him the chairmanship of the Subcommittee on Space Transportation, too."

"It *is* unusual to have a newly elected Congressman as a House committee chairman," mused Alan. "Even if it is just a subcommittee."

"What was the date of appearance on the subpoena?" asked Randy.

"Tuesday of next week. But our lawyers have been able to push that date off into next month."

"Tell them I'll be there next Tuesday," said Randy firmly. "It'll be a pleasure to give Oscar a piece of my mind."

"What?" said Alan, perplexed. "If you were willing to testify, then why did you have our lawyers try to quash the subpoena?"

"If I'm going to testify, I want to do it of my own free will," said Randy heatedly. "I don't want some dustbrain Congressman telling me I *have* to be there—especially if the dustbrain is Oscar. He was always ordering me around as a kid, and I'm not going to take it anymore."

"I'll tell the lawyers about your decision," said Alan. He shot out his cuff-comp to take a look at the time. "It's after midnight their time. I'll call them tomorrow."

"You could have known that by just looking out the window," said Randy, pointing to the Earth steadily rising up past the top of the view window.

"I don't understand," said Alan, frowning.

"If it's sunrise in Africa, it's midnight in New Jersey." Randy pointed at the continent emerging from the shadow line. "Once you've been out here a few days, you get a different mental picture of the continents. Instead of just static shapes pasted on a globe, your mind changes them into moving shapes, like fish, with a 'front' end and a 'back' end. North America, South America, and Africa all look like seahorses, with pointy leading chests, blunt trailing backbones, and hanging tails, while Australia looks like a piranha. When the front of the continent is coming out of the dark, it's sunrise. When the front goes into the dark, it's sunset."

Rose came into the room and greeted Alan with a peck on the cheek. "I'm so pleased you came to visit us," she said. "I had the cook prepare us a lovely dinner—not too heavy, since you're not used to low gravity yet."

"I might try some," said Alan. "I didn't eat much on the way up and I'm famished."

"White wine?" said the robobutler, coming up to them with a tray holding three glasses.

➤　➤　➤

It was late Monday afternoon when Randy and "Red" Hurley, the senior senator from New Jersey, walked down the echoing halls and into a meeting room on the House side of the Capitol Building. Some technicians were setting up television cameras for tomorrow's meeting. Senator Hurley was nearly bald, but instead of wearing the white "English barrister" wig most of the other senators affected, Red Hurley wore a bright-red Paul Revere tied back with a formal black bow.

"This is where you'll be giving your testimony tomorrow," said Senator Hurley.

"Just as I thought," said Randy, visibly irritated as he looked over the meeting room.

"What's wrong?" asked Senator Hurley, looking around in puzzlement.

"The witness table."

"It's one of the standard large tables," the senator said. "But it looks as though someone has had wheels added to the legs."

"The witness chair, too," continued Randy, pointing.

"It's just one of the standard large chairs . . ." The senator's eyebrows raised. "Except that someone has had the wheels taken off the feet." He looked down at Randy's grim face.

"It doesn't take much guessing to know who that someone was," said Randy furiously. "If *I* sat in *that* chair before *that* table, I'd barely be able to get my chin up over the edge. I'd look like a kid getting a lecture at the principal's office."

"I'll talk to the Speaker of the House and have them replaced immediately," said Senator Hurley, very annoyed with Congressman Barkham. Barkham, with his billions, didn't care that Mr. Hunter was one of New Jersey's most important constituents, but the senator did.

"Wait," said Randy, thinking. "Just leave the table and chair the way they are. If we change them, Oscar will just come up with some other way to humiliate me." He shot his cuff-comp from his sleeve and punched away on the touchscreen.

"But how are you . . . ?" started Senator Hurley.

"Tony?" said Randy to the image in the cuff-comp. "I need the beam cutter and the sportsman's chair. At the Capitol steps, before nine A.M. tomorrow."

➤   ➤   ➤

Oscar Barkham was in his element. Television lights glaring in his eyes, he banged his gavel loudly on the table before him, causing the microphones to make overload splutters in protest. He had grown even handsomer as he grew older, and today, a boyish wisp of blond hair had escaped his Paul Revere and was dangling seductively down his forehead.

"The meeting of the House Subcommittee on Space Transportation will come to order!" he said. "The purpose of our meeting today is to discuss the hazards of the so-called Terravator space transportation system being constructed by Reinhold Astroengineering Company. Our first witness is Mr. Harold Randolph Hunter, the owner of the company. Is Mr. Hunter here?" He looked around the room. There was no sign of Randy.

"Randy-y-y?" he called out into the room, peering through the lights with one hand over his eyes. "Are you hiding behind a toadstool somewhere?" Laughter spread around the room, which he allowed to continue for a while before belatedly bringing it to a halt with a few bangs of his gavel.

"Since Mr. Hunter has chosen to ignore the subpoena of this subcommittee," Oscar intoned, "I hereby find him in contempt of Congress."

The meeting-room doors opened and Randy walked in. "You're absolutely right when you say I'm in contempt of Congress, Oscar." He waggled a finger at him. "But remember—you said it, I didn't." He strode to the front of the room until he was standing in front of the too-tall witness table. He put a small black case down on the floor beside him.

"I had the subpoena quashed," said Randy belligerently to Oscar. "So I cannot be forced to testify."

Someone behind Oscar leaned forward and whispered in his ear.

Oscar turned back to look at Randy. "The Subcommittee's legal counsel informs me that the subpoena was not quashed, merely delayed a month. In that case, Mr. Hunter, we will see you next month and force you to testify."

"If you wish to do it that way," said Randy with an unconcerned shrug. "But since you are here ready to listen and I am here ready to testify, why don't you just *ask* me to testify? I'm more than willing."

Without waiting for an answer, he turned his back on the subcommittee and took a look at the witness table.

"Just what I needed for my first demonstration!" he said loudly, patting one of the huge legs of the table. Turning around to face the subcommittee, he took a crystal disk the size of a hockey puck from his pocket and stuck his finger through a crystal ring-tab that extended from it. He pulled out a glittering thread from the reel and showed it to the members of the subcommittee.

"One of the reasons that the Terravator will never be a hazard to Earth is that it's being made of the strongest material that can be manufactured by man. Gentlemen, this is a Reinhold isopure diamond fiber, containing a core of isotopically pure, perfect diamond crystal, coated with a thin layer of isopure diamond glass. It is the strongest, hardest, toughest material known."

He went to the table and hooked the tab to one leg, about a foot off the floor. He then walked around the table, threading the diamond fiber around all four legs. When he got back to the first leg he picked up the tab and inserted it into a notch in the side of the crystal disk. He pushed a button in the center of the disk and a small internal motor started to reel in cable. Soon the disk was suspended between two of the table legs and the whirring sound changed in pitch as the thread tightened.

"It can cut through anything!" said Randy with a flourish. The committee and audience watched in amazement as, one by one, the thick oak table legs were sliced through by the diamond thread. Soon the last leg was cut and the crystal disk clattered to the floor and turned itself off. Randy picked it up and put it in his pocket, at the same time giving the table a heave with his shoulder. The table clattered to the floor, now a foot shorter. Randy kicked the amputated leg ends underneath, picked up the black case, and walked around to where the large witness chair stood.

"I won't need this," he said, sliding it heavily aside. "I brought my own chair." He opened the case and took out a folded cluster of crystal rods and shapes. He gave it a shake and it unfolded into a tall stool with a curved seat, curved backrest, and curved armrests. "Made of grown diamond structures," he explained to the audience. He sat down, elbows resting comfortably on top of the table, hands clasped, smiling, and waiting for Oscar to speak.

"You have gotten off to a bad start, Mr. Hunter," said Oscar severely. "Destroying government property . . ."

"I just 'modified' it, Mr. Barkham," said Randy calmly, "so it serves its purpose better. Besides . . . this table had already been 'modified' by someone else previously. Would you like to go into a discussion of that topic?"

Oscar frowned. "No! Our topic today is that monstrosity that you call the Terravator and the hazards it will present to life on Earth, and especially to people living in the United States of America."

"Nothing is absolutely safe," Randy countered. "But the Terravator is a safer Earth-to-escape space transportation system than any other yet invented. Rockets can explode and beamed power laser drives can suffer punch-through and tumbling."

"While all the Terravator can do is break up on reentry and scatter hardware halfway across the country," Oscar retorted.

"Most of the mass of the Terravator is in orbit, high above the atmosphere, where it will stay even if it came completely apart," said Randy. "May I show my first image?"

"Very well," said Oscar. "The display screen is set to receive on Channel 100."

Randy fingered in the numbers on his cuff-comp, and it broadcast the first of the stored images. It was a table listing the characteristics of the completed Terravator system. Randy used the point of a pen on the touchscreen of his cuff-comp to push a leaf-green arrow icon across the image as he talked. The image on his display was replicated in the large screen display at one end of the meeting room.

"The center of the Terravator is in a fairly high orbit, six thousand three hundred seventy-eight kilometers, or exactly one earth radius. The cable itself is twice that length, since each end must be able to reach down nearly to the Earth's surface. The orbital period of the center of the Terravator around the Earth is close to four hours, while the ends touch down once every two hours."

"Does that mean it only touches down twice per orbit?" asked some other member of the subcommittee. "I thought rotovators touched down six times per orbit, like the one on the Moon."

"A minimum-mass rotovator is one that touches down six times per orbit," replied Randy. "And we initially considered that option for the Earth rotovator, or Terravator. But I vetoed it. People riding on that version would be subjected to nearly two-gees acceleration all during their ride. Instead, I decided to make a longer, heavier, and more expensive version that only subjected its passengers to a maximum of one-point-two gees. This version has a cable taper of fifteen to one, a total mass of twelve thousand tons, and end stations of one hundred tons each, fully loaded with passengers. It can lift and deposit thirty tons of passengers or cargo at a time."

"So!" interrupted Oscar. "We're going to have a hundred tons of deadweight dropping down out of the sky over Jerseyork, creating a horrendous sonic boom, and, sooner or later, crashing into the populace below."

"The way I've designed the system, most of the touchdown points are above water," Randy explained. "Let me show you." He punched the icons on his cuff-comp screen, and the static image on the large screen display was replaced with a moving image of the Terravator rapidly orbiting around a more slowly rotating Earth. The Terravator was touching down directly at the north and south poles while the Earth rotated beneath it.

Everyone in the room was watching the moving display on the wall screen except Randy, who was keeping his eyes on Oscar because he was talking to him. Thus, only Randy saw Oscar's body drop into slow motion, except for the eyes, which were flickering back and forth at high speed. Oscar's ZED-flashback attack didn't last long, but Randy was appalled. It took him a second to get back into his standard patter that went with the animated video segment.

"The simplest version is to have the Terravator visit just two points on the Earth's surface, the North and South Poles. The orbital period is four hours, so at each pole we can pick up and land a capsuleful of passengers six times a day. Unfortunately, there aren't many customers near those regions."

He switched the display to a new video segment. "If we move the touchdown points away from the poles and toward the equator, then the Terravator still only touches down at two points, one north of the equator and another south of the equator, so each hemisphere gets visited once every four hours. The Earth, however, has rotated sixty degrees during that four hours, so each successive touchdown point in each hemisphere is sixty degrees west of the preceding one. After six touchdowns, or twenty-four hours, provided we have timed everything right, the pattern starts all over again with the same six touchdown points in each hemisphere. These will be the twelve new spaceports of the future."

"Can I arrange a spaceport for northwest Nevada?" asked Congressman "Dusty" Miller. "Congressman Barkham may not want the Terravator visiting Jerseyork, but Nevada could certainly use more business."

"The laws of orbital mechanics limit our choices," replied Randy. "Let me show you the best arrangement I have been able to find." A polar map of the Northern Hemisphere appeared on the large screen display, with six blinking red dots on it spaced at equal intervals of sixty degrees.

"By selecting the touchdown points at thirty-seven degrees north and south of the equator, we cover most of the world's population. In the Northern Hemisphere, we will have spaceports in the oceans off New York City and San Francisco, in the Pacific northwest of Hawaii, in the Yellow Sea between Japan, Korea, and China, in the Caspian Sea to serve Russia and the Near East, and near the Strait of Gibraltar to serve Europe and North Africa." He switched to the Southern Hemisphere. There were only three bright-red blinking dots, with three smaller pink dots in the middle of large seas with no landmasses in sight.

"For the Southern Hemisphere, three of the points are essentially worthless, while the other three touch down in the interior of Australia, south of the Cape of Good Hope, and the South Atlantic off Buenos Aires. That pretty much covers the world, while keeping the actual touchdown points well away from populated areas," Randy concluded, smiling proudly.

"Very nice," said Dusty Miller. "But suppose we shift the San Francisco one inland some ten or fifteen degrees."

"Then everything else gets shifted on the globe the same amount," warned Randy. "I'll be glad to entertain any suggestions for arrangements of touchdown points, but don't forget, in order to make the Terravator pay, I've got to serve the whole world, not just the United States."

"If the touchdown points are mostly over oceans," said Congressman Clyde Peterson, "how does one board them? From boats?"

"Special airplanes," said Randy. "The end of the Terravator only dips into the upper atmosphere of the Earth. You use one of our high-flying capsule airplanes to go up to meet it. It transfers two capsules, usually one cargo and one passenger, to the end station on the Terravator at the same time it accepts two capsules to bring back down."

"My technical staff says that when a disaster occurs on the Terravator, the debris will drop to the west," interjected Oscar. "That means that all of Jerseyork is in danger from the touchdown point in the ocean east of New York City."

"*If* the Terravator has an accident, the debris *will* fall west," admitted Randy. "But, first of all, it is designed with high redundancy so that even if a large spacecraft collides with the cable, only a small fraction of the support strands will be severed. Second, even if something breaks, most of the debris will remain in orbit. Third, even if something falls in, most of it will be burned up in the atmosphere. Fourth, even if something falls to the Earth's surface, most of it will land in the oceans or unpopulated areas."

"But there *still* could be a number of large pieces that land on Jerseyork," persisted Oscar.

"Rockets from Canaveral are more likely to crash into Jerseyork than the Terravator," replied Randy, keeping a tight rein on his temper.

"But the Terravator touches down twelve times a day, while we only fire rockets from Canaveral every few days," said Oscar. "The potential for disaster is dozens of times greater."

"You mean the potential for low-cost access to space is dozens of times greater," retorted Randy.

"I'm not going to take the responsibility for letting this whirlygig threaten these United States without protecting our populace," said Oscar. "I will inform the Secretary for the Environment that Congress insists on a full environmental-impact report on the effects of the operation of the Terravator on all parts of the United States and its territories."

"That'll take forever!" Randy protested. "You can't do that! The Terravator is an orbiting spacecraft. It doesn't come under the jurisdiction of the Environment Department."

"You yourself said it penetrates the atmosphere," said Oscar. "Anything that penetrates the atmosphere at high speed is certainly going to impact the environment, and we in Congress need to know what that impact is. In addition, we shall also require that liability insurance be in place before you go into operation."

"I've already got liability insurance. It covers everything up to ten billion dollars," replied Randy.

"Ten billion dollars in New York City will only buy you a few city blocks," said Oscar. "You will need liability insurance with no upper limit."

"You're crazy!" exploded Randy. "No insurance company will issue such insurance."

"And I don't want some dinky kid playing space-Tarzan over my district without full insurance!" Oscar shouted back.

There was a shocked silence in the meeting room. Randy's face was dangerously solemn.

"Very well, Mr. Barkham," he said slowly. "It is obvious that the Congress of the United States is not willing to take risks in order to expand our last frontier. I have explored a secondary option for the placing of spaceports around the Earth. You will be glad to know that if I use this constellation of ports, at *no* time does *any* portion of the Terravator touch the atmosphere above the United States or its territorial waters."

Randy hopped down from his diamond crystal stool, collapsed it, and put it back into its case.

"Where are you going!" demanded Oscar. "We're not through with you yet!"

"Yes, you are," said Randy calmly. "Since my Terravator will be neither disturbing the United States nor serving it, I do not need your permission to operate it."

"Not serving it!" Dusty Miller exclaimed.

"In the secondary option, all of the touchdown points are at twenty-five degrees north or south of the equator," said Randy. He flashed his last image on the screen. It was an equatorial map of Earth unrolled into a wide band. There were bright-red blinking dots in the Australian outback, the ocean near Hong Kong, the Red Sea, the ocean off Namibia in South Africa, the ocean off Morocco in North Africa, the jungles outside Rio, and the lower Gulf of Mexico. "I will be contacting with the various equatorial countries for use of their airports for movement of passengers and cargo to the high-altitude touchdown points of the Terravator."

"How come the touchdown point near Hawaii is pink instead of red?" asked Dusty, looking at the map.

"Pink means no operations from that touchdown point. To service that point I would have to fly out of a U.S. airport on Hawaii. Can't do it." Randy raised his hands and shrugged. "Can't get the insurance . . ." He turned to go.

"Wait!" said Dusty. "If you're not going to operate out of Hawaii, then where do U.S. citizens go when we want to use the Terravator to get into space?"

"Havana Airport," said Randy over his shoulder as he stalked out the gigantic committee-room doors.

"Havana Airport!" exploded Dusty Miller. He turned to yell at Oscar. "Now you've done it, Oscar. Castro's nephew will be chortling in his rum over this. He'll want diplomatic relations, relaxation of sanctions, probably even aid, before he opens up his airports to U.S. travelers."

"Well . . ." said Oscar, trying to salvage something out of the mess he had made, "we could fly to Rio or Morocco instead."

A low groan passed through the meeting room.

➤   ➤   ➤

Randy next visited the Reinhold Research Laboratories to be briefed on the latest findings on the Silverhair and its magical gifts of negmatter spheres. The conference room was full as Randy walked in and took his seat at the end. There was a pause as the chair raised him up to table level. The first to speak was Hugh Smith, the acting director of the Laboratories when Randy wasn't there directing things himself. Hugh was a retired admiral who had kept the short haircut and full beard worn by men in the navy.

"We have learned quite a bit during the month you were on vacation," said Hugh. "The prospector ship with the negmatter drive that you returned with has already made three trips out and back with scientists and diagnostic equipment. Steve Wisneski has been the contact point for the laboratory, so I've asked him to summarize for you."

Steve rose from a chair along the wall and went to stand at the head of the table in front of the display control console. A wry smile flickered under his twisting caterpillar mustache as he stood looking at his tiny boss at the other end of the table. Steve was a young theoretical genius who obviously resented working for someone younger than he. He was so good, however, that his supervisors and Randy tolerated his brash manner.

"You sure are a lucky bastard, Randy," started Steve. "One little find, and you end up owning a space warp, a reactionless space drive, and a nearly infinite source of free energy."

"Free energy?" Randy repeated, a little taken aback.

"Yep," said Steve. "When negative matter and positive matter interact through long-distance forces, the negative matter gains negative kinetic energy, while the positive matter gains positive kinetic energy. Take a drop of highly charged negative matter, push on it with electric fields until it is going at nearly the speed of light, and in return you get electrical energy back. The only limit on the amount of energy you can get is how close to the speed of light you can push the negative matter before losing control of it."

"That could cause a serious hazard," said Randy. "The whole solar system contaminated with high-speed negative-matter particles."

"Simple solution," replied Steve. "Just direct the high-speed negative matter into a beam stop. Generic dirt will do. The negmatter with all its negative kinetic energy will just disappear when it hits the dirt and nullifies."

"Hmmm," said Randy. "Looks like I had better start an energy production division."

"There's more than electrical or mechanical energy," said Steve. "There's also nuclear energy. The Silverhair has shown us it can be done, since it feeds that way, but we're still trying to figure out how it does it."

"The Silverhair feeds on nuclear energy?" asked Randy. "That doesn't sound right. If I remember, there wasn't any significant gamma radiation around it when it was being fed from the plasma gun."

"That's because it was using a *negative* nuclear reaction process," said Steve. "We finally found out why it likes iron. Iron is at the bottom of the nuclear energy curve. The Silverhair somehow breaks the iron nuclei into individual protons and neutrons."

"But that requires energy," interrupted Randy, puzzled.

"Exactly," said Steve with a broad, superior smile. "While the iron nuclei are gaining positive nuclear energy by 'un-fusion,' the Silverhair is gaining *negative* nuclear energy. It uses that negative energy to make the complex negative-matter molecules it needs to maintain itself and grow."

"What are those silver spheres of nonliving negative matter that it emits?" asked Randy. "Does it need them? I hope not, as I could sure use as many as I can get."

"They seem to be inert drops of negative-matter particles with no molecular structure and with most of the negative energy taken out of them," said Steve. "If I were a negative-matter biologist, I'd call them the Silverhair's equivalent of *shit*." He laughed at the gasps that arose around the conference room.

"If you don't mind the idea of being called a shit collector, Randy," said Steve, still chuckling, "I'm sure the Silverhair doesn't mind you cleaning up after it."

Randy started to chuckle too. "For free energy and reactionless drives you can call me anything you like," he said. "What's the status of the negmatter-drive development program?"

"Hiroshi Tanaka has completed the preliminary design of a second-generation negative-matter space drive," said Steve. "As you requested, it can propel a much larger spacecraft, one ultimately suitable for rapid interstellar flight. The major new feature is that the ship contains one of the Silverhair buds electrostatically suspended in a vacuum chamber in the hold. The Silverhair bud will provide a space-warp connection from the spacecraft to another Silverhair bud left behind around Earth."

"There are more than two Silverhairs now?" exclaimed Randy.

"Siritha has learned how to bud new Silverhairs at will," said Steve. "Each bud seems to be able to grow as large as the first one we found. We have already used them to demonstrate long-distance warp transport of small objects over many kilometers. The Silverhair space warp seems to work fine, except after about eighteen hours the Silverhairs at each end start to call plaintively for their trainers to come and feed them. If they aren't fed, they give up and pull their bodies back through the wormhole. Without the negative matter of the Silverhair body in the wormhole throat to keep it open, the warp closes up."

"That doesn't sound like a very reliable device to have on an interstellar spacecraft," said Randy.

"Reliable enough," said Steve. "Once a day you just shut down the drive for a half hour, and while you're coasting in free-fall the Silverhair can float free from its suspension system. You feed the Silverhair and play games with it to keep it happy, then put it back in the suspension system so you can start up the drive again."

"Play games with it?" asked Randy in disbelief.

"Well, besides dancing, it loves to play peekaboo, zap-the-trainer, and poof-ball," said Steve.

"This is getting ridiculous!" Randy groaned.

"It'll behoove you to stay on the good side of it," said Steve, smiling. "Especially when you're sliding through the space warp in its belly." He paused to look thoughtfully at his boss. "You know, with your small size, you'd be the ideal candidate for the first human warp transfer. The bigger the object, the harder the Silverhair has to work to transfer it. That is, if you aren't scared . . ."

"Being scared has nothing to do with it, Mr. Wisneski," said Randy, turning boss. "Tell me more about the space-warp experiments."

"Well, as you demonstrated with the tape measure," said Steve, "the Silverhairs are interconnected through a space warp, and it's possible to go through one and out the other. The distance through the inside is smaller than the distance around the outside. In fact, it's near zero."

"Zero?" echoed Randy.

"As near zero as we can measure it. The length of the warp tunnel starts out about equal to the size of one of the Silverhairs, and doesn't grow at all as the two ends of the warp get farther apart. Effectively, it's instantaneous transport—a space warp from one point in space to another. The two Silverhairs are not equivalent, however; one is the older Silverhair and the other is the younger one that budded from it."

"How do you tell them apart?" asked Randy.

"It's not possible to tell just by looking," Steve admitted. "If you initiate a warp through the younger bud, the warp always comes out the older Silverhair. But if you initiate a warp through the older Silverhair, it doesn't come out the younger one, but out the even older Silverhair from which it budded previously."

Randy stroked his chin thoughtfully. "Hmmm . . . And if you initiate a warp in the very first Silverhair?"

"It comes out somewhere else," Steve answered. "We don't know where yet, but Elena Polikova is working on it." He paused. "There is something else you should know about these space warps. If you handle them right, you can make a time machine."

"A time machine!" said Randy in amazement.

"Yep." Steve flashed a sly smile. "All you have to do is take one of your Silverhair pets on a short relativistic ride in one of your magic negmatter-drive ships, bring it back to sit next to its partner on the other end of the space warp, and you have built yourself a time machine. A fast journey of, say, a few light-weeks will make the traveling Silverhair a week younger than the stay-at-home Silverhair. Then, all you have to do to make a killing on the stock market is to warp through the younger Silverhair into next week, buy a copy of the *Wall Street Journal,* then warp back into the past to place your orders with your broker."

"I don't believe that," Randy murmured, frowning.

"It's true," said Steve. "The theory was worked out long ago."

"But suppose I met myself in the future?" asked Randy. "Would I annihilate myself or something?"

"Probably nothing will happen," said Steve. "Unless you tried to do something foolish like shoot yourself."

"Probably?" repeated Randy. "You mean you don't *know* what will happen?"

"There are some theories . . ." Steve replied hesitantly, "but not much work has been done on them since the 1990s. No one believed that time machines would ever be possible, so work on the theories dropped out of style."

"What did the theories predict?" asked Randy.

"Once any time machine starts operating, the whole future of the universe is constrained so that events happening around the time machine are consistent. For instance, the universe will arrange itself so you can't go back in time to kill yourself, no matter how hard you try."

"Are you sure?" asked Randy.

"No," Steve admitted. "That's just what the theory predicts."

"If we're not sure, then we're not going to mess with time machines," said Randy firmly. "I don't want to go down in history as the man who loused up the entire future history of the universe by opening up a Pandora's time box." He turned to look around the room at everyone. "I want you *all* to understand that we will only use these space warps for moving through space. Any employee found trying to use them to meddle with time will be fired *and* reported to the proper authorities."

"But think of all the money you could make with just a one-day time machine . . ." protested Steve.

"I don't need to cheat to make money." Randy dismissed the topic. "Now . . . continue with your report on the space warp tests."

"Well, Siritha has managed to bud off a number of new Silverhairs and we now know enough to attempt the first transfer of a human."

Randy turned to look at Hugh. "When will a test be ready?"

"They're preparing for it now, out in the asteroid belt," said Hugh. "It's mostly a matter of getting the test diagnostic instrumentation ready and into position at both ends."

"Schedule me for the next flight out," said Randy.

"You needn't bother, Mr. Hunter," said Hugh. "Siritha is quite small, and has already volunteered to be the first human through."

"Siritha may be small . . ." said Randy, lowering his chair and getting out of it, "but I'm smaller. I'll go first." He walked across the conference room and paused at the door. "I'll be home packing. Give me a call when the ship is ready."

"Yes, Mr. Hunter," Hugh sighed, knowing it was useless to argue with Randy when he was in this mood.

➤   ➤   ➤

"We are ready to start, Siritha," said Hiroshi Tanaka. "Is the Silverhair ready?"

<<Me move me self here, and there, and here . . . >> murmured the Silverhair to itself.

"I've got it on waltz music," said Siritha. "And it's responding normally. If you're ready, I'll warn it to expect a probe to open up the warp."

"What do you use?" asked Randy. "The fancy equivalent of a tape measure?"

"Used to," said Siritha. "But occasionally we would goof and touch the Silverhair—hurting it. We use a laser beam now." She changed the music from a waltz to a synthesized warning signal that sounded like a siren wail. A slight distance away, Hiroshi Tanaka flicked a switch on an inertially stabilized instrument package. A laser on the front of the package gave off a red glow. A large red spot showed up on the side of the Silverhair a short distance away. Hiroshi adjusted some knobs, and the red spot started to shrink in size while gaining in intensity. As the spot grew smaller, the Silverhair developed a depression as if the light beam were a physical probe.

"The laser bean is poking a hole in it!" said Randy in surprise.

"Steve Wisneski tells me it probably feels like cold toes in bed," said Siritha. "Any positive energy absorbed by the Silverhair nullifies an equivalent amount of negative thermal energy in its body, making it cold."

"It's through!" came a voice over the intersuit radio.

Randy and Siritha jetted over to the other Silverhair a short distance away in space. On the other side of that Silverhair was a copy of the instrument package. There was a spot of red laser light on it. The laser spot started to grow in size, while developing a dark spot in the middle. Soon it was a large ring of red light, slowly growing in radius as it enlarged the hole made in the Silverhair. The technician monitoring the operation of the instrument package motioned to Randy to come over.

"The monitor screen is showing the view through a telescope boresighted with the laser," he said as Randy came to a halt next to him.

"It's Hiroshi Tanaka!" said Randy, looking in the monitor.

"A hundred meters closer in that view," said the tech.

"When will it be big enough for me to go through?" asked Randy.

"It isn't easy for the Silverhair to expand," said Siritha, who had followed Randy over. "The maximum growth rate seems to go as the square of the diameter of the warp. The first few centimeters is easy. Getting it up to a meter takes a couple of hours."

"I only need a foot—a half meter at most," Randy said.

"Philippe warned me about that," said Siritha. "I have firm instructions that the warpgate must exceed one meter before any human can attempt to pass through. Come back this afternoon and we'll be ready."

➤   ➤   ➤

When Randy returned later, Philippe and a camera crew came with him. So far, the news organizations had been kept away. Tomorrow, however, the evening news would have videotapes of Randy passing through a warpgate, his head coming out of one end while, a hundred meters away, his feet were still going in the other end.

"Put your jetpack on inertial," said Hiroshi Tanaka. "I'll feed it the coordinates." A few seconds later he said, "Increase the velocity control when you are ready, Mr. Hunter."

Randy reached up to his chestpack and carefully moved a control. Tiny gas jets fired and he started moving slowly down the hollow tube of laser light toward the hole in the nearest Silverhair.

"I can see laser light on one of your elbows," reported Hiroshi over the suit link. Randy quickly pulled his arms in closer to his body.

"I'm getting nearer . . ." Randy reported as he approached the Silverhair. "Entering the near end . . . Tunnel only two meters long . . . Everything fine . . . no funny sensations. Head out other side . . . clear!" He moved the velocity control back and the jetpack fired again to bring him to a halt just a short distance away from the instrument package.

"Are you OK, Mr. Hunter?" asked Hiroshi over the radio suit link as he collapsed the laser beam.

<Ah!> said the Silverhair in what sounded like relief.

"More than that, Hiroshi," said Randy. "Exhilarated would be a better word. How about setting up the next warpgate between here and Earth? I've got a new bride I need to pay attention to."

"That's going to be a little more difficult, Mr. Hunter," said Hiroshi. "We need to bud off a new Silverhair from this one and take it to Earth first."

"I guess I'll just have to take the slow way home, then," Randy sighed.

Philippe gave a snort, then chided him. "In the olden days of space travel—before the invention of the negmatter drive—people would have thought three days from the asteroid belt to the Earth was a pretty fast trip."

"I guess I'm just spoiled," said Randy, nodding his head in agreement.

Suddenly a large white sphere moved by Randy's helmet, spiraled around him, and stuck to one of his elbows.

<Ball!> came the voice of the Silverhair over their radio suit links. <Play!>

Randy just floated there, looking bewildered at the softball-sized plastic-sponge sphere clinging to his elbow. Philippe reached over, plucked the ball from Randy's arm, and threw it back at the Silverhair. In the vacuum and weightlessness of space, the lightweight ball moved as fast and as straight as a hardball.

At first, Randy was concerned that the ball of normal-matter plastic would touch the Silverhair and hurt it, but as the ball approached the Silverhair, the alien stretched out a number of silvery tendrils to meet it. Sparks flew from the ends of the silvery threads to the ball, accompanied by a loud burst of static from the radio. The multitude of threads backed away and got control of the electrostatically charged foam sphere in a backwards scooping motion. Then, with a continuous whipping motion, the tendrils fired the ball back at a human—Siritha this time. Siritha expertly fielded the ball and threw it back at the Silverhair. Hiroshi was next. He reached for a high one and expertly tossed it back under one leg.

<Ha!> yelled the Silverhair in excitement, and fired the ball back at Hiroshi again, almost out of his reach. Hiroshi was up to the challenge

and the poof-ball was soon back on its way to the Silverhair. The next thing Randy knew, the sponge ball was coming straight at him. The ball turned out to be easy to catch, because the electrostatic charge it gained from each zapping interaction with the Silverhair almost pulled it to his waiting fingertips. He wasn't prepared for the static spark, however, and shook his hand in surprise after attempting the catch. The poof-ball sailed out of his hand over his head, and with nothing to stop it, kept on moving. Randy turned his back on the group and jetted off to retrieve the ball.

"Po-o-o-r Mr. Hunter!" came a chorus of voices from the three other humans.

ZAP!!! Randy was struck in the rear by what felt like a bolt of lightning. *"Yeow!"* he yelled, and turned around indignantly.

<Oik! Oik!> came a tiny laugh in the voice of the Silverhair. Randy looked at the large alien, still many meters away in the distance. It was looking as innocent as it could, considering it was nothing but a faceless ball of silver threads. Then he noticed two tiny, disembodied silver threads tiptoeing rapidly away through space, like pixie toes dipping down through the surface of a pond.

"Zap-the-trainer is its favorite game," said Philippe with a suppressed laugh.

"Just who is training whom?" asked Randy as he jetted back with the poof-ball. His next throw had a vicious speed on it, but the Silverhair was more than up to the catch.

After a few more zaps, one inflicted on Philippe, Randy had to call a halt to the poof-ball game.

"My jetpack is nearly out of fuel," he reported. Siritha was just catching the ball, so instead of throwing it back, she crumpled it up and stuffed it out of sight in a chestpack pocket.

<Ball?> said the Silverhair plaintively.

"No ball," she said firmly.

<Dance!> said the Silverhair, changing the subject but wanting to keep the humans around.

"How much fuel do you have, Mr. Hunter?" asked Siritha.

"Eighth of a tank," said Randy, looking down at the telltales in the neck of his helmet.

"Enough for a short dance. I'll slave your nav system to mine." Siritha punched some buttons on her chestpack. Within a few seconds, Randy found his jetpack firing short bursts that brought him closer to the Silverhair. The lively beat of "La Cucaracha" came out over the radio waves from Siritha's audio chip, while the jetpacks of the four humans moved them in a slow circle around the dancing Silverhair, and the humans jerkily moved their arms and legs to the beat. Over the trumpets and rhythm section of the orchestra could be heard the strange melodic radio voice of the Silverhair, singing to the music in a still undeciphered tongue.

<<Me move me out here, me move me out here . . . then, me move me in . . . >>

Randy leaned back in his office chair at Reinhold headquarters and put his tiny size-four feet up on his desk. He gave a bored sigh and looked grumpily over at Alan Davidson, sitting quietly on the couch across the room.

"It sure is easy running a company with monopoly control over a bunch of new technologies that generate more cash flow than you can spend," said Randy.

"Within a year you should be the richest man on Earth," said Alan.

"One down," muttered Randy to himself, thinking of the goals that he had set himself. He had once thought they were all impossible, but very shortly he would be the richest man in the solar system, and soon after that he could be traveling to the stars . . . if he wanted to.

"What?" asked Alan.

"Nothing . . ." said Randy. He thought for a while longer, then pulled his feet off the desk and sat up.

"Order a new chair for the desk," he said to Alan.

"Certainly," said Alan. "Is the lift broken on that chair?"

"Nope," said Randy. "This chair is too small to fit you. Running Reinhold Astroengineering Company isn't any fun anymore. No challenge. I'm turning this job over to you."

"What are you going to do?" asked Alan.

"Spend all the money you make for me," said Randy. "I'm going to build me an interstellar spacecraft and explore the stars!"

5 »»

Ad Astra!

A few months later, Randy was at the Reinhold headquarters building being given a briefing by Andrew Pope. Randy had hired Andrew away from Boeing-Lockheed to be the new head of the recently formed Interstellar Transport and Trade Division of Reinhold Astroengineering Company. It wasn't hard. Andrew had been in charge of the Advanced Propulsion Department at Boeing-Lockheed for almost two decades, but because of low budgets, the only thing he had been allowed to produce during his long professional career was a large pile of paper studies. When Randy offered Andrew the chance to build a real interstellar spacecraft, Andrew jumped on the next plane to Jerseyork.

Andrew Pope was a typical aerospace engineer-manager, in his early fifties, with a slightly overweight, stocky build that exuded authority and competence. He wore a conservative suit of expensive brown silk in the new short-tail cutaway style, with a conservative brown-on-brown choker and matching hair ribbon. His only concession to jewelry was his MIT school 'ring on his right ear. His Paul Revere was slightly unusual; instead of letting his forelocks grow long, then brushing them back in a standard pompadour, he had short bangs hanging down to help cover a balding forehead.

In the room with Randy and Andrew were three transferees from other divisions of Reinhold Astroengineering Company, Hiroshi Tanaka, Steve Wisneski, and Elena Polikova, and a new hire picked by Andrew Pope from the long list of competent professionals Andrew had gotten to know over the years. He was C.C. Wong, a thin, reclusive aerospace engineer and test pilot Andrew had hired away from the Chinese Space Agency. He was proudly wearing the form-fitting bright-red jumpsuit and black-leather zipper boots that constituted the unofficial uniform of a space test-pilot.

"There's no question we can build you an interstellar vehicle, Mr. Hunter," said Andrew. "It will just take some time to build one that we can be sure is reliable enough to get you there safely."

"We've already demonstrated the negmatter drive at one gee," complained Randy. "It's just a matter of running it for a year instead of a few days. It never runs out of fuel and has no parts to wear out or break down."

"I'm afraid you are not aware that the negmatter drive failed on our first trip," interjected Hiroshi Tanaka apologetically. "One of the electrostatic power supplies failed halfway back to Earth. Fortunately, I was able to switch it with one of the transverse-direction power supplies that weren't being utilized and we were able to continue the mission."

"I don't recall that!" Randy said, sitting up in his chair.

"You were asleep at the time, sir," said Hiroshi. "Mr. Pilcher made the decision not to tell you, for fear you would worry."

"Thanks," Randy said sarcastically, slumping back down.

"Mr. Wong and I have outlined a design and test program to thoroughly test out the drive electronics," said Hiroshi. "We can assure you a high-reliability system, but it will take many months of test flights by Mr. Wong before we know how reliable it really is."

Steve Wisneski's mustache twitched in irritation as he listened to Hiroshi. "The electronics are the easy part," he insisted. "What are you going to do about the most unreliable part of the whole system, the Silverhair itself?"

Andrew, who had been coping with Steve's personality for only a few weeks, was nevertheless on top of the situation. "I agree that a living creature is usually not the most reliable component in a complex system, Steve. But would you mind giving us a summary of the tests the Silverhair trainers have carried out?"

"Well . . ." started Steve reluctantly. "Siritha and the rest of the trainers now have considerable experience with the Silverhairs." He paused.

"And?" prompted Andrew.

"They get better with training," admitted Steve. "At first, they weren't housebroken. They would void a small ball of negative shit whenever and wherever they wanted. That's OK when they're floating all by themselves out in space, but if they did that while they were suspended in the hold of a spacecraft under acceleration, the ball of negative shit would nullify its way out through the hull and leave a nice big hole where the outside vacuum could pour into the ship and fill it full of nothing, making it difficult to breathe. Now, however, one of them has been kept in an electrostatic suspension under high centrifugal gees for over fourteen months and hasn't broken training."

"And they never seem to forget," added Andrew, turning to Randy.

"Never forget?" asked Randy, slightly puzzled.

"Interconnected elephant clones," said Steve, as if that explained it. "Like an elephant, once they learn a routine, they can repeat the performance again after many months off. Like a clone, if you bud a new Silverhair from an old one, the new one has all the memory and capability of the old one. And since they are all interconnected through space warps, once one Silverhair learns something, soon all of them have the ability. As I said, interconnected elephant clones."

"How many Silverhair clones do we have now?" asked Randy.

"I've lost count," said Steve. "A couple of dozen, I guess. We have four pairs busy as warpgates between Earth orbit and various portions of the asteroid belt, three pairs in a triangle between the Earth, Moon, and Mars, and a number being milked for silver shit balls."

"I hope they aren't using Bob Pilcher's rock-music shock technique," said Randy, wincing. "That'd be cruel."

"Siritha wouldn't allow it, anyway," said Steve. "Instead she has induced a Pavlovian-type controlled-reflex response in the Silverhairs that accomplishes the same thing whenever she broadcasts the ringing of a bell—in this case, Big Ben chiming one o'clock. The carillon tune gets the Silverhairs ready, and at the stroke of one it ejects a silvery blob. Two strokes gets you two blobs, but the second one is tiny compared to the first. The optimum output is one large blob of some twenty tons of negmatter every eighteen hours. It's an elephant-sized, string-feathered goose that lays silvery eggs."

"A string-leaved plant that drops silvery fruits," retorted Randy. "Don't forget, I want to get that international plant patent! You can't patent wild animals that you find, but you *can* patent a new plant variety you have discovered."

"Good luck on that one, Randy," said Steve. "Now that Oscar

Barkham has bought his way into the presidency of the Animal Rescue Front, you're going to have a tough time getting that patent issued."

"At least it's better than having him in Congress where he can throw laws at me," said Randy. "It sure didn't take the voters long to throw him out after he had another ZED-flashback attack during that Nancy Queen interview on national television." He looked around the room. "Anything else new that we've learned about the Silverhairs?" he asked.

Elena Polikova raised her hand. It had a videodisk in it. "I have some data," she said, walking to the front of the conference table and putting the videodisk in the machine. Elena, a professor of astrophysics at the University of Moscow on an exchange visit to Reinhold Research Laboratories, was a regal-looking dowager in a shapeless grey dress, with sharp grey eyes in an aging face and her greying hair in a Mongolian bun.

"My colleagues at Moscow University and Glavcosmos do experiments with Silverhair you loan to us," said Elena, turning on the video. "Instead of opening up warpgate with laser beam, we have been using physical probe with tiny television on end. Let me show you."

The videoscreen on the wall showed some people floating in space suits near a Silverhair in high Earth orbit. The suits were of Socialist Eco-Bloc design. One figure carried a probe consisting of a small box with a short telescoping rod sticking out from it. There was a tiny TV camera built into the end of the rod. The cosmonaut pointed the rod at the television camera and the view switched to that of the tiny camera, showing another cosmonaut pointing a large television camera at the screen. The view switched back and the cosmonaut showed how the probe could extend out about five meters and then back again.

"If we send probe straight into a Silverhair," said Elena, "it always comes out parent Silverhair—the Silverhair it bud from. No matter what direction probe goes in—it comes out same Silverhair, just in different direction. This probe instrument is just like laser beam you use. Probe, however, have more capability than laser beam."

Elena continued to narrate as the video switched to an animated sequence that showed the operation of the probe bending at an angle inside a cartoon Silverhair. "Probe can turn at angle once inside and continue to extend from tip. It always comes out somewhere, but *not* from parent Silverhair. We take picture with TV from inside tunnel, then withdraw probe." She stopped the animation segment and switched to a still picture of a star pattern with a distant red sun in one corner.

"This is one of first pictures we take. We put picture of stars in computer. Computer match pattern with stars in memory. It is view from near Betelgeuse."

"Betelgeuse!" exclaimed Randy. "That's light-years away!"

"Six hundred fifty light-years," said Elena dryly. "Here is other picture." The screen was suddenly ablaze with tens of thousands of stars.

"Where is that?" asked Randy, awed.

"We do not know," replied Elena. "It is obviously near center of globular cluster, but computer has not made match yet. Could be near cluster, could be far cluster."

"How far away from Earth have you been?" asked Randy.

"Very far," said Elena. She put up the next image. The screen was almost black except for some faint wisps of light spread out over the distant background. "Very strange place, this one. No stars at all. We have to take one-hour exposure to see anything. All we see is galaxies, very far distant. But computer was able to find match."

"Where is it?" asked Randy, now excited.

"Is center of Boötes Void," said Elena solemnly. "We suspect Boötes Void caused by cloud of primordial negative matter that push primodial positive matter out to spherical surface of void. There, positive matter collect into galaxies of stars which we can see. Negative matter does not form into stars."

"A region of negative matter," mused Randy. "That's probably the original home of the Silverhairs."

"And home to lots of other negmatter life-forms besides Silverhairs," interjected Steve.

"How do you know?" asked Randy. He turned to look at Elena. "Have you seen any evidence of other life-forms?"

"No," replied Elena, also looking puzzled. She turned to Steve. "We have seen nothing. Why you think there are other life-forms?"

"Because the Silverhairs are intelligent," said Steve. "Not very intelligent, I admit, but more intelligent than most animals. The only reason a plantlike creature like the Silverhair would ever evolve intelligence would be if it had a predator and needed intelligence to escape that predator. Ergo, there is at least one more negmatter life-form, and probably many of them."

"Perhaps," replied Elena, thinking over what Steve had said, "but why haven't we seen any?"

"Probably because the predators haven't learned to use wormholes," replied Steve.

"Steve may have something there," said Randy. "I remember Kip Carlton saying a Silverhair is like an octopus backed into an amphora in a Mediterranean shipwreck. How much would we know about the life-forms on Earth if our only view of Earth was an occasional look out through the bottleneck of an amphora in the hold of a wrecked ship at the bottom of the Mediterranean? Once in a while we might be lucky enough to see a shark swim by, but the shark certainly can't get through the neck of the amphora to visit us, even if the octopus can."

"Negmatter sharks!" exclaimed Andrew with a grimace. "I certainly wouldn't like to meet one."

"We will keep open the link to the Boötes Void to see if we can spot any other creatures," said Elena.

"How far away is the Boötes Void, anyway?" asked Randy.

"Distance to Boötes is substantial fraction of distance across entire *universe*," said Elena.

"Y'know," mused Randy, looking at Andrew, "maybe we don't need to make interstellar spacecraft. If we could use Elena's technique to open up a warpgate with the right bend in it, we could pop out almost anywhere in the entire universe."

"Nice try, Randy," said Steve with a condescending sneer, "but no biscuit. The Silverhair at the other end is moving with respect to the Silverhair in orbit around Earth. An object entering one mouth nearly at rest with the rest of the universe exits the other mouth having high kinetic energy and momentum. Compensating for that change in energy and momentum puts a terrific internal strain on the Silverhair. The larger the diameter of the wormhole and the higher the differential velocity, the less mass it can pass without collapsing. At the high velocities encountered when warping over interstellar distances, the Silverhair is just barely able to pass a small TV camera a few millimeters across. Humans are out of the question."

"Is there any way around the problem?" asked Randy.

"Actually, the problem is not supposed to be there. There is nothing known in the Einstein General Theory of Relativity that would lead one to suspect such an effect. In general relativity theory, the throat of a wormhole does not know, and in fact has no way of knowing, whether or not the two mouths of the wormhole are, in the long-way-around geometry, moving with respect to each other. What these experiments with the Silverhair are telling us is that the Einstein theory is not the last word in space-time-gravity theories. There must be something else that needs to be added to general relativity, that somehow globally takes into account the existence and topology of the rest of the universe. Personally, I suspect it has something to do with a theory of inertia."

"Theory of inertia?" said Randy, bewildered. "Never heard of it."

"That's not surprising," replied Steve. "There *is* no theory of inertia . . . yet. But I'm working on it now that I know there must be one." His mustache twitched. "In the meantime, we are stuck with the fact that if the ends of the wormhole have significant relative velocity, the Silverhair can't open more than a few millimeters. That's enough to send a laser comm beam through, but not people. Once you start off on a ship, you are stuck on that ship until you bring it to a halt with respect to the Silverhair mouth back in the solar system."

"Damn!" Randy said in exasperation. "I guess we'll just have to do it the hard way." He leaned back in his special chair. "All right, Andrew, tell me more about the design for the good ship *Rosita*."

"Well," started Andrew, "because *Rosita* will have a built-in warpgate connection back to Earth, it will be an interstellar vehicle unlike any imagined before—even in science fiction. The old 'twin paradox' situation just doesn't apply to these ships. In the past, if you made a ten-light-year journey, even if you could travel at the speed of light, it would take a minimum of ten Earth years to travel there and ten Earth years to travel back or send a message back. In either case, Earth would not learn what you found there for a minimum of twenty years—twice as many years of time as light-years of distance."

"With the warpgate, we can cut that in half," said Randy. "The spaceship, carrying one end of the warpgate, only has to go one way. Once there, you open up the warpgate, and Earth instantly knows what you found."

"It's better than that, Randy," interjected Steve. "The Earth shares in the astronaut's time dilation. Once the spacecraft gets up to speed, where the time-slowing factor gets large, then the spaceship can travel many light-years of distance in just one year of ship proper time. For example, if the spacecraft pulls thirty gees and gets to, say, ninety-nine-point-five percent of the speed of light in a hurry, then the time-slowing factor is ten to one. The ship would cover ten light-years in one year ship time. When the astronaut uses the warpgate to return home, he will find he has been gone only one year Earth time, yet in that one year, he has opened up a warpgate to a point ten light-years distant."

"Like traveling at ten times the speed of light," said Randy, impressed.

"I'm afraid *Rosita* is not going to let you travel faster than the speed of light, literally or figuratively," said Andrew. "We have a live Silverhair aboard that wasn't designed to take gees, and then there is the radiation hazard from moving through the interstellar gas and dust."

"Radiation hazard?" asked Randy.

"A hydrogen atom moving at relativistic speeds is a deadly high-energy particle," Steve explained. "Even if you could turn it aside with magnetic fields so it doesn't burn a hole through you, it would emit a burst of bremsstrahlung X rays that would do almost as good a job of frying you all over."

"We will be working hard on the radiation shielding problem," said Andrew. "But I'm afraid that the design speed of *Rosita* will be limited by the radiation hazard to eighty percent of the speed of light, while the design acceleration will be one gee. We can push both limits, but one leads to increased risk to your health, and the other leads to increased risk that we could lose control of the Silverhair, with drastic conse- quences for the Silverhair, *Rosita,* and you, when the negative matter of the Silverhair contacts the sides of the containment vessel in the hold."

"What is the trip time to Alpha Centauri, then?" asked Randy.

"From takeoff to warpback—five years," said Andrew. "But it's better than the thirteen years it would have taken to make a round trip at one gee the old way."

"Five years . . ." repeated Randy. He sighed heavily. "Rose isn't going to like it."

➤   ➤   ➤

Randy had avoided attending the trial. It had been getting enough publicity from the newspapers, and if he were visible to the newspapers, then the headlines—RICH BRATS IN "SLAVER" COURTROOM BRAWL— would start again.

Oscar Barkham was creating enough headlines all by himself. He staged a news conference every day after the court session was recessed, as celebrity after celebrity paraded up to the witness stand to condemn Randy and the Reinhold Astroengineering Company for making slaves of the Silverhairs. As a result, Oscar's ruggedly handsome face was now seen daily around the world on television.

Oscar had latched onto the very popular Animal Rescue Front in order to make a public comeback after his ZED-flashback debacle on the Nancy Queen show. Oscar now basked in the media attention and the daily close association and new friendships with video, music, and publishing superstars. Memberships in the Animal Rescue Front increased dramatically. The increase in donations, however, was nowhere near sufficient to pay the hefty appearance fees of the superstars. Oscar covered those costs.

After two weeks of depositions, the Animal Rescue Front completed its arguments, and it was now time for Reinhold Astroengineering Company to present its side of the case. Randy had chosen Red Hurley, recently retired senator from New Jersey, as his attorney.

"I'd like to be in the courtroom," said Randy. "But I won't come if you think it will be detrimental to our case."

"Since this is a patent court," said Senator Hurley, "and the case is decided by the judge, not a jury, having you there would show the judge that you think the case is important."

"It won't be for long, anyway," said Randy.

"No, it won't," said Senator Hurley, smiling. "Your idea for our first witness was most surprising when you first suggested it, but I think it was a stroke of genius. I remember what a fool you made of him at that Congressional hearing on the Terravator. He'll never forgive you for that. Was he mad! And still is."

"Mad, hell," said Randy. "That guy's crazy!"

"He'll be even madder once I finish with him on the witness stand," said Red. "If things work as we planned, we won't need the rest of the expert witnesses we've lined up."

When Randy's small form walked into the courtroom, passed through the gate, and sat down at the defendant's table, a cloud of hisses and mutterings billowed up behind him as the spectators recognized the diminutive body. Randy sat in a special chair that Senator Hurley had arranged for him, and soon was raised up to where he could put his arms comfortably on top of the table. Before he rested his arms, he took a packet out of his jacket pocket, ripped it open, and removed a wiping paper soaked in cleaner. After cleaning his hands, he wiped the top of the table. Depositing the spent wiper in a nearby trash basket, he put his arms on the now-clean table, interlocked his fingers, and sat quiet and motionless. Soon the noises from the spectators dwindled to muffled whispers.

The judge entered, sat down, and picked up the docket from her bench.

"We will now hear the arguments by the defendant, Reinhold Astroengineering Company," said the judge, looking over her half-lens reading glasses at the defendant's table.

Senator Hurley got up from behind the table and walked up to the bench.

"Our first witness will be the president of the Animal Rescue Front," said Senator Hurley. "Will Mr. Oscar Barkham please take the stand."

Randy could see the judge's eyebrows raise when she heard the name; then her jaw cocked to one side as she considered the ploy and obviously thought it a good one. The noise from the spectators' area grew as a confused Oscar Barkham had a hurried conference with the bevy of lawyers at the plaintiff's table.

The judge gaveled the courtroom into silence as a reluctant Oscar Barkham took the stand and was sworn in. Senator Hurley came close to the witness stand and gave Oscar a disarming smile.

"This is really a very simple case, Mr. Barkham," started Senator Hurley. "My client maintains that the Silverhairs are plants and subject to protection under the new Standardized International Patent Law provisions—"

"Some protection!" blurted Oscar. "Slavery is more like it!"

Senator Hurley ignored the outburst and continued, "—while your organization maintains that the Silverhairs are wild animals obtained directly from nature without genetic manipulation, and therefore cannot be patented."

"They are intelligent, sensitive . . . *caring* animals," said Oscar. Remembering some phrases from the pamphlets and press handouts the Animal Rescue Front had generated for the case, he went on. "They deserve a better life than slavery to serve a brutish master who tortures them with tissue-damaging probes to make them serve his will"— Oscar turned to look at Randy—"and satisfy his base desire to dominate large animals to compensate for his diminutive stature!"

Randy nearly exploded at the remark, but kept his temper under control. The judge spoke out tiredly.

"In the future the witness shall confine his remarks to direct responses to questions put by counsel," she said.

"Now," said Senator Hurley, "let us come to an agreement on a description of a Silverhair."

"It's an animal!" persisted Oscar.

Senator Hurley didn't look to the judge for help, but simply ignored Oscar's remark and went on. "Please answer yes or no. A Silverhair is a living object, is it not?"

"Yes . . ." said Oscar slowly, suspecting a trap.

"A single Silverhair consists of a central body that branches out into many hundreds of tendrils all similar in structure, although differing in length and diameter."

"Yes," replied Oscar.

"A Silverhair reproduces by bifurcation of an existing Silverhair."

"So do simple animals!" blurted Oscar.

"Yes or no," said Senator Hurley.

"Yes," admitted Oscar.

"All Silverhairs are interconnected through warps in spacetime."

"Yes," said Oscar. "That's why they are being enslaved by Reinhold Astroengineering Company." Senator Hurley ignored the outburst.

"The original Silverhair was found floating in space, and neither it nor any of its dozens of budded replicas have shown any signs of locomotion."

"Yes . . . but oysters don't move either."

"A Silverhair eats rocks and prefers iron, especially iron atoms from a plasma gun," said Senator Hurley.

"Yes."

"The Silverhair can detect light with its tendrils."

"Yes!" said Oscar, now feeling more confident. "And detect radio waves."

"I was coming to that," said Senator Hurley. "The Silverhair can both detect and transmit radio waves with its tendrils."

"Yes!"

"In fact, using its radio-wave detection and transmission ability, a Silverhair can communicate with humans."

"Yes!" said Oscar, feeling pleased with the turn of the questions.

"The level of communication, however, is limited to single words and simple concepts," said Senator Hurley.

"Yes . . ." said Oscar reluctantly, still looking for a trap.

"Now," said Senator Hurley, changing tack. "All living objects are either plants or animals, is that not so?"

"Yes," said Oscar. "And the Silverhair is an animal."

"The witness is warned," said the judge. "He is to confine his future remarks to direct responses to questions by counsel. If he does not, he will be found in contempt of court." Oscar was now under great strain. Randy saw the ZED-flashback attack coming, but most of the rest of the people in the courtroom missed it, including the judge and even Senator Hurley, who was busy looking at his notes and not watching the witness. Oscar went into a trance, his body moving in slow motion while his eyes darted wildly around the courtroom, as if he were a trapped wild animal looking for some way to escape.

"Both plants and animals are sensitive to light," read Senator Hurley from his notes. "But animals have complex seeing organs called eyes, while plants have no eyes and sense light with their leaves and body. Is that true? Yes or no."

Oscar didn't answer.

"The witness will answer the question," said the judge, clearly annoyed.

Fortunately for Oscar, the attack didn't last long. He had heard the question and figured out the correct answer, but had avoided responding since his slurred, lowered voice would have been a direct giveaway. He finally came back to normal.

"Y-e-s," he said slowly.

"Both plants and animals eat food. But animals eat by ingesting living or formerly living food made of complex molecules into their gut, while plants eat by absorbing simple elements like iron or compounds like minerals through their skin."

"Yes," Oscar murmured reluctantly.

"Now let me read you the scientific definitions of plant and animal taken from the Encyclopaedia Britannica," said Senator Hurley. "After I have read the definitions, I will ask you a simple question." He consulted his notes again.

"An animal is a living organism that ingests complex organic material into a gut to obtain energy and raw materials for growth and maintenance of its body. It has a highly differentiated structure, with many different and separate organs for processing food, sensing the environment, and locomotion. It propagates by sexual reproduction." He shifted to another piece of paper.

"A plant is a living organism that absorbs simple minerals plus energy through its surface to make complex molecules used for growth and maintenance of its body. It has a relatively simple cellular structure, with no separate organs for processing food, sensing the environment, or locomotion. It can reproduce either by sexual reproduction, buds, runners, or shoots." Senator Hurley lowered his notes and looked at Oscar, who was staring furiously at him.

"Now, Mr. Barkham. Is the Silverhair a plant or an animal?"

"But they're intelligent creatures!" yelled Oscar.

Senator Hurley lifted his two sheets of notes and looked at them in mock bewilderment. "There is no mention of intelligence in either of these two scientific definitions," he said. He lowered the notes and advanced on the witness stand.

"Come, Mr. Barkham," he snarled. "Is the Silverhair a plant or an animal?"

"I'm not going to allow those beautiful intelligent aliens to be enslaved!" yelled Oscar. Turning maniacal, the ex-football player grabbed Senator Hurley by the throat and started to choke him, sending his red wig flying to the floor. The judge rose and tried to intervene, but Oscar sent her flying to the floor with a jab from his elbow. The marshal for the courtroom rushed over and started struggling with Oscar, trying to free Senator Hurley from his grip. Randy, slipping around behind everyone, finally stopped Oscar with a vicious judo chop to the back of his neck.

➤ ➤ ➤

After Oscar had been taken away by the marshal, Senator Hurley turned to the judge, bald head shiny with sweat. "Based on the testimony of the plaintiff himself, Your Honor, I submit that even the plaintiff would have to admit that the living objects known as Silverhairs are plants. I also have a long list of biology and zoology experts ready to give testimony that the Silverhairs are plants. Since they are plants, they are subject to patent coverage and to monopoly ownership and control for the term of the patent under the terms of the Standardized International Patent Law statutes."

"You won't need to call your expert witnesses," said the judge, looking ruefully at her reading spectacles, broken when Oscar had knocked her down. "I've heard enough."

➤ ➤ ➤

"Coo," said Harold Randolph Hunter, Jr., his pudgy fingers trying to grab hold of the buttons on his daddy's shirtfront. Randy looked down at his son, nestled against his chest in a dark-blue belly-hugging carrier harness. Junior had been born ten months after their marriage, making Rose's mother happy in more ways than one. Randy gave Junior a long loving hug and kissed him on top of his head. Then, while walking slowly to the edge of the ha-ha moat around the make-believe castle on his estate, he unconsciously wiped his mouth with the back of his hand. Randy grinned with pleasure and started to rock the baby from side to side as he looked out at the brilliantly sunny countryside stretching out for miles around the small hill they were on. Behind him, Rose was busy tidying up after their family picnic.

"I wish you wouldn't go," she said plaintively.

"I've *got* to," said Randy. "I've already told you that a thousand times. I've dreamed of doing it my whole life."

"I know," said Rose with a resigned sigh. "I just never thought it would happen."

"Neither did I," said Randy, looking out at the horizon and giving his baby a few absentminded pats.

"But *five* years!" exploded Rose, slamming the picnic basket lid shut in frustration.

"It takes a year to get up to speed," said Randy. "And the radiation shields are only good to eight-tenths cee. During the coast phase, I make up a little due to the time dilation, but then it's time to decelerate again. I'm lucky it's only five years of travel for a four-light-year journey."

"*Lucky!*" yelled Rose at his back. "Junior will be in *first* grade when you finally get back." She calmed herself and walked over to join them at the edge of the moat. Tears streaming down her face, she pleaded with him, "Can't you use the warpgate to trade places with someone so you can come home to visit once in a while?"

"The warpgate can't be dilated when I'm moving," said Randy. "In an emergency I could decelerate, match speeds with Earth, then arrange a trade with someone, but every time I did that, it would add two years to the length of the trip."

"U-u-h-h-g-g," grunted the baby.

When he heard the noise, Randy panicked and started undoing the straps on the belly carrier. Rose came to his rescue.

"Here!" said Randy, handing the smelly baby to her.

Hurriedly wiping the tears from her eyes, Rose took the baby and put him down on his blanket. "Are you sure you don't want to change this diaper?" she asked. "It'll be your last chance before you go."

"No. Thank you," said Randy. He took out one of his handkerchiefs and wiped his hands. He started to put the handkerchief back in his pocket, then dropped it in the diaper bag.

"I sometimes think you're going to Alpha Centauri to avoid having to cope with the messy stage of Junior's life," said Rose as she raised the baby's legs and wiped its bottom.

Randy said nothing, but went back to look out at the countryside from the top of the moat. He knew that he shouldn't be doing this to his wife and son. He knew he was being selfish, and it made him feel rotten inside . . . but he *had* to do it. An opportunity like this only happened once in a lifetime . . .

He would be the *first* man to travel to the stars!

➤   ➤   ➤

It took a little over thirteen months before Randy reached eighty percent of light speed. The radiation indicator was already in the yellow zone. He switched off the drive and, floating weightlessly, made his way through the tiny combination control deck and living quarters crammed behind the radiation shield. Gidget was making up

Randy's narrow bunk, taking advantage of free-fall to put bright-blue grasping manipulators on all eight appendages instead of having to use magnetic grippers on four of them for feet. Randy made his way down past the negmatter drive at the center of the ship to the spherical room in the hold that held the ship's Silverhair, put on his tightsuit, and cycled through the vacuum lock. Reaching out from the walls of the vacuum chamber were six insulating posts with large metallic plates at the ends. When they were under acceleration, the plates became charged and pushed on the Silverhair to keep it centered in the room. But now, there was nothing there. The Silverhair was gone.

The first time that had happened on the way out, Randy's heart had skipped a beat. With the warpgate gone, Randy would have lost his link back to Earth. But it was only the Silverhair playing peekaboo.

"My goodness!" exclaimed Randy in feigned surprise. "I wonder where Sil has gone . . ."

<Eek! Eek!> came a suppressed giggle over the radio receiver.

Randy started to look in an exaggerated fashion behind each electrode support post, all the time keeping up a constant patter. "I wonder where Sil is? Is Sil behind this post? No . . . I guess Sil is gone! Maybe Sil is behind *this* post. No . . ."

It didn't take him long to spot, out of the corner of his eye, a tiny silver thread hiding behind the plasma gun fastened to its bracket on the wall, but he continued his exaggerated search routine and passed by the plasma gun without looking at the thread. He tensed his buttocks for what he knew would come next . . .

ZAP! came the lightning bolt, followed by an explosion of alien laughter. <Oik! Oik! Oik! Oik!>

"*Yeow!*" yelled Randy, not really having to fake it. He turned around, and as he did so, the tiny silver thread exploded into a large silver dandelion seed.

<Here!> said the alien. Then, using a laborious step-by-step warpbudding transfer process, it moved itself back to the center of the room and grew to full size. <Dance!> it said.

"OK," said Randy, picking up the plasma gun and turning on the music. The pompous oompah of a German polka band came over the suit comm link.

<Food!> said the Silverhair.

Randy now used the six posts to augment his suit jets as he did a polka around the Silverhair, plasma gun swinging back and forth as he sprayed plasma at the silver threads swaying in time to the music.

<<Me go here, me go there, me go out, me go in . . . >> sang

the Silverhair. Randy heard the musical muttering coming over the radio and knew the Silverhair was singing to itself, but none of the trainers had yet been able to unscramble the alien language. The Silverhair had demonstrated that it could learn and use simple single-syllable human words, but complex communication between the two species was still very far away.

After about fifteen minutes, the Silverhair said, <No food!>

Randy turned off the plasma gun, but kept on dancing with the Silverhair for a while until its searching tendrils had cleaned out all the iron atoms floating in the cavity. The dance over, Randy fastened the plasma gun back into its wall bracket next to the vacuum lock and turned off the music.

"Godget!" he said through his suit link. "Are you ready with the laser communicator?"

"I am in the vacuum lock," said Godget in a deep voice. Randy cycled the lock door and the bright-yellow body of Godget floated through, its eight yellow manipulators pulling a small instrument package with it. Godget set up the communicator on a wall bracket and pointed the laser at the body of the Silverhair. It pushed a button on the side of the communicator, and over the radio came a warning buzz. The Silverhair, hearing the sound, remembered its training and stopped still. Shortly afterwards the silver tendrils spread apart like the petals of an opening flower. A red beam sprang from the end of the laser and struck the silvery body in a red-speckled millimeter-sized spot.

<Cold!> said the Silverhair. <Oo! Cold!>

Its body rapidly developed a depression, then a deep hole. In just a few seconds the laser beam had punched a warpgate through to Earth. In response, a tiny laser beam from Earth came shining back through to bathe the communication apparatus with speckled red light carrying video messages from Earth. Randy's video monitor now showed the face of Andrew Pope in a vacuum helmet. Standing behind him was Hiroshi Tanaka.

"How is the radiation level?" asked Hiroshi in a concerned tone.

"In the lower part of the yellow zone," said Randy. "I could probably go a little faster."

"I wouldn't if I were you," said Hiroshi.

"I don't intend to," said Randy. "Wouldn't save that much time, anyway, and I might hit a gas cloud. Is Rose available? I'd like to talk with her."

"You got up to speed a little faster than we had estimated," said Andrew. "We didn't expect your link until tomorrow. Rose and

Randy, Junior, are in New York City today. I know where they are, however, so it will only take me a few seconds to set up a link. Don't forget, although there is no time delay through the warpgate, there will be a quarter-second delay in the comm link to Earth and back."

A few seconds later, Rose's image appeared on the screen. She was holding a naked child; it was Junior. He was twisting and turning and leaning over, trying to get away from her and get down on the floor. There was a woman in a white coat in the background.

"Rose!" exclaimed Randy. "And Junior . . ." He waved at the camera and called, "Junior, it's Daddy. Hi, Junior. It's me, Daddy." Junior ignored the screen and wiggled and squirmed to get down. "Harold Randolph Hunter Junior!" yelled Randy, trying to get the child's attention.

"He doesn't recognize your voice, Randy," said Rose quietly. She let little Randy escape down off her lap. He crawled away across the floor, but the woman doctor came over and picked him up. He squirmed in her arms, trying to get down again.

"It's good to see you again, Randy," she said with a loving smile. "Is your trip going OK?"

"No problems," said Randy. "Only three and a half more years to go."

Rose's smile faded and a glistening of tears started to show on her crinkled face. Randy became concerned.

"But now that I'm up to speed, I can call you every day," he said, trying to make his wife feel better.

"That'll be nice," said Rose, swallowing hard and putting on a smile again. The doctor paced back and forth behind her, trying to calm young Randy down.

"Where are you?" asked Randy. "Is that a doctor?"

"We're at the clinic," said Rose.

"Clinic! What's wrong?"

"Don't worry," Rose said reassuringly. "The doctors have been monitoring Junior's growth rate since you've been gone. They projected his final height at five feet. I just brought him in for more tests before they start giving him growth-hormone therapy."

"Growth hormones!" said Randy. "That could give him cancer!"

"The doctors assure me that the new hormones don't have that problem," Rose said firmly.

"Besides," blustered Randy, "being small didn't hurt me. As my mother said, 'Everybody has to have something wrong with him.' I was short. Let him be short."

Rose straightened up. "I don't agree with your mother, Randy," she said. "And since you left me in charge of raising our son, I'm going to do it my way."

"Rose!" Randy protested. "Let's talk it over."

"I'll be glad to talk it over, if you'll come back here and talk with me face to face."

"I can't do that!" said Randy. There was a long silence.

"I love you, Randy," Rose said finally. "But I love our son too. And I'm going to do what I think is best for him."

"Rose!" hollered Randy.

"I'll talk to you again tomorrow, darling," Rose said sweetly as she reached out to turn off the link.

Her image was replaced by that of Andrew.

"Anything we two need to discuss?" Randy asked.

Andrew's face clouded up. "Our problems with the Animal Rescue Front are becoming serious," said Andrew. "It started after they lost their case in patent court. First, it was just demonstrations in front of the various Reinhold buildings around the world. Those soon escalated into paint balloons thrown at Reinhold trucks and into lobbies. Next came vicious computer viruses introduced into our networks by sympathizers who took jobs with the company. Now it's worse."

"What have they done now?" asked Randy angrily.

"Three days ago, a mail clerk at Reinhold headquarters was seriously injured by a letter bomb," said Andrew. "The letter was addressed to you."

"Those murderous bastards!" yelled Randy.

"A telephone call from someone claiming they were from the Animal Rescue Front told us there would be more bombings if the Silverhairs weren't freed immediately," said Andrew. "Oscar Barkham denies the A.R.F. was involved and insists that the organization only condones 'civil' violence, like property damage."

"I don't believe him," said Randy. "With those ZED flashbacks making him unstable, he is capable of anything."

"I *think* I partially believe him," said Andrew. "I suspect the real problem is that his organization has lost control over some of its more violent members, but Oscar doesn't really care enough to do anything about it."

"We've got to do something!" Randy cried.

"Alan has implemented all the antiterrorist procedures that the police recommend," said Andrew. "But even the police have to admit that there isn't much you can do."

"Break the link," Randy snorted in frustration.

The red laser beam from Earth blinked off, and Godget slowly lowered the intensity of the laser beam on the ship's communication gear. The hole in the Silverhair disappeared.

<Ah!> said the Silverhair.

Randy turned his radio link to the Silverhair back on.

"Good-bye, for now," he said.

<Bye!> said the Silverhair.

Randy shut the vacuum port on the Silverhair's spherical chamber and ottered his way back up around the drive room toward his cramped quarters. Gidget and Gadget helped him off with his tightsuit in the bottom engineering deck, and after dressing in a jumpsuit he went up to the living deck and strapped himself in the pilot's seat. Floating weightlessly in his seat, Randy rotated the ship around until it was facing backward along its direction of flight from Earth to Alpha Centauri. He started the drive again, this time at a half-gee. That would give him enough acceleration for good footing. He would rotate the ship around again every day, just before breakfast, so he would keep near eighty percent of the speed of light while always being under gees.

By the time Randy had completed the ship maneuvers, Gidget had finished making breakfast. Bright-blue manipulators flashing, Gidget laid out breakfast option number seven, yellow scrambled eggs and crisp brown English bangers, toasted, floury white scones with orange shred marmalade, light-green reconstituted apple juice, and strong brown tea with real demerara sugar and thick UHT double-cream.

Since the pilot's seat was the only place to sit in the cramped quarters other than the bunk and the toilet, Randy simply swiveled around from the pilot's video console against one wall to face the all-purpose table in the center of the room. On the other side of his plate, hanging from the ceiling, was another videoscreen.

Normally, Randy would eat slowly and deliberately, enjoying the good food the robots had prepared for him out of the many options available from the frozen food locker that made up a large portion of the weight of the good ship *Rosita*. Today, however, he just shoveled in his food, for his mind was busy watching the first of the video messages from Rose that had been linked through from Earth during their last brief contact through the warpgate.

➤　　➤　　➤

Randy had the telescope pointed in the proper direction as he approached the first star in the three-star Alpha Centauri system, so it wasn't long before he picked up the largest planet orbiting Proxima Centauri. The planet was a large, cold, blue-green gas giant far distant from the small, reddish star. It had been seen from the observatories at Backside on the Moon many decades ago and named Hercules. The blue-green disk in the telescope monitor stayed nearly featureless as *Rosita* zoomed past it, still decelerating.

Knowing where to look, Randy easily found the three other known planets around Proxima Centauri, and set the telescope controller to take pictures of Hercules and the other three planets every hour. The pictures would be transmitted back to Elena Polikova and Andrew Pope, who would turn them into a scientific paper for *Astrophysical Journal Letters* and a publicity release for the Sunday science sections of the major papers around the globe.

Randy then set the telescope controller to take high-magnification pictures of the small region near the star that constituted the "life zone," where water on a planet would be warm enough to be a liquid but not so hot as to be evaporated into space. For many hours the search revealed no new planet. Then the alert bell rang and Randy looked up from his lunch at the monitor screen.

Randy would never forget the thrill he felt when he saw *his* planet. It was still a small disk on the screen, but distinct features were already visible. Fortunately, *Rosita* was still moving toward it, so it would grow larger for the next few hours. Randy's lunch grew cold as he watched—enthralled—as the telescope took picture after picture of the rapidly rotating planet. After gazing in awe at the strangely shaped continents and oceans, hidden here and there behind swirls of clouds, Randy finally came to his senses and initiated the preprogrammed science routine in the telescope controller. The controller would now alternate visual photos with infrared and ultraviolet photographs, and high-resolution spectroscopy scans over the whole spectrum.

After a short period of time, the orbital elements, physical properties, and major constituents of the planet had been identified. The orbital elements were most unusual—the planet was in a very close, near-polar orbit around Proxima, while all the rest of the known gas giants were close to an "ecliptic plane" that passed through the equator of Proxima. The high inclination and close distance was probably why the planet had been missed despite deliberate searches with infrared telescopes on Backside for "green" planets. The orbit was slightly elliptical and had a "year" of only 33 hours. Although the tidal forces of Proxima on the planet were thousands of times stronger than the Sun's tides on Earth, the planet was not tidally locked, with one side always facing the star. Instead, like Mercury, the planet was stuck in a 3:2 spin-orbital tidal resonance, giving it a sidereal day of 22 hours and a solar day of 66 hours.

"I don't understand that," Randy muttered, a puzzled look on his face. Being an amateur astronomer, he understood the interaction of the spin rotation of the Earth and its orbital rotation about the Sun. The Earth spun on its axis once every sidereal day, which was 23 hours and 56 minutes, but because the Earth was orbiting around the Sun once every 365 days, the solar day from noon to noon was longer—four minutes longer. He tried to picture the planet spinning with a sidereal day of 22 hours, moving with an orbital rotation rate of 33 hours, and coming up with a solar day that was 66 hours—twice as long as the "year." He couldn't do it.

After two days, the telescope had taken enough pictures of all sides of the planet so that the scientific data bank could generate a virtual image of the planet on the videoscreen for Randy to play with. Randy got out the virtual-world helmet and gloves that he used for entertainment and put them on. Ahead of him was the blue-brown planet, and off to one side was the small red star, looming large in its proximity. Manipulating the imaginary joyball control in his virtual-glove fingers, he zoomed his imaginary airplane across the computer-generated landscape.

There was a large continent at the north pole with a thin shield of layered ice in the center. The south pole had no continent and no pack ice—the strong tidal flows prevented any buildup. The whole southern hemisphere was mostly ocean, with two Australia-sized island continents connected by a chain of very large Mars-sized volcanic islands, hundreds of kilometers in diameter and twenty kilometers high.

The north-pole continent was connected by another chain of large volcanoes to a long, flat continent that went almost two-thirds of the way around the equator. The continent had a large rift in the middle that nearly split it in two, like the Red Sea splitting off Africa from Eurasia. Within a few million years there would be two continents.

At the east end of the continent was one of the two "hot" poles of the planet, those places where high noon occurred at closest passage to Proxima. Randy flew his plane to the hot pole and landed his imaginary airplane on the top of a curved mound of weathered mountain that had once been a volcano.

As he waited in the early-morning twilight, he looked east over the rolling landscape. It looked like good real estate, even if it did get hot every "summer." Randy shot out his virtual cuff-comp from his virtual sleeve in his virtual jumpsuit and used the cuff-comp to turn off the weather and hasten the passage of time to one hundred times normal. The light on the horizon increased and Proxima rose rapidly. Randy knew it was much redder than the Sun, but his eyes automatically adjusted to the color, and everything looked normal except that the blue jumpsuit that he normally wore in virtual-world was now black.

Although physically smaller than the Sun, Proxima was much closer, and so looked larger than the Sun. It covered over ten percent of the sky. It grew even larger, and slowed down, as the planet moved toward periapsis and noon approached. The stars were moving through the sky three times faster than Proxima. Randy was taken aback when Proxima came to a stop, reversed its course to pass back through the zenith, then turned around and came back again before proceeding toward the western horizon, decreasing in size and increasing in speed until it set, thirty-three hours after it had risen. Even though he had seen it, Randy still didn't understand it. He took off the helmet and, shaking his head back on the "real" world of *Rosita,* touched the menu on the control screen to bring up the temperature data that had been collected.

The temperature data was surprising, since the radius of the planetary orbit was technically far outside the "life zone" of the very-low-luminosity star. Fortunately, the large tides supplied a lot of heat to the planet, keeping the water from freezing.

The planet was bigger than Mars and smaller than Earth, with forty-five percent Earth gravity. The ratio of continents to oceans was also about forty-five percent. Except for its quantity, the atmosphere was a disappointment. It was mostly carbon dioxide, nitrogen, and water vapor, with traces of rare gases. There was plenty of it, almost two Earth atmospheres' worth, but no oxygen, no hydrogen, no methane, no ammonia, nothing reactive and short-lived that would indicate life was there, exhaling.

"A large, warm, wet, gassy Mars," Randy finally concluded. "Ripe for terraforming." He mused on that thought, then dictated a memo into his cuff-comp to have Andrew change the name of the division to the Interstellar Transport, Trade, and Terraforming Division.

The last picture the telescope on *Rosita* took, as it turned away from the receding Proxima Centauri system and turned its attention to the approaching Alpha Centauri system, was that of the newly discovered and newly named planet, "Hunter."

➤ ➤ ➤

The exploration of Alpha Centauri A and B was less exciting. The close double-star system had two Sun-like stars, but the two stars had swept up into themselves or blown away most of the primordial planetary nebula, leaving very little remaining to make planets out of. The only planets Randy found were those already discovered by the telescopes on Backside, either baked rocks orbiting close to one of the two stars, or frozen gas giants circling around the pair at great distances. After doing a careful scientific survey, Randy returned to Proxima Centauri and the planet Hunter.

His first task was to match velocities with Earth so the warpgate could be dilated and he could warp home. Proxima Centauri had a significant differential velocity with respect to the Sun, some twenty-four kilometers per second in transverse motion and minus-sixteen kilometers per second in radial motion. In anticipation, the Reinhold crew monitoring the Silverhair at the other mouth of the wormhole had taken their Silverhair across to the other side of the solar system and accelerated it up to twenty-nine kilometers a second to temporarily cancel out most of the velocity difference. It was now up to Randy to adjust the speed and direction of *Rosita* to bring the differential motion to near zero. By measuring the frequency of the light from a laser beacon sent by the solar weather polestat sitting motionless over Sol, Randy and the ship's computer set themselves in motion to track the Silverhair sitting in the other end of the space warp back in the solar system.

"Everything seems right," said Randy as he measured his motion with respect to Proxima and found it was near zero. "Time to suit up, Gadget," he called, unbelting himself from his swivel seat and floating across the room. Gadget was waiting there, bright-red manipulators holding the relaxed tightsuit for him. While Gadget checked him out, Gidget cycled the lock leading to the hold and opened the inner door. The bright-yellow form of Godget was waiting there, ready to accompany Randy into the hold.

With Godget leading the way, Randy made his way through the narrow passageway around the drive room and down to the spherical chamber in the hold that held the Silverhair. The Silverhair was glad to see him.

<Rand!> it called, spreading its silvery tendrils out toward him. <Food! Rand! Food!>

Randy started some slow waltz music, fired up the plasma gun, and commenced a half-hour-long feeding dance with the eager, hungry Silverhair, weaving his way around the support posts for the drive plates that kept the Silverhair safely centered in the spherical chamber. The feeding dance was time-consuming, but the Silverhair's obvious enjoyment of his company made it endurable. Over the suit radio, Randy could hear it singing to itself.

<<Me move me self here, and there, and here. Me move me self round, and back, and round . . . >>

When the Silverhair started to play with its food instead of unfusing the iron into protons and neutrons, Randy turned off the plasma gun, replaced it in its bracket, and turned on the laser probe.

<Cold!> complained the Silverhair, but it knew how to avoid the cold.

"The warpgate is opened," said Godget, looking at the indicators.

"Good!" said Randy. "Widen it up so my replacement can come through. I'm ready to go home!"

The transmitting lens on the laser probe changed shape, and the solid laser beam changed into a hollow laser beam and started growing larger.

<Oo! Cold!> complained the Silverhair, the hole through its body getting larger.

"It will take a number of hours before the warpgate is large enough to transmit humans," Godget reminded as they both watched the warpgate widen.

"Watching the Silverhair eat made me hungry," said Randy. "I think I'll go have lunch."

≻   ≻   ≻

By the time Randy had finished lunch and returned, the hole through the warpgate was large enough to peer through. Randy looked through the video monitor boresighted with the hollow laser beam and saw space-suited figures clustered around the laser probe instrumentation at the other end of the short, silvery tunnel that was two meters long on the inside and 4.3 light-years on the outside. One of them was tiny and slim—that was probably Siritha, his replacement. One was wearing a Chinese Space Agency-style tightsuit—that was probably C.C. Wong. He couldn't figure out the others, but they probably included Hiroshi Tanaka and Andrew Pope. He had already been informed that Rose had decided that she and Junior would wait for him back on Earth.

Soon the tunnel through the Silverhairs was large enough that Randy's tiny body could have floated through, miniature space suit and all. But he waited. The semi-intelligent Silverhairs only responded well when human trainers were around. If he were to leave now, and the Silverhair were to get lonely and discouraged by his sudden absence, the warpgate might collapse. Then, since the warpgate had to be opened from the Proxima end, it would be up to Gidget, Gadget, or Godget to do it, and experience had shown that the probability of the Silverhair cooperating with a robot was less than ten percent. If a robot insisted on trying to force open up a warp when the Silverhair didn't feel like cooperating, the Silverhair would simply eject a jet of negmatter excrement at the annoying robot and nullify a hole through it.

Finally the tunnel was large enough for Siritha. She stretched out in free-fall inside the hollow laser beam. Her jetpack fired a burst and she floated through. Randy caught her as her jets brought her to a stop. She gave him an excited hug.

"I did it! I did it!" she squealed, her dark-brown eyes flashing with excitement. The large dot of seductive red makeup on her forehead and the feeling of her lithe body against his through the thin tightsuits sent Randy's hormones into high gear.

I'd better get back to Rose in a hurry, he thought to himself.

<Sir!> chimed the Silverhair when it saw her appear. <Dance!>

Siritha's eyes lit up again. She pushed some buttons on her chestpack, and the radio waves carrying the melodic strains of the "Blue Danube Waltz" filled the large chamber as the limber body of the master trainer danced with the waving fronds of the gigantic alien. Randy bore the delay, knowing full well that he owed a great deal to this semi-intelligent being.

Plant! he reminded himself. *Semi-intelligent plant.*

When the dance was over and the Silverhair had quieted down, Siritha came to help Randy warp through. He put on the miniature jetpack with its beam riding autopilot, straightened out inside the hollow laser beam, and rode through back to the solar system. The first round-trip interstellar journey had been completed. Hiroshi and Andrew caught him on the other side.

"Why aren't you back at the office minding the store?" Randy asked Andrew in a bantering tone.

"You can't tell me what to do!" said Andrew, unafraid of his diminutive boss. "You're only the owner, president, and CEO. I'm a division manager and get to do what I want until you fire me—and I wasn't going to miss this event for anything. After we've done all the necessary things, I'm going to warp through myself, go outside in my space suit, and look at Proxima and Hunter with my own eyeballs. I'll consider that my bonus for the year."

"Be my guest," said Randy, pointing at the warpmouth. "Save me the five-million bonus I was going to pay you for pulling off a successful mission."

"It'll be worth every cent," said Andrew, grinning.

They were interrupted by Hiroshi, who had been monitoring the slow increase in the warpgate tunnel diameter.

"The warpgate is now large enough for you to pass, Mr. Pope," he said.

"Great!" said Andrew, reaching for Randy's jetpack. "I'm going through."

"You have fun," said Randy, heading for the vacuum lock in the spherical chamber. "I'm going to catch the next ship home to my wife and son."

6 ➤➤

Welcome Back

The stench and dirt of crowded humanity closed in on Randy the second he took off his helmet. The spacecraft that had husbanded the Silverhair at the solar-system end of the Sol-Proxima warpgate had been built about the same time as Randy's exploration ship, six years ago. Although it was not as small as the tiny one-man exploration craft, it had been crowded every second of those six years with dozens of scientists, engineers, and visitors who had set up and monitored Randy's five-year trip to the stars.

Randy could see two brightly colored clones of Gidget and Gadget busy cleaning, but the scratches on the wall from six years of contact with the sharp edges of equipment were now filled in with dirt, and the whole inner surface of the ship was darkened by an impervious coating of grey grime. The cold blast of freshly filtered air coming from the ventilator system still retained the moist taste of sweat and the rancid smell of dirty human bodies. Randy grimaced, but managed to shake hands all around, thanking everyone for the good job they had done.

"I really need to get out of this tightsuit, use the head, and clean up," he finally said, trying to bring the welcome to a halt.

"Your room is at the end of the hall where it has always been—waiting for you to return," said someone. Randy ottered quickly down the hallway, entered the master stateroom, and shut the door thankfully behind him.

The air in the room was stale with disuse, but it was clean and dry, so he didn't turn on the air conditioner. There was a slight hint of Rose's strong perfume in the air, for she had been the last one to use the room. Randy quickly floated to the small private toilet, found his stash of handwipes, and tore open one of the packets. The solvent had leaked out during his long absence, but he reactivated the wipe with a small ball of water from the sink and carefully cleaned off his tightsuited right hand where it had recently met so many fervent but grimy palms. That taken care of, he put his room Gadget to the task of thoroughly scrubbing the shower, while he relaxed his tightsuit, peeled it off, pulled off the codpiece, and tossed everything to the room Gidget. With a sigh of relief, he closed the door to the free-fall bathing stall and took a long hot shower until he felt clean again.

Randy's arrival on Earth to a hero's welcome as the first true astronaut was marred by one ugly demonstration after another organized by the Animal Rescue Front. Frustrated everywhere he tried to travel, Randy finally had to cancel all of his invitations and go directly home. The last A.R.F. demonstration was inside the Princeton Enclave, right outside his property line. Oscar Barkham's father had died two years ago, and Oscar's mother was in a rest home, leaving the Barkham billions and property in Oscar's control.

"You had better fly in from the northeast, sir," said the pilot of the Reinhold Astroengineering Company VTOL jet as he let his diminutive boss handle the controls of the powerful airplane from the copilot seat.

"But the wind is the other way," protested Randy.

"Mr. Barkham has the southwest approach blocked by makeshift barrage balloons, sir," said the pilot.

"I can't believe that guy!" said Randy angrily. "I've got to see this."

They flew a few minutes longer, and soon the Princeton Enclave was in sight. All along one side, where the Barkham and Hunter properties touched, was a string of large weather balloons tethered to the ground by strong steel cables.

"That's kind of stupid," said Randy. "Even a novice pilot could avoid those."

"If we had our customary afternoon low clouds, those balloons would be hidden in the cloud bank, and those steel cables are strong enough to slice this aircraft in two," said the pilot grimly.

"That murderous bastard!"

"We tried to get an injunction," the pilot said. "But the Animal Rescue lawyers argued that the injunction would impair Oscar's right to free speech. And if you were stupid enough to fly into the balloon tethers, it would be all your fault, especially since you would have been flying too low over his property."

Randy flew along the long row of balloons. They had messages on them, each message separated from the next by a balloon carrying the jet-black and scarlet-red symbol of the Animal Rescue Front: a vicious, large-toothed dog biting the bloody hand of a human with the words BITE BACK underneath. The messages were large enough to be seen from the interstate, and varied from trite to vicious:

FREE OUR SILVERY ALIEN FRIENDS.

SILVERHAIRS ARE ANIMALS, NOT PLANTS.

STOP THE EXPLOITATION OF INTELLIGENT BEINGS.

KILL THE DWARF SLAVER!

Randy was taken aback by the last one. "Can they say that?" he exclaimed. "Can they come right out and say 'Kill someone'?"

"According to our lawyers, the only time the authorities will prosecute someone for saying 'Kill that person' is when it is said to someone who has a gun pointing at that person, and the gun goes off."

"Lot of good that does," Randy grumbled. He flew the VTOL to the end of his private strip and started the nearly vertical drop downward. "Besides," he continued in a mutter half to himself, "I'm not a dwarf. I'm just small."

➤   ➤   ➤

The airplane was met at the strip by a limousine. The pilot stayed with the plane while Randy rode back to the house on the other end of the estate. They were passing by the training stables when Randy suddenly reached forward and turned on the intercom to the chauffeur.

"Stop here, William," he said. "I want to take a quick look at my horses."

The limousine turned into the driveway and made its way past the homes of the stable crew. There were a few horses on the grounds and a number out taking turns around the track. He found Curly near the finish line, timing a horse.

"Two-thirty for the mile and a half," said Curly, resetting the watch.

"Who was that?" asked Randy.

"Winter Zephyrs," said Curly. "One of the newest from Winter Winds."

"Oh . . . right," said Randy knowledgeably. "Those charts on him you sent me looked excellent. Good lines on both sides and good performance to date. Legs still good?"

"Couldn't be better," said Curly. "You've got another winner there, Mr. Hunter."

"*We've* got another winner," corrected Randy. "I couldn't do it without you."

"But it's your money, so you get the cup," said Curly. "Don't forget to drop by my office and pick it up."

"What cup?"

"You won a cup last year for 'International Horseman of the Decade,' " said Curly. "I flew over to Ascot and accepted it for you from King William himself. Didn't Mr. Davidson pass the message on to you?"

"I guess he didn't think it was that important," said Randy slowly, his mind in a mild state of shock. *I had four impossible dreams,* he thought to himself. *And now three of them have come true . . .* He shook his head at the next thought that came to his mind. *Naw! That's crazy. Nobody can live forever . . .*

"I'm going to have Billy take Summer Zephyrs, twin sister of Winter Zephyrs, around for time," said Curly. "Want to stay to watch?"

"Nope," said Randy. "Got to get to the house. Rose and Junior are waiting."

After the limousine had pulled back out onto the drive, the aroma of the stable lingered in the car, getting stronger. Randy sniffed, then looked down at the soles of his shoes.

"An occupational hazard of being the best horseman of the decade," he muttered disgustedly. He gingerly took off the offending shoe and tossed it out the window. He would never be able to put it on again anyway. Shooting his cuff-comp from his sleeve, he set it to comm mode.

"Get me James," he said into it.

➤   ➤   ➤

When the limousine drove Randy up the driveway to the front door, Rose was outside waiting. He got an enthusiastic hug from his slightly teary wife, who quickly wiped away her tears.

"Sorry we couldn't come to meet you at the strip, darling," she said. "But Junior has a bad cold and I wanted to keep him out of the drafts." She looked down at his stockinged foot.

"What happened to your shoe?" she asked.

Just then James appeared, carrying Randy's loafers.

"Your shoes, sir," said James, putting them down. Randy kicked off his other shoe and stepped into the loafers.

"Tell you later," he answered Rose.

She led the way into the house and up the large main stairs to Junior's room. Junior was now almost six years old, and had long ago left the crib room. Rose softly opened the door and they tiptoed in. Junior was lying in bed, his eyes open, looking out the window.

"Hi, Junior," said Randy. "It's Daddy!"

The child didn't stir, but kept looking out the window. Randy walked around to the other side of the bed and sat down. He put his hand on Junior's shoulder.

"Hi," he said again. "Daddy's here . . ."

Junior gave a grunt and, avoiding Randy's eyes, turned over and looked the other way.

"Junior!" said Rose, exasperated. "Say hello to your daddy!"

"That's all right, Rose," Randy said gently. "He's punishing me for being away so long."

"But he's seen you nearly every day on the video letters you sent to us."

"You've got to admit that's not the same thing as being here in person."

Rose thought of the years and years of empty beds she had endured and said nothing.

Randy leaned over, put his arms around Junior, and gave him a long hug, murmuring softly into the back of his neck.

"I love you, Junior," he said. "I love you more than anything in the world. I think you are terrific, wonderful, stupendous, the best boy in the whole universe. I love you very, very much."

The tiny body started shaking, and Junior broke into long, heart-rending sobs. Randy just held him tight until they abated.

"I . . . I . . . thought," he sobbed, "you . . . were never coming back."

"But I *did* come back, didn't I?"

"You were gone so long."

"But I'm back now. Give me a hug."

Junior sat up in bed. His eyes were dripping tears, and long streams of snot dribbled down from his nose. Randy hesitated for a second at taking the messy child in his arms, but he quickly recovered, pulled out one of his two handkerchiefs from his hip pocket, wiped the nose mostly clean, and hugged the boy close.

Now Junior had started talking, it was impossible to get him to stop. "I thought you were dead, and Mr. Davidson was trying to fool us with make-believe videos of you talking to us . . ."

Rose, with a little bit of help from Randy, got Junior dressed while he showed his dad all the cutouts and other projects that he had been doing to while away the time in his sickbed. On the way downstairs, he talked all about his classmates in the first grade at the Enclave School, then spent most of dinner disparaging "gurls," particularly those who made his life miserable by chasing him around the playground trying to kiss him. Then, as they took him back upstairs and sent him off to an early bed, he and his dad planned what they would do together that weekend.

"Can we go fishing in the pond in the middle of the track?" asked Junior excitedly. "Curly showed me where the big ones hide."

Randy didn't relish the thought of handling worms and slimy fish, but if they took Curly along . . .

"Sure, big guy!" he said cheerfully.

"I am big, aren't I!" said Junior, jumping up out of bed and running over to the doorway. "Measure me again, Mommy."

"Not now, dear," Rose said. "It's time to go to bed."

"I want Dad to see how big I've grown," said Junior. He looked at his father with eager, sparkling eyes. "I take my growing pills every day—and they're working."

"Junior, dear, time to get into bed," said Rose, trying to deflect the conversation.

"That's all right, Rose," said Randy, straightening up to his full four feet eleven inches. "Let's see how tall the boy is."

Rose got the straightedge from its accustomed place on the bookcase shelf while Junior put his back up against the doorjamb and stood tall. The doorjamb had a cloth tape measure glued along its length. Randy placed the straightedge on top of Junior's head. The boy's head was already up to Randy's chin.

"Got it!" said Randy. Junior slipped out from under the straightedge and Randy peered at where it met the tape.

"Hundred and thirty-five centimeters—four feet five inches," Randy read, feeling a little queer.

"Now to bed!" commanded Rose.

Junior hopped into bed and they turned out the lights, shut the door, and went downstairs.

"How tall is he going to get?" asked Randy.

"The doctors predict he'll get to five feet four, taller than his mother."

"I've always wanted a son I could look up to," Randy said wryly.

➤   ➤   ➤

Randy spent Sunday afternoon fishing with Curly and Junior, and Sunday evening in his three-meter-wide bed getting reacquainted with Rose. On Monday morning, he was up early, watching the household routine from the breakfast table as Rose and Anna, the downstairs android, got Junior ready for school.

"I've got some shopping to do," said Rose, "so I'm going to go along to school in the limo with Junior. That way I can be at the mall when it opens."

"Fine with me," said Randy, sipping the coffee with relish—it was fresh, not aged five years in a can. "I'll drive over to the headquarters building and get a briefing from Alan."

Randy watched as William chauffeured Rose and Junior off in the limousine to the center of Princeton Enclave. After they had gone, he looked around with pride at his estate. It was a beautiful day— he checked the sky and found a small fingernail moon shining palely in the blue sky in front of the sun. A silvery thread rotated slowly in space to one side of it. It would also be a beautiful night for observing if the weather kept clear. The only thing that marred his enjoyment was the sight of the balloons off in the distance above the trees.

He was almost tempted to take a walk through the woods to the headquarters building, but it had been even longer since he had driven one of his cars. He went to the garage and looked them over, James trailing along behind him. Since William had gone into town, James used his master key to open the key cabinet.

"Mr. Davidson purchased a new Mercedes-Benz in anticipation of your arrival, sir," said James. "The previous one was six years old and getting out of style. Would you like to drive that one?"

"Don't think so," said Randy, looking past the Mercedes at his other cars. "It's really only meant for show. Not that much fun to drive."

"How about the Rolls-Royce, sir?" asked James. "You have always enjoyed that car."

"I'll take the Duesenberg," Randy said finally. "Now that's a *big* car—and it's been some time since I've taken it for a spin."

James got out the large, gold-plated key to the modern reproduction of the original sixteen-cylinder Duesenberg convertible and handed it to his diminutive master. Randy took a big step up onto the running board and another big step into the tall, block-long monster. The seat was already adjusted forward and up as far as it would go, and Randy looked down from on high like the driver of a fire truck. With a grin of pleasure, he started up the thundering engine, lowered the top, backed the long car out of the garage, and took off down the driveway at high speed, throwing gravel behind him at the turns.

➤   ➤   ➤

Randy spent the whole morning hearing nothing but good news from Alan and his group and division managers.

"In summary, the Cable Transportation Group is continuing to make excellent profits," said Anthony Guiliano. Randy noticed that Tony's hair was greying around the temples. "And although its growth rate has slowed, we expect it to continue to expand as we add new rotovators around Earth, Moon, and Mars to handle increased demand."

"I presume they're in the same orbits, just half an orbit apart," said Randy.

"No," said Alan. "They actually go in opposite directions. That cuts down on the travel time when you want to go east instead of west."

"Sounds dangerous," said Randy, slightly concerned.

A shrill voice piped up from the back of the room. It was Mary Lewis, manager of the Rotovator Division. There was a vexed look on her face as she pushed her owl glasses back from where they had slipped to the tip of her nose.

"I can assure you that the laws of orbital mechanics preclude any collisions."

Alan switched to another chart.

"Our biggest money machine is the Negmatter Energy Division. Since we have a monopoly on the source of the negmatter, there is no competition. Although we get our energy for essentially nothing, we set our energy prices just below what it would cost to generate energy using other techniques, such as solar, electric, and nuclear. Of course, no one is allowed to burn organic fuels anymore, even if they could afford them. As you can see, this division alone produces a profit of two hundred billion a year. We plow a good deal of it back into new energy-production facilities and keeping the Interstellar Division afloat, but there is plenty left over. You are close to being the world's first trillionaire."

"That brings up something I've been thinking about for a while," said Randy. "I've got more money than anyone could spend in a lifetime . . . wisely, that is. Perhaps I ought to do some good with some of it."

"But most of your money is invested in businesses that supply good jobs to people," said Alan. "That's positive."

"That's not enough," said Randy. "I'd like to start a charitable trust. Sort of like Howard Hughes did. He set up the Hughes Medical Foundation and funded it by breaking out his aircraft division from the Hughes Tool Company, calling it Hughes Aircraft Company, and giving all the stock in the new company to the Medical Foundation."

"We could certainly do something like that," said Alan. "What are you thinking of?"

"I'll keep all the solid profit-making divisions under Reinhold Astroengineering Company," said Randy. "So Rose will be taken care of and Randy Junior will have a good start if something happens and I go too soon. But I'll keep the Interstellar Division separate and use that for funding the trust. Admittedly, it is still in a risky, negative-cash-flow state and will require pump-priming from my own pocket. But it ultimately could be the biggest and most profitable of all my enterprises—after all, its growth potential is effectively unlimited."

"Have you decided on a name for the charitable trust?" asked Alan.

"Yes," said Randy. "I'm going to call it the Hunter Institute for Aging Research. It's to be modeled along the lines of the Hughes Medical Institute, but instead of supporting medical research in general, it's to concentrate on medical solutions to the problems of aging." Randy gave a wry smile. "Since—as much as I want to—I can't live forever, perhaps the researchers can find a way for me to stay around longer than normal."

"Unless you kill yourself off in an accident sooner," chided Alan. "The VTOL pilot said that he didn't get a chance at the controls during your entire flight home."

"That reminds me," Randy said. "Who are the pilots for the second wave of interstellar warpmouth transport vehicles?"

"I'll let Andrew Pope tell you those details," said Alan. Andrew took over the video console with an air of authority.

"We have four ships almost ready to go," said Andrew. "They are being reworked slightly to correct the design problems that cropped up during your journey."

"I sure hope you've finally developed a good zero-gee toilet," muttered Randy.

Andrew read from a chart on the videoscreen. "The first one off will be going to Barnard, six light-years away. With the eighty-percent-cee velocity limit, it will take a little over five and a half years to get there.

The pilot is C.C. Wong. Like you, he decided he would rather travel alone than cope with someone."

"Probably wise," said Randy.

"Next off is a ship going to Lelande at eight light-years," said Andrew. "It's going to have a crew of three, pilot Robert Pilcher and two girlfriends."

"Really!" said Randy, his eyebrows raising slightly.

"They have been living together for a number of years," said Andrew. "The company psychiatrists say the situation should stay stable."

He consulted the chart again. "The next mission is purely a scientific one. It's going to set up a warpmouth near the giant star Sirius and its white dwarf companion. I wasn't going to send a ship there. The Backside telescopes show that the planetary nebula of the system was blown away during the formation of the two stars. With no planetoids to exploit and the high level of radiation from the large main star, it has very low commercial value. The International Space University, however, wants to set up an observing post. We sold them a ship at cost and they will be supplying their own pilot. In return, we get to use their warpgate to launch follow-on missions to stars further out, like Procyon."

"What's the next one?" asked Randy.

"It'll be a long mission visiting two star systems, UV Ceti and Tau Ceti," said Andrew. "The ship will be a custom model since it has to carry two Silverhairs, one to leave in each system, so it won't come off the production line until next year. No pilot has been chosen yet." He turned off the videoscreen and stepped back. "That's about all the production we can afford until we start generating some positive cash flow with business to and from the Alpha Centauri system."

➤   ➤   ➤

Rose knew it was coming. Every time Randy attempted to leave the Enclave, he was followed by airplanes or automobiles or helicopters from the Barkham estate carrying loads of raucous, shrill Animal Rescuers who hounded him at every stop. He had given up trying to travel anywhere, and was essentially imprisoned on his own estate.

Randy's cleanliness fetish was also getting worse. Rose noticed that he was now surreptitiously wiping his mouth with his handkerchief after kissing her. That hurt, and she spoke to him about it.

"It's getting to the point it's compulsive," she said. "Perhaps you ought to see a doctor."

"It's nothing!" Randy snapped. "I just like to be neat, that's all. I don't need to see some shrink." Angry and frustrated, he turned away from her. "I'm going to go out and get some fresh air." He slammed out the door leading to the garage, and the next thing she heard was the sixteen-cylinder roar of the Duesenberg as it raced down the driveway at top speed.

After leaving Princeton Enclave and turning onto the interstate to Atlantic City, Randy lost the carful of animal activists by deliberately deactivating the automatic pilot on the Duesenberg. This caused the expressway safety system to shunt him off the high-speed autopilot lanes through an emergency exit onto the human-driver lanes. His pursuers weren't able to follow him since their more modern car had a built-in autopilot that couldn't be switched off. Free of his pestiferous trackers, Randy took side roads to the beach and drove down to the end of the road at Cape May, where he parked at the little place he often took Rose to. After staring gloomily at the sea for a while, he came to a decision. Shooting out his cuff-comp, he said, "Get me Andrew."

"Hello, Mr. Hunter," said Andrew. "What can I do for you?"

"Tell C.C. Wong he'll have to wait a year and do the two-star Ceti mission," said Randy. "I'm getting out of this place and heading for Barnard."

➤ ➤ ➤

When Rose saw Randy driving slowly up the driveway in the Duesenberg convertible she grew worried. He looked grim and tired rather than smiling and relaxed as he usually did after a ride in one of his vehicles. She decided she would tell him her little bit of good news. She had wanted to wait a while and be sure, but perhaps it would cheer him up. She put on a happy smile and went downstairs to greet him. When he came in from the garage, however, he was distant and refused to look her in the eyes.

"I'm going!" he blurted out. "I can't stand this place anymore. I'm piloting our next ship out to Barnard and there's nothing you can say that can change my mind—so don't even try." He stomped off to his study and slammed the door behind him.

Rose was furious. Here she was, trying to make him feel better, and he was yelling at her for no good reason. A vindictive look appeared on her face as she stared at the closed door.

Going off again, are you? Just for that I'm going to keep my good news to myself.

Randy had expected Rose to follow him into his study to try to argue him out of his decision. He was ready for yelling and screaming and tears and pleading, and had hardened his heart in preparation. When she went away instead, he wondered at her strange behavior.

➤   ➤   ➤

The next few days were a flurry of packing and last-minute preparations. There were a lot of things to take care of, for he would be gone nearly six years this time. Junior bore the news well for a six-year-old—although Rose knew that she would be soothing his bruised spirit for years to come.

Rose had known what she was getting into when she had married this self-centered man. Poor Junior had no choice. *You can choose your husband, but you don't get to choose your father.* She tried to make the best of it and, for Junior's sake, kept a bright, unaccusing tone in her voice during the daily videolink connections with the geosynchronous orbit station where Randy and the crew were preparing the ship *Golda* for its flight to Barnard.

Underneath, however, Randy could sense an angry, vindictive edge in her voice. She was still mad, and would strike back at him somehow. Randy knew that she wouldn't get a divorce. Divorce was out of the question. Rose had made that clear before they got married. That was one of the reasons she had taken so long to say yes. Well, he had to admit to himself, whatever she did, he would deserve it for being such a selfish stinker and running off to explore instead of staying home to take care of his family.

➤   ➤   ➤

Finally the day came.

"Good-bye," said Randy. "I'll talk to you again in a month when we have our first warpgate comm link."

The videoscreen went blank and Rose was alone . . . again. The years of loneliness stretched seemingly endlessly ahead. She looked at the grandfather clock in the corner of the living room. Junior was already asleep, but it was just after ten o'clock—too early to go to bed. She'd better find something to read. She went to the bookshelf and looked for a classic—one of those books your teachers in high school had said would be good for you. She found a book by Rudyard Kipling, *Puck of Pook's Hill*, and sat down to read it. The fantasy of two children meeting Puck the fairy took her thoughts far away from her problems. She was really enjoying herself until, about a quarter of the way through the book, she came to the poem "Harp Song of the Dane Women."

What is a woman that you forsake her,
And the heart-fire and the home-acre,
To go with the old grey Widow-maker? . . .

She has no strong white arms to fold you,
But the ten-times-fingering weed to hold you—
Out on the rocks where the tide has rolled you . . .

Then you drive out where the storm-clouds swallow,
And the sound of your oar-blades, falling hollow,
Is all we have left through the months to follow . . .

Putting the book down, Rose wept bitterly. Finally, when the grandfather clock struck midnight, she went to her lonely bed and fell asleep, her arms cradling the spark of life growing in her belly.

➤   ➤   ➤

"Rosita Carmelita Cortez Hunter, Junior," said Rose defiantly.

"Junior!" exclaimed Randy. "You can't name a girl Junior!"

"I can and I did!" Rose declared haughtily. "This is my baby and I'll name it what I want."

"But it's my baby, too," argued Randy.

"All you did was supply half the seed," said Rose. "I did the rest. If you want this to be your baby, then come back and help take care of it."

"You know I can't do that!"

"You wouldn't be much help anyway," Rose said sarcastically.

"You could have at least told me," complained Randy.

"I was going to, but . . . but . . . you took off before I could." Rose pouted, her face starting to crinkle up.

"Rose . . ." implored Randy. "I'm sorry I left . . . but I *had* to. I love you, and I love Randy, Junior, and I love Rose, Junior, too. I promise that when I come back from this trip I'll stay home forever."

"Don't make promises you can't keep, Mr. Buck Rogers Hunter." Rose was turning contumacious again.

➤   ➤   ➤

After five years and seven months of travel, the *Golda* finally reached her destination, a close orbit around Barnard. Unlike Proxima, which had a terraformable planet, the Barnard planetary system was exactly what the planetary scientists had predicted. Randy reported his findings back to Elena Polikova through the laser comm link as the autopilot on *Golda* matched velocities with the ship back in the solar system that carried the other mouth of the warpgate.

"There're a few large, cold gas giants some distance away from Barnard," said Randy. "And a few airless dirtballs either too cold or too hot for life."

"Are there large moons around the gas giants?" asked Elena. "Some of those might have water and an interesting atmosphere."

"Nope," said Randy. "Earth-like moons around gargantuan gas giants in the Barnard system are only found in science fiction stories. No Rocheworld double-planets either."

"Doesn't sound very profitable to me," came Andrew Pope's voice over the link. "Perhaps we should not even bother to open the warpgate, just write the mission off as a loss."

"Wait 'til I get back *through* first!" joked Randy in mock fright. Then his voice changed. "But it isn't that bad. I think we can make money out of the asteroid belt. It's not only much larger and much thicker than the asteroid belt around Sol, but the asteroids themselves are mostly carbonaceous chondrites full of organic material, frozen ices, and other volatiles."

"Hmmm . . ." said Andrew. "It might be a lot easier to mine those Barnard asteroids and warp the valuable organics and volatiles back to Sol than attempt to find and extract the same materials in the dry stones that make up most of the asteroid belt here."

Slowly the hollow, cylindrical laser beam through the Silverhair grew in size while Randy waited. On the other side of the warpgate he could now see the large, rotund tightsuit of Andrew Pope and the smaller suits of Siritha, Hiroshi Tanaka, and two other people.

Finally the tunnel was large enough for Siritha. "Straighten out your legs!" came Hiroshi Tanaka's voice through the warpgate over the suit radio links.

Siritha straightened out. Her small jetpack fired a short burst and she floated through. Randy caught her and pulled her out of the laser beam as her jets brought her to a stop.

With Siritha safely through to take his place at keeping the Silverhair happy, Randy activated his jetpack and easily slipped through the warpgate back to the solar system. Now that he wasn't peering through a tunnel, he recognized the wasp-waisted figure in the tightsuit in front of him.

"Rose!" he exclaimed, taking her into his arms, their helmets getting in the way of their hugs. The two were in turn grabbed by the long arms of a third, taller person.

"Daddy!"

"Junior!" said Randy. "What a surprise!"

"Mr. Pope said I could come," said Junior. "Rosey is too little and had to stay at home." The three hugged each other again.

"OK," said Andrew in a mock-serious tone, "that's enough mush. You civilians get in the lock. We engineers have some work to do."

The lock door opened and the happy family squeezed into the vacuum lock. Andrew cycled them through.

➤ ➤ ➤

It was only six months before Randy started to get itchy feet again.

"You're not going to get away from me so easily this time," said Rose. "I'm going with you."

"But Rose, these exploration ships are only designed for one person," protested Randy.

"Then have Andrew make a bigger one," said Rose. "And I want it nice and comfortable, not some tin can."

"But that'll cost a fortune!"

"The last time I talked to Alan, he said you were worth a million ordinary fortunes," Rose retorted. "Have you ever thought about spending some of them for the enjoyment of yourself and your family? You can't take it with you, you know."

Randy was taken aback by Rose's remarks. She was right. He was nearly thirty-seven—almost middle-aged—and the world's first trillionaire. It was time he stopped working so hard and started enjoying life.

"That's a good idea, Rose," he finally said. "With a negmatter drive, it doesn't really matter how massive the spaceship is; you just use more negmatter in the drive room. I'll have Andrew build us a large explorer ship with a couple of comfortable rooms."

"Make sure he includes a nice kitchen," said Rose. "It doesn't need to be a big one. After all, we won't be doing much entertaining."

"Sure," Randy said expansively. "A nice kitchen."

"With a view over the sink."

"We can easily add a viewscreen over the sink with living video images taken from every scenic spot in the solar system," said Randy agreeably.

"That'll do fine." Rose looked around their large living room. A roaring fire was burning in the fireplace in the far wall, ostensibly warding off the cold autumn evening. "And a fireplace," she added.

"A fireplace in the kitchen?!" exclaimed Randy, waking up from his reverie.

"Of course not, darling." Rose looked at him indulgently. "In the living room, of course."

"A fireplace in the living room," Randy repeated, nodding thoughtfully. "I suppose you'd also like a fountain in the garden."

"A small waterfall would be nice," said Rose.

"Why not?" Randy was getting into the spirit of the discussion. "And some rosebushes, so I can stop and smell the roses as I rush through life at relativistic speeds."

"That would be nice, dear."

The grandfather clock next to the fireplace struck ten.

1 ➢➢

Epsilon Eridani

IT was a year later when Randy was taken on a tour of the new ship the Interstellar Division had built for his trip to Epsilon Eridani. The cylindrical spacecraft was floating some distance from the Reinhold orbital space station. It still had a crew of teleoperators and robots checking out the instrumentation and putting on the last touches, such as painting its name, *Spacemaster*, on the side. Randy, Andrew Pope, and chief engineer Hiroshi Tanaka rode out to the ship in a flitter. Hiroshi was piloting the flitter, and he flew it in a circle around the spacecraft as he explained the new features of the radiation shield that would protect the ship during its high-speed travel through the not-so-empty vacuum of space.

"Whereas the first-generation explorers were limited to a safe upper speed of eighty percent of the speed of light," said Hiroshi, "the shielding on this ship is good enough to allow travel at up to ninety-nine-point-five percent of light speed."

"Impressive!" exclaimed Randy. "What's the gamma for that?"

"The time dilation factor is ten," said Hiroshi. "Although we don't recommend extended travel at that speed until we have a lot more experience with particle concentration variations in space."

"You're right," said Randy, nodding. "Hit a molecular cloud at that speed and you could get fried in a hurry."

Hiroshi suspended the flitter and pointed toward the spacecraft. "Do you see those lumpy portions at the front and rear?"

"The things that look like Turkish knots?"

"Right," said Hiroshi. "Those are force-free coils made of the new supermagducting wire. They generate the magnetic field for the primary radiation shield. The outside of the ship, of course, is plated with the same metal to keep the magnetic field inside the ship to near zero. The primary shield extends out to ten thousand kilometers and essentially takes care of all incoming atoms or molecules by stripping off their electrons and deflecting the resulting ions away."

Hiroshi activated the flitter and moved it to the front of the interstellar spacecraft. "What really concerns us, however, is the larger dust grains and ice crystals. At those speeds, they can penetrate the primary field before the field can break them up into individual atoms. Now, notice the smaller lump on the front end of the ship."

"I see it," said Randy. "A smaller Turkish knot on the end of a short boom."

"That coil generates the secondary shield," said Hiroshi. "When the ship approaches relativistic velocities, the boom extends out a kilometer ahead of the ship and the coil is turned on. Its concentrated magnetic field breaks apart the dust grains and smaller meteorites into individual atoms and molecules at a sufficient distance away from the ship that the primary shield has time to deflect them. Particles that come right down the magnetic axis will not be deflected, of course, but will be collected by a patch of activated metallic foam. That will supply the small amount of positive mass input needed for control of the mass balance of the ship, while insuring that the radiation generated in stopping the matter is kept far from the crew."

"What about the larger meteorites?" asked Randy. "They're pretty rare, though . . . I guess I'll just have to take my chances with them."

"They are taken care of by the third shielding system," said Hiroshi. "If they are large enough to penetrate the magnetic shields, they are large enough to be seen by our laser radar system at over one thousand kilometers distance. Even if the meteoroid has a significant velocity of its own, so the closing rate is three nines, the meteoroid will be lagging the laser radar return by more than a kilometer, giving us whole microseconds of warning time so we can zap it into small fragments. The magnetic fields then take care of the fragments."

"Whole microseconds . . ." Randy said, bemused at the thought. "I hope I never have to test it."

"Finally, there is the last layer of shielding," said Hiroshi. "Notice the color of the top of the ship around the boom."

"It's a smooth silver," said Randy.

"An electrostatically levitated pool of liquid negmatter. Anything that gets through the first three shields will strike the ultradense negmatter and be nullified. No particle left and no energy released." Hiroshi gave a proud smile.

"Terrific!" said Randy. He turned to Andrew Pope. "I hope you appreciate what a talented engineer you have here."

"Oh! I do, Mr. Hunter, I do." Andrew patted a now embarrassed Hiroshi Tanaka on the shoulder.

"And will show your appreciation in his paycheck next week," continued Randy.

"Oh! I will, Mr. Hunter, I will," Andrew vowed with a grin.

"I will now take you to see the inside of the ship," murmured a thoroughly flustered Hiroshi as he reactivated the flitter. They entered the free-falling spacecraft at the center airlock.

"This is the drive room," Hiroshi said as they floated into a large space dominated by bulky boxes of high-power electronics surrounding a large sphere at the center. "It has the usual collection of six negmatter blobs for six-axis acceleration and torque capability, except that these negmatter blobs are ten times bigger, since your spacecraft is ten times more massive than our first one-man explorers. The drive is capable of five gees, although the recommended acceleration is three gees."

"You could go at one gee and take it easy on yourself," interjected Andrew Pope.

"Takes too long to get up to speed that way," said Randy. "I want to get to Epsilon Eridani in a hurry." He patted one of the power supplies. "With *Spacemaster* here, I can accelerate at three gees, and in nine months I'll be at ninety-eight percent of cee and traveling five lightyears per year. Then I can cut back to one gee, bring in Rose, and live in style as I whisk my way to Epsilon Eridani. By the way, can I see my living quarters?"

"Since they are only designed to withstand one gee, they're all folded up," said Hiroshi. "After we get back to the station, I can take you on a virtual walk-through of the computer design data. Right now, all I can show you is the drive cockpit with the high-gee acceleration couches."

"If you've seen one cockpit, you've seen them all," said Randy. "Besides, I've been practicing in the virtual simulator cockpit for the past month, so I know it well. You did a good job on the design. The drive controls are nearly foolproof."

"Thank you, Mr. Hunter," Hiroshi said. In order to divert attention from himself he changed the subject. "Now let me take you to the Silverhair chamber to show you the transfer pods that Steve Wisneski invented."

"The invention that finally made spacewarp transportation a civilized way to travel," Randy remarked as he followed Hiroshi down the corridor.

"I'll see you back at the flitter," said Andrew, heading the other way. "I have some things to check on."

As they cycled through the vacuum lock into the chamber, they were greeted by the Silverhair.

<Hir! Rand! Dance!> said the Silverhair.

"It was fed and danced with just two hours ago," said Hiroshi. "Ignore it."

"I'm going to have to live almost three years with this Silverhair," said Randy, adjusting his suit radio so it broadcast some rumba music. "It behooves me to stay on the good side of it." Arms and legs moving with the syncopated beat, Randy swung around the electrode support posts that kept the Silverhair centered while the ship was under acceleration. The Silverhair joined in the dance, its long silver tendrils developing traveling waves in them as they moved jerkily to the beat.

<<Me move me up and down. Me move me round and round . . . >> sang the Silverhair in its mysterious, melodic voice.

After about three minutes the tune came to an end, and Randy didn't start another. The Silverhair, contented, stopped wiggling and relaxed into its normal spherical shape. Randy kicked over to where Hiroshi stood patiently waiting beside a long oval egg of silvery-colored negmatter resting inside what looked like a small electromagnetic gun. The oval was about three meters long and a half-meter thick at the center, just big enough to hold a person in a stretched-out position.

"A normal-matter inner shell coated with an electrostatically levitated skin of negmatter," said Hiroshi. "Crack the pod open around the middle, stretch out inside, seal it up again, adjust the amount of negmatter until the net mass is zero, and you're ready to go. As soon as the acceleration at both ends of the warpgate is zero and the gate through the Silverhair has been expanded until it is large enough to pass the pod, the electromagnetic launcher charges up and fires you through the warpgate, to be caught by the electromagnetic catcher on the other side. All done automatically, without involving humans and all their potential error sources. Even if there is an error and the pod brushes the inside of the tunnel, the Silverhair is not hurt, since it only contacts negative matter."

"Still have to stop the ship before you can transfer, I notice," said Randy.

"Yes, I'm sorry to say, Mr. Hunter," Hiroshi said. "Because of the negative matter surrounding the transfer pods we transfer zero net mass through the Silverhair. Since we transfer no mass, we automatically conserve energy and momentum during the transfer, even though the Silverhairs at the two ends of the warpgate are traveling at different velocities. Because energy and momentum are conserved, there is no internal strain on the Silverhair when the pod transfer takes place, and the warpgate doesn't collapse. Unfortunately, we've been unable to find a way to dilate a warpgate while it's under acceleration. Steve is working on it, though."

"Good enough for now," said Randy. "Let's go back to the station so you can give me a virtual walk-through of my space mansion."

➤   ➤   ➤

Randy was lightly strapped to a large couch in the center of the cramped control deck of *Spacemaster*. He was wearing a virtual helmet and arm-length virtual gauntlets. In front of him the helmet produced an image of a control panel, and although there was nothing between the fingers of his right hand, they felt as if they were holding the metallic sphere of a joyball controller. Right now, the center of the screen was filled with an image of Rose. She was smiling pleasantly.

"It won't be long this time," said Randy. "In nine months I'll be up to speed and you can join me."

"Nine months is still a long time. I wish I could be with you now." Rose smiled wistfully.

"Normally I'd love to have you next to me in a waterbed," said Randy. "But at three gees it wouldn't be any fun. Bye now. See you soon."

"Good-bye," said Rose. Her image blanked out and was replaced by that of an elderly, bearded Russian man, the persona of the *Spacemaster* computer.

"Shall I initiate the acceleration program?" spoke the icon in Russian.

"Why should I let *you* have all the fun, Konstantin?" replied Randy, also in Russian. "I paid for this ship, so I get to drive it."

Randy's virtual left arm moved up to press the drive-control icon on the virtual screen. The icon grew in size and moved to the center of the

screen as the icon of Konstantin shrank into the upper left corner. The
drive icon was in the cylindrical shape of *Spacemaster*, centered in a
large three-dimensional cage of concentric spheres. Each sphere
represented two light-years of distance. There were eleven white
dots—star systems—scattered around the cage, most of them between
the fifth and sixth sphere. A faint green line ran from the ship icon to
one of the stars—his destination, Epsilon Eridani.

Nearly along that line was a short red arrow, indicating *Spacemaster*'s present velocity due to its orbital motion about the Earth and
Earth's orbit around the Sun. The launch time had been picked to take
advantage of this small start toward *Spacemaster*'s ultimate relativistic
speed.

Randy rotated the imaginary joyball with his virtual glove until the
icon of *Spacemaster* was lined up with the green line that was his
desired path. He pulled up on the joyball and his body started to sink
into the waterbed as a small yellow acceleration arrow grew from the
nose of the icon to point along the green line. In the head of the yellow
arrow was a number, indicating the acceleration level in meters per
second squared. Randy pulled the imaginary joyball upward until the
number read 29.4—three gees. Breathing heavily under the strain,
Randy effortlessly raised his virtual left arm to the screen to push the
drive icon back to the edge of the screen.

The icon of Konstantin grew and moved to the center of the screen.

"You were not quite correct in your choice of word for 'drive' in
your last sentence," said Konstantin in English. "That is more properly
used when you are moving herds of animals, not piloting vehicles.
Would you like a lesson in colloquial Russian?"

"*Horosho,*" Randy replied. "Anything to pass the time."

He breathed heavily again as he readjusted his body on the
waterbed. He was determined to last the four hours until his one-hour
lunch break, when he would cut the acceleration level back to one gee.
At least he wouldn't have to cope with the toilet in zero-gee.

➤   ➤   ➤

After nearly nine months at three gees, Randy was eagerly awaiting
his release from his near imprisonment on the high-gee waterbed. The
red velocity arrow on the drive icon was now pointed directly along the
green line, and the number inside the arrowhead read 0.979. When it
switched to 0.980, Randy pushed down on the joyball in his virtual
glove until the acceleration arrow read 9.8—one gee. The ship would
now maintain a comfortable one-gee acceleration, slowly increasing its

velocity from 98 percent of the speed of light to 99 percent in the next seven months until turnover.

"All yours, Konstantin," said Randy to the icon in the virtual screen. "Keep it at one gee and signal my cuff-comp if there are any problems."

"I will do as you direct," replied Konstantin in Russian.

Randy took off his virtual helmet and gloves and, climbing lightly out of the acceleration couch, heaved a sigh of relief.

"Didit!" he called. The door to a closet slid open. Inside was the rotund figure of an android butler modeled after Randy's human butler, James. Didit stepped forward out of the closet.

"Yes, Master Hunter?" queried the butler.

"It's time to live like a civilized being once again," said Randy. "Unfold the mansion."

"I shall so inform the engineering robots," Didit said. Almost instantly, Randy could feel vibrations coming through the metal deck as the floors below started to expand from their collapsed shape.

"Now that I'm off work for a while, I should like a beer with lunch," said Randy, walking to the elevator. Didit followed him into the elevator and pressed the button for the main floor.

"I'm afraid your first lunch will be somewhat plain, sir," said Didit. "It will be a few hours before the full kitchen is unfolded and operational. I was planning a cold chicken sandwich with a glass of chardonnay."

"The cold chicken sounds fine," said Randy. "But I'd really prefer a beer—Anchor Steam Beer if you have it."

"Very well, sir," said Didit as the elevator arrived at the main floor. Didit held the door open with one hand. "I have it stored in one of the coolers in the basement. I will return with it shortly."

Randy stepped out into organized pandemonium as the elevator door shut behind him. To his right was the living room area with a fireplace in the far wall. On one side of the fireplace was a large view-window showing the woods outside his mansion back in the Princeton Enclave. There was a winter snowstorm in progress, and the wind could be heard whistling outside the simulated windowpane.

The flashing blue manipulators of Gidget were unfolding the back of his recliner chair from where it had been packed between the armrests. The seat cushion was on the floor next to the seat cushions from the already unfolded sofa, while the magazine table and the other tables were still in a folded stack next to the liquor cabinet. On the far wall, easily visible from both the sofa and the recliner chair, was a viewscreen that nearly covered the entire wall from floor to ceiling. The grandfather clock on the other side of the fireplace was already assembled, and its pendulum was ticking away the seconds in the constant one-gee acceleration.

To his left was the dining room area, separated from the living room by floor-to-ceiling solid-oak folding panels on an overhead track. When fully extended, they formed a wall that separated the living room from the dining room, and one panel had a door that allowed passage between the two rooms. With the oak doors folded back into the wall, the fireplace could provide heat to both rooms.

In the dining room, Gadget was putting the legs on the large mahogany banquet table that could easily seat twelve people, while Godget was removing the form-fitting packing around the dishes in a replica of a Chippendale china cupboard. The dining room also had a large view-window showing another snowy view from his home.

Randy turned and made his way around the central elevator column with its circular staircase leading to the bedrooms above. The kitchen was unfolded, but nothing had been unpacked yet. The view-window over the sink was already on. It was duplicating the scene outside the real kitchen window in his Princeton Enclave mansion. It was snowing there, too. From the living room came the sound of the grandfather clock striking the quarter-hour.

Randy walked into his study, which took up one-fourth of the main floor. There was a corner of it reserved for Rose and her painting, with a large view-window giving a northern exposure for proper lighting. This view-window was apparently perpetually set on some ideal day for best lighting. Instead of showing a snowstorm, it looked like spring outside, and birds could be heard in the bushes.

The study was obviously the first thing that the robots had unpacked, for everything was out and in its proper place. To the right side of his desk was a view-window of the same size and in the same position as the real window in his study at his mansion in the Princeton Enclave. The view-window was in phase with the others; it was snowing out this window too. To the left side of his desk, in a deliberate attempt to counteract the illusion that he was living on Earth, there was a large, thick glass porthole in a conical depression in the half-meter-thick metal double hull of *Spacemaster*. The porthole looked out on the reality that surrounded the cozy, Earth-like interior on all sides—a star-studded black vacuum.

Didit appeared at the doorway. "Lunch will be ready in ten minutes,

Master Hunter. Would you like to freshen up? I have your clothes laid out in the master bedroom."

Randy had been planning on eating in his jumpsuit, but now thought better of it.

"Since it's only a cold chicken sandwich and a beer, it can wait a while," said Randy. "I'm going to take a long hot shower first."

"Very good, sir," said Didit. "Because of the inclement weather, I added a bowl of hot clam chowder to the menu, but I can put the saucepan on simmer while you shower."

Randy looked at the snowy scene outside his study. "Sounds like a great lunch," he said. "Instead of having it in the dining room, how about setting it up on a small table next to the fireplace in the living room?"

"Excellent suggestion, sir," said Didit, turning to leave. Randy followed him to the door and, whistling cheerfully, stepped lightly up the circular staircase to the bedrooms above.

⤜　　⤜　　⤜

The master of *Spacemaster* paused on his slow descent back down the circular staircase. He was clean and warm from the hot shower and wearing his comfortable charcoal-grey flannel slacks and a charcoal-grey, V-neck cashmere sweater over a light-blue cotton turtleneck. A matching light-blue hair ribbon held back his hair while a cluster of whitish-blue star-sapphire earrings climbed up to his left ear.

Randy had paused because he had smelled something strange, yet distantly familiar, coming from the living room. It wasn't the aroma from the bowl of chowder steaming on the small table set in front of his chair—he had enjoyed many bowls of chowder during his one-gee meal breaks on the long trip out. Then he recognized the smell. It was burning wood—normally a smell that would cause serious concern on any ordinary spacecraft, but not on *Spacemaster*.

Didit had placed a real pine log on top of the artificial logs in the gas fireplace. Randy smiled, walked down the rest of the circular staircase, strolled into the living room, and with a poker gave the log a couple of pokes to make it sizzle and send the sparks flying up the chimney. Then, with a broad smile and a contented sigh, he sank into his comfortable overstuffed chair and took a sip of hot clam chowder while the cold wind whistled outside the view-window.

⤜　　⤜　　⤜

"It's just a little scary," Rose said over the laser video link, her wide eyes looking even wider in the fishbowl helmet.

"Come on," coaxed Randy. "There's nothing to it. You've podded through a warpgate before in the practice sessions, and Hiroshi is right there to make sure everything goes perfectly."

"But the practice sessions were only a few kilometers," said Rose. "And this is almost one and a half light-years."

"Only on the outside," said Randy. "On the inside you are just a few meters away. Now get in that pod and let Hiroshi shoot you through. I'll be waiting here to catch you and help you out."

"OK . . ." Rose turned away from the camera. Randy, floating in free-fall, watched in the video monitor as Hiroshi helped the wasp-waisted figure in the tightsuit get into the transfer pod. Rose placed her feet in the foot stirrups at one end and reached up to grab the handholds at the other end. Hiroshi checked her position, then touched a button on a control panel. The two halves of the pod came together around her and silvery liquid negmatter flowed out of a storage container to cover the outside of the pod.

"You must clear this area before transfer can occur," said a warning voice in Randy's helmet. He looked around and suddenly realized that he was standing in front of the electromagnetic launcher, right in the path of Rose's incoming pod. Pulling on his handhold, he quickly moved himself out of the way. The laser-beam-filled hole through the Silverhair was dilated almost as much as it could be at this differential velocity. It wasn't easy for the Silverhair, as it frequently let them know.

<Oof! Cold!> it complained.

There was a warning buzz, a flash of silver coming through the warpmouth, and suddenly the transfer pod was in its cradle on *Spacemaster*. The laser beam flashed off and the Silverhair relaxed.

<Ahh!>

Randy drained the negmatter off into storage and cracked open the pod. Rose was stretched out inside, eyes tightly shut. Randy, feet in wall stirrups, reached up to grab her around her waist. He gave her a couple of squeezes.

"Either Hiroshi is getting fresh or that's Randy," Rose mumbled through the suit links. She opened her eyes, saw Randy, and then let go of her grip so he could pull her free. They hugged, enjoying the feel of each other's nearly naked bodies through the tightsuits.

<Rose!> said the Silverhair. <Dance!>

"I'll dance with you," said Randy. "You were a good Silverhair to hold open that long."

Randy took Rose over to the vacuum lock. Godget, yellow manipulators busy, was cycling the door. "Why don't you go through," he said, giving her a pat on the rear. "Gidget will help you out of your tightsuit and Didit will show you where your clothes are stored in the suit room. I'll be there as soon as I dance the 'Minute Waltz' with the Silverhair. It'll take me a few minutes since my jetpack is too slow to allow me to rush through it in just one minute."

➤   ➤   ➤

"It's lovely, Randy," Rose said as he showed her around their mansion in space. "It's even better than the virtual simulators." She walked over to the kitchen cupboards and opened a few drawers and doors. "And everything is in the same place as at home!" she squealed in delight. The sun was shining in the view-window over the sink and the the hum of an android grounds-keeper operating the snowplow could be heard from the driveway.

"This is the way upstairs," said Randy. "I'm afraid we couldn't fit in a grand suitcase. But you can either take the elevator or climb the circular stairway around it." The elevator was at the main floor and the door was open, so they took it up to the second floor. The door opened onto a circular hallway. Arm in arm, Randy led Rose around the corridor, pointing out doorways as they passed.

"This is the first bedroom, for either a kid or a guest; then a bathroom; a second bedroom; another bath; a third bedroom . . ." He opened the door. "This one even has a crib in one corner in case we have a wee visitor." He closed the door and went on. "Next is the master bath, and finally"—he paused with his hand on the doorknob to the last door—"let me show you my latest crib—no bars on this one—and three meters in diameter . . ."

➤   ➤   ➤

"Don't slurp your soup, Junior," said Rose.

"Aw, Mom," Junior whined. "How'm I gonna eat it?"

"Quietly," said Randy.

"You slurp sometimes, Dad," Rosey said sanctimoniously. "And I never do."

"Children!" said Rose to the two images in the viewscreens sitting across the dining room table. She sometimes wondered if these Sunday afternoon videolink suppers together were worth the effort.

Rose and Randy's two children were at the Princeton Enclave boarding school, but every Sunday afternoon William would drive them back to the mansion for a long-distance videolink dinner with their parents. Junior and Rosey really looked forward to the dinners, since Cook's meals were much better than the offerings at the boarding-school cafeteria.

Fortunately, since the videolink between *Spacemaster* and Earth suffered no time dilation effects when brought through the warpgate, the family didn't have to cope with slipping calendars, shifting clocks, and red-shifted voices. The only evidence that the children were light-years away from their parents was the quarter-of-a-second time delay introduced by the long hop between the Princeton satellite dish to the Reinhold geosynchronous station that held the other end of the warpgate.

"Junior High graduation will be in a few weeks," said Junior. "Will you be coming, Dad?"

"I'll see it on video," Randy answered, not really wanting to face the crowds. Besides, his presence at the graduation would be likely to provoke a protest action by the Animal Rescue Front activists. "I've got to stay on the ship in case there's a problem."

"I'll be there, Junior," said Rose with a sweet smile. "I've been here with your father for over four months now."

"How long will you be staying with us, Mommy?" asked Rose.

"All summer," said Rose. The faces of the two children brightened.

"Great!" said Junior. "I was afraid I'd be stuck in this place having to go to summer school." His image turned in the viewscreen to look at his father. "I was talking to Curly this afternoon and he said I could help out at the stables this summer if it was OK with you. Can I, Dad?"

"It isn't all just riding horses," warned Randy. "You've got to learn how to clean out their hooves, brush them down, and check them for injuries. Then there's the job of cleaning out their stalls. Just because you're my son doesn't mean you escape learning about *that* part of being a horseman."

"Working with the horses themselves is just for fun," replied Junior maturely. "This year, for my term paper in biology class, I did a review of gene clipping and insertion techniques. My teacher put me in touch with a biology professor over at Princeton who gave me a copy of his gene-mapping program to play with. I was thinking of applying it to the horses in our stable to see if we can improve our lines by controlled gene insertion instead of just letting nature take its course."

"Hmmm. Sounds like it might be a good idea . . ." said Randy, impressed with his son.

Junior frowned, then shook his head in discouragement. "The problem is, the program is so big it almost fills up the memory in my computer—and that makes it run slow."

Randy thought for a second. "Say!" he said. "I'm about to order the

latest MacIBM personal computer for my home office. I was going to
trade my old computer in, but why don't you take it instead?"

"Great!" said Junior, looking extremely surprised and pleased.
"Your machine has twenty times the RAM and ten times the speed of
mine. I should be able to try a dozen gene permutations a day with that
machine."

➤   ➤   ➤

Rose had been gone about two months when Randy's cuff-comp
vibrated on his wrist. He put the hard copy of the latest quarterly
earnings report for Reinhold Astroengineering Company down on the
magazine table in the living room and stretched out his arm until the
wide, flexible viewscreen showed below his shirtsleeve. It was
Konstantin, the icon for *Spacemaster*'s computer.

"We are approaching the midpoint of our journey," said Konstantin
in Russian.

"Horosho," replied Randy. "Commence turnaround. I presume
you'll use the constant-acceleration J-hook turn? Or should I have
Didit secure the china and other loose items?"

"It will be a twelve-hour J-hook turn," said Konstantin. "Only a
half-degree per minute. You should not notice anything unusual, since
the living quarters are so close to the center of the ship."

"I'll be in bed during most of it, anyway." Randy yawned. He
picked up the earnings report as the grandfather clock on the far wall
chimed eleven. After the chimes had finished, Randy could almost
swear that the steady *tick-tock, tick-tock, tick-tock* of the pendulum had
become slightly asymmetrical. He checked grandfather's time against
his cuff-comp, and noticed the date. Another two months to go before
Rose podded back to his side.

➤   ➤   ➤

Rose woke up expectantly. Today was Sunday. A special day, and
not just because the children would be joining them on the video-
screens for tonight's supper. She rolled to the edge of the large circular
bed in the master bedroom on *Spacemaster*, and sat up on the edge.
Randy was still quietly snoring away in the middle. She looked at him.

I wonder if he'll remember? she thought to herself. She shook her
head resignedly. *Probably not.* She got up and went into the master
bath, taking off her nightgown and handing it to Didit as he held the
door open for her.

Rose and Randy spent a peaceful, busy morning together in the
study. Randy was reading and making editorial comments on some
of Reinhold's latest patent applications on the newly invented

supermagductor-coated diamond fibers. The supermagnetic, supercon-ducting material constrained a strong magnetic field in the diamond inside, and the magnetized diamond in turn was three times as strong as unmagnetized diamond. Some of the Reinhold engineers now wanted to use the new cable material to construct a "suspension bridge" from the South Pole on Earth to Nearside Base on the Moon. Randy looked at his cuff-comp and quietly got up and left the study. Rose was engrossed in working on her latest watercolor painting in the corner and didn't notice him leave.

Her watercolor was of a garden scene with bright sunlight striking a jetting water fountain in the center of a shaded rose garden. Above her easel was a viewscreen with a still video image of Junior and Rosey in their rose garden at home, but she was rearranging the bushes and leaving out the children as she copied it. The knees and thighs of her fashionably faded jeans were covered with colorful spots of paint where she had occasionally wiped her brush to remove excess paint. Around her was a foot-deep pile of failed attempts on crumpled sheets of partially colored paper attesting to the difficulty of the task she had undertaken. Finally she was finished—with no errors and no drippy streaks, every rosebud sharp and crisp around the edges, every drop of water sparkling in the sunlight, every shadow in its correct place.

"Beautiful!" she said proudly. "Randy, come see!" She turned around toward his desk, but he wasn't there. Slightly puzzled, she called out again. "Randy?" Just then she heard the elevator door opening on the other side of the center column.

"Be right there, darling," he said. He came around the column with a self-conscious half-smile on his face.

When Rose saw the sappy grin, her heart melted. *He did remember after all.* She tried not to notice that he was hiding something behind his back.

"Did you call?" he said, strolling nonchalantly up to her.

"I wanted to show you my latest painting," she said, playing along.

"Say!" said Randy, impressed with the painting and its complexity. "That's really good! Look at those roses!"

"Why, thank you for the compliment," said Rose, pleased at his sincerity. "It would have been easier if I was at home where I could look at real roses instead of video images."

"Then I should have given you this earlier." Randy brought forth what he had been hiding behind his back. It was a single perfect, long-stemmed Picadilly rose, with rust-red and sand-yellow petals.

"Randy!" exclaimed Rose, taking the flower gently from his fingers.

"A rose for my Rose," Randy said lovingly. "Happy birthday, darling."

"Where did you get it?" she asked. "Did you have it warped through?"

"Nope. Can't use the warp. We're still under acceleration." He grinned. "I picked it from our rose garden—here on *Spacemaster*."

"We have a rose garden on the ship?!?" Rose said incredulously. "Where? Why didn't you tell me before?"

"Because it wasn't ready before," said Randy. "A garden needs time to grow and flower before you can use it. But it's ready now. Come with me and I'll show you where it is." He took her by the arm and lifted her from her chair. "We'll go for a walk and smell the roses as the stars go rushing by."

"Sounds delightful," said Rose happily. "What a wonderful birthday present."

As they left the study they were met by Didit, who was holding a large wicker picnic hamper. Randy took the hamper and led the way around the corner column to the elevator.

"After our stroll through the rose garden, I thought we would stop by the brook and have a picnic lunch," he said nonchalantly.

"A brook!" Rose looked at him in surprise as the elevator door opened.

Randy punched one of the lower buttons and the elevator went down. "The hydroponics level?" said Rose. "I went down there when I was first exploring around, and I didn't see any brook or rose garden. Only floor-to-ceiling trays of vegetables and dwarf fruit trees."

"You only saw the working half of the hydroponics deck," Randy explained. "For safety reasons, the deck is divided in two with a pressure bulkhead in between. If one side gets holed and the plants are killed and the water lost, we can always survive using the other side. The chances of that happening are so slim, however, that on the alternate side I only keep a small selection of food plants to get started with. The rest is for fun." He spoke into his cuff-comp as they arrived at the hydroponics deck.

"Open the rear elevator door this time, Konstantin," he said. The elevator door opened, and the smell of flowers and sound of rushing water came flooding in.

"Your garden, my lady," he said, bowing.

Rose, wide-eyed, still holding her birthday rose, stepped through into a garden glen.

There were high walls all around of stone, dirt, and greenery. Plants, shrubs, and trees grew in such profusion that the blue-painted "sky" high overhead was barely visible. A bright "sun" shown down through some palm branches. Off to the right side was a flowing torrent of water, falling ten meters from the edge of a cliff into a deep pool.

Randy followed her through the elevator door and it shut behind him, blending invisibly into the rocky cliffside. He pointed at the waterfall.

"You said a small waterfall would be nice."

"It's a good thing I didn't ask for a big one," said Rose, blinking in the warm mist blown by the wind exiting a cave half hidden under the falling water. Soaking in the mist were long strands of ivy hanging down the cliffside, and below them, terraces of ferns, ivy, violets, baby tears, and grass that led down to a shaded bank of firm mud around one side of the pool. On the opposite shore was a dry sandy beach edged with a grassy lawn. The beach was in full sunlight and contained a pair of colorful deck chairs, while the lawn held a shadow-dappled picnic table.

"Look at the flowers on that far bank," Rose breathed. "Rhododendrons and azaleas. And over there, primroses and camellias."

"Periwinkle, too," said Randy. "Let me put the picnic basket on the table and I'll show you the rest of the place." He led the way to a small stone bridge that arched over the burbling brook that flowed from the end of the pool.

From the bridge, Rose could now see a small octagonal building downstream on an island half hidden in a screen of willow trees.

"That's the cottage," said Randy. "We can even stay overnight here."

"How romantic!" said Rose, more and more pleased with what she saw.

"Let me take you around." Randy put the basket on the picnic table, and together they weaved their way along the path through the thick stand of birch trees to another little bridge that led to the island. Along the way they passed more tiers of flowers—cyclamen, begonias, pansies, and geraniums watered by tiny springs that started high up on the rocky hillside, then turned into rivulets that merged together at the bottom to flow into the brook.

Randy led the way over the arched wooden bridge to the island. The brook burbled noisily over its moss-covered rocky bottom as it flowed rapidly below the windows of the cottage, its banks green with mint and watercress.

"It's so tiny and cute," said Rose as they approached the cottage. "Can't have many rooms."

Randy opened the cottage door. "A dressing room and bathroom to the left for me, and another dressing room and bathroom to the right for you," he said, opening the two doors on each side. Rose just glanced in the dressing rooms, then walked ahead into the main room of the cottage.

"And one master bedroom with nothing in it but a three-meter bed," she said with a wry smile. "When you said we could stay here overnight, you really mean 'night,' didn't you? Suppose I wanted to do something other than climb in bed with you? Like sitting down and looking at the beautiful garden."

"We can do that too," said Randy. "Let me show you the view from the gazebo." He walked back out of the cottage and across the bridge. Rose stopped to open the closet doors in her dressing room. Everything she could possibly want was there, including two swimsuits, one quite skimpy.

They retraced their path through the birch trees almost to the beach; then Randy started up a narrow, rocky pathway that led up the side of the stone cliffs. Rose noticed that Randy said something into his cuff-comp as he started up the path. They climbed above the terraced gardens of cyclamens and geraniums until they were halfway to the "sky." Just beyond the stand of birch trees, perched high above the glen, was a small round gazebo with a shake roof. In the center of the gazebo was a round bench covered with a thick round pad. Rose noticed it was only two meters in diameter.

From the gazebo you could see practically everything in the glen. No sooner had they sat down on the edge of the round bench to admire the view than the "sky" started to darken and a cool wind rose up.

"Looks like we're in for an afternoon shower," said Randy. "Good thing I left the lid closed on the picnic basket."

There was a flash of light and a crack of thunder.

"Oh!" gasped Rose, clutching at Randy. Then the "heavens" opened and they watched the rain front start over the pond and sweep toward them until they were under the downpour, with the raindrops drumming on the roof above them. The lightning flashed again and again, while Randy held Rose tightly. The shower lasted five minutes, then ended as quickly as it had started, and the sun came out.

"Looks like it's over," said Randy, putting his hand out to feel the last drops falling from the treetops. "Let's go see the rest of the garden. Watch your step, the path is slippery."

Hand in hand, they made their way down from the gazebo to the other end of the glen. There, outlined with boxwood hedges, was a large, beautiful rose garden. Each rosebush was a different variety. Rose went around to each one, smelling the fragrant blossoms.

"I never promised you a rose garden, but here's one anyway," said Randy expansively.

"Oh, Randy," said Rose. "How lovely." They finally came to the end of the path where it was blocked by the brook. On the other side of the brook was another cliff with a six-tiered waterfall splashing down its face. The brook widened into a small, shallow pool before it disappeared into a wide crevasse at the base of the cliff. In the pool were red and yellow carp swimming slowly among the water lilies, rushes, and cattails.

"There's more," said Randy, leading the way across the fish pond on a series of stepping stones. He parted the thick stands of rushes and stepped onto a bed of thick green moss. The moss covered a small island in roughly circular shape that was completely surrounded by a privacy wall of tall rushes and cattails.

"The moss here is really thick and springy," said Randy, kneeling down to demonstrate by giving it a push with his fingers. "As soft as a mattress."

"It's interesting that this bed of moss is almost exactly circular," Rose mused, one eyebrow raised. "Could it possibly be three meters in diameter?"

Randy looked around the island. "Why, so it is!" he said in feigned surprise.

"Do you have anything else to show me?" Rose asked archly.

"The orchard." Randy walked across to the opposite side of the moss bed and pushed through the rushes. A winding grass path lay ahead of them. On each side of it were dwarf fruit trees, most of them laden with fruit.

"Apples, cherries, peaches, apricots . . ." said Randy, pointing them out. "Only these are growing in dirt instead of hydroponics tanks."

Rose stopped at the orange tree to smell the blossoms. "I'm going to come down here every day just to smell the flowers."

"Make sure you drag me along," said Randy. "Even though I'm traveling through space at two-nines-cee, I've got to learn to stop and smell the roses."

They had come to the end of the path through the orchard. They were back where they had started from. Ahead of them was the pond and the thundering waterfall.

"I'll make sure you come," Rose said pensively. She looked at the cool, inviting pool glimmering in the hot sunlight. "I think I'll take a dip before we have our picnic lunch."

"Great idea!" said Randy. "There are bathing suits in the dressing rooms in the cottage."

Rose looked at him. "Who needs a bathing suit?" she said, unclasping the large turquoise belt buckle holding up her paint-covered blue jeans.

➤   ➤   ➤

Didit had to come down into the garden to remind them of their imminent video dinner with their children.

➤   ➤   ➤

It was another quiet morning on *Spacemaster*. Rose was painting a still life of a bowl of various fruits from their garden, while Randy read the morning business mail scrolling up the screen of the video display at the back of his desk.

"Another star system opened up," he said out loud. Then, as he watched more information flow up the screen, he added, "Not much money, though."

"What did you say, dear?" asked Rose.

"C.C. Wong has finally arrived at UV Ceti on his way to Tau Ceti," said Randy. "Not much there, since the two stars in the system are so small."

"That's nice, dear." Rose was thinking of something else. "I ought to be going home again soon," she said. "The children's spring vacation is coming up, and they both do so much better being at home."

"It's almost time for me to decelerate *Spacemaster*, so you'd have to go home soon anyway," said Randy. "We have to fold up the living quarters since the ship will be at high gees."

"What happens to the garden when you decelerate the ship?" asked Rose, now concerned.

"We do what we can by supporting the larger plants and inducing a nine-month 'winter season,'" said Randy. "But only some of the plants can survive that kind of treatment. In fact, Konstantin started fall earlier this week. The birch leaves are starting to turn yellow."

"That sounds lovely," said Rose. "Let's take a stroll through the woods and look at the autumn colors from the gazebo."

"I'll bring along a warm blanket," said Randy. "In case we want to dally a while."

➤   ➤   ➤

The nine-month-long deceleration period was finally over and *Spacemaster* had arrived in the Epsilon Eridani planetary system. Randy got up off the deceleration couch, shed his virtual helmet and gauntlets, and took his seat at the pilot console. *Spacemaster* was still decelerating at one gee.

"Have your telescopes found anything unusual, Konstantin?" Randy asked the icon on the videoscreen.

"Nothing that the telescopes on Backside had not identified before we left," said Konstantin in English. "Four gas giants and two dirt balls. The second one out looks interesting."

"Let me see it," said Randy. The icon of Konstantin shrank, moved to the upper left corner of the screen, and was replaced by the picture of a red-and-yellow planet with small white spots and gigantic polar caps that went halfway down to the equator.

"It is larger and more massive than Earth," said Konstantin. "So it has kept most of its volatiles, including its nitrogen, producing an atmospheric pressure of nearly one atmosphere. But it is further out, in the equivalent of a Martian orbit, so most of its water is in the form of ice in the large frozen lakes or snow in the large polar caps. At spots near the equator the lakes show evidence of being ice-free during the summers. Over the years, they have probably converted most of the primordial carbon-dioxide atmosphere into carbonate rocks."

"Any sign of life?" asked Randy.

"No," said Konstantin.

"All it needs is warming up and some oxygen, and it would be a pretty good substitute for Earth," said Randy. "We could manufacture large space-mirror sails to hover over the dark side of the planet and reflect sunlight back on the polar caps and frozen oceans. The extra heat will have the planet warmed up in no time and we could start planting. Even before that, people could start colonizing using simple oxygen masks."

" 'No time' is not correct," said Konstantin. "Assuming the aluminum content of the nearby asteroid belt is similar to the solar-system asteroids, and assuming a modest investment in automatic film fabricators to make the space mirrors, it would take a full twenty-three years to get the average temperature of this planet up to ten Celsius."

"In terms of the age of the planet, twenty-three years is as close to 'no time' as you can get!" said Randy, pleased to hear the computer's estimate. "Let's get the experts here and start terraforming!"

"I shall set a course that will match speeds with our station back in the solar system," said Konstantin. "That way, equipment can be sent through the warp without having to enclose it in negative-mass pods. Fortunately, the relative velocity between Sol and Epsilon Eridani is small, so we can stay in formation for many months without leaving the planetary system here."

"How long will it take to match speeds?" asked Randy.

"Considering our present velocity, twenty-three minutes at one gee."

Randy got up from the pilot's seat. "I'm going to put on my tightsuit," he said to the icon. "As soon as we've matched speeds and you put us in free-fall, I'll dance with the Silverhair and open up the warp."

"Very well, sir," said Konstantin. Randy felt the motion as the ship's computer turned the ship to its new heading.

"Hmmm," Randy mused as he passed a small door in the wall. "It's going to be a long day. Stuck in a tightsuit to boot. Better make a pit stop while I'm still under gees."

➤   ➤   ➤

As Randy floated out the vacuum lock into the large, spherical chamber, he was greeted by the Silverhair.

<Rand! Dance! Bol!>

Randy groaned. Just before she had left, Rose had taught the Silverhair to dance to "Bolero," and it had been the Silverhair's favorite tune ever since. Randy suspected the reason the Silverhair liked the tune was because it ran so long. The Silverhair never seemed to tire of dancing, even though its human keepers did. Randy set his suit radio so it would broadcast the "Blue Danube Waltz" and he started to waltz around the room, but the Silverhair just drew in its silver threads.

<No!> it said. <Bol!>

I'd better give in, Randy thought, coming to a halt. *I'm going to need its cooperation to open up the warpgate back to Earth. If only someone could come up with a mechanical method for holding open a warpgate mouth so we don't have to depend upon trained animals*—he corrected himself—*plants.*

Randy changed the music chip selection to the opening beats of "Bolero" and started the jerky dance around the electrode support

posts. The Silverhair joined him, twisting its strands of silvery tendrils
as it sang along in its melodic tongue.

<<Me move me here . . . then me twist and twirl round. Me
move me there . . . >>

By the next day, the Silverhair's spherical chamber in the hold had
become a cargo transfer station. With the two ends of the warpgate
moving at the same speed, there was now no strain on the Silverhair as
cargo was transferred back and forth. Under urging from the cold touch
of the red column of laser light, the Silverhair dilated until cargo two
meters in diameter could be floated through the warpgate, then out a
cargo door that opened into space. Most of the cargo was one way, but
tightsuited humans floated back and forth over the eleven-light-year
distance as if a trip to the stars was a short stroll down the office
hallway. The continuous stream of cargo was going to be used to
assemble a spaceport station and a fleet of ships to fully explore the
new planetary system.

Once every eighteen hours, the warpgate traffic was shut down and
the Silverhair was allowed to relax a little. For the next hour the
Silverhair was danced with and fed. Then, after a vigorous game of
poof-ball, it was back to work. Fortunately, the Silverhair didn't need
sleep, just food, entertainment, and human company.

After the first few rooms of the space station had been constructed,
a special container was sent through the warpgate. Randy, Hiroshi,
Siritha, and some roustabout robots were waiting for it on the space
station. The cargo inside the container was another Silverhair, its
tendrils shrunk in length so it would fit inside. Siritha was right there
to greet it.

<Sir!> said the Silverhair, seeing her. <Food!> it demanded.

"Just a minute," said Siritha through her intersuit radio link.

"Lift it out gently," Siritha instructed the robots on another channel.
Their six long arms had large electrodes at the ends. Using electrostatic
fields to push on the electrically charged negative-matter creature, they
lifted it from the pod. Using their built-in negmatter drives, they
moved the Silverhair to the center of a spherical room in the central
hub of the space station. The room had electrodes to maintain the
Silverhair in the center of the room and electromagnetic guns for the
transfer of cargo pods. Siritha swung out a large machine with multiple
ports from its holder on the wall.

"You'd better turn down the volume on your suit radio," she

warned. Suddenly Randy's ears were blasted by the overamplified screeches and staccato drumming of a heavy-metal rock group. In addition to the usual instrumental sounds, there was an electrical zapping and crackling tone, with an occasional lightning bolt thrown in, but all in time to the music. The singer had an amazing vocal range, although the words were unintelligible.

"What in hell is *that!*" yelled Randy.

"The Silverhair's favorite sound track," Siritha said in a resigned tone. "The Deadly Scum wangled a visit to one of the Silverhairs in Earth orbit. The visit turned into a combination free-fall dance and electronic jam session—with the Silverhair supplying the vocals and the electrical sound effects. The videotape of the session is now a worldwide best seller." She pointed to the machine. "This gun is a multiplasma generator the Deadly Scum sent the Silverhair as a thank-you present. They've also given the Silverhair a share of the video royalties. Alan Davidson is holding the money in trust for all the Silverhairs."

Randy and Hiroshi watched as the Silverhair fed, and then Hiroshi turned to Randy. "Now that we have this Silverhair set up in a cargo transfer room on the space station, we can release yours so you can travel around freely in *Spacemaster* and look at all the planets."

"Good!" said Randy. "I'll warp Rose and the kids through, and we'll all take a little vacation tour around the system."

⊱   ⊱   ⊱

Rosey and Junior were thrilled by their first warp-through. Randy had put on a tightsuit to welcome his family. Rosey was nine and still a tomboy. She wore her hair in a long ponytail, even though she knew it annoyed her father. Junior was approaching sixteen and his voice couldn't decide what register to settle in. He must have been using Randy's gym at home, for his chest and shoulders were almost as muscular as those of his father.

After they had gone to the dressing rooms and changed out of their tightsuits into street clothing, Randy was appalled by the children's clothes, even though Rose assured him they were the latest style at the Princeton Enclave school. Junior wore an open-necked purple velvet tunic, a broad black leather belt with a large silver buckle, black tights with a grotesquely large codpiece, and black swashbuckler boots. His ears were covered with purple amethysts, and his long bobbed hair, wavy chestnut-brown like his father's, was topped with a purple velvet cap sporting a long feather. Randy had to admit that the outfit looked good on the kid, although the tights looked a little sissy.

"What's with the codpiece, Junior?" he asked. "Even mine isn't that big."

Rose interceded. "The principal tried to put a stop to it, but some of the older boys really needed something that large. And of course none of the other boys would want to admit that they didn't . . ."

"Well, OK . . ." Randy sighed.

Rosey was more acceptably dressed in a pseudo-fifties outfit. White blouse, white wool sweater, pleated skirt, bobby sox, and white tennis shoes. Her dark brown ponytail looked good with the outfit, but Randy thought it looked too mannish. He would try to do something about that while she was here.

While Konstantin took them off at one gee to see the other planets in the Epsilon Eridani system, Randy and Rose showed the kids around the ship. Junior and Rosey were pleased with their bedrooms, especially since they didn't have to share a bathroom but could mess up their own private bathroom to suit themselves. Junior soon had pinups on the walls of his room, while Rosey installed a terrible picture of the Deadly Scum on one wall that made Randy sick every time he saw it.

Junior had brought along two HoloHelmets, and soon he and his dad were stalking wild animals in the garden. The HoloHelmet projected three-dimensional color laser images against the scenery around them, taking into account the real foliage in the background to hide the animals and adjusting the laser light intensity to compensate for the variances in reflectivity.

"This is even better than a virtual game," said Randy, looking carefully around as the two of them walked side by side across the circular mossy island. Each was carrying a laser pistol. A peccary scurried off through the orchard beyond, and Randy and Junior both fired at it, but they missed. The HoloHelmets were also good for World War I dogfights and *Star Wars* space battles. Randy flew his recliner and Junior flew the sofa. They did well working as a team, except when the enemy attacked from the direction of the fireplace. The laser projector couldn't compensate well for the pitch-black soot, and the enemy craft were often on them before they could see them coming.

Randy also spent a lot of time with Rosey. She had brought along a maglev space chessboard. It was the standard three-dimensional chessboard, except that the pieces were made of room-temperature supermagductor material, and the board had a complex magnetic-field pattern generator in it that allowed the chess pieces to float in arrays in empty space. Randy was impressed with Rosey's chess-playing skills. Her sharp analytical ability had also shown itself in her science and math grades in school. In fact, both kids made good grades, which pleased their parents.

Randy kept bugging Rosey about her hair. Every morning at breakfast, he would walk around behind her on his way to the head of the table and tug lightly on the end of her ponytail.

"Hmmm . . . getting a little long," he would say. "Like me to give you a little trim?" Finally, Rosey had had enough. One morning after Randy had sat down, she pointed her cereal spoon at him.

"Look, Dad," she said, "I'll make you a deal. You beat me at space chess, and I'll let you cut my hair. If you lose, you shut up about my hair for a whole year."

Randy paused. It wasn't much of a risk for Rosey. She had been beating him at space chess five out of six games. But he really had been getting obnoxious about her hair and ought to quit bugging her about it anyway. Hair length wasn't really all that important.

"It's a deal," he promised.

Rosey eagerly hurried through her breakfast and had the chessboard ready before Randy was done. It was a hard-fought contest, and the advantage passed back and forth many times. Late in the game, Rosey moved a piece.

"Check!" she said gleefully. Then she gasped as she saw something she had missed before. "Oh my God!" she groaned. "What a *stupid* move! I was too eager . . . I should have looked around the board before I took my hand off the piece."

Randy thought it had been a very good move. His king was in check and he didn't see a way out of it. He had been about to concede, but if Rosey had seen something, then it was there.

"Hmmm . . ." He frowned, looking carefully around the chessboard. He finally found what Rosey had seen, and reached out his hand. His space bishop slid all the way across from the other side of the board to simultaneously block the check and pin Rosey's queen on the diagonal to her king.

Rosey put up a good fight, but with her queen gone, she didn't have a chance.

"Oh, well . . ." she said as she finally gave up. "It was getting too long anyway."

Randy set up a stool in the kitchen and a sheet on the floor, draped a towel around Rosey's neck, and took the comb and scissors that Didit handed him.

"I can't stand to watch," said Rose. "I think I'll go into the living room and watch the Lunar Olympic Trials with Junior." She left the room, leaving father and daughter together.

"Don't make a mess of it, Daddy," Rosey pleaded, although her dad had cut her hair before when she was little.

"I won't," promised Randy. "When it comes to the delicate parts, I'll have Didit do it." He undid the ponytail and started combing out the shoulder-length hair.

Rosey enjoyed the attention and made a humming sound in her throat.

"What?" asked Randy.

"Nothing," said Rosey. "Just purring . . ."

"Oh." Randy kept up the combing. After a moment he said, "I suppose you and your mother have had a talk about growing up and sex . . ."

"Of course," said Rosey. "A couple over the past years. I even brought along some supplies in case I should start early."

"Good," said Randy. "Now . . . let me give you some advice about boys, and all the lines they will try to hand to you when you get older . . ."

➤　　➤　　➤

Rosey also joined her dad in the daily visits to the Silverhair. She still looked like a young boy in her tightsuit, but now that Randy had cut her hair short, you could at least tell she was a girl.

"I brought along a new chip," she said, holding up a petarom cartridge, then inserting it into her chestpack.

"Not the Deadly Scum, I hope," replied Randy with a grimace.

"Don't be silly, Dad," said Rosey. "The music the Deadly Scum plays is great for concert shows, but you can't dance to it. This is a chip of Simon and the Bolivars' latest hit, 'Dancing on the Moon.' It's climbing to the top of the chip charts." As they cycled through the airlock into the chamber of the Silverhair, she turned on the music. It was a spirited, rapid melody that made your feet move. After all the electronically modified popular music that Randy was used to hearing, the simple woodwinds and drums the Bolivars had adapted from the music of their Bolivian Indian forerunners had a refreshing newness. Yet the tunes and beats of the Bolivian dances were not simple; they were very complex, indicating significant embellishment over the centuries. Randy found himself enjoying his chore as he followed his slim daughter in and out among the suspension electrodes, trying to imitate the intricate dance steps her feet were making. The Silverhair enjoyed it too.

<More!> it called, after the music stopped.

"That's enough," said Randy, panting. "I'm pooped."

"I'm not," said Rosey. "You rest and watch." She started the next tune. "This one is called 'Sun Fairies,'" she said, and started dancing with the Silverhair again. Randy watched her lithe movements with pride.

She will be a beautiful woman, he thought. *Like her mother . . .*

He watched her some more, and the bouncing bob of short hair on her head reminded him of his month-long battle with her over the length of her hair. *Feisty, too . . . like her mother . . .*

➤   ➤   ➤

"Of all the planets, I like this one the best," said Rosey. She was sitting on the sofa in the living room between her parents as they all looked at the image of the surface of the planet moving by on the living room view-wall. Yellow sand dunes, rust-red mountain ranges, grey-white icy lakes, and white polar caps alternated in the view as *Spacemaster* moved in a terminator orbit that followed the shadow line around the planet.

Spacemaster was in an acceleration-augmented close orbit that decreased its orbital period from a nominal ninety minutes to sixty minutes, while at the same time producing a comfortable one-gee environment on the ship instead of the free-fall environment normally associated with orbiting a planet.

"Anyone want the last marshmallow?" said Junior, holding up the toasted brown delicacy from his seat in front of the fireplace. When no one answered, he popped it in his mouth.

"What are you going to name it, Dad?" asked Rosey.

"Well," said Randy, "it is mostly rust-red and sand-yellow, like a Picadilly rose . . ."

"You aren't going to name it 'Picadilly,' are you?" asked Rosey in disgust. "That's a groaky name for a planet!"

"No," said Randy, smiling. "I'm going to call it 'Rose.'"

"Wow!" said Junior, impressed. "Mom is going to have a planet named after her."

"It's named after me, too," Rosey piped up.

"No, it isn't," said Junior. "He didn't say Rose, Junior, he said Rose."

The grandfather clock chimed.

"Ten o'clock," said Rose. "Time to go to bed. We have to warp back tomorrow and catch the two o'clock rotovator to Havana Spaceport. Then, day after that, school starts again."

"Groan," said Junior, getting slowly up and brushing the fireplace ashes off his tights.

➤ ➤ ➤

After the children were off in bed, Rose and Randy cuddled on the sofa in front of the fireplace, watching the surface of the planet Rose pass by on the view-wall.

"I wish you could come back with us," said Rose.

"Afraid not," said Randy. "Tomorrow I start a three-day long-term strategy meeting with my top executives to plan our development of the Epsilon Eridani system. I'm holding it here in the system to get across the physical reality of the magnitude of the problems and the prospects that lie before us."

"It *is* a big job, isn't it?"

"Only the first of a lot of big jobs," Randy said confidently.

Rose sighed. Never had she known a person with so much ambition and drive. Fortunately, the warpgates now allowed her to catch up with him occasionally.

Randy had really been a good father and husband during the ten weeks they toured the Epsilon Eridani system. He had played with the kids and paid attention to her. She now realized that she had made the right choice of husband. Randy really loved them all.

Yet she also had to admit that it wouldn't be long before he left them to go off exploring again. He had to. It was in his blood. For the same reason a mountaineer *had* to climb the cliffs to the mountaintop, Randy *had* to fly through space to the next planet . . . "Because it's there."

She sighed again. He certainly wasn't a perfect husband and father, but he was more than good enough. She snuggled closer to him and purred into his chest. He took her head in his muscular arms and gave her a squeeze.

8 >>

Timemaster

THERE it *is*, ladies and gentlemen, the Epsilon Eridani planetary system . . ." Randy intoned as he turned on the colorful, rapidly rotating, three-dimensional display. The six major planets orbited the star, while smaller moons orbited the four outer gas giants. The display was contained within a crystal sphere that sat on a small pedestal in the center of the conference table in the meeting room on the space station.

All the senior executives and scientists in every division of Reinhold Astroengineering Company had been warped through to take part in the three-day planning session. Because the space station was not large enough yet for rotation to be applied, everyone was floating in their seats or hanging from some convenient handhold. Some of them hadn't been in space much, and were not very comfortable in free-fall.

"We have opened up the gate to this new frontier," continued Randy. "Our job in the next three days is to come up with a long-range plan for turning this system into a commercially viable enterprise. We need to design and set up the transportation system, identify and develop the resources, and open up the land to settlers so we have future customers." Randy looked over at the tall figure of Bull Richardson.

Bull looked sick. He had strapped himself tightly in his conference chair, and the chair was anchored firmly to the deck, but that hadn't helped much. Bull's skin was greenish-white, and his normally ugly red rash spots were a sickly yellow.

"Since having transportation between the planets is an essential first step, I was going to call on you first, Bull," Randy said. "But if you'd like, I'll be glad to postpone your presentation until later."

Randy began to think that having the meeting on the space station had been a mistake. At the lunch break, he would shift the meeting to *Spacemaster* and have Konstantin operate the ship at one gee during the sessions.

"I think you'd better," Bull said through clenched teeth.

"I'll give his presentation for him!" piped up a loud, shrill voice from a handhold up near the ceiling. "I've certainly heard it enough during his practice sessions at home."

Randy looked up at Mary Lewis. She was obviously enjoying the free-fall environment, except that her large owl glasses kept drifting up off her perky nose and she kept jamming them back on. She fluttered down to where Bull could hand her his videodisk, then took it to the presenter's podium, where she stuck it in the slot and activated the wall screen.

"Since the major center of commerce in the system is going to be the planet Rose," said Mary, starting Bull's presentation, "the first cable catapult center will be established there . . ."

➤   ➤   ➤

It was lunch break, and the attendees of the planning session were enjoying vegetable soup and sandwiches in the one-gee environment of *Spacemaster*. Most of the executives were seated at the large oak dining-room table, but a few had taken their sandwiches with them and were wandering around Randy's mansion in the sky, admiring the furniture, investigating the garden, or enjoying the warmth of the fireplace.

"These are great sandwiches," said Steve Wisneski, his caterpillar mustache munching along a tuna-fish-on-white. "Especially the bread."

"It's homemade bread," said Randy. "We don't have Wonder Bread factories here, so we have to struggle along like the old pioneers. Fortunately, grain keeps well in storage, so every few days Didit grinds up some fresh flour and bakes a loaf or two. The yeast is special—a new genetic strain."

"This vegetable soup is great, too!" said Andrew Pope, slurping up the last from his dish and reaching for the steaming pot in the center of the table. "I think I'll have another bowl."

"That's homemade, too," said Randy. "Those vegetables were

fresh-picked this morning from the hydroponics garden. With Rose and the kids gone, we have a surplus."

"Space travel is sure rough," said Anthony Guiliano, looking up from his corn-beef-on-rye to admire the fine crystal and china in the Chippendale cupboard and the solid-oak folding wall.

"No fresh meat, though," Randy reminded him.

His cuff-comp buzzed the arrival of a personal message and he bent his left hand down under the edge of the table to take a peek at the viewscreen. It was from the deep-space laser communication center on the space station.

Since all normal communications went instantaneously through the warpgate directly to Earth, the usual function of the deep-space comm center was merely to transmit a laser beacon signal. In return it collected information on the position and relative motion of the distant laser beacon signals coming in over deep space from Sol, the various star systems that had already been visited, and the various spacecraft on their way to new star systems. The laser beacons, however, could also be used to send messages.

"It's a message from C.C. Wong," said Randy. "I'll project it up on the living room view-wall." Randy worked his way through the seldom-used menus on his cuff-comp, and soon it was broadcasting the video message to the view-wall receiver.

"I've finally arrived at UV Ceti on my way to Tau Ceti," said the image of C.C. Wong. "I'm afraid there's not much here, since the two stars in the system are so small . . ."

"That's the same message I got ten months ago," said Randy, slightly annoyed. He turned off the view-wall and picked up his soup spoon. As he lifted the spoon, he paused, suddenly perplexed.

"Say!" he said. "How come that message got here so soon? He's over five light-years away. That message should have taken five years to get here, not ten months."

"It's obvious," Steve said patronizingly. "The warpgate system from UV Ceti to Sol to Epsilon Eridani almost forms a time machine. The UV-Ceti-to-Sol warpgate has a time jump of about minus four years, while the Sol-to-Epsilon-Eridani warpgate has a time jump of about plus eight and a half years. That means the net time jump between UV Ceti and Epsilon Eridani is plus four and a half years, while the normal space-time delay between the two stars is a positive five-point-three years. The difference is only eight-tenths of a year, or ten months."

"If you say so . . ." said Randy, not quite understanding.

"Yep," said Steve, speaking up so everyone could hear. "If UV Ceti had been only one light-year closer to Epsilon Eridani, that laser beacon message from C.C. announcing his arrival at UV Ceti would have gotten here before people on Earth knew he had arrived."

"That can't be right," Andrew interjected. "How could he arrive before he arrived?"

"Because the system would be an automatic time machine," said Steve. He leaned over, pointed his soup spoon at Randy, and lowered his voice to a conspiratorial whisper. "Y'know, if you would just take *Spacemaster* here and fly it one lightyear closer to UV Ceti, then you could read electronic versions of the *Wall Street Journal* a week before it's printed back on Earth. I've been monitoring a couple of stocks, and . . ."

"No!" said Randy firmly, now annoyed with Steve. "I said it long ago and I'll say it again. I am not about to fool around trying to make a time machine until we know a lot more about these warpgates. I'll use them to make space commerce easier, but I'm not going to allow them to be used to meddle with time."

"OK, OK," said Steve, leaning back and taking the last bite of his tuna sandwich. As he chewed away, frustrated in his plans, his mustache wriggled furiously under his nose.

➤   ➤   ➤

The afternoon session of the planning meeting on *Spacemaster* was coming to a close. Anthony Guiliano of the Cable Transportation Group had just finished outlining his plan for setting up a cable-fabrication facility on Thorn, the small, carbonaceous chondrite moon orbiting Rose. The day would now finish with a presentation by Duncan Scott, president of the Triple-L subsidiary. He would discuss the plans for the electromagnetic launchers that were to be set up on Thorn as well as on Periwinkle, the small, innermost dirt planet around "Epsidani"—the nickname that had evolved for Epsilon Eridani.

A deliberately annoying buzz came from the cuff-comp under Randy's sleeve, and Randy peeked at the telltale. It was an urgent message from Alan Davidson back on Earth. He got up from the conference table and slipped into the kitchen.

➤   ➤   ➤

"First let me assure you that they are not hurt badly," started Alan's video image on the small screen.

Randy's heart skipped a beat. Rose and the kids must have been in an accident.

"As William, your chauffeur, was driving Rose and the children back from the airport, the limousine was hit by an antitank rocket," Alan reported.

"My God!!!" gasped Randy.

"The rocket penetrated the driver's compartment and William was killed instantly. Fortunately, last year I purchased you a new limousine with an armored passenger compartment. Rose and the children are only suffering from shock, bruises, and temporary deafness."

"It was those murderous Animal Rescue terrorists, wasn't it!" shouted Randy furiously, his voice carrying into the living room. The lecturing voice of Duncan Scott stopped.

"I'm going to *kill* Oscar Barkham!" Randy shouted even louder.

"Oscar wasn't there," said Alan. "He has been in Washington, D.C., for the past few weeks. The governor of New Jersey appointed him to the U.S. Senate to finish out the term of Senator Black, who died last month. Oscar seems to be as shocked as you are, and has ordered the police to clear all the protestors off his estate as soon as they have captured the killers."

"Have they found them yet?" asked Randy.

"They got away through a hole in the fence leading to the main highway. It was obviously well planned, with a getaway car waiting for them. That's the trouble with these terrorist groups. They strike at innocent people and they're too smart, too small, too dedicated, and too mobile to find and capture easily. If only I had been given some warning that they were going to strike—I could have taken precautions."

Randy's furious face turned grim as he thought.

"I'm going to give you that warning," he vowed menacingly. He turned off the cuff-comp and walked out of the kitchen into the now-silent living area of *Spacemaster*.

"Steve?" said Randy softly as he entered the room, his face full of rage and determination.

"Yes, Mr. Hunter?" replied Steve, for once awed by his diminutive boss.

"Tell me about time machines." Randy sat down once again in his special chair at the head of the table. "Specifically, I want to be able to foretell what someone is going to do in the future, before it happens, so I can do something about it."

"Well . . ." started Steve, his mustache twisting furiously as he tried to think of the best way to explain the problem. "The time machines we can make using warpgates don't quite work that way . . ." Randy glared at him. "However . . ."

➤   ➤   ➤

"So, to sum up," said Steve much later, "you can't change the past. But the word 'past' now has a multiple meaning. It not only means the past you have just lived, but any past you can observe through a time machine that looks into the future. If you get a newspaper from next week and read that you were killed by a terrorist or bought the wrong stock, then next week you will be killed by a terrorist or buy the wrong stock."

"But suppose I call the police . . . or tell my broker not to buy the stock?" persisted Andrew Pope. His logical engineering training had been rejecting all that Steve had been trying to tell them.

"Next week the newspaper will say you were killed by a terrorist or you bought the wrong stock," Steve repeated. "*Something* will happen to make sure that the future past is not changed. The terrorist will slip by the police, the stockbroker will get your order wrong, or it could be the newspaper got the wrong information, and what is printed is not true."

"But those are such low-probability events," complained Andrew.

"Once time machines exist, no event is low probability if it is needed to make the past consistent," said Steve. "The simplest example I know of is called the Moravec Paradox Box. It consists of a simple inverting amplifier and a timegate between the future and the past. In an inverting amplifier, if you feed a logical 'zero' into the input, after a short time delay it produces a logical 'one' at the output, and vice versa. In the Paradox Box, the output of the amplifier is fed into the future end of the timegate, while the past end of the timegate is fed into the input of the amplifier.

"Now suppose we assume there is a 'zero' applied to the input of the amplifier. A 'one' will appear at the output. The 'one' goes into the timegate at the future end. The 'one' comes out the timegate in the past sometime earlier. The 'one' then goes into the input and creates the paradox, since we assumed there was a 'zero' at the input."

"Which proves that time machines cannot exist," said Andrew.

"I'm not done yet, Andy," said Steve, waggling his finger at his supervisor. "If the positive time delay through the amplifier is larger than the negative time jump of the timegate, then what we have is an oscillator. A 'zero' goes into the input, turns into a 'one' two microseconds later, jumps back through the timegate by one micro-second, and the 'one' replaces the 'zero' one microsecond after the 'zero' was applied. We have an oscillator. As the magnitude of the timegate negative time jump approaches the amplifier positive time delay, the frequency of the oscillation increases to infinity. The average output is then neither 'zero' nor 'one' but the normally impossible 'one-half.' If you want to look at it from a quantum-mechanical point of view, the output of the amplifier is a mixed state of the 'zero' state and the 'one' state."

"I *think* I'm beginning to see . . ." said Randy, a puzzled frown still on his face.

"Let me try to explain it another way," Steve suggested. "In quantum mechanics, electrons in an atom can only occupy certain orbits around the nucleus. Those allowed orbits are those where the wave function of the electron just fits into the orbit an integral number of times so the beginning of the wave function matches the end of the wave function. If it were otherwise, a point on the orbit would correspond to two different values of the wave function. Since this situation is not self-consistent, that orbit is not allowed.

"In general, if a wave function has a certain value in one region of spacetime, then the value of the wave function at some other region is determined by the path between those two points. Once a timegate exists, there are two paths, one through the timegate and one through normal space. If the paths have different lengths, then there could be two values of the wave function in the second region. However, the only wave functions that are allowed to exist are those that produce the *same* value in the second region, even though, a priori, that wave function would have a very low probability of existing." He paused. "When timegates exist, things become likely that would otherwise be nearly impossible."

"I still think it's crazy!" said Andrew, shaking his head.

"You're beginning to talk like Steve used to," chided Randy, who had been listening eagerly. He leaned back in his chair and started to fiddle with the row of diamond studs climbing his right ear. "Tell me, Steve," he said, "if I can't change the past, then how can I use a time machine to at least avoid unpleasant futures, like my family getting killed by terrorists?"

"Think of it as a telescope," said Steve. "Before telescopes, Viking raiders could sneak up and attack a town when it was unprepared. After telescopes were invented, they allowed the townspeople to see the Vikings coming at a great distance, and that gave them time to organize the defense of the town."

"So it isn't a cure-all," Randy mused. "You've got to be constantly keeping an eye out for potential problems, and set things in motion to counteract those potential problems. But once you have observed something happen, you can't 'unhappen' it."

"But you *can* take advantage of something you know will happen in the future," said Steve. "In my plans to beat the market, I was going to look up the prices of the various shares in the financial pages I obtained from the future and compare them with the present prices on Wall Street. I would tell my broker to buy a few shares of the stocks that were presently low in price, and sell them again when they were high."

"You could make a killing that way," said Andrew.

"Not really," said Steve. "If I bought too many shares, I would just raise the price of the stocks to where I didn't make any net profit."

"I'm sure the Securities Exchange investigators would also find a way to apply insider trading laws to the transactions," Randy scolded. "But that's interesting . . . If everybody had a time machine and had access to future issues of the *Wall Street Journal*, then everybody would be trying to do the same thing, buy low and sell high."

"And the market would stabilize itself," said Steve. "No wild swings in prices."

"The stock market would finally become what it is supposed to be, a convenient and efficient method for people with excess money to supply working capital to businesses," said Randy. "All the present problems with the market are due to people with get-rich-quick personalities trying to use it as a substitute for gambling." He leaned back in his chair and thought for a while. "If that's what time machines will bring to the world—stability and order and sensibleness—then perhaps they aren't such a bad thing after all . . ."

"I can't be sure of that," Steve warned. "We still don't understand the theory well enough in detail to be sure there won't be some catastrophic problem."

"Well, my real problem is terrorists," said Randy. "How can I use 'time telescope' to protect against them?"

"That's going to be tough," said Steve, pulling thoughtfully on his mustache. "You could have someone keep an eye on them and report the instant they did something suspicious. Even though normally there wouldn't be enough time to bring in the police to stop them, if you could use your advance knowledge to warn the police ahead of time, they could be there set up to stop them."

"Not very good. Besides, we don't really know which ones are the dangerous ones until they strike."

"Yeah . . ." said Steve, still thinking. "Even if you know who they are, you can't just go around arresting people because they *might* do something."

"And if you let them make the attack so you have the reason for arresting them, you aren't accomplishing what I want to do—which is stop them in the first place!" said Randy in frustration.

Steve stroked his chin for a moment before he said, "Let's think this through. Rule one: You can't change the past."

"But what exactly *is* the past?" asked Randy. "Perhaps the solution to our problem lies there."

"Whatever you have lived in your present timeline and whatever you can observe through the timelink connecting you to some future timeline," said Steve.

"*Can* observe, or *have* observed?" said Randy. "Suppose I have a timelink to the future. Certain pieces of information come over that timelink, such as the animal activisits launching an attack on someone. I can't change the fact that they launched the attack, because it has already happened, and as you said, you—"

"—can't change the past."

"But because of the limited bandwidth of the timelink communication channel, I don't know *everything* that happened in the future past," continued Randy. "For instance, unless someone tells me, I don't know the attack was successful. It could very easily have been thwarted instead."

"Hmmm," said Steve. "You might have a good idea there, Randy. Normally, one would think that either the attack succeeded or it didn't. Whether or not you personally didn't know about the success or failure shouldn't have any effect on the actual result. But it could be the situation is like the paradox of Schrödinger's cat—who was neither dead or alive, but in an undecided state, because no one had looked in the box to check. And since the wave function for the attack event can couple back on itself through the timegate, what actually happens could depend upon what parts of the wave function were allowed to come through the timelink communication channel."

"And *I* will be controlling what goes through that channel," said Randy. "If I let myself know that an attack has taken place, but not what the outcome of the attack was, then maybe I can feed back a warning about the attack and make sure it fails!"

"I'm not sure that's going to work. . . ." said Steve, his mustache crooked over to one side of his face as he puzzled the problem through. "I'll have to think it over."

"You do that," said Randy, dismissing him. "In the meantime, I'll give it a try." He turned to Andrew.

"I want you to refit my ship as soon as possible for another interstellar trip," he said. "Add a good deep-space laser comm system that will allow me to get wideband data from our new warpgate station around UV Ceti. As soon as I get close enough to UV Ceti, I'll have a time telescope that will let me keep a future eye on those animal rescue Vikings."

"If you head directly for UV Ceti, you'll start getting future news from the UV Ceti warpgate in about six months," said Steve.

"Not much profit in going to UV Ceti," said Randy. "Nothing much in that star system to develop. I'm not taking off on a long boring trip between stars just because I'm angry—I intend to make a profit off the journey. It would make better sense for me to head for Tau Ceti where we know there's future business potential. I'll take along an extra Silverhair mouth to leave there. That way we'll end up with a direct warpgate between Epsilon Eridani and Tau Ceti, and cut down on the traffic passing through the Sol gateway station."

"Good idea, Randy," said Steve. "Since Tau Ceti is in the same general direction as UV Ceti, it'll still only take about six months of travel before you can access the future through the UV Ceti comm link."

While Steve and Randy had been talking, Andrew Pope had been thinking. "It will take us only a week to insert an extra chamber to *Spacemaster* to hold the second Silverhair, Mr. Hunter," said Andrew. "I'll just reassign a Silverhair containment chamber designated for one of the negmatter spacecraft being constructed at the space station."

"Good," said Randy. He then turned to the silent group of executives sitting around in his living room and dining room. "Sorry for the interruption, ladies and gentlemen," he said expansively. "Duncan? Please continue with your briefing."

He suddenly had another thought, and held up his finger.

"Wait just a second, Duncan." He leaned over to talk to Andrew. "One other thing . . ."

"Yes, Mr. Hunter?" said Andrew.

"Find someone with a can of paint and have him change the name of my ship from *Spacemaster* to *Timemaster*."

➤　➤　➤

Eight days later, Randy was lying on the acceleration couch, head encased in a virtual helmet and arms in virtual gauntlets. The virtual screen in front of his eyes contained the icon of the revised persona for the computer of *Timemaster*. It was a kindly-looking old German gentleman dressed in an opennecked shirt and a rumpled sweater, with a busy mustache under a bulbous nose and wise eyes under a high forehead crowned by an unkempt mane of bushy white hair.

"The spacecraft is ready," said the icon in flawless German. "Shall I initiate the acceleration profile?"

"Nein, Herr Professor Doktor Albert," replied Randy in German. "I am paying for it, I get to drive it."

Randy raised his virtual left arm up to the screen to press the acceleration control icon on the virtual screen. The icon of Albert shrank and moved to the upper left corner while the acceleration icon grew and took the center of the screen. The acceleration icon contained the cylindrical shape of *Timemaster* centered in a large three-dimensional cage of concentric spheres, each sphere representing two lightyears. Off in the distance, just at the outer twelve lightyear sphere, were two stars, Sol and Sirius. Closer in were three stars within the six lightyear sphere, 40 Eridani, UV Ceti, and Tau Ceti—his target.

Randy rotated the imaginary joyball with his virtual glove until the icon of *Timemaster* was lined up with the faint green line that was his desired path. He pulled up on the joyball and the acceleration rose until the ship reached a steady three gees. Using his virtual left hand, Randy pushed the drive icon to the edge of the screen, and the icon of Albert grew and moved to the center of the screen to take its place.

"You were not quite correct in your choice of word for 'drive' in your last sentence," said Albert in English. "That is more properly used for driving automobiles along the autobahn, not piloting spacecraft through space. Would you like a lesson in colloquial German?"

"*Ja,*" replied Randy. "Anything to pass the time."

➤   ➤   ➤

Six months later the icon of Albert rode up on his bicycle while Randy was in the midst of a virtual stroll around a small lake on the planet Rose. High in the sky was a bright new sun, the first of one thousand Reinhold-built, one-hundred-kilometer-wide reflectors that would hover over the dark side of Rose, capturing sunlight from Epsidani and sending it down to warm up the planet and unfreeze the oceans. Blades of a hardy grass from the northern plains of Mongolia were just poking their first shoots out of the ground.

"We are approaching the Cauchy horizon," Albert said as he circled his bicycle around Randy.

"The what?" asked Randy, turning his head around to follow him.

"Where the news from Earth via the UV Ceti laser link is about events that happen in the future time of the news from Earth via the direct Silverhair link," said Albert. "Alan Davidson is in the timelink-control room back on Earth and would like to converse with you."

"I'll be right there," said Randy. "Reduce the acceleration level to zero."

Randy took off his virtual helmet and gauntlets, and sat up on the acceleration couch. When the ship's acceleration stopped, he floated over to the pilot's chair and activated the viewscreen. There were two images of Alan Davidson there, side by side. One came from Earth via the video comm link through the warpgate in the Silverhair down in the hold of *Timemaster*, while the other went from the same camera through the warpgate to UV Ceti, where it was then sent by laser beam over the five-light-year distance between UV Ceti and *Timemaster*. Randy could talk with the direct image, since there was no time delay in the communication link through the warpgate in *Timemaster* directly to Earth. But any attempt to converse with the indirect image involved a long time delay because of the nearly five lightyears back to UV Ceti.

The direct image of Alan was looking him straight in the eyes and waiting patiently for him to speak, while the indirect image was obviously not seeing him, but was talking to Albert's icon instead. The mouth in the indirect image was moving very rapidly because *Timemaster* was moving toward UV Ceti at a good fraction of the speed of light, causing a strong blue shift in the signal and a speed-up of motion. The ship's computer couldn't do much about the rate at which Alan's words came, but it could downshift the frequency of Alan's ultrasonic voice to the range where Randy's ears could hear it.

"WouldyoupleaseinformRandolphthatIwishtospeakwithhim, Albert?" said the indirect image of Alan in a rapid, staccato voice. The image then waited, and was still waiting in the direct image. Randy knew that Alan was always calm and composed, but in the sped-up indirect image, he looked like he had a bad case of the fidgets.

A special, locked, timelink-control room had been constructed in the Reinhold space station around Earth for Alan's use. All communication in and out of the room was encrypted, along with the communication links. Randy didn't want to take any chances that something might leak into or out of the timelink that he didn't have control over.

"Hello, Alan," said Randy to the direct image.

"Are the two signals getting through?" replied the direct image of Alan at a normal rate. Even though *Timemaster* was moving rapidly with respect to Earth, there was no relativistic frequency shift or any time delay in this signal, since the communication beam came through a warpgate rather than through normal space.

"The two links are working fine," replied Randy. "The indirect link is still showing what you were doing a few minutes ago, but at a very rapid pace. It should catch up with your direct image shortly."

"Arethetwosignalsgettingthrough?" chirped the indirect Alan, now looking directly at Randy's eyes.

"This is a momentous occasion," said the direct Alan. "Too bad we have to keep it secret. I wonder if I'll notice any difference when we pass through the crossover point."

The direct image of Alan was interrupted by the indirect image, which rapidly repeated the direct image's first two sentences, and caught up with it in the middle of the second sentence.

"There's the answer to your question," Randy said to the direct image. "I now see—"

"Thatisspooky!" interrupted the indirect image.

"—what you are doing in the future," continued Randy.

"That is spooky!" said the direct image of Alan.

"It sure is," said Randy, impressed and a little scared. "Now remember, I want to go into the future-prediction business slowly and carefully. My main purpose is to see if we can't thwart the violent activities of those Animal Rescue terrorists. It's going to be tough, since we can't change the past, so we can't undo any harm they do. I think I have a way to anticipate their actions so they can be stopped before they do anything bad."

"Verywellsir," interrupted the indirect image of Alan. He got up, unlocked the door to the timegate-control room, and ran stiffly out, slamming the door behind him. Randy turned off the indirect image and enlarged the direct image.

"Since I am the key element in the feedback loop, I'm going to assume that only what *I* know is what is important, not what everyone else knows. At least it's worth a try," said Randy. "The next time the Animal Rescue Front attacks someone, send me an electrofax through the indirect link with just the time and place of the attack. Don't tell me the results, and don't read it over a videolink. I might subconsciously glean something from the look in your eyes, or your tone of voice, distorted as they are by the blue shift. Remember, just an electrofax with the time and place of the attack. I will then inform your past self, who can pass the information on to the police. After I have had sufficient time to contact you in the past and pass on the information, send me another electrofax with the full details of the incident, so I can determine whether my intervention was effective or not. To make sure, wait a full hour."

"Very well, sir," said Alan. He got up, unlocked the door to the timegate-control room, and strode slowly out, closing the door behind him.

➤   ➤   ➤

Two days later, Randy's cuff-comp buzzed. He pushed his sleeve back to expose the wide display screen that was held on his wrist by its diamond-studded, jet-black plastic catch. It was an encrypted message from the future Alan.

"Street in front of Interstellar Transport, Trade, and Terraforming Division headquarters building in Los Angeles at 1715 Pacific Daylight Time, Friday, 9 May 2053." The message was sent at 1903 PDT on 9 May 2053.

"That's a week from now," said Randy. He brought the icon of Albert up on the display. "Tell Alan to call me from the timelink-control room," he said. About ten minutes later, Alan called in through the direct link and Randy passed on the information.

"I'll warn Interstellar Division security and tell the Los Angeles police," said Alan. "I hope the police believe me."

"I'll soon find out," said Randy.

➤   ➤   ➤

An hour later another electrofax came from the future. Randy's face fell as he read it.

"At 1715 PDT on Friday, 9 May 2053, the steps and lobby of the ITT&T Division headquarters building were raked with bullets from an automatic rapid-fire gun fired from a high-speed vehicle. The target was Andrew Pope, who was supervising the placement of security guards at the entrance. Andrew was seriously injured and a security guard was killed. The police were not present and the killers got away."

"It didn't work!" said Randy in frustration, shrugging the cuff-comp back up his sleeve. "You can't change the past. I'll just have to figure out some other way to stop those murderers."

A little while later, Randy's cuff-comp buzzed again. It was another electrofax from the future.

"The police are now asking me how I knew of the attack beforehand. There was even some suspicion that somehow I am involved with the Animal Rescue terrorists. As you instructed, I told the police chief about the timelink through your ship. He was very dubious, but semibelieves it because of your reputation. He said he would pay attention to the next warning, so I gave the second warning to him."

"Hmm," said Randy, a chill running through him as he realized he was hearing about things he had done that he hadn't yet done. "I guess I'm going to try to stop them again. Wonder when? And will I be successful next time?"

➤   ➤   ➤

It was four days later ship time, and nearly two weeks later future time, when the next warning came.

"1440 GMT Thursday, 22 May 2053, receiving dock, Morocco Rotovator freight terminal. Box with bill of lading #A12114930 for shipment to Reinhold Space Station from Arcorp."

Randy passed the message on to Alan over the direct link.

"Sounds like a bomb," said Alan.

"Don't give the message to the police just yet," said Randy. "Wait until the Los Angeles police chief comes to visit you to discuss the first warning, then tell him about the existence of the timelink and give him the second warning. Let him pass it on to the Moroccan police, who are more likely to pay attention to him than to you."

"The first warning didn't work, did it?" said Alan, guessing from the look in Randy's eyes.

"You can't change the past," Randy said brusquely as he blanked the screen. The next hour crawled interminably, but finally the follow-up message arrived.

"Success! Moroccan police officer in a Reinhold Rotovator uniform was holding the bill of lading #A12114930 in his hand when two men walked in with large box from Arcorp to be shipped to Reinhold Space Station. The two men were surrounded and police asked them to open the box. One of the men started to open it, but the other stopped him, telling the police it would explode when opened. The two men were arrested and the bomb squad took the box away. The two men were both active in the Animal Rescue Front."

➤   ➤   ➤

Over the next few weeks, Randy and Alan foiled one attack after another by Animal Rescue terrorists. With the more violent of the activists in jail, the attacks became fewer and less violent. The Animal Rescue Front, its major source of funding turned off by a now careful Senator Barkham and its failures trumpeted in every newspaper, was essentially defanged.

Unfortunately, news of the existence of the timelink leaked out during a press conference with the Los Angeles Chief of Police. Many people refused to believe it, but Wall Street became paralyzed by fear.

Articles in the *Wall Street Journal* expressed concern over what Harold Randolph Hunter might do if he decided to use his knowledge of the future to get rich off the errors in judgment of other investors. Speculators deserted the market and it stabilized at rational levels.

There were other repercussions as well. The headquarters office of the Reinhold Astroengineering Company was flooded with letters to Randy, asking him for predictions of the outcome of sports events or whether a certain person was alive or dead at some point in the future. Leaders of nations pressured Randy for access to the timelink to avoid future catastrophes. Scientists speculated on what the consequences of time travel would be on the world and future science. Scaremongers pointed to strange coincidences as evidence that Randy was already tampering with the future. Finally, Randy was forced to issue a statement through Alan to the press.

"I never wanted to use the spacewarp concept to construct a timelink. I was driven to it by an attack on my family by the vicious and murderous so-called Animal Rescue Front. I vowed to put them out of business and I have. I have deliberately limited the knowledge passing through the timelink to that needed solely to stop the A.R.F. It is because of that limitation that the world has not changed more, except perhaps for the recent rational behavior of the stock markets, which in the past never behaved rationally anyway. I want to assure everyone that I have not used in the past, and have no future intention of using, the timelink for personal profit, and I will resist all attempts by others, including governments, to gain access to it."

The worldwide discussion about the timelink rapidly reached the corridors of Congress. The newly appointed Senator Barkham even introduced a bill to outlaw the construction and operation of time machines and to expropriate the existing timelink for sole use by the U.S. government. Oscar was summoned to the office of the Senate Majority Leader, Wismer (Wiz) Jones.

"Senator Barkham," said Wiz, "I want you to drop your timelink bill."

"No!" Oscar replied hotly. "That megalomaniac little twerp has got to be stopped before he tries to take over the world!"

"You read Hunter's statement," Wiz said calmly. "He only used the timelink to stop the A.R.F. and has no intention of doing anything more with it."

"I don't trust him!" shouted Oscar. "I notice that he isn't destroying the timelink, only promising not to use it. I want it either destroyed or taken over by the U.S. authorities."

Senator Jones snorted. "I'd rather trust the timelink in the hands of Hunter than the U.S. government. More trustworthy, in my opinion."

"Not in mine," replied Oscar. "My bill will make sure the timelink is either shut down or put under proper control."

Senator Jones gave a weary sigh. "Look, Oscar, you are a freshman senator, and appointed at that. You've got to realize that passing a law doesn't always solve a problem. Your bill is a case of trying to close the barn door after the horse was stolen. The timelink already exists, so you can't prosecute Hunter for illegally building one, because he did it before the law was passed. You can try to prevent him from using it further, but he has already said that he isn't going to. Besides, it is bad policy to make a law that you can't enforce. Your bill would only apply to the United States, and Hunter is operating the timelink in deep space, well outside our jurisdiction."

"We've got to do *something* about that blasted time machine!" Oscar railed. "The papers are speculating that he could destroy the future universe if he creates a paradox with it."

"According to what my science experts have told me, it is not possible to create a paradox with it," replied Wiz. He got up from behind his desk and put a friendly arm about the junior senator. "I tell you what we should do . . ."

"What?" asked Oscar, calming down a little.

"You grew up with Hunter," said Wiz. "You know him and how he works. Why don't you go visit with him and have a chat, boyhood chum to boyhood chum . . . get him to see your concerns and agree to close down the timelink voluntarily."

"I don't know," said Oscar dubiously. "He's so pigheaded he will probably say no just because it was me that was asking."

"Well, make it clear that all of us are asking," said Wiz.

"OK," Oscar said reluctantly. "I'll try." He turned to leave.

"Oh, Oscar," added Wiz. Oscar turned around. "Don't lose your temper like you did at the patent trial. If you do, I can guarantee you will never win the next election, even if I have to finance your opposition opponent out of party funds."

9 ➤➤

Visit

At first, Randy refused to let Oscar visit him. But finally he gave in to pressure from his friend, ex-Senator Red Hurley, who passed on a personal request from the President asking Randy to at least listen to Oscar.

"OK . . . if she wants to make a federal case out of it," said Randy, breathing heavily on the three-gee couch. "But he'll have to wait until I've reached ninety-eight-percent cee and can unfold the living quarters."

➤   ➤   ➤

Three weeks later, life on *Timemaster* had reached normal and Randy was waiting for Oscar to arrive. He wasn't about to stand around in a tightsuit waiting for the bastard to warp through, so after a vigorous game of vacuum poof-ball with the Silverhair, and getting the warpgate started, he let Didit and Gidget monitor the dilation while he dressed and got himself some lunch. The ship had to be in free-fall while the transfer took place, so he was reduced to opening a cold can of corned beef and cutting off slices to nibble on. It wasn't one of his favorite meals, and it made him dislike Oscar's coming even more.

As he ate, Randy watched Oscar's progress on his cuff-comp via the video monitors mounted at strategic locations around *Timemaster*. In addition to the small bag that carried his folded dress clothing, Oscar was hauling along a bulky package wrapped in butcher paper. Didit helped Oscar through the vacuum lock and out of his tightsuit. Randy grinned as he watched Oscar remove his codpiece.

At least there's one *part of me that's bigger than Oscar's,* he thought in amusement.

By the time Oscar had gotten dressed, Gidget had collapsed the warpgate and Albert had the ship under one-gee drive again. Randy unlatched Grandfather's pendulum, set it ticking again, and reset the time.

He welcomed Oscar at the elevator as he arrived at the main floor. "Greetings, Senator Barkham," he said, shaking hands perfunctorily. He reached for the bulky package under Oscar's left arm. "Here—let me take that off you," he said.

"I'll be glad to get rid of it," said Oscar, handing it to him. "It must weigh twenty pounds. What is it?"

"Dinner!" said Randy, breaking the tape and unrolling the butcher paper to reveal a fresh turkey. "A beauty!" He grinned and handed it to Didit, who took it off into the kitchen.

"When your wife gave it to me, I thought it was something important," Oscar grumbled.

"But it *is* important," said Randy. "I certainly wouldn't want to inflict an ordinary defrosted fillet of beef on such an important guest as you."

"But the ignominy of being asked to haul a turkey around . . ."

Randy was going to make a quip along the lines of "it takes one to haul one," but decided not to.

➤   ➤   ➤

The visit started well enough, with Oscar taking an interest in seeing Randy's mansion among the stars. He was impressed with the living quarters, although the rooms were sort of small compared to the typical billionaire's mansion, and he asked lots of intelligent questions about the hydroponics deck. The garden was just recovering from being under three gees, but he could see and appreciate the potential. Oscar's eyes didn't miss the number of circular patches scattered here and there about the garden, and Randy got some good-natured kidding about them. By the time the afternoon was over, Randy was even beginning to see a good side to Oscar. All that disappeared, however, when Randy took out a handkerchief to wipe off his hands as they left the garden.

"There you go . . . wiping your hands again," Oscar sneered. "You're such a *cleany-weeny* . . ."

Cleany-weeny . . . The childish taunt in the childish voice dredged up a long-hidden memory from Randy's early childhood, when he was a tiny, immature four and Oscar was a terrible six—large, hyperactive, and strong as a young bull. Randy had been dressed in his white Sunday suit, and Oscar and his parents had dropped over after church to visit.

"Keep clean," his mother had warned him. But Oscar had other ideas. In the garage was a barrel full of soot left by the chimney cleaners. Oscar had climbed on a box, removed the lid, stuck in an inquisitive finger, and started writing bad words on the garage wall. Randy had threatened to tell, then suddenly found his tiny body hanging by its heels over a soot-black hole.

"Afraid of a little dirt, cleany-weeny?"

Randy had kicked and screamed. His kicking had caused Oscar to lose his grip, and Randy's screams had been choked off by smothering soot. The rest of the nightmare was mercifully gone from his memory, except for the humiliating ending—Oscar had been praised for rescuing little Randy, while Randy got a whipping from his father for ruining his white suit. Randy doubted that Oscar even remembered the incident.

"I just like to be clean, that's all," he said.

> ➤ ➤ ➤

The two of them sat down to a delightful dinner. There was roast turkey with stuffing made of chestnuts and homemade bread crumbs, fresh coleslaw and sweet yams from the hydroponics tanks, and fresh-baked pie made with cherries from the orchard. Randy made a production out of carving the turkey, sharpening the carving knife beforehand on the steel sharpener, and handing out large slabs of steaming white meat to them both. It wasn't until the coffee that Oscar brought up the purpose of his visit. The conversation soon became heated.

"The world will never be the same again!" complained Oscar.

"The *universe* will never be the same again," corrected Randy, an unconcerned tone in his voice. "Once a timelink is created, from that moment on, the future happenings at that location are determined by the actions of those in the future as well as those in the past. All of future time and space will be one self-consistent, logical whole."

"You are destroying free will!" Oscar insisted. "What good are a man's thoughts—his dreams—his aspirations—if all the future is predetermined?"

"You have a parochial view of time, Oscar," said Randy. "A person will still have dreams and aspirations—and carry out actions to make those dreams come true—only his actions can now cause effects that take place in the past as well as the future."

"But the paradoxes!" exclaimed Oscar. "Like going back in time and killing your grandfather. If, by accident, you create a paradox with your blasted timelink, no one knows what would happen. Time might stop. The universe might be destroyed. *Anything* could happen . . ." Oscar's voice took on a frenzied edge. "You've got to destroy that infernal machine!"

"You are not being logical," replied Randy, infuriatingly calm and self-assured. "The beauty about timelinks is that they obey the Novikov Self-Consistency Principle—that anything involving a timelink must be self-consistent. You exist, so therefore you did not kill your grandfather, no matter how much you want to, or how hard you try."

Oscar sputtered, "But . . ."

"That's the thing I like best about setting up this timelink," continued Randy. "For the first time, the future workings of the universe will be determined by logic rather than the whims of some illogical but powerful human. Reason, not emotion, will prevail in the new universe I am creating."

"That's what you *really* want, isn't it?" Oscar growled. "I knew you couldn't control that much power without using it. You little Napoleon . . . you're not satisfied being the richest man in the solar system. You want to use your timelink to become ruler of the universe!"

Under the stress Oscar slipped into a ZED-flashback, and Randy became scared. The last time Oscar had had a flashback, he had lost control of himself and tried to choke Red Hurley. There was no telling what he would do now.

"You're up to something . . . I'm *sure* of it," Oscar said savagely, rising from his chair. "I'm not going to let you do it! I'll *kill* you first!"

Moving at manic speed, Oscar grabbed the carving knife from the table and was suddenly on Randy, pinning him in his armchair against the wall. The only things keeping the carving knife from penetrating Randy's throat were Randy's strong hands holding tightly to Oscar's right wrist and one of Randy's feet in Oscar's belly.

Didit appeared in the kitchen doorway, and for a second Randy felt a sense of relief. But Oscar, who had learned the trick as a kid, screamed *"Stop!"* and the robot was instantly frozen into immobility by its built-in safety circuits. Oscar turned back to look again at Randy. His eyes started flickering wildly. Randy, having seen that crazed look before, came close to panic. For once in his life, he was really scared, for his judo tricks were useless with his opponent right on top of him.

"I've got you now!" Oscar rasped, his muscles straining against Randy's weakening grip. Slowly, the knife tip came closer and closer to Randy's face. Randy felt his heart pounding as he stared at death.

I'm going to die! he thought. *If I could just think of some way to save myself!*

Just then, Randy was very surprised to see a heavily bearded man tiptoe through the door from the living room beyond. The man was dressed in red spacesuit outeralls and black space boots. He was helmetless, and his face and suit were smudged with black soot. In his tightsuit-gloved hand the man held the poker from the fireplace tool rack. Randy watched as the man crept up behind Oscar.

"Better put down that knife," Randy warned Oscar. "There's someone behind you!"

"You aren't going to fool me with that one, you miserable midget," said Oscar, pulling his knife hand free in order to strike again at Randy.

The stranger leaped forward and the heavy metal poker smashed against the back of Oscar's hand, sending the carving knife thudding onto the ornate rug.

"YEOW!" yelled Oscar, letting go of Randy to grab his injured hand. He tried to straighten the obviously broken fingers and cried out in pain again. "Ow-w-w-w!" he howled, stamping his feet in agony.

Randy quickly bent down and picked up the carving knife. Using the knife to keep Oscar at his distance, Randy clucked disapprovingly and used his napkin to wipe up the grease stain from the expensive Oriental rug.

Oscar, still holding his injured hand, turned slowly around to look behind him.

"Surprise . . ." said the stranger. With his bearded face, soot-covered bright-red outeralls, and black boots, the man looked like Lewis Carroll's version of Saint Nick—except, of course, for the fireplace poker he was tapping in his sooty left hand.

Oscar's eyes widened and his face blanched as if he had seen a ghost. The shock of seeing the bearded man combined with the physical shock of his broken hand were too much—he fainted.

"Sissy," said the bearded man, kicking at the collapsed body with his toe.

"Thanks, mister," said Randy with great relief.

"Help me tie him up. We'll put him in the transfer pod and send him back," said the bearded man.

"No need to soil our hands with that animal kisser," said Randy. "I'll have Gidget do it." He stretched out his left arm and touched an icon on his cuff-comp. Off in the distance there came a clatter of metallic manipulators moving toward them down the corridor.

"We'd better do something about his hand before we send him off," said the man. He, too, stretched out his left arm and raised his cuff-comp to his mouth. "Godget, please bring the medical kit. Our guest has suffered a broken hand."

Randy stared at the man's cuff-comp. The catch that held it on the man's wrist was made of jet-black, shiny plastic, set with dozens of diamonds of various sizes and tints to outline the constellations in the sky. The man's cuff-comp was identical to the one his father had given him! Randy looked down at his left wrist. His cuff-comp was still there . . .

Suddenly it all clicked into place: the identical cuff-comp, the identical small stature, the identical chestnut-brown hair, the way he ordered the robots around . . .

It's me! thought Randy, turning pale. He started to feel dizzy and sat down weakly in the nearest chair. The last thing he remembered was the bearded man saying, ". . . and we'll probably need some smelling salts for the youngster."

➤   ➤   ➤

"Get in the pod," Randy ordered. Oscar glared back at him with sullen fury from inside the fishbowl helmet of his tightsuit. The right glove fingers of Oscar's tightsuit were crinkled up into little wormlike appendages that sprouted from the rounded cast that protected Oscar's broken hand. His wrists were bound together with a knotted piece of cord, as were his ankles.

"Before I go, I insist that you promise you will close down that infernal timelink and never use it again," said Oscar.

"I'll hold off using the timelink for a while and think about it," promised Randy. "Now get in the pod."

"I insist!" Oscar yelled.

"Don't try to bully me," said Randy. "I'm not afraid of you anymore. Every time you've tried to get in my way recently, I've made a fool of you. In the future, you had better stay away from me, or I'll do it again."

"Besides," added the bearded man, tapping the fireplace poker in the palm of his tightsuit glove, "you aren't in a position to insist on anything. You heard him . . . get in the pod."

Grudgingly, Oscar stretched up in free-fall to grab the handhold at the top of the transfer pod and eased into the foot stirrups at the base of the pod. As he did so, Randy gave him a warning.

"Now remember . . . if you tell anyone about what happened today, I'll tell them the whole truth—including your ZED flashback—*and* I'll file criminal charges for attempted murder. That should be more than enough to end your political career."

They closed the pod on Oscar and shot him through the warpgate back to Earth.

"I wonder if we've seen the last of him?" mused Randy.

"I can guarantee that we haven't," said the bearded man. "He's really mad now . . ."

"Mad? That ZED has made him an unpredictable crazy. He's liable to do anything."

"You don't know the half of it," said the bearded man with a sigh. They collapsed the warp, danced with the Silverhair for a while, then cycled through the lock.

➢   ➢   ➢

"One thing has been bothering me," said Randy as he relaxed the electrolastic in his tightsuit back in the dressing room. "Where in hell did you come from? You couldn't have warped through. We were still under acceleration."

"Came from UV Ceti in my ship, the *Errol Flynn*," said the bearded man. "It's flying in formation right alongside your ship."

"Why didn't Albert or Didit tell me you were coming?"

"I told them not to," said the bearded man. "I was afraid that Oscar might overhear and be forewarned that I was coming. Although logically I knew he would be surprised, I still have a tough time really believing that you can't change the past."

The man had stripped off his tightsuit, which was now a relaxed pile of fabric around his feet. He pulled his combination codpiece and antibind protector from between his legs, and Randy was impressed with what fell out. Then Randy noticed the jagged scar on the man's belly. His groin clinched up reflexively in sympathy for the ancient injury. The bearded man saw Randy staring at his scar, then turned and stretched it out with his hands so Randy could see it clearly.

"Convinced?" he asked.

Randy hesitated for a long moment as he thought. "Up in the hayloft at the stables . . ." he said, a challenging note in his voice as he dredged up a very embarrassing incident that only a certain young lady and he knew about.

The bearded man instantly blushed all over his body at the

long-suppressed memory, the old scar standing out in white contrast on his pink belly.

"With a very sympathetic but very frustrated Mary Lou Preswick," he said, shaking his head at lost opportunities. He looked down between his legs and hollered. "She was willing . . . why weren't you!"

"Convinced," said Randy.

"Say, can I borrow some underwear?" said the bearded man. "Mine are all back on my ship."

"I don't know," started Randy hesitantly, then broke into a broad grin. "I'm a little short . . ."

He ducked as a sweaty, sooty tightsuit flew across the dressing room at his head.

After dinner, Randy led the way into the living room. Didit had put out two glasses of port and a bowl of walnuts. A real pine log was crackling on top of the artificial gas logs. The bearded man started to head for Randy's recliner, then changed his mind and sat on the sofa. Randy sat down in his chair, reclined slightly, took a sip of port, then reached for the nutcracker.

"Rose will be podding in tomorrow," he said after a while.

"You'd better meet her by yourself," said the bearded man. "I'll stay on my ship and you can tell her about me after she's had a chance to settle down."

➤   ➤   ➤

"You ought to warp through more often, Rose," said Randy as he downed the last of the gewürztraminer in his glass. "That fresh salmon you brought with you was superb."

"I had Franklin stop by the fish market in New York City before going on to the airport," said Rose.

"Franklin?" said Randy.

"Our new chauffeur."

"Oh . . ." Randy had put the death of William out of his mind. Unpleasant memories now flooded back, most of them involving Oscar.

"How did your visit with Senator Barkham go yesterday?" she asked, her mind moving in the same channels as his.

"Come on into the living room," said Randy, getting up from the dining room table, "and I'll tell you about it."

➤   ➤   ➤

". . . and so I was saved by my own self—from the future," Randy recounted, taking another sip from his snifter of cognac.

"Unbelievable . . ." whispered Rose, eyes wide with wonder. She stared at her snifter. It was still full, untouched as she had listened to Randy's tale. She took a large gulp of cognac and let it slowly slide down her throat, burning on the way.

"Where is he?" Rose asked finally.

"In his ship," said Randy. "You can see it from the porthole in my study." Rose quickly got up off the sofa and headed for the study while he followed along after her.

"Down to the left," he said as Rose approached the porthole.

"It doesn't look like a typical Reinhold ship," said Rose.

"It's a third- or fourth-generation model," said Randy. "Don't forget, he's from the future."

"How fascinating!" Rose turned to look at Randy. "Is it OK for me to talk to him?" she asked.

A twinge of jealousy shot through Randy. He tried to rationalize it away. After all, the man was himself. Why shouldn't Rose be allowed to talk to her husband? Then the thought that the man was her husband evoked even stronger stings of unreasoning jealousy.

"Sure . . ." he said, trying to be nonchalant. He went to his desk and activated the videoscreen. A few flicks on the screen icons and the bearded face of the man on the other spaceship appeared. He had obviously been sitting at his pilot's console, waiting for the link to be opened. Rose slipped quickly into the chair in front of the desk and looked intently at the image.

"It's hard to tell for sure because of the beard," she said. "But the eyes sure look like Randy's."

"It's me, all right," said the bearded man. "Just a little older, a little wiser, and a lot hairier. It's good to see you again, my lovely rosebud."

"It sure sounds like you!" giggled Rose.

The pangs of jealousy came flooding back into Randy.

Rose turned and looked at him. "I'd like to ask him a few personal questions . . . just to make sure," she said. "Would you mind leaving the room? It won't be long." She turned her back on him and looked again with intense interest at the man on the screen.

"Of course I don't mind!" replied Randy, minding furiously. He stalked from the study and closed the door loudly behind him.

➤   ➤   ➤

Rose was still bubbling with excitement when she finally opened the study door two hours later.

"It really *is* you," she said, smiling happily. "From almost four years in the future. We're still happily married, and the children are doing well, and so is the rest of the world in general."

"I know, he told me," Randy said curtly.

"He also told me about his long, harrowing trip through space to get to you in time to save you from Oscar," she said. "Weeks at a time at thirty gees, drowning all the time in a high-gee protective tank."

"I've been through it," said Randy unsympathetically. "It's not so bad."

"The poor dear," said Rose. "He's been all alone for eight months." She paused, then added hesitantly, "I felt sorry for him and told him I'd go over to visit and keep him company for a while. I hope you don't mind."

"I've been all alone too," Randy protested. "And it was for nine months, not eight months."

"But he said that he has to leave again tomorrow. Oscar is still trying to stop you and he has to go ahead and arrange some sort of protection."

"I don't like it!"

"He saved your life!" said Rose, starting to get annoyed. She looked him in the eyes. "Say, you aren't jealous, are you?" she asked. "How can you be jealous of your own self?" She came up to him, put her hand on his chest, and gave him a peck on the cheek. "Besides, it will only be one night. After he leaves tomorrow I'll be with you every day for four months."

"Well . . . OK," Randy agreed reluctantly.

➤   ➤   ➤

Randy went down with Rose to the dressing room to help her get into her space suit for the short trip over to the other ship. His groin began to tingle as he watched her strip until she was naked. Her custom-molded antibind protector was much narrower than a man's, for in women all it had to do was fill in the concave crevasses in the crotch area so the tightsuit would fit tightly without binding or pinching. He helped shake her into her leggings, then slowly released the relaxing voltage on the electrolastic as she smoothed out the last wrinkles in the tightsuit and set the fingers on the built-in gloves.

With a resigned smile, Randy helped Rose on with her outeralls, boots, and helmet, then cycled her through the airlock. He watched through the porthole as she was met on the other side of the airlock by a space-suited figure. Randy continued to watch—his body flooded with frustrated jealousy stronger than any emotion he had ever felt before—as the bearded man led his willing wife off by the hand to his ship for the night.

➤   ➤   ➤

Rose and the other man didn't get back until late the next morning. The three had a polite but strained lunch together, eating the remainder of the poached salmon from yesterday's dinner as a cold entree. After lunch, Rose left the two men talking at the table while she went to the study to talk to the children over the videolink.

"Being around you makes me nervous," Randy said. "Not that I'm not glad you came when you did, mind you."

"You're right. It's like talking to yourself in a mirror," said the bearded man. "Plus the fact that I've heard all this conversation before. Besides, I'm sure you'd like me to leave so you can have Rose all to yourself. I know I did when I was sitting there."

"Stop that!" said Randy, a little irritated at the cocksure attitude that foreknowledge gave the other man.

The bearded man shot his cuff-comp out of his sleeve to look at the time. Randy noticed once again how brilliant the diamonds were on the jet-black plastic clasp. Because the diamonds on his cuff-comp were on the outside of his wrist, he never saw them himself except when he combed his hair in front of a mirror.

"It's nearly two o'clock. I'm expecting a shipment, so I'd better get back to my ship," said the bearded man.

"What is it?" asked Randy.

"Why don't you come over to the *Errol Flynn* with me and see?" said the other man, getting up and leading the way to the elevator down to the dressing room.

➤   ➤   ➤

When they arrived at the *Errol Flynn*, they didn't bother taking off their tightsuits, but just hung up their packs, outeralls, space gauntlets, and boots in the suit rack. In a storage net above the suit rack were two green metal boxes with strange lettering on them. Randy was going to ask about them, but the bearded man was already on his way out the door. They made their way through the narrow corridors to the warpgate deck.

As they exited the lock into the evacuated warpgate chamber, the bearded man pointed to the center of the room. "An artificial warpgate," he said. "Just what you ordered—back when you got tired of dancing with the Silverhair."

Randy looked around in amazement. The evacuated spherical room was similar to the ones used to hold Silverhairs, but slightly smaller. There were the six electrodes that kept the negmatter warpmouth in the center of the room, but instead of a large living ball with long silvery tendrils, the artificial warpmouth was a small frame of what looked like thick silver wire in the shape of a dodecahedron, twelve pentagons enclosing a nearly spherical volume.

The warpmouth was hard to look at, for each pentagon presented a different view through the warpgate into a large spherical room similar to the one they were in, and the different views didn't match up with each other or the background. Randy then noticed that the containment room was not exactly spherical, but was also in the shape of a dodecahedron, with twelve flat pentagonal walls that seemed to be lined up with the pentagons in the warpmouth frame.

"The first artificial warpgates were cubical in shape," said the bearded man. "Later it was found that any regular solid will do for a negmatter Visser frame. The main idea is to hold the warpgate throat open with a rigidized frame of solid negmatter rather than completely filling the throat with fluid negmatter like the Silverhair does. Hiroshi and Steve found it was slightly easier and faster to expand the pentagons in a dodecahedron than the squares in a cube."

"Who invented it?" asked Randy. "Steve?"

"Of course," said the bearded man. "Late last year. His invention is based on some ancient papers published by two scientists named Garfunkle and Simon . . . or something like that. They showed that, in theory, you could create a wormhole through space if you started with ultradense, oppositely charged matter in a strong electromagnetic field. They did their calculations assuming two black holes with opposite magnetic charge in a strong magnetic field. The theory of quantum gravity hadn't been developed yet, so they couldn't take their calculations very far. Then Elena Polikova and her University of Moscow colleagues discovered the negatively charged Silverhair. It produces negmatter with an electrical charge that is opposite to the Silverhairs we have."

"Where is this new Silverhair?" asked Randy, a little overwhelmed.

"Somewhere in the Boötes Void, they tell me. When Steve heard about the negatively charged Silverhairs, he said 'Of course!' and within less than a day he had used Nakashima's Theory of Quantum Gravity to figure out not only how the Silverhairs worked, but how to build an artificial space warp without having to use Silverhairs."

" 'Of course . . .' " said Randy, tossing up his hands in amazement.

"Of course . . ." the bearded man repeated, imitating Randy's motions. "Then the Russians added a radio transmitter to their TV probe, sent it into the Silverhair with a negative electric charge, and broadcast the Big Ben carillon and one o'clock bong. The Silverhair, having learned the proper response from our positive-electric-charge Silverhairs, dumped a multiton blob of ultradense negative matter with negative electric charge. The Russians fished it back through the spacewarp using electric fields, while at the same time squirting through an equal amount of positively charged negmatter to equalize the mass flow and excess electrons to equalize the charge flow. Once they had significant quantities of negative matter with both positive and negative electric charge, it was simplicity itself to follow Steve's prescription and make a small spacewarp out of nonliving negative matter."

"I see," said Randy, shaking his head slowly in disbelief at the rapid evolution of technology. "Simplicity itself . . ."

"Well," admitted the bearded man, "getting the necessary very strong electric fields took some time, but the work went quite fast. The nice thing about the Wisneski Warps is that you can expand them fairly rapidly to any size you want."

The bearded man went to a control panel and activated some controls with his tightsuit-gloved fingers. The *Errol Flynn* stopped accelerating and the two men went into free-fall. The tiny warpgate in the center of the room then expanded until the pentagons were about a foot across. A figure in a tightsuit appeared on the other side of the warpgate. Randy recognized Hiroshi Tanaka inside the bubble helmet. Hiroshi passed through a rectangular metal box and the bearded man reached for it.

"Watch out!" shouted Randy. "The negmatter will nullify your fingers!"

"No negmatter needed," said the bearded man, taking the box in his fingers. "That's the other nice thing about the Wisneski Warps. Since they are made of rigid negmatter instead of liquid negmatter like Silverhairs, they can withstand the stresses induced when you transmit matter through warpgates with the two mouths moving at different velocities. No negmatter pods needed." He pushed some other buttons on the control panel, the warpgate shrank, and the *Errol Flynn* resumed acceleration.

"I notice that we still have to stop accelerating before we can use the warpgate," said Randy.

"I'm afraid so," said the bearded man. "Even artificial warpgates can't be dilated very far while they are under acceleration. They can, however, pass objects while they are moving at constant relative velocity, like this box."

"What's in the box? Something for tomorrow's dinner?"

"Something a lot more important than dinner—your and my salvation, sent from the future," said the bearded man. He opened the long top of the rectangular box and let Randy peer inside. The box was divided into two compartments. In each compartment there was a tiny dodecahedral frame made of silvery metal. The two frames were levitated in the center of the compartments by electrostatic fields generated by electrodes sticking out from the walls of each compartment. In many of the pentagons Randy could see either a portion of his helmet or a portion of the bearded man's helmet—each view seeming to be at a different angle.

"A matched pair of warpgate mouths," said the bearded man. Randy gasped as the man stuck his tightsuit-gloved index finger into one of the tiny pentagons. Then he felt slightly sick as the fingertip appeared out of one of the pentagons on the dodecahedron in the next compartment. The finger wiggled at him.

"Stop that before you hurt yourself! Us, I mean!" said Randy. The bearded man removed his finger, none the worse for the experience, then carefully closed the lid on the box.

"Well, I'd better get moving," said the bearded man. "I have to build the trap for the rat that's following us. It has to be a big trap for such a big rat, and it'll take some time to grow it."

"Grow it?" asked Randy.

The bearded man sighed. "I'll explain it all to you later when I have the full-grown trap to show you."

"When will that be?" asked Randy. He was a little worried about being left alone.

"A couple of months," said the bearded man. "I'm going to run on ahead at high gees and set up the trap. *Timemaster* couldn't match *Errol Flynn*'s acceleration anyway, so you might as well take it easy. Just stay on your present course, decelerating at one gee, until you catch up with me. By the time you get there, I'll have the trap built and you can be the cheese that attracts the rat to the trap."

"Anything else I should know before you go?"

"I don't remember me telling you anything else," said the bearded man. "So I guess not." He stuck out his hand. "Good luck—I know you had it. Speaking of luck, I'm not going to press mine by coming back to your ship to give Rose a good-bye kiss." He smiled at the annoyed look that suddenly appeared on Randy's face. "You give it to her for me," he said, patting him on the shoulder in a brotherly fashion while leading him to the vacuum lock.

10 ➤➤

Avenger

WHEN Oscar podded through from *Timemaster* to the Reinhold Space Station, which contained the Silverhair at the other end of the warpgate, he was met in the dressing room by Alan Davidson and two security guards.

"My instructions are to see that you are returned to Earth as rapidly as possible," said Alan curtly. "I'm sure you will want a doctor to examine that hand." His tone changed to one of mock sympathy. "We are terribly sorry about your accident."

As Oscar was led away by the security guards, Alan raised his cuff-comp and said, "Get me the head of security." Almost instantly, the security officer of the day was on his screen.

"For the next month, I want a red intruder alert at all Reinhold installations, especially those containing warpgate mouths and space-ship docking ports. In addition, I want you to personally contact each Reinhold spaceship. Make it clear that unless I give personal authori-zation, no non-Reinhold employees are to be allowed aboard *any* Reinhold ship."

➤   ➤   ➤

A little while later, the security officer of the day was halfway through the list of spaceships on his screen. While he was waiting for

Icarus to respond from its orbit near Mars, he looked at the next name on the list. It was the freighter *Jupiter*.

"I wonder if I should bother?" he muttered. "It's still under construction and it doesn't even have its radiation shields installed. A person would have to be crazy to fly it in that condition . . ." He decided he would call it anyway—just to be on the safe side. Just then, his relief came in.

"Time for your break," she said. He got up and pointed to a message at the top of the screen. Below the message was the list of ship names.

"We're on a red intruder alert. We're also to give that message to every ship on that list. I've done up to *Jupiter*."

He left for his break and she took his place at the console. "Let's see now," she murmured, looking at the list. "He said he did up to *Jupiter*, so I guess the next one I call is the *Monitor* . . ."

➤   ➤   ➤

Later that day, Oscar was back at his home in the Princeton Enclave, nursing his aching hand and seething with anger.

I'm sure *that power-hungry no-good has some devious plan up his sleeve. The only way to stop him is to* kill *him! But* how . . .

He was sure that Randy and that supercilious trust officer would have left instructions with the Reinhold security force not to let Oscar visit any of their installations, especially the space stations that controlled access to Randy's spacecraft, warpgates, and the timelink-control room. Then he remembered that his pharmaceutical company was in the process of negotiating a lease for a Reinhold space freighter. It would probably take some time for Alan's warning to filter down to every engineer and salesperson in the Reinhold Company. But, if Oscar acted quickly . . .

"What was the name of that Reinhold salesgirl?" he muttered to himself as he raised his cuff-comp to check through his appointment calendar for the previous month. Shortly he had her on the telephone.

"Good evening, Miss Jabbar," he said, flashing her his "dazzle 'em" smile. "I happen to be coming up to the Barkham Pharmaceuticals Space Station early tomorrow morning, and I was wondering if you would happen to have a freighter similar to the one we are going to lease. I would like to take a look at it."

Oscar smiled evilly as he broke the connection. She hadn't yet been alerted and he had an appointment! He quickly punched in another telephone number. It was the secret line to the Animal Avenger Army, the illicit terrorist arm of the Animal Rescue Front. After the answering machine had made its noncommittal reply, he punched in a secret access code. After a single ring, a gruff voice growled, "Hello?"

"This is Oscar," he said. "I need three men tomorrow morning. Armed."

➤   ➤   ➤

The next morning, Marcie Jabbar floated into the small control deck of the Reinhold freighter *Jupiter*. The ship was still under construction as it floated near the Reinhold Space Station in geosynchronous orbit around the Earth. Hans van Ewijck was belted into the pilot's seat and was manipulating the complex keyboard of a robogang controller while he watched the results on the videoscreen in front of him. His team of robotic roustabouts were loading a complex tangle of machinery into the hold under the control of his fingers.

"The shuttle with Oscar Barkham from the Barkham Pharmaceutical Corporation will be here shortly," said Marcie. "Is there any part of the ship that's too dangerous to take him into?"

"My robogang should be through loading the Miranda 'lectromagnetic launcher shortly," said Hans. "As soon as they're done, I'll seal and pressurize the cargo hold so you can show our prospective customer around. Is it a sale or a lease?"

"Long-term lease," replied Marcie. "He wants to set up a supercryo pharmaceutical research station in the shadow cone of Pluto, then later explore Charon for exotic ices."

"Then this ship is a good model of what they'll get," said Hans. He touched some control icons on the pilot's display and the cargo doors closed. "Make sure you show him the Miranda launcher in the hold. A similar model would do for Charon."

"How long before we could deliver?" asked Marcie.

"Since it would be similar to this ship, I would estimate one year," said Hans. "But for an exact date, you'd have to ask Hiroshi Tanaka." He motioned upwards with his finger. "He and his robogang are outside working on the installation of the secondary magnetic shield."

Marcie's cuff-comp buzzed under her sleeve. She read the message on the screen and headed for the outside airlock. As she waited for the computers of the two ships to complete the attachment of a passageway between the two airlocks, she took a quick look at herself in the black porthole window. She fluffed out a flat spot in her Afro with her fingers and straightened up the Harvard MBA 'ring on the right side of her broad brown nose. There was a hissing and a click, and the lock cycled.

"Welcome!" she said as she greeted the contingent from Barkham

Pharmaceuticals. She frowned a little as three bodyguard types pushed their way through the passageway between the ships and spread out to look around. It would be expected that a billionaire would need bodyguards—but in space? They were followed by a tall, handsome blond man whom Marcie instantly recognized as the most eligible bachelor in the world. Oscar gave her one of his famous disarming smiles and Marcie's heart skipped a beat. When she saw the cast on his right hand, a motherly feeling flowed over her.

To business, Marcie, to business . . . she told herself as she got her emotions under control and started her spiel.

➤   ➤   ➤

After Marcie had taken Oscar around the whole ship, his bodyguards trailing behind, she returned to the control deck. Oscar had asked many more questions than the usual company CEO. Nearly all were intelligent, penetrating questions, as if he were going to pilot the ship himself.

"The ship has a standard negmatter drive with the new feature of an artificial warpgate," said Marcie. "Unlike the Silverhairs, the artificial warpgate needs no tending."

"You still need to torture the poor animals to make them give you the negative matter for the artificial warpgates," blurted Oscar, his face hardening into a scowl.

"The Silverhairs are plants, sir," replied Marcie firmly, parroting the Reinhold Astroengineering Company line. "As so judged by the patent courts. Obtaining negmatter balls from the Silverhairs is no more harmful to them than picking apples from an apple tree."

She turned to point to the pilot's console. "To cut operational costs, the whole ship is designed to be run by one person from this room. This is the pilot console for normal one-gee operation, while next to it is the five-gee acceleration waterbed for reaching cruise speed. Over there is the thirty-gee immersion tank for emergencies." She paused and looked at Oscar. "Do you have any more questions?"

"Yes," said Oscar. "Is the immersion tank in working order?"

Marcie turned to look at Hans.

"This is a standard control deck," answered Hans. "It comes from the robofactory with everything installed and operational." He frowned. "But why do you ask? This isn't the ship you're going to get. *This* ship is going to be used on the Uranus run."

"Not anymore," said Oscar, his eyes suddenly turning dangerous. He pulled his left hand from his pocket, and the tips of ten triangular ceramic bullets pointed at Hans from ten triangular holes in the rectangular end of a ceramic disposa-pistol. The bodyguards also drew their box-shaped guns and soon a very frightened Marcie and Hans were facing forty ceramic bullets.

"Stay still and don't say a word, and you won't be hurt," commanded Oscar. "And stick out your cuff-comps." Two of the bodyguards moved forward, removed their cuff-comps, and turned them off.

➤   ➤   ➤

Floating securely in his construction pod, Hiroshi Tanaka saw the shuttle from Barkham Pharmaceuticals leave. He was a little puzzled, however, for its course seemed to be taking it directly to Earth rather than back to the Barkham Geostation. Urgent-sounding beeps suddenly drew his attention back to his robogang control screen. Emergency circles were flashing around every robot working on the spaceship.

"The ship is moving!" he gasped. He jabbed a communication button.

"Hans! What the devil is going on!" There was no answer. The ship was now moving even faster. With an experienced flicker of his fingers over the controller keyboard, Hiroshi sent his crew of construction robots into an emergency escape pattern. A few seconds after that, the *Jupiter* was gone, leaving behind an expanding cloud of tumbling robots and two inflated rescue bags with their emergency beacons beeping distress calls into space.

➤   ➤   ➤

Oscar kept the ship at five gees for as long as he could stand it. After about five hours he pulled down on the joyball and lowered the acceleration to one gee. Exhausted from the strain, he climbed off the acceleration couch and collapsed into the pilot's chair to check the screen. He had traveled a tenth of an AU and was moving at nearly a thousand kilometers a second.

"Fast enough to prevent any immediate pursuit," he panted. "But I've *got* to go faster if I'm going to catch up to him." He brought up the instructions for the use of the immersion tank. It sounded dreadfully uncomfortable, but he would have to do it.

The default persona for *Jupiter* had been an icon that looked like the Roman god. Oscar found it inhibiting and turned it off in favor of a mechanical voice.

"The flight plan you have proposed exceeds safety standards," warned the voice. "Full radiation shielding has not been installed in this ship. Velocities in excess of point-nine cee will produce radiation doses exceeding minimums."

"Damn!" said Oscar. "I should have waited a few more days." His face grew grim and determined. "But there's no helping it now. I'm going to stop that goddamn bastard if it's the last thing I do." He scrubbed down, struggled into the tank suit, adjusted the helmet, and lowered himself into the immersion tank.

Breathe deeply, he reminded himself as his helmet filled with oxygen-bearing fluid.

The next five weeks passed in increasing misery. Oscar limited his one-gee rest breaks to thirty minutes every eight hours. That gave him just enough time to cough his lungs out, cram some tasteless pap down into his shriveled stomach, see if he could make his constipated bowels move, then climb back into the tank again for another eight hours of drowning at thirty-gee acceleration.

Even his underwater sleep periods were miserable. He had a recurring dream where he was marching to his destruction like a tiny tin robot toy, while towering above him was a gigantic, laughing Randy, controlling his every motion with a remote-control box. The only difference in the dreams was the method by which he was destroyed.

➤ ➤ ➤

"The radiation dose on the pilot deck has now reached a rem a day," warned the ship's computer.

Oscar looked at the virtual screen projected in his helmet. The head of the velocity arrow had the figure "0.995c" in it. It would have to do. He still had a year of travel to go even at that speed. But at a rem a day, he probably wouldn't survive the trip. Six hundred rems killed most people, and even a few hundred rems made a person awfully sick. He pushed down on the virtual joyball and brought the acceleration down to a comfortable one gee. Weakly, he got out of the tank, took off his helmet and suit, and coughed his lungs dry. After a long, hot shower, he came back to talk to the ship's computer.

"Where's the safest place on the ship?" he asked.

"There is a 'storm cellar' in the center of the water storage tank on the hydroponics deck," said the mechanical voice. A map appeared on the screen, showing him how to find it.

Oscar crawled through the doubly twisted tunnel that led to the cramped, cylindrical room. There was a toilet, three bunks, a pneumatic tube connecting to the robokitchen, and a stripped-down pilot's console that allowed the ship to be operated from inside. There was no acceleration couch, so the acceleration was limited to what the pilot could stand. The radiation dose inside the storm cellar was a tenth of what it was in the rest of the ship. Oscar decided to stay.

Normally, life in a storm cellar was boring. But Oscar had plenty to keep him busy. On one of his brief excursions he brought back the robogang controller keyboard that the technician had been using when he had boarded the ship. He found an instruction program that taught him how to operate the controller, and within a week he had brought back to life the gang of robot roustabouts that had been left abandoned in the cargo hold when he had stolen the ship.

"First things first," said Oscar, now very pleased with himself. "What color paint do we have on board?" he asked the ship's computer.

"There is a good supply of all-purpose white base paint with additives to produce any color," said the mechanical voice.

Oscar had one of the ship's crablike mechanical robots mix up some paint while he got used to operating an android roustabout through a virtual suit and helmet. He put the ship into free-fall, and used the android to take a trip out to the front of the ship. There, he painted out the name *Jupiter* and replaced it with the name *Animal Avenger*. Next to the name he painted the logo of the Animal Rescue Front—a large-toothed dog biting a bloody human hand. Oscar was a little disappointed in the result. His version of the dog didn't look anywhere near as ferocious as the ones he remembered.

While he was outside, Oscar took the opportunity to use the android's eyes to take a good look at the kilometer-long mast sticking out of the end of the ship. He used the android to climb to the end where the secondary magnetic shield was normally installed. There was some debris there, generated during his abrupt departure. He used the android to clear away the debris and to document the exact status of the attachment brackets that were left.

For a month the *Animal Avenger* stayed in free-fall while Oscar used the crew of android roustabouts to jury-rig a one-kilometer segment of the Miranda electromagnetic launcher to the long mast. Finally it was done. Oscar used the controller keyboard to bring the androids back into the cargo hold, then donned a virtual suit to get inside one of them.

Using the android's built-in negmatter drive, he floated over to a rack and took out a massive cylinder, almost as long and as big around as the android's body. It was a bucket made of silvery supermagducting metal with a rounded point and a blunt tail. It was designed to hold ore as it was being accelerated by the launcher.

"A silver bullet to exorcise that chihuahua-sized werewolf," gloated

Oscar. Tucking the silvery bucket under the android's arm, he took it outside, where he inserted the bucket into the end of the launcher and activated its supermagnets. The bucket snapped to the center of the breech and vibrated there, levitated by its strong magnetic fields.

"Fire!" yelled Oscar inside his virtual helmet as he pressed a button on the console in front of him.

The bucket was gone so rapidly that even the eyes of the android didn't see it leave.

"It worked!" yelled Oscar with joy. Inside the virtual helmet he smiled maliciously as he brought the android back inside.

"Now all I have to do is set up a feeding mechanism so I can shoot it rapid-fire . . ."

➤   ➤   ➤

"I would really feel better if you would pod home, Rose," said Randy at dinner. It was their engagement anniversary, and the table sparkled with candles, crystal goblets, and champagne. "Albert can see Oscar's ship on the radar and it's closing on us at close to the speed of light. I don't know how he's managing it. According to the message from Earth, the ship he took didn't have a complete shielding system. He must be getting a horrific radiation dose."

"He can be a very determined man," said Rose.

"ZED-crazy, is more like it," Randy said contemptuously. "He also doesn't seem to be slowing down any, so I don't know what he intends to do when he gets here. I've checked with Albert and he informs me that *Jupiter*'s computer will refuse to ram *Timemaster*, since the collision will kill Oscar. Oscar could deactivate the computer and fly the ship himself, but if he does that, Albert is confident it can outdodge a mere human. Besides, Oscar may be mad enough to want to kill me, but he's not crazy enough to commit suicide while he's doing it."

"I'm not worried," said Rose calmly. "I know you survived. I talked to the older you myself."

"But we aren't sure what happened to you," said Randy.

"Yes, we are," said Rose. "He said that I and the kids were just fine and doing well."

"I still wish you would pod home," Randy persisted.

"No!" said Rose defiantly.

➤   ➤   ➤

Oscar, having had problems with objections from the ship's computer, had taken the computer out of the control loop and was now flying the *Animal Avenger* himself. He still used the computer for calculations, however.

"What is the maximum acceleration of Randy's ship?" he asked.

"My records show that *Timemaster* had a first-generation drive," responded the mechanical voice. "Maximum acceleration would have been five gees."

"Good!" gloated Oscar. "If he started accelerating now, show me the volume containing all the points he could reach by the time we get there."

Shortly a picture appeared on the screen. In front of the icon of the distant ship, right at the intersection of its trajectory with that of *Animal Avenger*, there appeared a shaded volume labeled "Escape Sphere." Because of the high relativistic velocity of Randy's ship, the "sphere" was squashed into a flat ellipsoid.

"Now," commanded Oscar, "calculate how many buckets I have to fire to make sure that at least one of them *hits* the bastard."

Almost immediately a pattern of lines sprayed from the point showing Oscar's present position to pierce every portion of the flat ellipsoidal volume. "One hundred thirty-four," said the mechanical voice. "The number required slowly decreases as we get closer and there is less time for maneuvering." The voice sounded stern as it added something generated by its security monitor subroutine. "You are warned, however, that there is a high probability that the distant ship has human beings on board. Since the probability of the ship being hit by one of the ore buckets exceeds ninety-nine percent, there is a high probability of a human being suffering injury, and perhaps death. You are warned that you must not launch the buckets."

"But you can't stop me, can you?" asked Oscar.

"No," admitted the computer in its mechanical voice.

"Good!" Oscar reached for the firing button jury-rigged to the rapid-fire mechanism of the electromagnetic launcher. Holding the button down with his left hand, he manipulated the joyball carefully with his right hand, rotating the nose of his ship until the line on the display indicating the orientation of the ship had passed over Randy's escape ellipsoid four times. Shortly thereafter, five hundred silver bullets streaked silently ahead through space in a deadly pattern of destruction.

➤   ➤   ➤

The next day Randy and Rose were up on the bridge of *Timemaster*, watching Oscar's approaching ship. As a precaution, they had donned tightsuits and helmets and were strapped side by side in the waterbed acceleration couch. The image of the approaching ship on the videoscreen in front of Randy was drastically blue-shifted and grew rapidly as it came straight toward them.

"I can now detect a cloud of objects in front of the ship," said Albert. A cloud of yellow specks appeared on the screen in a spiraling pattern.

"What are they?" gasped Randy. Rose shut her eyes and prayed silently.

"Massive metal objects," said Albert. "A strike from any one of them would be enough to hole the ship. Even the negmatter barriers would be ineffective against objects this size."

"Can you vaporize them with your laser cannon?" asked Randy.

"I can get perhaps a dozen," said Albert. "But there are five hundred of them. The laser system was designed for coping with an occasional micrometeorite, not a meteor swarm."

Randy recalled the last meteor swarm he had watched back on Earth. It had been an exceptional display of the Perseid stream a number of Augusts ago. He had let the kids stay up late and they had all gone out to lie on the lawn and watch. The rate had peaked at almost one a second. Now he was facing five hundred in less than a second.

I was safe then, he thought to himself. *I had the Earth's atmosphere to protect me. I wish I had it now. Those deadly missiles would turn into a harmless fireworks display.*

"There is another ship approaching," said Albert from the upper left of the screen. "It is coming from the direction of Tau Ceti. I had not picked it up before, since I was concentrating nearly all my radar power in the direction of Oscar's ship."

"Who is it?" said Randy.

"I have received a message from the ship," said Albert. "It is from you."

"Let me see the message," Randy said. It appeared at the top of the screen.

"Hold the fort! The cavalry is coming! (Even if you can't see it.)"

"Will the ship get here in time?" asked Randy.

"No," said Albert. "It is decelerating at thirty gees and in fact is now going the other way. I calculate it will match speeds with us in a few days."

"What good is that?" yelled Randy, now genuinely worried. "Where's the cavalry he promised?"

"I think he dispersed it long ago," said Albert calmly. "There seems to be a cloud of hydrogen gas coming toward us. It will pass right between us and Oscar's ship, creating a temporary artificial atmosphere. It should be thick enough to vaporize the pellets."

"Hooray!" Rose piped up. "Randy to the rescue! I knew he'd think of something!"

I wonder when I thought of it? thought Randy. Then he had another thought. *Just a little while ago, stupid!* Still another thought followed. *How could that be?* Randy decided to stop thinking and just watch.

⊱   ⊱   ⊱

"Any second now . . ." Oscar murmured as yellow display dots indicating the position of the torrent of buckets closed in on the slowly expanding blue-shifted image of his target. He had slowed down and changed the course of his ship slightly so that he could witness the strike but keep his ship clear of the resulting debris.

"What the hell!" he blurted as the yellow dots were rapidly replaced by bright streaks of evaporating metal.

"Hold on!" warned the mechanical voice of the computer. The computer had noticed the cloud of hydrogen gas through the ship's sensors, as well as the distant ship that had dispersed it, but since Oscar had blocked the computer from controlling the ship, the computer had done nothing about it. Because of imminent danger to a human, however, its safety monitor subroutine had overridden Oscar's blocks enough to shout out a warning.

Oscar was jerked forward in his seat belt as a glowing hemisphere of light appeared just ahead of his ship. The bowl of light grew brighter and contracted toward him as the acceleration increased. Groaning audibly under the stress, the ship glanced off the tenuous cloud of hydrogen gas, its multikilometer-diameter magnetic shield acting as a giant shock absorber.

Oscar blacked out.

⊱   ⊱   ⊱

. . . A sharp pain in his right shoulder jerked Oscar awake. Dazedly he reached a hand up. There, under the large bruise from the shoulder belt, was an extremely tender spot where he could feel the broken end of a collarbone just under his skin.

"Did I get him?" he asked groggily.

"Fortunately, something happened to your buckets, so no human beings were killed," said the mechanical voice of his computer. "Your activities did result in the injury of one person, however—yourself. My safety monitor subroutine will be forced to report your actions when I next undergo periodic maintenance and upgrade."

"Shut up!" shouted Oscar angrily. He took control of the joyball and turned the ship until it was pointed in the direction of Tau Ceti. The star shone brightly off in the distance, while slightly off to one side were the red-shifted images of two ships. One was the large, plush space mansion of Randy's ship, while the other was a one-man working ship, like his.

"Can I catch up to them before they reach Tau Ceti?" he asked.

"Only if you go at maximum acceleration . . . and even then it would take four months," said the mechanical voice. "That course of action is forbidden, anyway. The radiation levels on the flight deck will reach five rems a day. Considering you already have accumulated over one hundred rems, you would have exceeded six hundred rems by the time you catch up. There is a high probability you will be dead before you get there."

"What are my chances of survival?" growled Oscar sullenly.

"I have some medications that will help alleviate some of the radiation damage," said the computer. "Your chances of survival are less than fifty percent."

Oscar almost gave up. All he had to do was go down to the warpgate deck, activate the emergency escape mode of the artificial warpgate, and step through to surrender to the Reinhold employees sure to be waiting at the other mouth.

"I'm *not* giving up!" he roared, shaking his fist at the two ships on the screen. The angry motion brought a sharp pain to his shoulder, and he reached up to touch the sore spot over the broken collarbone. With an exhausted sigh, he got up from the pilot's console and shuffled over to the rack next to the immersion tank. Because of his broken collarbone, he had to get one of the ship's robomechanics to help him on with his suit. As he lowered himself into the tank and his aching body started to float in the buoyant fluid, he heaved a sigh of relief.

I could almost enjoy this, he thought, as he forced his lungs to accept their first breath of liquid. *If it weren't for the constant sensation of drowning.* He drifted off into fitful sleep.

He was a tiny tin robot again, and Randy was a huge giant controlling his every action with an electronic control box. But now he was being forced to carry the giant Randy on his tiny, aching shoulders . . .

➤   ➤   ➤

Four days after the attack, Randy and Rose were waiting at the airlock while a space-suited figure jetted across on a cable strung between the two ships. He was carrying two green metal boxes. Randy could now read the name on the other ship; it was *John Wayne.* The

John Wayne was sheltered in the magnetic field of *Timemaster*, since it had to turn off its own shielding fields in order for the two ships to approach each other. Both ships were under one-gee deceleration to give comfortable footing on board, only now they were facing away from Tau Ceti and were decelerating instead of accelerating.

The man cycled through the airlock, and put the green metal boxes into the storage net above the suit rack. When he took off his helmet, Randy was prepared. It was certainly himself, all right, but he had grown a mustache. The mustache was a chestnut brown and made the man look very debonair. Rose ran to greet him.

"Thank you for saving us!" she said, embracing the visitor and giving him a big kiss. As they separated, she wiped her upper lip and grinned at the man's mustache.

"Say," she said, giggling. "That tickles . . . and it looks very nice."

Gee, it does look good, Randy thought. *I think I'll grow one.*

"Hi, youngster," said the man, coming over and shaking hands.

"Thanks for coming to our rescue," said Randy.

"*John Wayne* and I were glad to help," said the man. "For a while there, I thought I might not have hauled enough liquid hydrogen to do the job." He gave Randy a friendly clap on the shoulder. "I was afraid I'd be short."

"Stop that . . ." Randy groaned, giving the man a punch on the shoulder in return. "Say, what's in the green boxes?"

"They're called 'feeders'," said the man. "They came from the future. According to the instructions that came with them, I'm going to need them later." He gave his helmet to Godget and hung up his outeralls on the hook next to Randy's. Then, still in his tightsuit, he crowded into the elevator with Randy and Rose.

"Why don't you go upstairs and change," said Randy, punching the buttons for both the main floor and the bedroom floor of the mansion. "Rose and I will wait for you in the living room. I'm sure Didit can help you find something comfortable."

"At least I don't have to worry about it fitting," said the man.

➢ ➢ ➢

"What shall I call you?" Rose asked as she sat on the living room sofa with their visitor. Randy handed them both glasses of champagne and, taking his, sat in his recliner chair. The grandfather clock ticked quietly against the wall as the man thought.

"Randy the Elder?" he finally suggested.

"That would make me Randy the Younger," said Randy, not liking the idea. "We already have a Randy the Younger at home—Junior."

"Then there is the even older Randy with the beard up ahead of us," reminded Rose.

"He could be Randy the Eldest," the man suggested.

"I don't think it matters," said Randy. "Each of us knows which is which. Rose can just holler 'Hey, you,' and we'll come just as fast."

"Shouldn't we be coming up on Randy the Eldest soon?" said the mustached man. In nearly simultaneous motions the two men shrugged their identical cuff-comps out of their sleeves and interrogated Albert. Albert, unfazed, answered them both.

"The *Errol Flynn* has backtracked to join up with us," said Albert. "It should arrive about an hour after dinner." The grandfather clock chimed half past six.

"Well, in that case," said Randy, drinking the last of his champagne, "we might as well not wait for him. What are we having for dinner tonight, dear?"

"Corned beef and cabbage, with smash on the side," said Rose.

"Again?" Randy complained. "We had that last week."

"Sounds good to me," said the mustached man, getting up and gallantly holding out his hand to help Rose up out of the sofa. Rose gave him a loving smile and led the way to the dining room. Randy followed glumly behind.

➤   ➤   ➤

The three were waiting at the airlock door when another space-suited figure arrived, this time from the *Errol Flynn*. There was no surprise this time when the man took off his helmet. Underneath was the bearded man who had saved Randy from Oscar the first time.

And is supposed to save me again, thought Randy.

Rose grabbed the bearded man and gave him a big hug and kiss. Randy was instantly jealous again.

"Say," said Rose, stepping back to look at the man's beard, "you've let it grow longer, haven't you? Looks very nice now—not like you forgot to shave—but distinguished-looking." She scratched him under the chin and he rumbled a deep-throated purr at the attention. The mustached man stepped forward to interrupt.

"I don't believe we've met recently," he said, putting out his hand. "I'm Randy."

"I'd recognize you anywhere," said the bearded man, shaking hands. "Even with that puny excuse for a mustache." He twisted the ends of the monstrous handlebar above his full chestnut beard in obvious pride. He turned to look at Randy.

"If you'll send Didit down to the dressing room with something comfortable, I'll meet you three up in the living room shortly," he said.

Randy looked down at the clothing he was wearing. It was his most comfortable outfit, charcoal-grey slacks and charcoal-grey V-neck sweater over a light-blue, long-sleeved, turtleneck cotton jersey. The man with the mustache was wearing his second most comfortable outfit, light-grey slacks, open-necked white shirt, and a black blazer. In one ear was Randy's gigantic tiger's-eye.

"I'm afraid we two have all the comfortable stuff," said Randy. "Why don't you call Didit yourself, and discuss with him what's left?"

"OK," said the bearded man, pulling back the cuff on his space gauntlets to get to his cuff-comp. "See you upstairs soon."

➤   ➤   ➤

The bearded man came slowly down the circular staircase in a white "cricket outfit" that Randy used for summer-afternoon lawn parties back on Earth. It consisted of a white, sleeveless, V-neck wool sweater over a long-sleeved white cotton shirt, white cotton slacks, white suede shoes, and a white velvet hair ribbon. Climbing up his left ear was a graduated set of iridescent pearls, and from the right ear dangled Venus's Tear, the pride of Randy's jewel collection. Randy was annoyed at the impertinence of his guest, but tried not to let it show.

"I'm glad you could join us," Randy said from his recliner chair.

"I wouldn't miss this night for anything," said the bearded man as he sat on the sofa on the other side of Rose from the man with the mustache. Randy was a little puzzled by the remark, but then again, the man had been here this very night twice before, so naturally he couldn't miss coming back.

"Brandy?" Randy offered, getting up to go to the liquor cabinet. He got out four large crystal snifters, filled them generously, and passed them around.

"To Rose, the spot of joy in my life," Randy said, raising his glass.

"To Rose!" the others said, lifting their glasses to her. She smiled with pleasure.

"To my Randys," she toasted back. "I love you one and all." They all had a sip of brandy, then Rose leaned back.

"I was wondering," she said, "what the age difference was between you three. I know the Randy with the beard is the oldest, and the Randy with the mustache is the next oldest, and—"

"And that beardless youth hogging the recliner is the youngest," said the bearded man.

"But what *are* your ages?" Rose continued, looking alternately at the two older men.

"What's the date on this ship, young man?" asked the man with the beard.

"A few days short of New Year's Day, 2054," replied Randy, consulting his cuff-comp.

"Well, that makes you two months short of forty-two years old," said the bearded man. He turned to the man with the mustache. "What date does *your* cuff-comp have?" he asked.

The mustached man looked at his cuff-comp. "The twenty-fifth of July, 2056," he said. "That makes me forty-four . . . and a half."

"And mine says twenty-ninth of July, 2057," said the bearded man. "Which makes me forty-five and a half."

"I'll be forty-four soon," said Rose, looking surprised. "You two are *older* than me."

"I said I would put you on a relativistic rocketship so I could catch up with you," said the bearded man, laughing.

"So you did, Mr. Buck Rogers Hunter," she replied. Then, patting the comfortable sofa, she added, "But I have to admit, this is no tin can you put me on."

Randy noticed that his brandy was almost gone. Getting up, he went to the sideboard as the conversation continued. "Anyone care for another splash of brandy?"

≻   ≻   ≻

The pine log in the fireplace was now a broken pile of charcoal kept alive by the gas log underneath. The grandfather clock struck eleven. The bearded man yawned and stretched flamboyantly. "Time to go to bed," he said loudly. The room grew pregnant with silence.

"I assume you two gentlemen will be wanting to go back to your ships . . ." started Randy.

"Say, Rose," the mustached man interrupted, pulling on Rose's elbow. "I'll have to be warping back tomorrow, and I was wondering . . ."

"Just a minute!" said Randy angrily, getting up from his chair. "Rose is *my* wife, and she's going to bed with *me!*"

"Let *her* decide!" insisted the mustached man. Randy noticed that the bearded man didn't seem to be concerned at all, but was just sitting back comfortably on the sofa, his hands behind his head and a broad smile on his face, watching the action.

"Now *just* a minute!" Rose exploded, getting up from the sofa and getting between the two men. She pushed the man with the mustache back down on the sofa, then turned to Randy. Taking him by the arm, she led him to the center seat on the sofa that she had just vacated. "Sit down!" she said firmly.

Randy sat down, and the three men looked up from the sofa at an extremely indignant Rose. For a long while, nothing was said; then the indignation on Rose's face was slowly replaced by amused contemplation.

"I was just thinking about Chem 102," she said. Randy frowned, uncomprehending. She walked toward them, hips swinging, and sat down on Randy's lap, then stretched out until she was lying across the laps of all three men. "Remember?" she continued, looking up at the bearded face above her. "When you tried to teach me about solubility?" She wriggled comfortably, then reached up to scratch the bearded man under his chin while she looked down her body at the other two men.

The bearded man purred loudly.

"This looks like a very interesting concentration ratio," Rose went on. "Three Randy molecules to one Rose molecule . . ." She paused. "Why don't we four go upstairs and see if we can't snuggle all four molecules into one three-meter-diameter container?"

➤   ➤   ➤

"Well, good-bye, young man," said the mustached man as he shook hands with Randy. Then he slapped the bearded oldster on the shoulder. "I know I'm leaving you in good hands." He reached up to the inside of the top of the pod and grabbed the handholds, then stepped into the foot stirrups at the bottom. Between the two foot stirrups were the two green metal boxes.

Both Randy and the bearded man started to reach for Rose; then the bearded man pulled his hands away to let Randy do the job. Randy, feet in wall stirrups, took Rose by the waist and lifted her into the pod. There, she grabbed the mustached man around his chest and wrapped her legs around behind his.

"It's going to be a close fit . . ." said Randy as he used the wall controls to slowly bring the pod halves together. The bearded man moved around the closing pod to keep watch, tucking in Rose's elbows and knees as the two halves came together. Finally the pod was closed, and the two men waited as a silvery skin of negmatter flowed from its storage container out over its electrostatic bed in the outer surface of the pod until the pod became a long, featureless silver egg with net-zero mass.

"Stand back," said Randy, warning the bearded man. He activated the transfer switch and the pod shot through the hole in the Silverhair and disappeared.

"I feel a lot better with her out of danger," said Randy.

"Me too," said the bearded man.

The two looked at each other. Randy was used to being alone, but it *would* be nice to have some company.

"Why don't you stay here in comfort while we catch up to the warpmouths you left behind?" said Randy. "*I* get to use the master bed and the study, however."

"And the recliner near the fireplace," added the bearded man. "As a mere guest, I wouldn't want to deprive the master of the house of his favorite chair—he might be a little short with me."

"Stop that—" shouted Randy, laughing in spite of himself. He went to the controls and collapsed the warpgate through the Silverhair.

<Ball!> called out the Silverhair.

Still laughing, the two men got out the poof-ball and started an exhausting game of "keep-away" with the gigantic alien.

11 ⋙

Timetrap

FOR Oscar, the days stretched into weeks. Slowly, slowly . . . the *Animal Avenger* made its wide turn and started to creep up on the three ships moving at nearly light-speed toward Tau Ceti. To counter the boredom of high-gee flight, Oscar interrogated the ship's computer about the workings of timelinks. As usual, the ship's computer had practically everything that had ever been recorded in human history in its data files. Since it was a Reinhold Astroengineering Company spacecraft, it also had all the nonconfidential company files, too. Using obvious keywords, Oscar soon found a series of tutorial memos from one Stephen Wisneski. The memos were not easy to understand, but Oscar was not dumb, and had plenty of time to puzzle out the terms and understand their implications.

The timelink, which gave Randy indirect control of the past by messages sent through time, had been set up when Randy's ship got *near* UV Ceti and could receive messages from the future. Since then, however, Reinhold Astroengineering Company employee C.C. Wong had arrived at Tau Ceti, which was also Randy's destination. Suddenly, the horrible truth dawned on Oscar. If Randy were allowed to reach his destination, then he could use the space warp on his ship and the space warp that C.C. Wong had set up in the Tau Ceti system to create, not a timelink, but a timegate that would allow a *person* to go back and forth in time.

That's *his secret plan!* Oscar thought. *I* knew *he had something up his sleeve. Once he can send* himself *back into the past, there would be no limit to the power he could grab.* He became furious at the thought and his speculations grew wilder. *Randy would control* everything! *The world . . . the solar system . . . the entire universe . . . for all time!* His wild imaginings drove Oscar even crazier. *He* can't *be allowed to do it. I'll* kill *him first!* he vowed.

Suddenly, his stomach wrenched and he vomited up blood, which mixed with the oxygenated fluid in his helmet.

Damn! he thought. *I'll just have to take more antinausea medication.* Holding his breath to prevent the blood from being drawn into his lungs, he lowered the acceleration level from thirty gees to one and climbed laboriously out of the protection tank. He coughed his lungs clear—his coughs alternating with strained attempts to vomit. The robomechanic was waiting with the medical kit, its yellow manipulator holding a nearly empty bottle of antinausea medicine.

"This is the last of the medicine aboard," said the robomechanic. "It is strongly recommended that you abort this mission and warp back to Earth for medical treatment."

"No!" said Oscar angrily.

"Then it is recommended that you stop acceleration so that additional medicine can be warped in from Earth," continued the robot.

"Little chance of them doing that for me," Oscar mumbled. "I'm going on, I tell you!" Oscar was worried now. He had to be in good shape during the attack, since the ship's computer would refuse to help and he would have to do it himself. He must save the last of the antinausea medicine for then.

That meant, however, he couldn't use the acceleration tank. He would have to use the acceleration couch, where vomiting blood only meant dealing with a mess, not pneumonia. He stumbled to the bathroom to wash off the oxygenated protection fluid and get into some dry clothing. He washed his hair, and strands of it came off in his hands. His body, emaciated from his inability to keep food down, was covered with boils and sore spots. He tried not to think what the spots would turn into. After a long, hot shower, he donned a clean jumpsuit, then automatically stepped to the mirror, pocket comb in hand. His hand stopped—there was practically nothing left to comb. Even his eyebrows were gone. Oscar looked at the ugly, hollow-cheeked, balding head with the sunken, dead-tired eyeballs.

"I *curse* you, Randy," he rasped. "Look what you've done to me!" He slipped into another ZED flashback. Eyes flickering back and forth rapidly, he strode quickly to the acceleration couch, buckled himself in, eyes still flickering wildly. He rammed the joyball to its five-gee limit.

"I'll get you!" he screamed as the pain hit him.

➤   ➤   ➤

"There it is . . . the timetrap!" said the bearded man proudly. The two men had just finished a leisurely dinner of chateaubriand together, and Randy was getting out some glasses and the decanter of port from the liquor cabinet while the bearded man set up the living-room view-wall to show Randy what he had arranged.

Timemaster was approaching the region where the warpgate pair had been dropped off. The two artificial warpgates were now very much larger and thicker, and the large pentagonal openings could easily be seen in the long-range telescope. The bearded man manipulated the icons on his cuff-comp and the view zoomed to one of the warp-mouths, then to a tiny icosahedral structure nearby with a multitude of flexible metal hoses coming from each of its triangles.

"This is one of the feeders," he said. "The hoses carry positively charged negmatter to the vertices of one mouth of the timetrap. There is another feeder whose hoses carry negatively charged negmatter to the other mouth." He manipulated an icon on his cuff-comp, and the image on the viewscreen zoomed away from the feeder and followed a set of hoses leading to the large dodecahedral structure in the distance.

"This is the 'past' end to the timetrap," he said.

Randy began to appreciate the immensity of the structure when he noticed how large it was compared to the tiny robomechanics that were monitoring the feeding of the outputs of the twenty hoses into the twenty vertices on the gigantic frame.

"By the time they finish," the bearded man continued, "it'll be two thousand kilometers across."

"Why so big?" asked Randy.

"So the warpgate can pass a whole spaceship without causing too much compression of the ship's magnetic-field shielding," the other man said. "Besides, we have to make the opening big to make sure the rat falls through the trap without hitting the frame." He manipulated his cuff-comp again and the view zoomed away toward another structure in the distance. As the view enlarged, Randy could see it was another dodecahedral artificial warpmouth.

"This is the 'future' end to the timetrap," the bearded man said. "The two ends of the timetrap are separated by one-point-six seconds in time, and one hundred and twenty thousand kilometers in space— ten times the diameter of the Earth. Before I started the growing process, I took one warpmouth on a short trip and 'younged' it compared to the other end."

"Amazing!" said Randy, impressed by the future engineering.

"Now," said the bearded man, "in order to bait the trap, we want to bring our three ships to a halt near the center, flying in formation inside the protective region of the timetrap. But be careful that you move slowly as you go between the two warpmouths of the timetrap. There is a very low probability that your ship will activate the trap as it approaches, but if you are going very slowly, you won't get hurt even if it *does* go off."

"How does the trap work?" asked Randy.

"It's really fascinating to watch," the bearded man said with a smile. "But instead of spoiling it by telling you ahead of time, I'll just let Oscar demonstrate it for you."

"Well . . . OK," said Randy, a little disappointed. "Since we have to match speeds with the timetrap, and the trap is just coasting along, we'll have to drop into free-fall. I'd better have the robomechanics close down the ship, especially the waterfall in the garden."

The bearded man leaned back on the sofa. "No need to do that, me boy. Just put *Timemaster* in a planetless orbit. Get it moving in a large circle, say a thousand miles in radius, and turn on your drive so the acceleration is inward. You'll go into an orbit with a comfortable rotation period of about a half hour, while you enjoy one gee on board."

"Of course!" said Randy. "I did something like that when I took the family on that orbital tour of the planet Rose—but I never thought of doing it with no planet at the center at all."

"You just did," the bearded man reminded him.

"Stop that," said Randy, rolling his eyes in mock exasperation.

The bearded man downed the last of his port and got up from the sofa. "Got to go," he said. "The timetrap is about finished and I need to retract the hoses and pack up the feeders. I'll be done in a few weeks, and then we can wait and watch the rat get trapped."

➤ ➤ ➤

For Oscar, the weeks turned into months, but slowly he was gaining on his objective. The three ships ahead of him were now undergoing a crazy circular motion that had Oscar suspicious. It looked like they might be trying to confuse him with a new version of the old shell game: "Which ship holds the Randy?"

As Oscar approached the trio, he left the ship's sensors at high sensitivity, keeping a watch out for anything emitted by the three ships, or for any other approaching ships trying to deflect him from his course. The sensors found two large structures with unusual reflection characteristics. They were on opposite sides of the three twirling ships, but were quite far away. Oscar had the ship's sensors add the two strange objects to their watch routine, and changed the course of *Animal Avenger* slightly to stay equally far away from both of them.

"I'd better make sure my gun is loaded before I start trying to use it," he said, putting the ship in free-fall.

He switched his virtual helmet and gauntlets from the task of operating the pilot's console to that of operating one of the android roustabouts. He took the robot out into space and had it float along the kilometer-long spar coming from the nose of the ship, checking each of the electromagnetic accelerators. One of them wasn't working right, but all he had to do was disconnect it from the power feed. The supermagducting ore bucket would just fly on to the next accelerator and the only net result would be a slightly lower muzzle velocity.

"Damn! Only two hundred forty-nine buckets left!" he cursed, after using the robot to count the buckets in the rapid-load mechanism. "But the gun is loaded and ready. I'd better get moving again."

He switched the virtual helmet and gloves back to the pilot's console and jammed the joyball up to its five-gee limit again. The android, abandoned in space, was left behind.

➤　　➤　　➤

"Here he comes," said the bearded man. "He must have had some trouble with the high-gee protection tank. His acceleration for the past few months has been only five gees. Even though he's going at over ninety-eight-percent cee, his relative velocity with respect to us is only four percent of cee."

"That's still pretty damn fast!" said Randy. "Don't you think that we ought to be in the control room in our tightsuits and helmets, at least?"

"Naw," said the bearded man with obvious unconcern. "Nothing is going to happen to us, and the view-wall here in the living room will give us a panoramic view of the action." He leaned back in the sofa. He was wearing Randy's "cricket outfit" again, and had an ice-cold long-neck bottle of Bud Classic in one hand and a bunch of pretzels in the other.

"Our lives are in danger, and you sit there like a sofa sausage watching Sunday afternoon football!" Randy exploded.

"Relax . . ." said the bearded man, stuffing another pretzel in his mouth and watching the wall-sized screen. "The only one getting kicked around today is Oscar." He sat up suddenly. "He's opened fire!"

➤   ➤   ➤

Oscar was more careful with his firing this time. Instead of holding down the firing button and spraying a spiral of buckets, he carefully pointed the nose of his ship and emplaced bucket after bucket in a programmed pattern that would produce a maximum probability of a hit on each of the three ships.

Done! he thought grimly after a few minutes of firing. *I only wish I had more buckets . . .*

With three ships, any one of which could be holding Randy, Oscar was forced to distribute his buckets equally among the three, and the probability of striking all three had been lowered to about seventy percent. That meant there was about a thirty-percent chance that one of the ships would escape.

And with the luck I've been having, Randy would be in the one ship that wasn't hit. His sunken eyes burned fiercely behind the contact lenses in his immersion helmet. *But he won't escape me even then!*

In preparation for the attack, Oscar had taken the remainder of his antinausea medicine and a dangerous amount of stimulant to flag his failing body into one last spurt of activity. In case the silver bullets didn't do their job, he was prepared to ram the ship that survived. There wasn't much hope that he would survive the ramming, but Oscar had tried to increase his chances by climbing into the high-gee protection tank and breathing protection fluid instead of air. Standing by outside were the three robomechanics, each holding an open rescue ball with spare tanks of oxygen. If he had to ram, and he somehow survived the collision, he could breathe the oxygenated fluid in his tank helmet until the robomechanics could stuff him into a rescue bag. His ship's warpgate, being made of rigid negmatter and protected by its suspension system, had a good chance of surviving the collision. The robots were programmed to haul him to the warpgate in the rescue bag and shove the bag through the warpgate back to Earth.

Watching the receding buckets on the virtual screen in the immersion tank, Oscar felt a desire to retch. He willed it down. The three clusters of silvery buckets moved closer to their targets. Suddenly an alarm buzzer went off and Oscar looked at a blinking circle on the lower part of the virtual screen.

"What the hell . . ." he gurgled in his fluid-filled throat. The blinking circle surrounded one of the large, strange structures far off in the distance. A cluster of dots were coming out from one of the pentagons in the structure!

It's some sort of gun, he thought. He activated the ship's defense subroutine, and it automatically predicted trajectories for the incoming missiles. Oscar relaxed as he realized that the missiles were not aimed at him. Another cluster, then a third, emerged from the strange gun.

They're aimed at my buckets! he realized in alarm, then watched in frustration as the missiles from the strange object struck each and every one of his buckets, deflecting them away from their targets.

"Damn!" Oscar muttered in his throat. *There is now only one thing left to do . . .*

➢   ➢   ➢

"Beautiful!" cried the bearded man as he watched each bucket being deflected by its twin. "Their high acceleration capability and the built-in magnetic 'spring' surrounding them make them nearly ideal billiard balls."

"That kind of precision is impossible!" said Randy, staring in disbelief as bucket after bucket was deflected in exactly the same direction.

"Improbable things become probable once warpgates exist," the bearded man reminded Randy. "Now, watch . . . He's going to have to duck . . ."

➢   ➢   ➢

They're coming right at me! thought Oscar in panic. He activated the ship defenses at the same time that he jammed the joyball to maximum side thrust to avoid the incoming projectiles. He was successful in avoiding most of them, and the automatic laser cannon took care of the few that came near him. The immediate danger over, Oscar looked around. The silver bullets he had previously fired, which had been deflected by the swarm of missiles that had just passed him, were now off at a great distance, all traveling in the same direction.

They're going directly to that other gun structure, he thought. *At least they're going to hit something.* He then watched in bewilderment as they all passed through one of the pentagonal holes in the structure and disappeared.

It acts like a warpgate mouth! he thought, and for a moment he tried to puzzle out the strange behavior. *Never mind!* he remonstrated.

You've got more important things to think about! He moved his joyball back to high gees again, and drove the *Animal Avenger* at the larger of the three ships.

One chance out of three . . . to save the universe from this madman!

➤   ➤   ➤

"Now the timetrap is going to act in earnest," said the bearded man as he intently watched the action on the viewscreen. He turned to Randy.

"Remember, now. Oscar is bringing this all on himself. If he wasn't intent on ramming your ship at high speed in order to kill you, then nothing would happen to him."

He turned to look back at the screen. "He's avoiding getting near either of the warpmouths and is coming straight at us. He is coming in along the plane that is equidistant between the two warpmouths, and we are right at the center. Now, if he isn't trying to ram us, just come real close and scare us, say, the timetrap won't activate. His ship will take the high-probability path, which is the obvious one. He will shoot through between the two warpmouths, pass real close to us at the center, and continue on out."

"But what if he intends to kill me?" asked Randy. "Then what happens?"

"Something is going to happen to save you," replied the bearded man. "Something that normally is *very* unlikely to happen. But in order to maintain self-consistency in the universe, that highly unlikely event is about to take place. Watch the younger warpmouth on the left of the screen."

"There is a spaceship coming out of it!" said Randy in amazement.

"A copy of Oscar's ship," said the bearded man. "From the future . . ."

"It's on a collision course with Oscar!"

➤   ➤   ➤

The buzzing alarm sounded again in Oscar's ears and a blinking circle appeared around one of the strange objects.

Another missile! he thought with alarm, then calmed down as he realized that the quick response of his laser cannon would take care of it. The missile grew impossibly large.

Another spacecraft! It was a ship like his, with the wreckage of a kilometer-long silver cannon trailing behind. Before Oscar's human reflexes could respond, the superstrong magnetic radiation-protection fields in the space around the two ships collided with each other. The hull of the *Animal Avenger* creaked dangerously and loose items crashed against walls. Oscar, only partially protected by the immersion tank, nearly blacked out under the extreme acceleration.

➤ ➤ ➤

"Oscar's ship was deflected away by the copy! We're saved!" exclaimed Randy. Oscar's ship had been damaged in the collision, and its kilometer-long electric cannon was now trailing along behind.

"Notice what direction it's going," said the bearded man.

"It's going right toward the older warpmouth!" Randy said in astonishment. "While the copy was deflected off in the direction that Oscar came from!"

"Well, the action is all over," said the bearded man, reaching for his beer. "Oscar's ship will shoot through one of the pentagons in the older warpmouth and be warped back in time one-point-six seconds. His ship will emerge from the younger warpmouth at just the right time, with just the right speed, and just the right angle to hit Oscar on the way in, deflecting his ship to go through the older warpmouth at just the right angle and just the right speed and at just the right time to produce a completely self-consistent event. The net result is that after a collision with itself, a passage through the timetrap, and another collision with itself, Oscar's ship will be sent flying off in the direction it came. In effect, the timewarp 'repelled' Oscar from the region it was protecting. A highly unlikely event indeed . . . but it happened in order to keep Oscar from killing you and creating a paradox."

➤ ➤ ➤

A second after the collision, Oscar saw one of the huge structures growing in size ahead of him as he shot toward it. It was as big as a moon. Off to the right were the three untouched ships, Randy no doubt gloating in one of them. His ship shot into one of the gigantic pentagons in the structure and flew out the other side—but something was wrong; the three ships were still on his right, and in front of him was another ship on a collision course with him! Oscar then suffered his second high-gee collision in less than three seconds. This time, despite the protection of the high-gee tank, he blacked out . . .

When Oscar came to, a short while later, his ship was in free-fall. He heard hissing sounds that indicated an air leak somewhere. He would stay in the tank where he could breathe the oxygenated fluid until the robomechanics could fix the leak. He looked out through the liquid surrounding him in the protection tank. The control room was a shambles, broken pieces of equipment floating everywhere. Then

Oscar saw, making their way slowly through the floating debris, six softball-sized silvery blobs, moving in formation. A sheet of metal, drifting in the swift air currents created by the air leak, collided with one of the silvery blobs. The blob passed right through the sheet of metal, leaving a softball-sized hole where a small portion of its multiton mass had nullified the metal away.

The negmatter balls from the space drive are loose on the ship! thought Oscar with alarm. The blobs moved ponderously closer and trapped Oscar in the protection tank. The center blob started to eat its way through the tank, and then the protection fluid itself, heading straight for Oscar's face, now pale with fear . . .

Oscar raised a hand and futilely attempted to push the silvery ball away. His hand went right through the ball, leaving behind three fingertips—floating away in the fluid. Oscar stared at the bloody stump that was left of his hand, part of his thumb hanging from the stump by a strip of skin and blood spurting out of the middle, coloring the protection fluid a crimson red.

The silvery blob moved inexorably closer to his face. In panic, Oscar froze, and his eyes looked down in horror as the menacing silver blob approached his face. The onset of a painful tingle in his nose induced a loud gurgled roar as Oscar attempted to scream with a throat full of fluid. His head—trying to escape the pain—twisted from side to side as the silvery blob slowly ate its way through his nose, lips, teeth, palate, cheeks, jaw, tongue, and throat—nullifying enamel, bone, and tissue with equal impartiality. Oscar's terrified howl was mercifully cut short a few seconds later as the silvery blob of negmatter relentlessly nullified its way through his spinal cord and out the back of his neck . . .

➤   ➤   ➤

"See!" said the bearded man, taking another gurgle out of his bottle of beer. "All over in a few seconds. If Oscar hadn't tried to hurt us, he wouldn't have hurt himself." He munched down the last of the pretzels.

"Is he dead?" asked Randy quietly as he watched the red-shifted image of Oscar's damaged ship moving rapidly away from them, in the opposite direction from which it had come.

"I'm afraid so," said the bearded man without concern. "Alan told me that the engineers were finally able to overcome the computer control blocks that Oscar had inserted, and they instructed the robots in Oscar's ship to open up the warpgate." He paused as his face took on a pensive look. "He refuses to tell me any details about what they found."

"Thank God this nightmare is over at last!" Randy breathed.

"That's where you're wrong, me boy," said the bearded man. "I've done my part—and I get to go back and live a happy future with Rose. You, however, have a lot of work left ahead of you, and if you're to be successful, you'd better get a move on."

"Me?" asked Randy. "Why me?"

The bearded man looked pensively at the soot-caked chimney in the fireplace. "It's a dirty job . . . but somebody has to do it."

Randy looked at him in bewilderment.

He sighed in exasperation. "Think, me boy . . . think."

It then dawned on Randy what lay ahead of him. He had survived so far, but only because the mustached man had deflected Oscar's original fusillade of missiles, and the bearded man had first knocked the poker from Oscar's hand and then set up the timetrap . . . and those two men were future versions of himself.

"You're right," Randy finally admitted. He then panicked a little. "But what am I supposed to do?!?" he asked.

The bearded man got up from the sofa. "The first thing *I'd* do is contact Andrew Pope and tell him to warp out some pilots to ferry the *Errol Flynn* and *John Wayne* to a safe landing at Tau Ceti." He headed for the elevator door. "I'll tell you the rest while we're waiting for your Silverhair to dilate so I can pod home."

➤   ➤   ➤

<Oo! Cold!> complained the Silverhair as the hollow laser beam slowly expanded in diameter. Randy and the bearded man had treated the Silverhair to a dance of the "Bolero" with two humans at once, fed it well, and then had turned on the laser, urging the Silverhair to open up so the bearded man could go home.

"Why didn't you warp back through the artificial warpgate in your own ship?" asked Randy. "It would've been a lot faster than waiting for this Silverhair to open up."

"Admittedly," said the bearded man. "But then I wouldn't be able to jump back as far into the past as I can with this warpgate, and I'd miss seeing my kids grow up." He pointed at the complaining Silverhair. "You don't realize how important that Silverhair is, me boy. Make sure you take good care of it as you fly it back to Earth."

"I've got to fly back to Earth? Why can't I just warp back like you're about to do?"

"I can see you don't quite understand yet," said the bearded man. "Let me go over it in detail . . ."

➤ ➤ ➤

"Well, it looks like the throat has dilated enough that I can pod through," said the bearded man finally. He stepped into the transfer pod and reached up to grab the handholds overhead. "Now remember," he cautioned Randy, "there isn't much leeway timewise, so don't dawdle!"

"But suppose I make a mistake and do the wrong thing?" asked Randy.

"I can assure you that you didn't," said the bearded man. "Besides, when you have time to think about it—and ahead will be lots of boring time in spaceships for you to think—you will find that what I have told you to do is the only logical path open to you. The main thing to remember is to watch the time . . ." Randy saw the bearded mouth spread into a sly grin. "You don't want to come up short."

"Stop that!!" Randy yelled over the suit radio as he slammed the pod shut around the bearded man.

➤ ➤ ➤

After he had closed down the warpgate and said good-bye to the Silverhair, Randy went immediately to the flight control deck and, with the assistance of Didit, changed into a comfortable jumpsuit and boots. He picked up the virtual helmet and turned to Didit.

"I'm soon going to have the ship under five gees. Better have the robomechanics collapse the mansion."

"Very well, sir," said Didit. Randy donned the virtual helmet and gauntlets. As he lay down on the water-filled acceleration couch he could feel vibrations coming from the lower decks. Within fifteen minutes he was breathing heavily, as *Timemaster* decelerated at five gees on its way to a stop at Tau Ceti a half-year later. The constant five-gee pull at his body was much tougher to take than the three gees he had used to get up to speed. Soon, Randy found himself looking forward to his daily poof-ball games and free-fall dances with the Silverhair. He didn't even mind dancing the long "Bolero."

➤ ➤ ➤

"It wasn't fun, but it had to be done," Randy said to himself as he finally pulled down on the virtual joyball and brought *Timemaster* to a halt at the Tau Ceti space station. He took off the helmet and gloves and floated over to a porthole. The slowly rotating space station was huge. In the center was a stationary spherical portion, with dozens of docking ports for spacecraft, while rotating around it was a large double torus. In the distance, extending from the remains of a partially mined asteroid, was a cable catapult under construction. Nearby were the two ships, the *Errol Flynn* and the *John Wayne*. Being capable of thirty gees, they had arrived long before *Timemaster* did. Next to them was a similar Reinhold spaceship, but it had been sliced in two, as if it were waiting for the insertion of an additional deck.

"That must be the *Rip Van Winkle*," said Randy. He then saw a cloud of robomechanics, androids, and human-piloted passenger flitters approaching to greet him.

"Looks like we have plenty of company coming," said Randy to Didit. "Too bad we can't unfold the mansion and have them to dinner, but I've no time to dawdle." He went to the airlock and waited for his visitors to float across the short distance between the ships in their tightsuits.

Andrew Pope was the first one through the airlock. Randy had talked to Andrew back on Earth not long ago, while setting up his weekly video laser link to Rose and the kids through the Silverhair in the hold. The date on Earth through that warpgate had been late 2054. This version of Andrew had come in from the warpgate between Sol and Tau Ceti, and was thirteen years older. He had lost some weight, and the bangs covering the front of his balding head were greyer and sparser.

The next one through was Siritha. She was still as skinny as ever, but her face was now much more mature, though still very beautiful. She too had a few strands of grey hair, and the makeup on her caste mark was less blatant than Randy remembered. She had a small, plain gold wedding ring welded permanently through her nose, and Randy wondered who the lucky guy was.

Behind Siritha was a older Hiroshi Tanaka, also in a tightsuit. He was operating a robogang controller and leading a cluster of android robots. Hiroshi had a similar plain gold wedding ring welded through his nose.

"Good to see you again, Mr. Hunter," said Hiroshi through his helmet. "I won't stay around to talk. My robogang makes it too crowded. I'll take them off to start working on the inside disconnects."

"I'd better go with him," said Siritha. "I want to stay with the Silverhair while we move its chamber over to the *Rip Van Winkle*. I'll tell it what's going on and reassure it you'll soon be back to dance with it."

"You can now talk with the Silverhairs?" said Randy in surprise.

"Not well," said Siritha. "For some reason their brains are only capable of coping with one syllable at a time. Two syllables without a pause becomes noise to them. There are some brain-damaged humans with a similar problem. They can read single words, but compound words are beyond them. Once we understood that, we made some progress." She shook her head. "But it is painfully obvious that they have a low IQ—about that of an octopus—or kitten." She put on her helmet as she followed Hiroshi's robogang off down the corridor.

"Everything is all set," said Andrew. His left arm held his helmet in an awkward fashion, as if it had been badly damaged some time in the past. "We should have the Silverhair transferred over from *Timemaster* in twelve hours, and by this time tomorrow you can be on your way in the *Rip Van Winkle*. Would you like a visit to the space station in the meantime?"

"Sure!" said Randy. "Let me get my tightsuit on."

➤   ➤   ➤

"Impressive!" Randy said as he looked around the gigantic, spherical room that formed the hub of the Tau Ceti space station. In the center of the room was a large artificial warpgate. Each of its pentagons had been opened until they were ten meters in diameter. The rigid negmatter frames of the warpgates had then been covered with welded normal-matter vacuum tubing that shielded the negmatter frame from dust, residual gas, and the occasional bump.

Most of the pentagons faced cargo hatches that opened out into the space around Tau Ceti. Out of some of the pentagons there flowed a continuous stream of instruments, portions of structures, rolls of supermagductor-coated diamond fiber, and other manufactured parts that were obviously designated for further construction of space stations, spacecraft, and space transportation systems. Into other pentagons flowed equally large streams of partially processed asteroid material.

"I don't see much passenger traffic," said Randy, looking in vain for a space-suited figure.

"Humans don't use the cargo pentagons," said Andrew. "Too much trouble getting in and out of tightsuits all the time. We use the passenger pentagon over there." He pointed up to one of the pentagons, where the tubular protective frame had been welded to a pentagonal corridor that led up to the central docking hub. Andrew led the way back to the exit door. "Come on, I'll show you."

After getting out of their tightsuits and dressing in jumpsuits and boots, Randy and Andrew pushed their way through the busy free-fall corridors to the docking hub. Andrew came to a halt in the middle of the pentagonal corridor.

"Up there," said Andrew, pointing up the corridor, "is the Reinhold space station serving the Tau Ceti system." He pointed down, and where Randy would have expected to see the far wall of the central sphere was another docking hub. "Down there," Andrew continued, "is the Reinhold space station servicing the solar system."

As Andrew talked, someone in a businessman's jumpsuit floated by and kicked down the short, air-filled corridor with leaf-green walls and pink trim that spanned the twelve lightyears between Tau Ceti and Sol. Randy noticed that businessmen's jumpsuits hadn't changed much in thirteen years, except that the lapel was narrower and the trim less flamboyant. Seeing the different clothing made Randy wonder what things looked like on Earth now that thirteen years had passed. Up in the space station, where things like clothing had to be functional, there didn't seem to be much that was different. But, unfortunately, he didn't have time to go down to Earth and be a rubbernecking tourist from the past. He was on an urgent mission to save his own life.

Then Randy saw someone coming the other way up the corridor. The young man looked familiar and was carrying a foam container. He was wearing a groundling's business suit, so he wasn't a regular visitor to the space station. Although the brown suit was obviously custom-robotailored out of expensive natural silk, the long tails on the coat looked funny flapping around in free-fall. The brown throat choker looked funny too. It had a hard knot tied in the middle, and was sort of halfway between a choker and an ancient bow tie. There was a large pearl in the middle of the knot that looked familiar, but he was wearing no other jewelry, not even 'rings on his ears.

"Dad!" said the young man.

"Junior!" exclaimed Randy. He gave the young man a hug and held him at arm's length. "My, how you've grown! I just talked to you by videolink yesterday and you were only seventeen. How old are you now?"

"Thirty," said Junior, looking slightly annoyed. He hesitated, then moved closer to his father so that Andrew couldn't hear. "Say, Dad," he muttered, "I'm grown now—and president of Reinhold Astroengineering Company . . . would you please stop calling me Junior? Just use Harold, will you?"

"Sure . . . Harold," said Randy, taken aback.

Andrew interrupted. "I invited Harold to join us for dinner." He pointed to the rotating portion of the central hub above them. "Shall we go out to the one-gee ring where dining is more comfortable?"

"That reminds me," said Harold, handing Andrew the foam container. "Have this broiled for the main course." He turned to Randy. "A trout from the pond in the center of the racetrack. Curly and I went out early this morning and caught it—a four-pound beauty."

➤ ➤ ➤

"Rosey apologizes that she can't come," said Harold as the three sat down to dinner. "She's having bouts of morning sickness and didn't relish the idea of free-fall."

"Then I'm going to be a grandfather!?!" said Randy.

"You already are, Dad," said Harold. "Harold Randolph Hunter the Third is seven years old this month."

"Whom did Rosey marry?" asked Randy, not sure that he liked the idea of his little girl getting married.

"No one you know," said Harold. "He's a nice guy, although a little immature," he said condescendingly. "He makes a good househusband for Rosey, though."

"What's Rosey doing?" Randy asked innocently. Andrew coughed self-consciously, and Harold grimaced.

"Chewing me out most of the time," he replied. "She's been chairman of the board of Reinhold Astroengineering Company since she was eighteen."

"And a good one, too," Andrew interjected between bites of trout.

"Everyone else is too awed by the Hunter name to suggest that I might be wrong in some decision," said Harold. "But Rosey isn't. She keeps me on my toes."

Not a bad idea, thought Randy. *I had been wondering how I was going to pass on the company to two kids.*

"And where's your mother? I expected her to come with you," said Randy, now a little worried.

Harold looked at Andrew. "I guess he doesn't know yet," he said. He turned to look at his father.

"She left with you some eleven years ago—into the future. They occasionally come back through time for brief visits with the grandchildren. They're both doing fine."

Randy had been hoping for at least one night with Rose. Now, the thought of Rose happily going off hand in hand with the bearded man brought back again a flood of unreasoning jealousy.

Andrew's cuff-comp beeped, and he looked at the message. "The work on *Rip* has proceeded faster than expected," he announced. "It'll be ready to go at oh-seven-hundred tomorrow. If you'd like to get a full eight hours' sleep at a comfortable one gee, you'd better go to bed soon."

12 ➤➤

Homeward Bound

B Y six-forty the next morning, Randy was in the high-gee protection tank and breathing liquid, head encased in a virtual helmet and arms in gauntlets. The virtual screen in front of his eyes contained the icon of the persona for the computer of *Rip van Winkle*. It was a skinny, bearded old man with an extremely long beard and mustache.

"The spacecraft is ready," said the icon in Dutch. "Shall I initiate the acceleration profile?"

NEE RIP, typed Randy in reply, trying to remember the little Dutch he had picked up in his youth. *I FLY IT.*

➤   ➤   ➤

After five weeks, the *Rip van Winkle* had reached 0.995 cee, and Rip interrupted a language lesson to pass on a warning from its safety monitor program.

"The radiation level on the control deck has reached ten millirems per day," said Rip. "You have reached the maximum recommended limit for even urgent missions."

HOW LONG BEFORE I REACH EARTH? typed Randy.

"Fifteen months ship time and not quite twelve years Earth time," said Rip. "If you continue to accelerate you can cut the ship time somewhat, but you are so close to the speed of light you will not cut the Earth time by very much."

Twelve years for an eleven-point-nine-light-year trip . . . thought Randy. *That's good enough.* He pushed the virtual joyball down and the *Rip van Winkle* stabilized at a comfortable one gee while the stars passed quickly by. His yearnings for Rose turned into jealousy as he remembered the last time he saw her—wrapped in an indecent body-to-body hug around that know-it-all with the mustache. Hmmm . . . Rose had liked that mustache . . . perhaps he should grow one. He certainly had plenty of time to do it.

➤ ➤ ➤

A few weeks later, Randy found himself plowing his way through yet another detailed quarterly earnings report for Reinhold Company. The company was now so large and had so many divisions it was nearly impossible for one person to keep on top of it all—especially if that person was trying to do it from lightyears away. Fortunately, Alan was there to manage things, but although he was a good bean-counter, he didn't have the innovative spirit and drive that was necessary to keep a high-tech business like Reinhold Astroengineering Company thriving.

What I need to do is to clone myself, thought Randy. He then remembered that he did have a clone of himself back on Earth. But the bearded old fart had insisted that he was "retired." He puttered around in comfort in the Princeton Enclave mansion, "writing his memoirs," while Randy slaved away at the double job of running Reinhold Astroengineering Company and traveling through space at dangerous speeds to save himself.

I wish I could retire, he thought. *But somebody has got to keep the company going.* Rip interrupted his thoughts with a message from the appointment calendar.

"Your son will be eighteen next month," reminded Rip. "What shall I arrange for you to give him as a birthday present?"

"Hmmm . . ." Randy fiddled with his new mustache as he thought. Then he came up with an idea. "See if you can't connect me through to old fuzzface at the mansion. I have something I'd like to talk to him about . . ."

➤ ➤ ➤

By the time Randy and the Silverhair were approaching the solar system, Randy had taught the Silverhair the samba and the Irish jig. Using the vocabulary Siritha had inserted in the ship's memory, Randy and the Silverhair had also learned to talk to each other, although in a limited way.

"Sir was right, Sil," said Randy, holding a one-sided conversation with the Silverhair after a laborious exchange. "Talking with you is like trying to hold a serious conversation with a cuddly pet kitten. Here I am, trying to find out more about the Boötes Void and what other creatures might live there, and all you want to do is play zap-the-trainer or talk about bagpipe music. Although I've got to admit . . . you imitate the bagpipes well."

As Randy crossed the orbit of Neptune on his way back into the solar system, he was still traveling at seventeen percent of the speed of light, but by the time he had reached the Reinhold Space Station around Earth, his thirty-gee deceleration had brought his speed to zero. He was feeling apprehensive as he matched speeds with the space station that held the twin of his Silverhair.

It's sort of like Rip van Winkle walking out of the hills back into his village after his long sleep.

He shot out his cuff-comp and looked at the date. He had checked it earlier during his daily discussions with Alan about company business via the videolink through the Silverhair.

Saturday the fifth of February in 2056, he thought. *Say . . . this is a leap year. I'll be having a real birthday in three weeks.* He paused to figure. *Gee . . . I'll be all of eleven years old.*

The videoscreen blinked and an image appeared on the screen. It was Hiroshi Tanaka, now grey and getting along in age. Above Hiroshi's image was the date: Saturday 16 September 2079. Randy was sure he would never forget how strange he felt when he read that date.

By making a round-trip journey from Earth to Epsidani to Tau Ceti and back, I've jumped over twenty-three and a half years of time!

"Welcome home, Mr. Hunter," said Hiroshi. "We have been waiting for you. Alan, Siritha, and I are on our way over in a flitter to help you dilate the Silverhair for your trip back in time. Say . . . that's an impressive mustache you've acquired."

➤   ➤   ➤

The flitter robomechanics, their colorful manipulators flickering at high speed, extended a passageway that fit against the airlock, and the three visitors floated through. Alan was wearing the semiformal business jumpsuit that had long replaced the one-gee-dependent Earth suit for businessmen and women in space. The suit hadn't changed much with time. The lapels had grown wider again, the neck cloth was now a flowing bow instead of a choker, and cuffs were back in fashion. What was really striking, however, was the subdued, pearly-colored, holographic herringbone pattern that shimmered just below the surface of the fabric.

They must have found some way to impress white-light holographic fringes right into the fabric, thought Randy as he looked at the ever-changing display.

Siritha and Hiroshi were in their tightsuits, ready to enter the vacuum enclosure holding the Silverhair. Their tightsuits had their names in pearly letters, holographically floating a centimeter or so above their chests. Hiroshi and Siritha were carrying sealed metal boxes. Hiroshi had two green boxes and Siritha had a red one.

"Where's Andrew?" asked Randy.

There was a moment's silence. "He died last year," said Hiroshi. "Harold appointed me to take over his division."

"Oh," said Randy. He shouldn't have been too surprised; Andrew would have been in his late sixties.

"The new medical treatments that you brought back through time are marvelous things," said Siritha with a resigned shrug. "But they can't help much if you're an overweight meat-eating workaholic. Now, Alan there is taking good care of himself. He's only eighty-seven and has many more decades left."

"She even has *me* eating vegeburgers most of the time," said Hiroshi wryly.

Randy was puzzled by Siritha's remark about his bringing medical treatments back through the timegate. He knew nothing of any treatments.

"Let's go down and visit your Silverhair," said Siritha brightly, trying to break the somber mood.

"You go ahead," said Alan. "I need to transmit some messages to Randolph first, and then he can join you." He shot his Rolex gold-and-titanium-grey cuff-comp from his sleeve. "Set your cuff-comp on receive," he told Randy. "You can read them later."

"What are they about?" asked Randy.

"Some welcome-home videos from your children and grandchildren," said Alan. "They realize that you can't spare time to visit Earth, and there wouldn't be room for them here. Most of the messages, however, are some amazing electrofaxes that recently arrived from the far future. You'll have to read them to believe them." Their cuff-comps chirped, indicating the end of the data transfer.

➤   ➤   ➤

"It's almost open," said Siritha, pointing to the widening hole in the Silverhair. "Fortunately, you don't need to bother with a pod, since the Silverhairs at the two ends of the warpgate are at the same speed." She handed Randy the two green metal boxes.

"Keep these with you," she said.

"What's in them?" asked Randy.

"Some things sort of like warpmouths, but they're called 'feeders,' " said Siritha. "They came through the timegate from the future yesterday. According to the message we got along with them, it is essential that you have them. I have no idea what they're for."

"I do." Randy nodded. They were the reason it had been essential that he come back to Earth. It would have been much easier for him to warp back into the past from Tau Ceti rather than having to fly all the way to Earth and make practically the same time jump from here.

"You go first," said Siritha. "I'll be following right behind with the red box."

"What's in that box?" asked Randy.

"An artificial warpgate mouth," said Siritha. "The other end of it is set up in the space station over there. As soon as I take it through the Silverhair into the past, it will be an alternative timegate into the future in parallel with the Silverhairs. We can then let the Silverhairs retire and enjoy their celebrity status."

"Celebrity status?" said Randy.

"Their first video with the Deadly Scum was such a success, they have produced four more," said Siritha. "The latest one is going osmium."

"Osmium?" said Randy, rapidly getting lost.

"A billion copies sold," said Siritha. "The Silverhair Trust Fund is making money faster than the Silverhairs can spend it."

"What do they need money for?" asked Randy, now thoroughly bewildered.

"Buying evacuated globes with electrostatic levitation systems so they can visit the surface of Earth—plus the costs of shipping the globes around in cargo craft," she said. "A Highland Game is not complete without a Silverhair playing along with the bagpipe band, and next month a Silverhair is going to conduct the Tokyo Orchestra in a performance of one of its own compositions, *Black Sphere*. It is an attempt to get across in atonal music the vast nothingness of the Boötes Void."

"I'll be . . . ." Randy was impressed with the capabilities of the aliens despite their limited language skills. "I was going to put them out to pasture in the asteroid belt, but it looks like they're taking good care of themselves. Say . . . did you ever really learn how to communicate properly with them?"

"I consider myself the world's expert in Silverese," said Siritha. "But who wants to spend the rest of their life talking to the alien equivalent of rambunctious zap-clawed kittens—even if they *are* supertalented billionaire musicians?"

"The timegate is open, Mr. Hunter," said Hiroshi from his position at the laser beam expander.

"I'll be coming through, then," said Randy. Holding the two green boxes in front of him, he positioned himself inside the hollow, cylindrical laser beam that was boring a hole in the Silverhair, and floated through.

On the other side of the timegate were Andrew Pope, Siritha Chandresekhar, Hiroshi Tanaka, and a few technicians. Randy experienced a slight shock when he saw Andrew alive. He was wondering how it would hit Siritha when she came through, although he was sure she would be more bothered by seeing her younger self and realizing how old and grey she had become.

Fortunately, Andrew left the Silverhair chamber with Randy before Siritha floated through. After changing into business jumpsuits in the dressing room, Andrew took him to the main part of the space station where the rotation supplied a firm footing of one gee. Andrew stopped at a door.

"Your family and the older version of you are on the other side of that door."

"Hold these," said Randy, handing him the two green boxes. They went through the door and Randy was immediately smothered with kisses from Rose and thirteen-year-old Rosey.

Rosey stepped back, giggling and rubbing her cheek. "That *tickles,* Daddy!" she squealed. Rose stayed in his arms and Randy gave her a long kiss. Over her shoulder, he could see the bearded man looking annoyed. Randy deliberately prolonged the kiss to bug the old geezer even more. The bearded man finally broke up the clinch by coming over to shake hands.

"Hello, young man," he said. "Glad to see you got *this* far in good time, at least."

After releasing Rose, Randy went over to his towering nineteen-year-old son, who was standing to one side with Alan. "How's business, son?" he said, shaking his hand and reaching up to slap him on the shoulder.

"Pretty good, Dad," said Junior. "Mr. Davidson has been tutoring me for the past year in corporate finance." He turned and gestured to the bearded man standing with Rose. "And . . . ah . . . Dad . . . has helped by arranging a series of technical briefings by the senior scientists."

"Even though he's only just turned nineteen, he's been doing a good job for the past year as president of Reinhold Astroengineering Company," said the bearded man proudly. "He even started a new Nanobiology Division recently."

"Nanobiology?" Randy repeated.

"Nanotechnology is finally going to become real after decades of failure," said the bearded man. "What Harold realized is that instead of approaching the problem from the viewpoint of an engineer, you should make the nanomachines out of the components that biology uses—carbohydrate molecules—but don't include all the evolutionary baggage of normal carbohydrate life-forms—like cellular structure and junk DNA."

"Say, that's a good idea!" said Randy. Junior gave a pleased smile at the compliment.

After the conversation had gone on for a while, Andrew looked at the time on his cuff-comp. "The next rotovator that connects to the space station holding the Tau Ceti warpgate will be arriving shortly," he reminded them.

"I guess I better say good-bye," said Randy. "Got to go off and rescue the kid in his mansion in the sky." He gave Rosey a big hug and Rose another long kiss—interrupted by a loud "Ahem!" from the bearded man. Then he shook hands with the men, ending with his son.

"I'll be keeping in touch through the videolink," he said. "But I'm glad to know the company is in good hands." He took his two green metal boxes from Andrew and followed him back down the corridor.

➤   ➤   ➤

At the Reinhold Space Station holding the Tau Ceti gate, the capsule bringing Randy in from the interstation rotovator had to pick its way through the heavy traffic flowing into the openings in the sphere at the central hub of the rotating space station.

"The warpgate to Tau Ceti opened only seven months ago," said Andrew. "So most of the traffic is outward while we build up the transportation infrastructure."

The capsule docked at the space station, and Andrew led Randy down one corridor and up another, with the gee level varying from normal to zero.

"When do we get to the warpgate?" asked Randy.

Andrew gave a startled look and burst out laughing. "We went through the warpgate from Sol to Tau Ceti two corridors ago. I should have stopped and mentioned it at the time." They came to a door. "This is the airlock leading to the ship you are going to use to fly to meet *Timemaster*."

Randy went to a porthole and looked out. Sure enough, the planet they were orbiting was not Earth. In the past few minutes he had traveled five short corridors and twelve long light-years. He looked to the right and saw his ship. It was a Reinhold freighter with a greatly elongated cargo hold. The name was visible on the nose: *John Wayne*.

"Are the tanks in the hold loaded?" he asked.

"Everything is ready as you instructed," Andrew assured him.

➤   ➤   ➤

Before an hour had passed, the *John Wayne* had been moved off a distance from the Tau Ceti base station, and Randy was in the high-gee protection tank and breathing liquid, head encased in a virtual helmet and arms in gauntlets. The virtual screen in front of his eyes contained the icon of the persona for the computer of the *John Wayne*. It was a rugged-looking cowboy with a confident grin on his face.

"The stagecoach is ready," said the icon in a western twang. "Shall I crack the whip?"

NOPE, MARION, Randy typed. *I'LL DRIVE IT.*

"OK, pardner," said the icon. "But don't call me Marion. The name's Duke."

Randy rotated the imaginary joyball with his virtual glove until the icon of the spacecraft was lined up with the faint green line that pointed at Epsilon Eridani. He pulled up on the joyball and the acceleration rose until the ship reached a steady thirty gees.

➤   ➤   ➤

On the way out, Randy had time to read the letters that Alan had transferred to his cuff-comp. Alan was right; they *were* nearly unbelievable. Most of them were invitations for him to be guest of honor at celebrations commemorating the opening of the first timegate in 2056. There were invitations from 2156, 2256, 2356, 2556, 3056, and even as far ahead as 5056. The phrasing of the last one was rather awkward, as if the language had changed so much that even the machine translators had difficulty translating the original version of the invitation into proper 2056 English. The thought of how strange the world would be that far in the future gave Randy the shivers.

The most amazing of the letters, however, was one dated 2133 from the director of the Hunter Institute for Aging Research.

Mr. Harold Randolph Hunter

Mrs. Rosita Carmelita Cortez Hunter

It gives me great pleasure to inform you that the International
Immortality Board has designated you to receive the first two
immortality treatments to be performed using the processes
recently perfected by the Hunter Institute for Aging Research.

Randy's heart skipped a beat. *I'm going to live forever!* His most
impossible dream was going to come true!

Randy finally calmed himself down. They could probably treat his
cells so that they wouldn't age, and they might even be able to make
him younger in the process, but they couldn't keep him from being
killed by an accident *someday* . . . or could they? With time machines coupling the past with the future . . .

Someday I'll probably just get tired of living and turn myself off, he
mused. *But it'll be a long time before I get that bored.* He started to
scroll up the rest of the letter. *I assume Rose and I will have to jump
forward into the future to get the treatment. I wonder who invented the
technique? Certainly he or she should be the first one to receive it. I
only put up the money.*

The last letter was also from the director of the Hunter Institute for
Aging Research. It was from a different director and dated twelve
years earlier than the other letter.

Mr. Harold Randolph Hunter,

This cover letter is followed by a long file containing
information about a number of medical treatments not available in
your time, including a complex treatment that is able to cure any
disease. Since the alleviation of human misery is a primary goal
of the Time Control Board, and takes precedence over the normal
Board task of limiting time travel in order to minimize
chronoshock and causal confusion of the past-time general
populace, the Board has authorized the contents of this file to be
transmitted as far back in time as possible, so that the treatments
therein can be developed and used as soon in past-time as
possible.

Since you will be traveling back into times that cannot be
reached through the existing timegates, it is requested that you
keep the file with you during your journeys. When you arrive
back in 2054, please transfer the file to the director at that time,
Dr. Angela Garibaldi.

"Medical treatments from the future, and I will be bringing them
back through time, just as Siritha said . . ." murmured Randy to

himself. "The world is never going to be the same again. Good thing, too. The old world had too much pain and suffering in it."

➤   ➤   ➤

Five months later, coasting along at just under the safe cruising speed of 0.995 cee, Randy was interrupted at dinner by the ship's persona appearing on the screen above the table.

"I can see the bad guy coming," drawled the icon. "He's got the gol-darnedest long rifle I've ever seen, and a bandoleer with five hundred bullets in it."

"Let's head him off at the pass," said Randy. For the past few days he had been limiting his meals to clear soups and non-gas-producing chewables. He disappeared into the head, and when he came out, the yellow manipulators of the ship's Gidget were holding up the high-gee tanksuit for him.

➤   ➤   ➤

"Bombs away!" yelled Randy as he vented the thousands of tons of liquid hydrogen into space. His ship was now decelerating and the liquid hydrogen vaporized into a cloud of hydrogen gas in front of him. His job done, he sent off a message to reassure the youngster ahead.

"Hold the fort! The cavalry is coming! (Even if you can't see it.)"

He climbed back into his high-gee protection tank and soon was back at thirty gees again. Only this time the acceleration was back toward Tau Ceti, so he could match speeds with *Timemaster* as it went past.

Got to get to that Silverhair on Timemaster *and go on to do the rest of the job,* he told himself. The thought of all the stress and loneliness that he still faced, months at high gees, stuffed in a cramped tin can, made him resentful of the spoiled young brat lounging around in his space mansion, waiting for other people to rescue him. It would be nice to see other human beings again, though . . .

". . . *especially Rose!*" Randy remembered what lay ahead.

Randy was too far away from the actual encounter to see any details of Oscar's attack, but he knew it was successful when he saw Oscar's ship deflected from its course long before it got to *Timemaster*. In the meantime, *Timemaster* was proceeding on its course without a hitch and without a distress call from Albert.

Four days after the attack, Randy pulled the *John Wayne* up to ride in formation with *Timemaster*.

"I'm turning the ship over to you, Duke," he said. "I won't be back.

Keep riding along with *Timemaster* until you are given further instructions."

"OK, pilgrim," growled the icon.

"Bye, Duke," Randy growled back in imitation. "It's been a pleasure riding the trails with you."

➤   ➤   ➤

When Randy arrived at the airlock to *Timemaster,* Rose and the younger version of himself were waiting for him. Randy put the two green metal boxes into the storage net above the suit rack. Rose came to greet him.

"Thank you for saving us!" she said, giving him a big kiss. As she drew away, she wiped her upper lip and grinned at him. "Say, that tickles . . . and it looks very nice."

Randy went over to the young man and shook hands. "Hi, youngster," he said.

"Thanks for coming to our rescue," said the youth.

"*John Wayne* and I were glad to help," said Randy. "For a while there, I thought I might not have hauled enough liquid hydrogen to do the job." He gave the young man a friendly clap on the shoulder. "I was afraid I'd be short."

"Stop that . . ." the young man groaned, giving him a punch in return. "Say, what's in the green boxes?"

"They're called 'feeders'," said Randy. "They came from the future. According to the instructions that came with them, I'm going to need them later." He gave his helmet to Godget and hung up his outeralls on the hook next to another pair that, from the size of them, obviously belonged to the young man. Then, still in his tightsuit, Randy crowded into the elevator with the young man and Rose.

"Why don't you go upstairs and change," said the young man, punching the buttons for both the main floor and the bedroom floor of the mansion. "Rose and I will wait for you in the living room. I'm sure Didit can help you find something comfortable."

➤   ➤   ➤

After some conversation and a tasty dinner of corned beef and cabbage, with smash on the side, the three were waiting at the airlock door when another space-suited figure arrived, this time from the *Errol Flynn.* Rose immediately grabbed the bearded man and gave him a big hug and kiss. Randy was a little jealous, but he was getting used to the idea, especially since it seemed to be making the young man even more jealous.

"Say," said Rose, stepping back to look at the man's beard, "you've let it grow longer, haven't you? Looks very nice now—not like you forgot to shave—but distinguished-looking." She scratched him under the chin, and the bearded man rumbled a deep-throated purr at the attention.

Hmmm, thought Randy. *It does look distinguished . . . and if Rose likes it, maybe I ought to grow one.* He stepped forward to interrupt.

"I don't believe we've met recently," he said, putting out his hand. "I'm Randy."

"I'd recognize you anywhere," said the bearded man, shaking hands. "Even with that puny excuse for a mustache." He twisted the ends of the monstrous handlebar above his full chestnut beard in obvious pride. He turned to look at the youngster.

"If you'll send Didit down to the dressing room with something comfortable, I'll meet you three up in the living room shortly," he said.

➤   ➤   ➤

The bearded man came slowly down the circular staircase in Randy's white "cricket outfit," Venus's Tear dangling from his right ear. Randy now wished that he had chosen the pearl instead of the tiger's-eye.

"I'm glad you could join us," said the young man in a stiff, formal tone from his place in the recliner chair.

"I wouldn't miss this night for anything," said the bearded man as he sat on the sofa on the other side of Rose. Randy knew exactly what the bearded man was thinking. He wouldn't miss tonight for anything himself. The young man, however, didn't know what was coming up . . .

➤   ➤   ➤

Later that evening, the grandfather clock struck eleven. The bearded man yawned and stretched flamboyantly. "Time to go to bed," he said loudly. The room grew pregnant with silence.

"I assume you two gentlemen will be wanting to go back to your ships . . ." started the young man. Randy decided to tease the youngster a little.

"Say, Rose," he interrupted, pulling on Rose's elbow. "I'll have to be warping back tomorrow, and I was wondering . . ." The teasing worked.

"Just a minute!" said the young man angrily, getting up from his chair. "Rose is *my* wife, and she's going to bed with *me!*"

"Let *her* decide!" insisted Randy, knowing full well what she was going to decide . . .

➤   ➤   ➤

"I know I'm leaving you in good hands," said Randy to the young man. He reached up to the inside of the top of the pod and grabbed the handholds, then stepped into the foot stirrups at the bottom. Between the two foot stirrups were his two green metal feeder boxes.

The young man took Rose by the waist and lifted her into the pod. There, she grabbed Randy around his chest and wrapped her tight-suited legs around behind his. Randy enjoyed the close embrace.

"It's going to be a close fit . . ." said the young man as he used the wall controls to slowly bring the pod halves together. The bearded man moved around the closing pod to keep watch, tucking in Rose's elbows and knees as the two halves came together. Once the pod was closed, Rose took the opportunity to give Randy a squeeze.

When the pod opened up again a few moments later, they were met by a youthful Hiroshi Tanaka, Andrew Pope, and Siritha Chandresekhar. Hiroshi pulled Rose free, and Andrew helped Randy to the wall.

<Rand! Rose!> said the Silverhair, glad to see them. <Oof!> it complained.

"If we're all done, then let the poor Silverhair relax," said Siritha with concern. Hiroshi went over to the laser expander and collapsed the warpgate.

<Ahh!> said the Silverhair in relief. <Ball!> it immediately shouted. Siritha found the foam-plastic ball and soon she and Hiroshi were engaged in a loud game of poof-ball with the alien, while Andrew cycled Randy and Rose through the vacuum lock into the dressing room.

"Don't bother removing your tightsuit, Mr. Hunter," said Andrew. "We have a flitter standing by to take you directly to the space station where the UV Ceti warpgate mouth is housed."

"Must you go so soon?" asked Rose, holding her helmet in one hand.

"Sorry, Rose," said Randy. "Got to hurry off and rescue that kid again, and there isn't any time to spare." He went over to give her a good-bye kiss. "This, time, however, I won't be away so long. See you in about four months." He gave her a long, hard kiss, then a loving smile. "And this time I promise I'll settle down and stay home."

"I'll believe it when I see it, Mr. Buck Rogers Hunter," said Rose, giving him a good-bye kiss back.

➤   ➤   ➤

It wasn't until he had almost entered the spacewarp to UV Ceti that Randy remembered the important message file from the future still stored in his cuff-comp. He called up Dr. Angela Garibaldi, director of the Hunter Institute of Aging Research, and transmitted the file full of medical treatments to her.

➤   ➤   ➤

When Randy emerged from the UV Ceti warpgate, his ship was ready for him. There was no heavy cargo this time, just the two green metal boxes containing the feeders, and himself—going off to parry knife thrusts with a sooty poker. It wasn't going to be fancy Hollywood swordplay where no one got punctured and blades were covered with ketchup, but a deadly serious business where throats could be ripped open by bloodstained knives if he didn't do everything right.

Saying good-bye to Andrew, he went out the airlock and floated over to his waiting ship, the *Errol Flynn*.

13 >>

...A Little Help from my Friends

BEFORE an hour had passed, the *Errol Flynn* had moved off away from the UV Ceti base station. Randy was in the high-gee protection tank, breathing liquid. The virtual screen in front of his eyes contained the icon of the persona for the computer of the *Errol Flynn*. It was that of an extremely handsome young man with a pencil mustache, a feathered pirate hat, and a daredevil smile on his face.

"The tide is high and the winds are favorable," said the icon in a clipped English accent. "Shall I set sail?"

NO, LESLIE, typed Randy. *I MAN THE HELM.*

"Very well, m'lord," said the icon, touching the brim of his hat in a sweeping gesture. Randy looked at the trim mustache on the icon. It really looked kind of effeminate. Randy wondered if *his* mustache gave that impression. A beard, now—beards were *never* considered effeminate, and Rose thought a beard made a man look more distinguished. He decided to stop shaving for a while . . .

> > >

Randy contacted Albert on *Timemaster* as soon as the two ships got within range. Albert was careful to check Randy's identity by having him put his eyes close to the monitor camera so that his iris pattern could be checked, but the computer didn't seem fazed either by Randy's full beard, the idea of time travel, or the fact that there were two Randys for him to obey. Randy explained the danger that the younger Randy would soon be in and his plans for rescuing him.

"He depends upon my sensor display for a view of the volume around the ship," said Albert. "I will merely remove information about your ship from the sensor data before I display it to him."

"I'll approach from behind so he won't be likely to see me out the portholes when you switch to cruise mode," said Randy. "Let me know when he has moved into the mansion. I'll drop my magnetic shields and come in close on the opposite side of the ship to the porthole in the study. During free-fall, when Oscar is podding through, I'll jet over and you can let me in."

"Gidget will be waiting at the airlock to cycle you through," said Albert.

➤   ➤   ➤

After having boarded *Timemaster*, Randy had to stay in the airlock and wait in order to avoid meeting the younger Randy and Oscar during their tour of the ship.

"We must hurry," said Gidget, as it finally cycled Randy through the airlock onto the engineering deck. "Didit reports they are already starting to argue." The blue manipulators of the robomechanic took Randy's helmet and placed it hurriedly in the rack beside the door. "This way," it whispered in its high-pitched voice. Still in his tightsuit, red outeralls, and black space boots, Randy followed the bright-blue body of the robot off down the corridor. They came to a robomechanic-sized panel that had been unfastened from the corridor wall and placed to one side. Randy paused to look at the hole in the wall. It was too small to pass an ordinary man.

I wouldn't be able to save myself if Mom had given me growth hormones . . . He squeezed through the tiny aperture.

Gidget turned on its lights and led Randy on a laborious climb up through the interior of the walls of the ship to the living-quarters deck. They went horizontally for a while and soon came upon Godget, its bright-yellow manipulators busily unscrewing some bolts and lifting off a round panel on what looked like a large air duct.

"This is the exhaust flue from the fireplace," said Gidget. "It comes up from a soot trap at the back of the fireplace. At the bottom of the soot trap, you will have to turn sharply up again to get to the hood area just above the fireplace. To get your body around the sharp bend, you will have to go in headfirst and backwards. You should have no problems, for the fireplace has been unlit for twenty hours."

Randy stared at the gaping, round, soot-black hole, and unreasoning fear surged over him. The robots were unaware of his suppressed phobia. He started to shake violently. "Isn't there some other way in?" he gasped in a trembling voice.

"No. Is there any problem?" asked the robot.

The distant voice of Oscar echoed up through the exhaust duct. He was angry and shouting.

"You are destroying free will!"

No time to find another way! thought Randy. He got control of himself and turned his back to the hole. After taking a deep breath and closing his eyes, he grasped the filthy, sooty edge on the far side and prepared to enter the hole.

Trying to be helpful, Gidget and Godget reached down, picked him up by the ankles, and lowered him headfirst down into the sooty blackness. Randy felt a scream of terror rising in his throat and strove to choke it off . . .

➤   ➤   ➤

I must have gone temporarily insane. Randy realized that, some-how, he was now crouched in the soot trap at the back of the fireplace looking down at the dusty gas logs in the grate instead of into a sooty blackness. He stepped down on the artificial logs and bent low to climb out into the living room. Oscar's agitated voice sounded loudly from the dining room.

"You want to use your timelink to become ruler of the universe!"

Randy grabbed the poker from the fire toolholder and crept across the living room to the door in the wooden folding wall, leaving a trail of sooty footprints on the priceless Oriental rug.

There was a commotion in the dining room, and then Oscar's voice rasped out, "I've got you now!"

Carefully Randy tiptoed through the door into the dining room, holding the poker in his tightsuit-gloved hand. Oscar had the youngster pinned in his chair, and the only thing keeping the carving knife out of the youngster's throat was a foot in Oscar's belly and two hands holding on to Oscar's wrist.

The youngster saw Randy sneaking up behind Oscar. *Now, if the stupid kid would only keep his mouth shut . . . but no . . .*

"Better put down that knife," the youngster warned Oscar. "There's someone behind you!"

"You aren't going to fool me with that one, you miserable midget," said Oscar, pulling his knife hand back in order to free it so he could strike again.

Now! thought Randy. He leaped forward and smashed the heavy metal poker against the back of Oscar's hand, sending the carving knife thudding onto the ornate rug. *Errol Flynn would have done that with more dash* . . .

"YEOW!" yelled Oscar, letting go of the young man to grab his injured hand. He tried to straighten the obviously broken fingers and cried out in pain again. "Ow-w-w-w!" he howled, stamping his feet in agony. He turned slowly around to look behind him.

Is he going to get the shock of his life! thought Randy. "Surprise . . ." he said to Oscar, tapping the fireplace poker in his sooty left hand and waiting for Oscar to recognize him. Randy could see by the look in the youngster's eyes that he still didn't know who Randy was. Like a feisty lapdog to whom all dogs were the same size, the kid thought all men were the same size. Oscar, however, knew only one person four feet eleven inches tall with chestnut-brown hair. It wouldn't take long for him to see through the beard . . .

Oscar's eyes widened, and his face blanched as if he were seeing a ghost. He fainted.

"Sissy," said Randy. He kicked at the collapsed body with his toe.

"Thanks, mister," said the youngster with great relief.

"Help me tie him up. We'll put him in the transfer pod and send him back," said Randy.

"No need to soil our hands with that animal kisser," said the kid. "I'll have Gidget do it." He touched an icon on his cuff-comp. Off in the distance there came a clatter of metallic manipulators moving toward them down the corridor.

"We'd better do something about his hand before we send him off," said Randy. He raised his cuff-comp. "Godget, please bring the medical kit. Our guest has suffered a broken hand." Randy paused as he noticed the kid staring at his cuff-comp.

It won't take long now . . . He watched the kid's eyes flicker first to Randy's cuff-comp, then to his own cuff-comp, then to Randy's hair . . . The kid turned pale and sat weakly down in the nearest chair.

"And we'll probably need some smelling salts for the youngster," he continued. He went over to poor frozen Didit, opened a panel on the robobutler's back, and pressed the reset button.

➤ ➤ ➤

After podding Oscar back to Earth, still nursing his broken hand, the two of them had a long dinner together. After dinner, the youngster led the way into the living room. There were two glasses of port and a bowl of walnuts waiting for them. A real pine log crackled on top of the artificial gas logs. Randy started to head for the recliner, then thought better of it and sat on the sofa. The young man sat down in the chair, reclined slightly, took a sip of port, then reached for the nutcracker.

"Rose will be podding in tomorrow," he said after a while.

"You'd better meet her by yourself," said Randy. He knew what was going to happen next. It would be better if the kid didn't think he had influenced it unduly by being aboard when Rose arrived. "I'll stay on my ship and you can tell her about me after she's had a chance to settle down."

➤　　➤　　➤

A little while later, Randy was at the pilot's console on the *Errol Flynn*, waiting eagerly as the link was opened. He watched as Rose slipped quickly into the chair and looked intently at him over the videolink.

"It's hard to tell for sure because of the beard," she said slowly. "But the eyes sure look like Randy's."

"It's me, all right," said Randy. "Just a little older, a little wiser, and a lot hairier. It's good to see you again, my lovely rosebud."

"It sure sounds like you!" giggled Rose.

Randy knew he had hooked her. Rose turned and looked off-screen. "I'd like to ask him a few personal questions . . . just to make sure," she said. "Would you mind leaving the room? It won't be long." She turned back and looked again with intense interest at him through the screen.

Randy heard the voice of the youngster hollering in the background, "Of course I don't mind!" followed by the sound of a door being slammed.

"I've been *so* lonely for you, my little flower," started Randy, pouring on the charm. The nice thing about this little tête-à-tête was that he knew he would be successful.

➤　　➤　　➤

As Randy floated over in his space suit from the *Errol Flynn* to *Timemaster* to pick up Rose, he felt as if he were a lusty, dashing pirate rogue abducting a not-too-reluctant woman off a passenger galleon. After Rose had exited the airlock and taken his hand, he looked back and almost felt sorry for the kid. The beardless face in the porthole looked wan and longing, watching forlornly as Randy led his willing wife off by the hand to his ship for the night.

➤　　➤　　➤

Randy and Rose didn't get back until late the next morning. The three had a polite lunch together. The cold fresh salmon was a real treat for Randy after the frozen and canned meats he had endured on his trip out from UV Ceti. After lunch, Rose left the two men talking at the table while she went into the study to talk to the children over the videolink.

"Being around you makes me nervous," said the youngster. "Not that I'm not glad you came when you did, mind you."

"You're right. It's like talking to yourself in a mirror," said Randy. Another attack of déjà vu came over him. "Plus the fact that I've heard all this conversation before. Besides, I'm sure you'd like me to leave so you can have Rose all to yourself. I know I did when I was sitting there."

"Stop that!" said the young man.

Randy shot his cuff-comp out of his sleeve to look at the time. "It's nearly two o'clock. I'm expecting a shipment, so I'd better get back to my ship," he said.

"What is it?" asked the kid.

Randy felt sorry for the other's ignorance. "Why don't you come over to the *Errol Flynn* with me and see?" The two of them went over to Randy's ship, where Randy explained about Steve Wisneski's invention of the artificial warpgates. While they were there, Hiroshi Tanaka reached through the warpgate from UV Ceti to *Errol Flynn* and handed Randy a box.

"What's in the box?" asked the youngster. "Something for tomorrow's dinner?"

"Something a lot more important than dinner—your and my salvation, sent from the future," said Randy. He opened the long top of the rectangular box and let the eager youngster peer inside.

"A matched pair of warpgate mouths," said Randy. The kid gasped as Randy stuck his index finger into one of the tiny pentagons. The fingertip instantly appeared coming out of one of the pentagons on the dodecahedron in the next compartment. Randy wiggled his finger.

"Stop that before you hurt yourself! Us, I mean!" said the kid. Randy removed his finger, then carefully closed and sealed the lid on the vacuum-tight box.

"Well, I'd better get moving," said Randy. "I have to build the trap for the rat that's following us. It has to be a big trap for such a big rat, and it'll take some time to grow it."

"Grow it?" asked the kid.

The kid sure has a lot to learn, grumbled Randy to himself. *I guess I'm going to have to teach him everything.* He sighed. "I'll explain it all to you later when I have the full-grown trap to show you."

"When will that be?" asked the youngster, looking a little worried.

"A couple of months," said Randy. "I'm going to run on ahead at high gees and set up the trap. *Timemaster* couldn't match *Errol Flynn*'s acceleration anyway, so you might as well take it easy. Just stay on your present course, decelerating at one gee, until you catch up with me. By the time you get there, I'll have the trap built and you can be the cheese that attracts the rat to the trap."

"Anything else I should know before you go?" asked the kid.

"I don't remember me telling you anything else," said Randy. "So I guess not." He stuck out his hand. "Good luck—I know you had it. Speaking of luck, I'm not going to press mine by coming back to your ship to give Rose a good-bye kiss." An annoyed look appeared on the kid's face. Randy smiled and gave the poor young man a brotherly pat on the shoulder. "You give it to her for me," he said.

➤   ➤   ➤

Randy accelerated the *Errol Flynn* at thirty gees until it was way ahead of *Timemaster*. He then decelerated until he had reached a cruise speed of ninety-eight-percent cee. After getting out of the tank suit and back into dry clothing he went to the control console and put the ship into free-fall. He looked at the icon of the ship's persona on the viewscreen.

"Time to start building our rat trap, Leslie," said Randy.

"I have Godget in the airlock with the warpgate box," said Leslie.

"Dump one of them out," said Randy. "And make sure you mark the spot." He watched, using the video monitor on the outside of the airlock door, as the yellow body of Godget exited the airlock and moved a short distance from the ship. Some of its manipulators had been replaced with electrodes. The robomechanic opened the box and used strong electric fields on its electrode manipulators to extract one of the dodecahedral warpgate mouths from one side of the box. It resealed the box and came back inside, leaving the warpmouth floating in space.

"Off we go on a visit to the fountain of youth," said Randy as he accelerated the *Errol Flynn* again at one gee. He needed a time difference of only a little more than a second, so there was no need to make himself uncomfortable by accelerating at high gees.

A few days later, the *Errol Flynn* returned to the waiting warpmouth. The boxed warpmouth that had traveled on the ship was now 1.6 seconds younger than the warpmouth that had stayed behind.

The timetrap is nearly ready, Randy thought. *Now all we have to do is make it big enough to catch our very big rat.* He made his way to the dressing room to don his space suit. He could have let the robomechanics handle everything while he watched from inside, but he didn't want to be left out.

Gadget followed him out of the airlock carrying one of the green feeder boxes. Randy opened the feeder box for the first time and looked in. The inside of the box was similar to one of the compartments in the warpmouth box, with electrodes coming from the walls to levitate the structure inside. In the lid of the feeder box, however, was a control panel with four buttons. Suspended in the center of the box was a frame of silvery rods of rigidized negmatter. The frame was about the size of a softball and was made of a large number of triangles.

"It looks very much like a standard warpgate mouth," Randy muttered, "except it's not a dodecahedron." He turned to Gadget. "Take it out and let's count the sides."

Gadget used its electrodes to remove the negmatter frame from the box and held it up.

"Twenty sides," said Gadget in its baritone voice. "It is an icosahedron." The robomechanic released the object so that it floated in space a few feet away from the warpmouth.

"That's funny," said Randy. "I wonder why they picked an icosahedron instead of the standard dodecahedron?" He stared at the control panel in the lid of the box. "Hmmm . . . I wonder what I do next?"

The control buttons had words below them. The letters were in a very strange font, with all the line ends and intersections tapering away to almost nothing, leaving just the center portions of the lines. *Almost antiserif,* thought Randy, looking at the futuristic letters.

The operating instructions were straightforward. One button said ACTIVATE, another said GROW, the third said SHRINK, and the fourth said STOP.

I feel like Alice in Wonderland, Randy mused as he pushed the ACTIVATE button. Instantly, twenty flexible metallic tubes grew out of the twenty triangles of the icosahedron until it began to look like a caricature of a Silverhair. Each tube was about the size of a small garden hose and had a complex, trilobed, flared connector at the end.

Although the tubes were shiny, they didn't have the impossible sheen of negmatter, but instead looked like stainless steel made of normal matter. The twenty hoses avoided Randy and Gadget, and stretched out for the distant warpmouth as if they had eyes. Within a few seconds, each of the twenty hoses had positioned itself next to one of the twenty vertices in the dodecahedral warpmouth.

"Oh . . ." said Randy, now understanding why the feeders had twenty sides. He waited for a second, but nothing else happened. He pushed the GROW button. Almost instantly the pentagonal sides of the warpmouth started to thicken and extend in length as more and more negmatter spewed from the ends of the tubes into the frame.

Randy watched in amazement. Somewhere, at some far distant time and place, large amounts of negative matter were somehow being gathered and warped over decades of time and light-years of space to feed his warpmouth. He wouldn't be surprised if the other end of the feeder were connected to a negative-matter collector set up in the Boötes Void, a third of the universe away. The amount of effort involved must be enormous. Randy was truly impressed. He left Gadget with the control box to monitor the growth of the warpmouth, while he went back to the airlock so Leslie could carry him over to where he would start the other warpmouth growing.

➤ ➤ ➤

"This one has to be positioned and oriented just right," said Randy to Gidget. "One axis must point along the line to the other warpmouth, and it must be rotated a hundred and eighty degrees with respect to the axis of the other one." Gidget took some sightings through a few of the warpmouth pentagons and made a few adjustments using its electrode manipulators, while Godget removed the feeder from its box and set it floating in space. Randy took the feeder control box and pushed the buttons in the lid to start the warpmouth growing. After it had gotten large enough that one of the pentagons could pass a robomechanic, he pushed the STOP button. Gidget passed through a pentagon, made a number of sightings, passed back again and made some more sightings, then rotated the now room-sized structure a tiny bit.

"You may continue growth, Mr. Hunter," said Gidget, and Randy pressed the GROW button.

Leaving Gidget and Gadget to monitor the growth of the warp-mouths, Randy and Godget headed back to the *Errol Flynn*. Soon the ship was under acceleration again as it headed back to link up with *Timemaster*.

➤   ➤   ➤

When Randy entered the airlock door back on *Timemaster*, Rose and the other two men were waiting for him. Rose grabbed him and gave him a big hug and kiss.

"Say," she said, stepping back to look at Randy's beard. "You've let it grow longer, haven't you? Looks very nice now—not like you forgot to shave—but distinguished-looking."

Randy felt pleased. He sure felt more distinguished-looking than the two bare-cheeked youngsters standing behind Rose. She scratched him under the chin the way she had done when they had spent the night together on his ship, and he responded with a deep-throated purr.

After some polite conversation, the other three went off to the living room to wait, while Randy went upstairs to dress in something comfortable. The only thing left in the bedroom closet was his white "cricket outfit." Randy always considered it slightly effeminate, but at least it gave him a chance to show off Venus's Tear.

"I'm glad you could join us," said the kid from his recliner chair as Randy came down the circular staircase and entered the living room. The youngster with the mustache was sitting on the sofa on one side of Rose.

"I wouldn't miss this night for anything," Randy said as he sat down on the other side.

➤   ➤   ➤

"Well, good-bye, young man," said the mustached man from inside his tightsuit helmet as he shook hands with the youngster. He slapped Randy on the shoulder. "I know I'm leaving you in good hands." Randy and the kid tucked the man and Rose into the transfer pod and shot them through the Silverhair back to Earth.

"I feel a lot better with her out of danger," said the kid.

"Me too," said Randy.

The two looked at each other. Randy was used to being alone, and he knew the kid was uncomfortable having him around, but he wouldn't look forward to another couple of months in the cramped quarters of *Errol Flynn*.

"Why don't you stay here in comfort while we catch up to the warpmouths you left behind?" offered the kid.

➤   ➤   ➤

Three months later, after a leisurely chateaubriand dinner, the two settled down in the living room and Randy adjusted the view-wall with his cuff-comp.

"There it is . . . the timetrap!" he said. He manipulated the icons on his cuff-comp and the view zoomed in to one of the warpmouths. Even Randy was amazed with the results. The growth of the warp-mouths had slowed as they had become larger, but they were now approaching two thousand kilometers in diameter, as big as a small moon. Although the warpmouths had gotten larger and the feeder hoses had lengthened to compensate, the feeder frames were still only the size of a softball. Randy, by adjusting the view with the icons on his cuff-comp, took the youngster on a tour of the timetrap and explained how it worked.

"Amazing!" said the kid, obviously impressed.

➤   ➤   ➤

It was a month and a half later when Oscar finally caught up with them. Randy had gone to the kitchen, found some beer and canned pretzels, and taken them into the living room. With Albert's assistance, he soon had a picture of Oscar's ship on the large view-wall screen, along with split-screen scenes showing what was happening near both warpmouths. The youngster had been slaving away in the study on Reinhold Astroengineering Company business all morning and Randy had to remind him to come into the living room to watch the action.

"Here he comes," Randy said. "He must have had some trouble with the high-gee protection tank. His acceleration for the past few months has been only five gees. Even though he's going at over ninety-eight-percent cee, his relative velocity with respect to us is only four percent of cee."

"That's still pretty damn fast!" said the kid, beginning to sound concerned. "Don't you think that we ought to be in the control room in our tightsuits and helmets, at least?"

"Naw," said Randy. "Nothing is going to happen to us, and the view-wall here in the living room will give us a panoramic view of the action." He leaned back in the sofa with his beer and pretzels.

"Our lives are in danger, and you sit there like a sofa sausage watching Sunday afternoon football!" exploded the youngster.

"Relax . . ." said Randy, having another pretzel. "The only one getting kicked around today is Oscar." Suddenly he saw some silver missiles streaking from the end of the long cannon on the nose of Oscar's ship. "He's opened fire!" he said, sitting up on the edge of the sofa.

Randy watched, admittedly with a little apprehension, as the silver buckets came closer. He held his breath while he kept an anxious eye on the split-screen showing the younger warpmouth. Finally he was relieved to see first one, then another, then a whole swarm of buckets coming out the warpmouth, heading straight for the incoming missiles.

"Beautiful!" Randy cried as he watched each capsule being deflected by its twin. "Their high acceleration capability and the built-in magnetic 'spring' surrounding them make them nearly ideal billiard balls."

"That kind of precision is impossible!" said the youngster as he stared in disbelief at the screen.

"Improbable things become probable once warpgates exist," Randy reminded him. "Now, watch . . . He's going to have to duck . . ." The two watched as Oscar dodged the outgoing stream of missiles from the younger warpmouth, while the ingoing stream was heading for the older warpmouth, where they disappeared. Oscar's ship changed its course, heading directly toward *Timemaster* in a deliberate attempt to ram; but two collisions and a few seconds later, the ship was heading directly away from them, deflected with a vengeance by the timetrap. Randy relaxed and took another gurgle of his beer through the long neck of the bottle.

"See!" he said. "All over in a few seconds. If Oscar hadn't tried to hurt us, he wouldn't have hurt himself." He munched down the last of his pretzels.

"Is he dead?" the kid asked quietly.

"I'm afraid so," said Randy, and mentioned Alan's report to him.

"Thank God this nightmare is over at last!" said the kid.

"That's where you're wrong, me boy," said Randy. "I've done my part—and I get to go back and live a happy future with Rose. You, however, have a lot of work left ahead of you, and if you're to be successful, you'd better get a move on."

"Me?" asked the youngster. "Why me?"

Randy looked pensively at the soot-caked chimney in the fireplace, and shivered internally at the memory of the soot-dark access hole above. *What a nightmare the poor kid has coming. I won't warn him, though. I'm sure glad the older Randy at that time didn't warn me. I don't know if I could have forced myself to board the ship, much less go down that soot-black hole.* He shuddered again at the thought.

"It's a dirty job," he told the kid, "but somebody has to do it." He sighed at the kid's denseness. "Think, me boy . . . think."

Randy watched the kid's eyes widen and a stricken look come over his face as he realized what lay ahead of him.

"You're right . . ." the youngster finally admitted. Then he panicked a little. "But what am I supposed to do!?!"

Randy got up from the sofa. "The first thing *I'd* do is contact Andrew Pope and tell him to warp out some pilots to ferry the *Errol Flynn* and *John Wayne* to a safe landing at Tau Ceti." He headed for the elevator door. "I'll tell you the rest while we're waiting for your Silverhair to dilate so I can pod home."

14 ➢➢

Off to the Future!

THE pod opened and Randy floated out into the spherical vacuum chamber that held the Silverhair at the Earth end of the warpgate. Siritha and Andrew reached out and pulled him over to the handholds on the wall. Off to one side, Hiroshi Tanaka was monitoring the laser beam coming through the Silverhair. As Randy watched, the beam shrank.

<Ahh!> said the Silverhair in obvious relief. It then noticed Randy. <Rand!> it called. <Food!> it demanded.

"I'll feed it," volunteered Siritha. "You and Andrew can cycle through and change. I'm sure you two have important business matters to discuss."

"Not really," said Randy. "The youngster I just left on *Timemaster* is running the company just fine through daily videolinks with Andrew and Alan. It wouldn't do to have two bosses trying to run the company, so I'm going to let him do all the work, while I get to dance with Silverhairs and have fun with my family." He reached for the plasma gun on the wall. "What's the latest dance you've taught the Silverhair?"

"The tango," said Siritha. She tapped some keys on her chestpack and the rhythmic beat of a tango came from her suit radio. The two danced around the Silverhair while Randy fed its waving tendrils with iron atoms from the plasma gun.

<<Me twist me up and down, me twist me round and round . . . >> sang the Silverhair as it fed and danced with the humans.

Randy let the pilot land the Reinhold Astroengineering Company VTOL jet at his private strip in the Princeton Enclave. He had taken the controls for about an hour on their way home from the Havana spaceport, but soon grew tired of it. Puttering along at a mere thousand kilometers an hour was kind of boring to someone used to traveling at near light-speed. He was met at the airstrip by Rose and the children.

"Home at last!" he cried as he tried to take them all into his arms. Junior, a mature seventeen-year-old who now towered over his dad, squirmed self-consciously out of his grasp, while eleven-year-old Rosey backed off sputtering.

"Poot! Dad, kissing you is like kissing a toothbrush."

"I don't mind," said Rose. So Randy gave her a kiss so long that the kids got embarrassed. Franklin escorted them to the limousine and they drove through the compound to their mansion.

"What's the date and time?" asked Randy, pulling out his cuff-comp. "Now that I'm back for good, I might as well be keeping the same time as everyone else."

Junior stretched out his cuff-comp. Spiraling across the blue clasp on his outer wrist were clusters of rubies, sapphires, emeralds, and white and yellow diamonds representing the various atoms in a segment of DNA. Randy had arranged for Alan to give it to him on his fifteenth birthday. "It'll be Wednesday, 18 March 2054, 1550 Eastern Standard Time . . . now!"

"Just lost about four years," said Randy as he readjusted his cuff-comp. "Or gained it—depending upon your point of view."

As they passed by the stables, Junior reached forward and pushed the button to signal Franklin. "Pull into the stables for a moment, please, Franklin. I want to show Dad my new colt." The limousine slowed and entered the driveway.

"Who are the sire and dam?" asked Randy.

"Winter Winds and Pollyana Parasol . . . mostly," said Junior.

"That breeding won't work," said Randy with a frown. "Winter Winds broke a leg from running too hard, and Pollyana has matchsticks for legs. That poor colt will snap a foreleg just trying to get up."

"Not my colt," said Junior proudly. "He has legbones like Ironman

Mike. That's why I said 'mostly.' I used a nanomachine to snip out Pollyana's legbone genes from one of her eggs, and inserted Ironman Mike's instead. It only took five tries before I got a viable egg."

"Say, what a great idea!" said Randy, highly impressed with his son. "That's going to raise havoc with the pedigree charts, though."

"Just an asterisk," said Junior. "The important thing is that all the genes come from thoroughbred horses. It isn't as though I cheated by inserting antelope or oryx genes. I merely got what Curly and I wanted in one foaling, instead of having to crossbreed the three lines for a dozen generations."

"There's Winds-O-Iron over there in that pasture," said Junior, pointing. Randy watched the large strong colt as it ran circles around the other colts in the pasture.

"You'll have to show me how that gene program works," said Randy. "So I can play with it while you're off at school."

➤　　➤　　➤

"I never thought I would be saying this," Rose said one day at lunch a few months later. "But I'm tired of having you around the house all the time. Why don't you go to work or something?"

"You married me for better or worse—but not for lunch?" Randy joked. "I *can't* go to work. The youngster on *Timemaster* is doing a fine job of running the company, even if he is pulling gees most of the time. If I went by the office, people would ask me for decisions, and things would get messed up—a classic case of too many cooks."

"How about taking up a hobby?" said Rose. "One that takes you out of the house."

Randy thought for a while. "Well, the playing around I've done with Junior's horse-gene program has gotten me interested in biology. I think I'll go bother the researchers at the Hunter Institute for Aging Research."

"Spend all the time away you want," said Rose, relieved. "Just make sure you come home at night."

"I wouldn't miss this night for anything . . ." murmured Randy, raising an eyebrow at her and giving her a knowing smile.

Rose blushed.

➤　　➤　　➤

That afternoon, Randy met with Dr. Angela Garibaldi and two of her senior scientists, Dr. Raymond Anderson and Dr. Charles Wentworth.

"We've had a number of months to study the message file, Mr. Hunter," said Dr. Garibaldi. "It contained a large number of different medical procedures, many of them simple treatments using new medicines or techniques that can be applied immediately. We passed all that information on to the World Health Organization, and they are using them even as we speak, to improve health all around the world."

Dr. Anderson interjected a comment from the other end of the table. "What is most interesting is that all the new medicines or techniques were already in existence in our time, but had either been neglected, abandoned, or not yet tried for that particular illness."

"What is even more interesting," added Dr. Wentworth, "is that in each case, without the intervention of the message, the probability of our ever trying that particular treatment for that particular disease was very low."

"When timegates exist," Randy reminded them, "low-probability events can become high-probability events."

"In addition to the relatively simple treatments for specific diseases, there is also a description of a much more complex procedure that we at the Institute are studying ourselves. It is a general technique for the repair and maintenance of human cells. Once we understand all the procedures, and more importantly have developed the background technology needed to carry out those procedures, we will be able to cure *any* disease."

"Even aging?" asked Randy.

"That will take some time," warned Dr. Garibaldi. "From our research to date here at the Institute, we know that aging is a very complex process, involving many different parts of the cell as well as the interactions of cells with each other. It could take a hundred years or more before we even *know* all the causes of aging, much less how to counteract them."

Randy gave a knowing smile. "I don't think it'll take that long."

"I hope not," said Dr. Garibaldi. "Our real problem with the message, however, is that it constantly refers to a technique called the 'McPhie Procedure' that the writers of the message assume we know about—but we don't!"

Randy's heart skipped a beat. Could there be something wrong? Could the past have somehow been changed—changed in such a way that the procedure didn't exist in this timeline? He felt a twinge of anxiety as he saw immortality slipping from his grasp.

"What are the clues in the message concerning the procedure?" he asked.

"Fortunately, the first paper written about the McPhie Procedure is referenced in the message," said Dr. Garibaldi. "It is dated four months from now."

"Then all we have to do is wait four months," said Randy, relieved. "In fact, if the reference includes the authors, we can call them up and ask them for an advance copy of their paper."

"*I* am the first author," said Dr. Garibaldi. "And not only am I not doing any research on the McPhie Procedure now, I haven't got the slightest idea what the McPhie Procedure is."

Randy's anxiety returned. "There must be some other clues," he said desperately. "Who are your coauthors on the paper? Maybe one of them knows something."

"There are several coauthors," said Dr. Garibaldi, "most of them physicians on the research staff here at the Institute. There are also two who aren't."

"Who are they?" asked Randy, hoping that would solve the problem.

"One of them is *you*."

"*Me!*" exclaimed Randy. "I don't even know anything about biology, much less about any McPhie Procedure."

"You must have contributed to the research in some significant way," said Dr. Garibaldi. "Institute policy does not permit 'honorary' authors on scientific papers."

"Who's the other outside author?"

"I've heard his name somewhere," said Dr. Garibaldi. "But I'm fairly certain he is not a biologist. It is Steven Wisneski."

Randy laughed. "Of course!" He shot his cuff-comp out from under his coat sleeve. "Get me Steve," he said to it. There was a pause and soon Steve's face was on the screen, his large black mustache twitching in irritation at the interruption.

"Randy the Eldest, I assume," he said. "I thought you were going to leave the pestering of company employees to Randy the Youngest."

"This isn't company business, Steve," said Randy. He turned up the volume on the cuff-comp so Dr. Garibaldi could hear Steve's reply. "Tell us about the McPhie Procedure."

"The McWhat Procedure?" replied Steve, his mustache coming to a bewildered halt.

Randy's heart sank. He looked up at Dr. Garibaldi. "I think we had better call a meeting of all the coauthors on that paper."

➤   ➤   ➤

"So no one here at this meeting has *any* clues as to what the McPhie Procedure might be," said Dr. Garibaldi. "Well, it is certain that *this* group is not going to be publishing a paper about the subject in only four months." She turned to Randy. "There must be something wrong with the theory behind timegates."

"Impossible," Steve blurted. "I've worked out every detail. The Novikov Self-Consistency Principle is inviolable. You cannot change the past. If those people from the future said that we published a paper on the McPhie Procedure in the *New England Journal of Medicine* four months from now, then we will write a paper on the McPhie Procedure, and it will appear in that journal exactly four months from now."

"That's crazy," Dr. Anderson protested. "The only thing I know about the procedure is that it's named after somebody named McPhie."

"There's a lead!" exclaimed Randy. "Does anyone know a person named McPhie? We can ask him if he knows what the procedure is."

"I once knew someone named McPhie," said Dr. Wentworth. "But we can't ask him anything. He's dead—killed in a car accident four years ago."

"I remember him now—one of our first postdocs," said Dr. Garibaldi. "Caused me all kinds of paperwork problems. He was driving an Institute car—and he had no living relatives."

"Did he ever publish anything on any sort of procedure?" asked Randy.

"Nope," said Dr. Wentworth. "He was working for me at the time on a dreary, time-consuming job—sequencing the gene that controls the differentiation of cells. Nothing really publishable in that work. I remember he kept complaining that there ought to be a better way of sequencing genes than chopping up DNA and inspecting the pieces. After he died in the accident, I turned over his Institute notebooks to another postdoc, who continued his work."

"Then his notebooks still exist?" said Randy eagerly.

"Show us where they are, Wentworth," said Dr. Garibaldi.

➤   ➤   ➤

"He seems to have been quite a cartoonist," said Dr. Garibaldi, looking over Dr. Wentworth's shoulder as he leafed through the old notebooks. "Drawings in the margins of practically every page."

"That one looks like a Silverhair with someone peering out of a warpmouth in its belly," Steve observed.

"That's McPhie," said Dr. Wentworth. "I'd recognize that nose anyplace. He seems to be holding a pencil and an Institute notebook. He's inside the nucleus of a cell and looking at a segment of DNA."

"That's crazy!" Steve snapped. "Silverhairs aren't that small."

Randy was thinking furiously. "Say, Steve . . . how small do you think an artificial Wisneski Warpmouth could be made?"

"Since they're made out of ultradense negative matter, theoretically, they could be smaller than an atom," said Steve. His eyes brightened as a thought came to him. "And, since the space between atoms is a vacuum, if we leave a little excess positive charge on the warpmouth, the atomic nuclei would be repelled from the warpmouth and nullification won't take place."

"If they can be made smaller than an atom, then we could pass a warpmouth through the wall of a living cell without hurting it," said Randy. "Once the warpmouth is inside, we can expand it enough to warp a nanomachine through. The nanomachine would do its job, then warp back out again. Since we don't damage the cell wall, the yield should be close to one hundred percent."

"There are an awful lot of cells in a human body," mused Steve. "But the way computer power is increasing every year, it should soon be possible to treat every single cell in a human body in a reasonable period of time."

"I think, Mr. Hunter," said Dr. Garibaldi, "you two have just described the McPhie Procedure."

➤   ➤   ➤

Summer was nearly over when Randy got a message from the youngster traveling back home on *Rip van Winkle*. After a long conversation, the two of them expanded it into a three-way conversation with Alan Davidson, and a decision was made.

That night at dinner, Junior said, "Dad? I'll be entering Princeton in a few weeks, and I was wondering if it would be OK for me to get my own apartment near the campus."

"Sure, son," said Randy. "We can certainly afford it. But I was going to discuss something else with you tonight that might have a bearing on that decision."

"What?" asked Junior, a little puzzled.

"You are also going to turn eighteen in a month," said Randy, pausing to wipe his beard with his napkin. "I just finished a long conversation with Alan and your other father. If you are willing to accept the responsibility, we would like you to take over as president of Reinhold Astroengineering Company on your eighteenth birthday."

"What!?!" cried Junior, completely overwhelmed.

"I'm sure you can do it," said Randy calmly. "I did it with even less preparation than you have."

"If he's going to get to be president of Reinhold Astroengineering

Company for his eighteenth birthday," interrupted Rosey, "what am *I* going to get for *my* eighteenth birthday?"

"You will see, Rosey," said Randy, smiling at her. "I can guarantee it will be just what you wanted." He turned back to Junior. "It'll mean that you'll have to take college courses part-time, but you'll be getting a lot of on-the-job training."

"OK . . ." Junior hesitated. "As long as I'll have you and Alan Davidson around to give me advice."

"I'm sure Alan Davidson will stay around as long as you want him," said Randy. "But your mother and I are going to have to leave in about fifteen months, right after your other father sets up the timegate."

"You're leaving!" said Rosey and Junior simultaneously.

"I've already told you that your mother and I are going to be the first ones to receive immortality treatments," Randy said. "We will have to go almost a hundred years into the future where they have the technology adequately developed. The treatments to produce immortality in the body are quite lengthy, and stretch out over almost five years. But once they are complete, we will live forever."

"I still think we should delay our departure, dear," said Rose. "At least until Rosey has gone off to college."

"As the message from the future explained," said Randy, "the one thing the treatments can't do is resurrect memories lost when a brain cell dies. The sooner we get under treatment, the more memory and capability we will retain."

"I'm thirteen—I can take care of myself, Mom," said Rosey. "You go get your treatment."

"I'll take good care of Rosey, Mom," Junior said.

"Phooey with that!" said Rosey contumaciously. "I want my own apartment."

"When you are eighteen, you can do what you want," Randy reassured her. "But until then, you had better stay at the mansion with Junior. Besides, it isn't that we are going to be gone long—at least as far as you two are concerned. As soon as we complete our five years of treatment, we will just hop back again through time. The only problem is that timegates jump over chunks of time. This first one covers twenty-three and a half years at a time."

Randy turned to look at Junior. "In the coming years, you will want to have the Reinhold engineers make timegates with different-length time hops, say twelve, six, and three years, then sixteen, eight, four, and two months, and smaller hops all the way down to a day or so. That way, by choosing the right sequence of timegates, we can come back to this time soon after we leave. Your mother and I can then live here in the mansion with you both until Rosey goes to college. Then, with you both properly launched, we can take off to explore the future."

"Even then," Rose added, "we will be coming back to visit often—especially to see our grandchildren."

"And great-grandchildren, and great-great-grandchildren, and . . ." Randy continued thoughtfully and quietly, awe in his voice. The somber realization of what it really meant to have true immortality as well as access to time machines was finally beginning to sink into Randy's consciousness.

Rosey broke the spell. "Fine thing!" she blustered. "I'm thirteen, have no boyfriends to speak of, and you two are already talking about me being a grandmother!"

"I'm sure you'll get married to a nice boy one of these days, dear," said Rose.

Rosey turned quickly to her dad. She wasn't dumb—her father had been in the future and probably knew if she ever got married or not. "Will I get married?"

Randy hesitated. Rosey was always quizzing him about the future, but for her own peace of mind he had avoided telling her too much—not that he had learned that much during his brief visits to the solar system between bouts of flying spacecraft at high gees. He had learned, however, about Rosey being married and having a househusband from Harold, Junior, over a trout dinner some twelve years in the future.

"Will I?" repeated Rosey, boring in.

Randy paused to think, then decided that it wouldn't hurt her to know. "Yes," he finally replied.

"What's his name?" persisted Rosey.

Randy was glad he didn't know—for sure Rosey would soon have it out of him.

"Mike? Jim? Pete?" queried Rosey, peering at her father's eyes for some clue.

"I honestly don't know," replied Randy with a relieved smile. "Harold didn't happen to tell me his name when we were talking about him."

"Who's Harold?" interjected Junior.

"The president of Reinhold Astroengineering Company," replied Randy, chuckling. "You don't call the president of a major company 'Junior.'"

"Oh!" said Junior, finally understanding. "Me!"

"Yes, you. And you can start learning about your new job as president tomorrow," said Randy. "You have an appointment with Alan Davidson and the company comptroller at nine."

"Right, Dad," said Junior, shooting out his cuff-comp and making an entry in his appointment calendar.

➤   ➤   ➤

"Well, we're all set," said Randy, standing with Rose on the porch, waiting for Franklin to bring the limousine around. "It seems so final," said Rose.

"It's just the beginning . . ." replied Randy, awed by the near infinity of lifetime that stretched before him. He looked up at the evening sky. There were now so many large objects in near-Earth space that he had long ago given up trying any serious ground astronomy from his backyard. He picked out the Reinhold Space Station, which would soon hold the two ends of the first timegate.

Franklin drove up.

"Are you two coming?" Randy hollered through the door at the youngsters.

➤   ➤   ➤

Everyone was waiting in the Space Station reception room when Andrew opened the door and the man with the mustache walked in.

Randy, in a bemused, almost paternal mood, watched the young man stride into the room. *I can't imagine that I was once that smart-aleck youngster, swashbuckling into the room sporting that silly-looking mustache. I must have thought I was Errol Flynn incarnate.*

Rose and Rosey smothered the man with kisses. Rosey stepped back giggling and rubbing her cheek. "That *tickles*, Daddy!" she squealed. Rose stayed in the man's arms and he gave her a long kiss.

What does Rose see in him, anyway? thought Randy, his mood becoming less paternal.

The clinch went on far too long. To break it up, Randy went over with his hand extended. "Hello, young man," he said. "Glad to see you got *this* far in good time, at least."

After the conversation had gone on for a while, Andrew looked at the time on his cuff-comp. "The next rotovator that connects to the space station holding the Tau Ceti warpgate will be arriving shortly," he reminded them.

"I guess I better say good-bye," said the mustached youngster. "Got to go off and rescue the kid in his mansion in the sky." He gave Rosey a big hug and Rose another kiss that went on far too long.

"Ahem!" said Randy, to break it up.

The man shook hands all around, ending with Junior. "I'll be keeping in touch through the videolink," he said. "But I'm glad to know the company is in good hands." The young man took his two green metal boxes from Andrew, stroked his mustache, waved good-bye, and left.

➤　　➤　　➤

Two days later, Alan and the children took Randy and Rose to the timegate room. The door to the room was built like a bank-vault door with a combination lock.

Alan explained. "We wanted to make sure that there is no unauthorized use of the timegate until we completely understand all its ramifications."

Junior punched in the combination and the door opened into a cubical room three meters on a side. They all went inside and Junior shut the door behind them. On the walls to the right and left of the rectangular entry door were two pentagonal doors, one labeled PAST, the other FUTURE. During the night, the artificial warpmouth that had been brought through the Silverhair from the future had been expanded and sealed in a tubular vacuum frame that had been prepared for it. One pentagon of the frame surrounded one of the pentagonal doors, while the rest of the pentagons had been blocked off and sealed into a doorless room on the other side of the wall. Each pentagonal door was also armored and had a combination lock. Above each door was an electronic clock with the date and time. On one door, the electronic clock was blank, and would stay blank for twenty-three years until the artificial warpmouth at the other end of the timegate was installed in the waiting frame. On the other door the electronic clock read *1252 GMT TUE 19 SEPT 2079*.

"Are you ready?" asked Junior.

"Are you?" asked Randy. "When you open that door, you three are going to see older versions of yourselves."

"I'd forgotten about that," said Junior. He punched in the combination and the pentagonal door to the future opened. The matching door in the future timegate room had already been swung back, and Randy glanced at the strangely silent Alan, Junior, and Rosey as their eyes widened at seeing themselves in the future. With them were some strangers and a number of children.

What struck Randy first was everyone's glowing health. The younger children, especially, had blemish-free skin, shining hair, intelligent bright eyes, healthy muscle tone, strong limbs, and beautiful faces and teeth. They looked like young Greek gods and goddesses. No makeup was needed for those vibrant, rosy-cheeked faces. With such beautiful hair to work with, everyone, men and woman alike, wore their hair long, men in shoulder-length curls and women in long braids that went down to their knees.

Men's fashions hadn't changed much, but nearly every suit had some sort of subtle holographic pattern either above or below the surface. The women's dresses, however, were spectacular. All the women and girls wore simple, long white sheaths that fell from the shoulder almost to the floor. Flowing over each sheath was a continuously moving, three-dimensional holographic image in living color. The skirt of one little girl had an image of a field of blowing flowers with bunny rabbits hopping everywhere. A matronly Rosey had a waterfall cascading down her body. Occasionally a salmon could be seen jumping up the falls.

"Hey, me!" Rosey called over to herself. "Like your braid. Think I'll grow one like it."

"Do it! You'll start a new fashion," replied the older Rosey with an amused smile.

"Shall we go, Rose?" said Randy, taking her hand and stepping through the door.

➤   ➤   ➤

When Randy and Rose stepped into the future timegate room, Rose immediately went to hug the matronly Rosey and the many grandchildren. Behind them, a mature Junior was closing the door that said PAST. The date on the electronic clock over the door was *0909 GMT SUN 06 FEB 2056*.

"Hello, Harold," said Randy, remembering that Junior was now a forty-three-year-old man who had been running Reinhold Company for nearly a quarter of a century. Standing next to Harold was an elderly Alan Davidson, a holographic tweed shimmering over his suit. "You're looking spry, Alan."

"Harold and Rosey keep me busy," said Alan.

"I'd like to stop and visit," said Randy, "but we'd best be getting on. We'll come back for a long stay as soon as we've finished our treatments."

"We've already enjoyed a number of your visits," said Harold.

Randy and Rose were then introduced all around to Harold's and Rosey's spouses and children. Randy stopped to chat with one teenage son of Rosey. His shirt was producing a moving three-dimensional kaleidoscope of brightly colored patterns. From each of his shoulders there emerged music directed at the boy's ears. The sound was so closely directed that the music couldn't be heard unless you were very close to the boy.

"Is that the Deadly Scum I hear?" asked Randy, wincing at the somewhat familiar guitar solo that often blasted out of Rosey's bedroom when she opened her bedroom door.

"Yezza, Granddad," replied the boy politely. "I switched my shirt to a nice quiet 'oldie-fogie' when I knew you were about to arrive."

"That's quite an amazing shirt," said Randy. "Moving three-dee images *and* sound."

"It's a Silvershirt," replied the boy.

Harold interrupted. "The Silverhairs turned out to have excellent artistic as well as musical talents. In addition to music videos, they now have their own line of designer holoclothing, with those unique synthesized three-dee patterns in them."

"They seem to be doing all right for themselves." Randy nodded in satisfaction. "Anything come of Elena's observations of the Boötes Void?"

"She has seen some occultations of background galaxies by distant objects," replied Harold. "But nothing definite yet."

"I'll soon know if she was successful in the future," said Randy.

When the introductions were all completed, Harold shooed the future family out. "The Timegate Control Board insists that sightseers be kept to a minimum." After he got the timegate room cleared, he turned to his parents.

"Are you ready?" he said.

"Are you?" asked Randy, holding Rose by the hand. "You're going to see a much older version of yourself on the other side of the door."

"I don't look anymore," said Harold. He punched the combination on the door that read FUTURE and slowly pulled the door open, staying behind it so the door blocked his view into the future. The heavy door from the other side also started to slowly swing open.

Holding Rose by the hand, Randy started for the opening door. The date on the electronic clock read *0126 GMT FRI 05 MAY 2103*.

Rose, looking with apprehension at the date, hesitated. "I'm afraid . . ." she said, holding back.

Randy came back to Rose, put his arms around her, and gave her a reassuring hug. Then, trying to lighten the moment, he stepped back, twisted his face into that of a hard-bitten cowboy, and tugged at her arm.

"Come on, Rose!" he growled in an imitation John Wayne voice. "Do you want to live forever?"

5 March 2056 and 18 October 2079

FINAL REPORT
TO THE

REINHOLD ASTROENGINEERING COMPANY
BOARD OF DIRECTORS

AND THE

REINHOLD TRUST
BOARD OF TRUSTEES

CONCERNING THE INTER VIVOS TRUST
OF HAROLD RANDOLPH HUGHES

Alan V. Davidson
Senior Trust Officer
Sequence National Bank

SUMMARY

With the resignation of Harold Randolph Hunter (HRH) as president of Reinhold Astroengineering Company in favor of his son Harold Randolph Hunter, Junior, the disbursement of most of his personal fortune to charitable works, and his permanent departure into future time, the necessity for a Trust Officer to manage his personal and business affairs through an Inter Vivos Trust during his frequent absences is no longer necessary.

This report summarizes the activities carried out by the Trust Officer during the duration of the trusteeship. A major portion of the report documents the important activities engaged in by HRH during the period of the trusteeship.

During the period of the trusteeship, HRH, through Reinhold Astroengineering Company, developed the techniques for rapid interstellar commerce between a majority of the "interesting" nearby star systems. A list of those star systems and a map of their relative positions in space are also to be found in the following pages.

At the end of the report are appendices, which by means of simple tables and diagrams give some of the important technical parameters and apparatuses mentioned in the body of the report.

EARLY INTERSTELLAR COMMERCE

The first interstellar voyages happened much differently than had been originally envisioned. Instead of initially exploring a star system with unmanned probes, then decades later sending exploration vehicles crewed by humans, the development of the Reinhold Negmatter Drive revolutionized space travel by allowing the initial exploration of the nearer stars to be carried out by a human crew (usually in the person of Harold Randolph Hunter) in less than a decade.

A Reinhold Negmatter Drive has the capability to operate at high accelerations, thus allowing relativistic velocities to be reached in weeks or months instead of years. The upper bound on the spacecraft velocity is limited only by the effectiveness of the ship's shields against the radiation generated by the passage of the spacecraft through interstellar gas and dust. The shields consist primarily of superstrong magnetic fields that surround the spacecraft out to great distances. The magnetic fields strip apart the gas molecules and smaller dust particles and deflect the resultant charged particles away from the rapidly moving spacecraft. The few larger dust particles, cosmic rays, and occasional stray molecule that slip through the magnetic field barriers are nullified by negative-matter shields. The early versions of the Reinhold spacecraft were limited to 0.8 c, while later versions could reach 0.98 c with no radiation danger to the crew, and 0.995 c under emergency conditions.

The first visit to an extrasolar star system was the exploration of the nearest system, Alpha Centauri, by HRH in 2042. Also known as Rigil Kentaurus, Alpha Centauri is the brightest star in the southern constellation Centaurus, and the third-brightest star in the sky after Sirius and Canopus. Alpha Centauri is not a single star, but a collection of three stars. The nearest of these, at a distance of 4.3 light-years, is a small red dwarf star called Proxima Centauri. The other two stars are one-tenth of a light-year farther away and are called Alpha Centauri A and B. Alpha Centauri A is similar to our sun, while B is slightly redder. These two stars orbit around each other every 80 years, while Proxima Centauri circles the pair with a period of millions of years. Proxima Centauri happens to be closer to the solar system at this point in its long orbit.

HRH traveled in one of the first-generation Negmatter Drive interstellar spacecraft, capable of an acceleration of one Earth gravity and a top speed of 80% of the speed of light. A disadvantage of the first-generation spacecraft was that the wormhole mouths carried in the ship were living Silverhairs. Because of the fragility of the Silverhair body, these wormholes could only be dilated for use when the relative velocity of the ship and Sol were near zero. Thus, although the person on board the ship could use laser links to communicate through the wormholes with the people back at Sol, the person had to stay on the ship until the ship had decelerated.

After successfully arriving at Proxima Centauri and discovering a potential earthlike planet, "Hunter," HRH then opened up a warpgate between Sol and the Alpha Centauri system. Shortly thereafter he demonstrated the rapid, economical transportation of people, goods, and raw materials over interstellar distances using the warpgates, thus establishing the economic feasibility of interstellar commerce. With a monopoly on the source of negmatter, HRH then committed Reinhold Astroengineering Company to a planned program for the installation and operation of a network of warpgates to the more commercially promising of the nearer star systems. Information on those star systems follows:

First is a listing of those Sun-like or otherwise interesting stars within twenty light-years, listed in order of their distance from the Sun. Multiple star systems are denoted by letters after the star name. Also shown are spacings between the stars when the distance is significantly less than the distance to Sol. Next is a three-dimensional plot of all the interesting stars within 16 light-years, showing their relative position in an Earth-oriented equatorial coordinate system, where the +Z direction is toward the north pole. Next is a projection on the equatorial plane of all the stars within 16 lightyears close to the equatorial plane of Earth. Dotted lines show the distances between neighboring stars, especially in the Ceti and Eridani sections of the sky. Note the commercially interesting "trade routes" with the two sunlike stars, Epsilon Eridani and Tau Ceti, as hubs.

SUN-LIKE (OR INTERESTING) STARS WITHIN 20 LIGHT-YEARS

| | | Dist. | Coordinates from Sun | | | Spacing |
| | | | X | Y | Z | |
	Type	(ly)	(ly)	(ly)	(ly)	(ly)
Alpha Cent. A,B,C	G2	4.4	− 1.7	− 1.4	− 3.8	
Barnard	M5	5.9	− 0.1	− 5.9	+ 0.5	
Lalande	M2	8.1	− 6.3	+ 1.7	+ 4.8	
Sirius A,B	A1	8.7	− 1.6	+ 8.2	− 2.5	
UV Ceti A,B	M6	8.9	+ 7.7	+ 3.4	− 2.8	5.3
Epsilon Eridani	K2	10.7	+ 6.4	+ 8.4	− 1.8	
61 Cygni A,B	K5	11.2	+ 6.3	− 6.1	+ 7.0	5.5 3.0
Epsilon Indi	K5	11.2	+ 5.3	− 3.0	− 9.4	5.8
Procyon A,B	F5	11.4	− 4.7	+10.3	+ 1.1	
Tau Ceti	G8	11.9	+10.3	+ 4.9	− 3.3	
Groombridge	K7	15.0	− 8.6	+ 4.6	+11.4	9.8
40 Eridani A,B,C	K0	15.9	+ 7.1	+14.1	− 2.1	
Altair	A7	16.6	+ 7.4	−14.6	+ 2.5	7.7
70 Ophiuchi A,B	K1	16.7	+ 0.2	−16.7	+ 0.7	
36 Ophiuchi A,B,C	K1	17.7	− 3.3	−15.5	− 7.9	
Sigma Draconis	K0	18.5	+ 2.5	− 5.9	+17.3	
Delta Pavonis	G6	18.6	+ 3.8	− 6.4	−17.0	
Eta Cassiopeia	G0	19.2	+10.1	+ 2.1	+16.2	

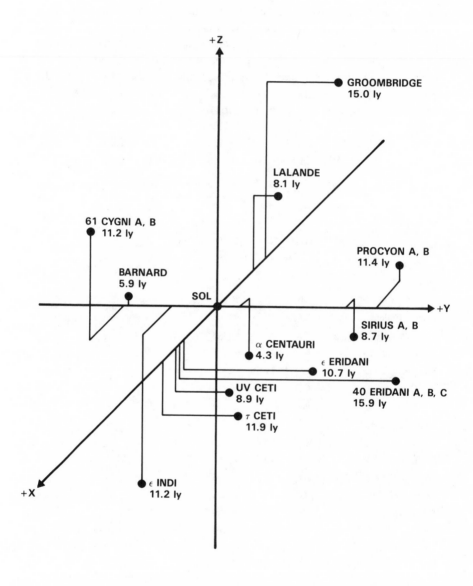

Interesting Stars Within 16 Light-Years

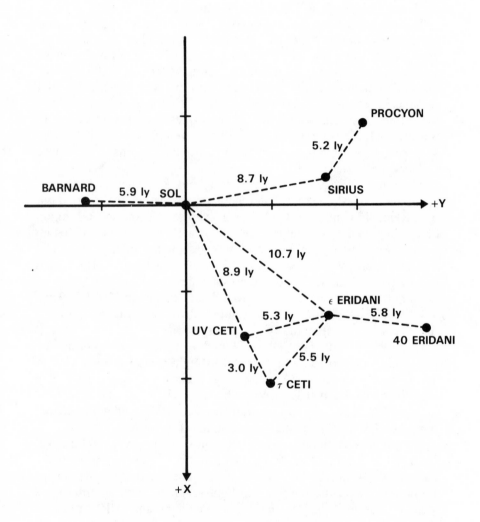

Interesting Stars Less Than 16 Light-Years With Z<R/3

HRH then undertook a second voyage, this time to the Barnard star system. He left in 2043, arriving at Barnard in late 2048. A half-year after HRH left, still in 2043, another Reinhold Astroengineering Company employee, Robert Pilcher, and two companions, started off on the third journey, to Lalande at 8.1 light-years.

The next trip undertaken was to the scientifically interesting star system Sirius in late 2044. This system is dominated by the very large, very bright, white-hot star, Sirius A; Sirius B is a small white dwarf star, with the mass of a star but the radius of the Earth. Because of the radiation hazard from the large star, this star system was not suitable for commercial exploration, and HRH made the decision not to explore the system with Reinhold employees despite its closeness to Sol. Instead, the system was explored for scientific reasons by a crew of research astrophysicists employed by the International Space University (ISU).

The fourth voyage sponsored by Reinhold Astroengineering Company, and the last one in a first-generation spacecraft, was carried out by a Reinhold employee, C.C. Wong, who set off for the Ceti region of the sky in 2044. Leaving Sol at Galactic date 2044, with two Silverhair warpgate mouths, Wong traveled the 8.9 light-years to UV Ceti at a speed of 0.8 c, arriving at 2056.1 Galactic time. He dilated one of the wormhole mouths and established contact with Sol. The wormhole mouth connected back to Sol at Galactic time 2051.8. Thus a Sol-to-UV-Ceti warpgate was established with a spatial jump of 8.9 lightyears and a time jump of 4.3 years.

C.C. Wong left UV Ceti at 2056.3 Galactic time carrying the remaining wormhole mouth over the 3.0 light-years from UV Ceti to Tau Ceti at a speed of 0.8 c, arriving at 2061.0 Galactic time. The wormhole mouth left at Tau Ceti connected back to Sol at Galactic time 2054.5. Thus a Sol-to-Tau-Ceti warpgate was established with a spatial jump of 11.9 light-years and a time jump of 5.5 years.

During these exploration trips, HRH finished his voyage to Barnard. He arrived at Barnard in 2051.3 Galactic time and set up a warpgate back to the year 2048.6 Sol rest time. The warpgate from Sol to Barnard had a spatial jump of 4.3 light-years and a time jump of 2.7 years. After exploring Barnard for a few months, HRH returned through the warpgate to Sol and Earth in 2049. A year later, in 2050, he was ready to take another trip.

EXPLANATION OF HRH CRITICAL TIMELINE DIAGRAM

Most of the important history of Reinhold Astroengineering Company and the Reinhold Trust occurred between the years 2050 and

2080, when Harold Randolph Hunter established the first major interstellar trade routes to and between the nearby Sun-like stars in the Ceti and Eridani sections of the Local Galactic Region. In the process he created the nearly-24-year timegate on Sol that has had a significant positive impact on Reinhold Astroengineering Company profits. The timegate also, incidentally, forever changed the future course of the entire universe. The actions of HRH during that time are depicted in the following spacetime diagram. The proper ages of HRH at each of the event points on the diagram are listed in the table following the diagram.

(In the diagram, distances are measured in light-years and time in years. Note that the scale length of a year is half as long as the scale length of a light-year, so the trajectories of light beams will not be at 45 degrees as is the usual custom with a spacetime diagram. Also, even though many of the star positions have a significant negative-Z component with respect to Sol (ranging from -1.8 ly for Epsilon Eridani to -3.3 ly for Tau Ceti), the Z component has been suppressed and all the stars are assumed to be at $Z = 0$ at time $T = 0$. The stars are assumed to be at rest, so that the proper time of each star system moves forward in the T direction at the same rate as Sol rest time. This is not strictly true since the stars are in relative motion, but is close enough that we can define an effective "Galactic" time and date that is essentially the same for all stars near the solar system.)

For his trip to Epsilon Eridani, HRH used a large personalized version of a Reinhold Negmatter Drive interstellar spacecraft called *Spacemaster*. The ship had acceleration couches for the crew that allowed acceleration up to 5 Earth gravities and improved radiation shields that allowed a top speed of 0.995 c.

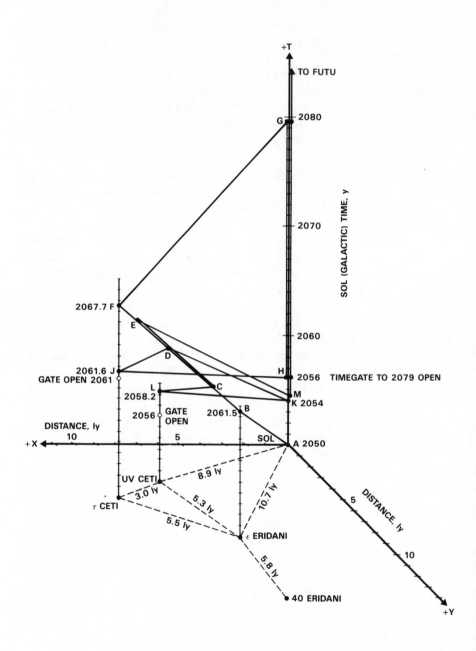

HRH Timeline Diagram

HRH TIMELINE AND AGES

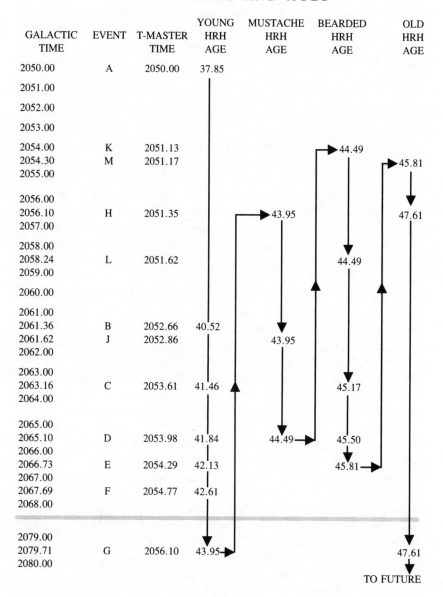

GALACTIC TIME	EVENT	T-MASTER TIME	YOUNG HRH AGE	MUSTACHE HRH AGE	BEARDED HRH AGE	OLD HRH AGE
2050.00	A	2050.00	37.85			
2051.00						
2052.00						
2053.00						
2054.00	K	2051.13			44.49	
2054.30	M	2051.17				45.81
2055.00						
2056.00						
2056.10	H	2051.35		43.95		47.61
2057.00						
2058.00						
2058.24	L	2051.62			44.49	
2059.00						
2060.00						
2061.00						
2061.36	B	2052.66	40.52			
2061.62	J	2052.86		43.95		
2062.00						
2063.00						
2063.16	C	2053.61	41.46		45.17	
2064.00						
2065.00						
2065.10	D	2053.98	41.84	44.49	45.50	
2066.00						
2066.73	E	2054.29	42.13		45.81	
2067.00						
2067.69	F	2054.77	42.61			
2068.00						
2079.00						
2079.71	G	2056.10	43.95			47.61
2080.00						

TO FUTURE

HRH left Sol in 2050.0 (Point **A** in diagram) and accelerated at 3 Earth gravities for 9 months until the ship reached 0.98 c. HRH arrived at Epsilon Eridani (Point **B** in diagram) at 2061.4 Galactic time. The wormhole mouth he left at Epsilon Eridani connected back to Sol at a Galactic time of 2052.7. Thus, a Sol-to-Epsilon-Eridani warpgate was established with a spatial jump of 10.7 light-years and a time jump of 8.7 years.

For a combination of personal, business, and humanitarian reasons, HRH decided to travel toward the Ceti system to shorten the distance between him and the warpmouth at UV Ceti so he could set up a communications link to the future. Since C.C. Wong had reported nothing of commercial interest at UV Ceti, HRH decided not to travel directly toward UV Ceti, but to the Sun-like star Tau Ceti instead. In this way he could open up a direct warpgate connection between the two commercially important Sun-like stars, Epsilon Eridani and Tau Ceti, at the same time he was setting up a future-time communications link. Renaming his ship *Timemaster*, HRH left Epsilon Eridani at 2061.6 Galactic time. The wormhole mouth on *Timemaster* connected back to Sol at 2052.9 Galactic time.

Senator Oscar Barkham objected to the idea of creating a future-time communications link, and went to discuss the matter with HRH (point **C** in diagram). Barkham argued with HRH, attempting to make him turn back, but HRH refused. Barkham attempted to stab HRH, but was restrained by an older HRH who had arrived from the future. The two HRHs forced Barkham to pod back to Earth, and directed the Reinhold Astroengineering Company workers in charge of the entire net of warpgates not to let Barkham through any of the warpgates.

A few days later, Barkham managed to steal a third-generation Reinhold Astroengineering Company starship under construction around Sol. In its hold were parts for an electromagnetic launcher. Barkham left the solar system in 2053.7 Galactic time and accelerated for a month ship time at 30 gees to reach 0.995 c. Disregarding the radiation dose, he continued to coast at 0.995 c for 14 months ship time. During this time, he used the ship's robots to convert the electromagnetic launcher into an electromagnetic gun that shot superconducting projectiles. Barkham caught up with the HRH ship at point **D** in the diagram along HRH's track from Epsilon Eridani to Tau Ceti.

Oscar Barkham attacked the HRH ship at point **D** with superconducting projectiles, but his projectiles were destroyed and his ship was deflected by a cloud of dense gas emitted by another Negmatter Drive ship that intercepted him. Barkham turned his ship around and accelerated after the HRH ship in a tail chase at relativistic speeds. Barkham caught up with the HRH ship and attempted one more attack at point **E** in the diagram.

Barkham was defeated by a timetrap set up at point **E** that repelled his remaining missiles and even his attempt to ram HRH's ship. Barkham did not survive the attack.

HRH finally arrived at point **F** at Tau Ceti in 2067.7 Galactic time with a wormhole mouth that connected back to Sol at 2054.8 Galactic time. HRH knew that it was important that he arrive back early enough to save himself from Barkham's attacks. The Reinhold employees had a third-generation ship ready for him, which he named *Rip Van Winkle*. He transferred the ship-Sol warpmouth from *Timemaster* to *Rip Van Winkle* and traveled back from point **F** at Tau Ceti to point **G** at Sol at maximum-safe acceleration and speed.

After traveling only 16 months ship time during the 11.9-light-year journey, HRH arrived at Sol at 2079.7 Galactic time. The wormhole mouth that had been traveling with him connected back to Sol at 2056.1 Galactic time. The side-by-side mouths of the wormhole now formed a timegate with a spatial jump of zero and a time jump of 23.6 years.

Since time was still of some urgency, as soon as the timegate had been sufficiently dilated, HRH stepped through the timegate from point **G** on the diagram in the year 2079.7 to point **H** in the year 2056.1. Shortly thereafter, he went to the mouth of the warpgate from Sol to Tau Ceti, and stepped through to arrive at point **J** around Tau Ceti at 2061.6 Galactic time. There he boarded another third-generation Negmatter Drive ship, the *John Wayne*, readied for him by Reinhold Astroengineering Company employees. The hold had been modified to hold liquid hydrogen. HRH flew the ship at maximum acceleration and speed toward point **D** in the diagram along the track of *Timemaster* from Epsilon Eridani to Tau Ceti.

HRH jettisoned his cargo of hydrogen prior to his arrival at point **D**. The cloud of hydrogen gas moved ahead of the *John Wayne* as it decelerated and turned to match speeds with *Timemaster*. The dense cloud of hydrogen gas burned up the projectiles and deflected Barkham's ship off its collision course with *Timemaster*. The older HRH then matched speeds with *Timemaster*, boarded it, and met the younger HRH. They dilated the wormhole mouth on *Timemaster* and the older HRH used the warpgate to go from point **D** to point **K** on Sol, arriving at 2054.0 Sol rest time. At Sol, the older HRH used the

Sol-to-UV-Ceti warpgate to go from point **K** on Sol to point **L** on UV Ceti, arriving at 2058.2 Galactic time.

HRH then boarded another Reinhold Astroengineering Company spacecraft, the *Errol Flynn*. HRH left point **L** at UV Ceti at 2058.2 Galactic time and went off to intercept *Timemaster* at point **C** on its journey from Epsilon Eridani to Tau Ceti. HRH arrived just in time to prevent the attempted stabbing of the younger HRH by Barkham at point **D**.

The older HRH then accelerated the *Errol Flynn* on ahead toward Tau Ceti. Once the *Errol Flynn* was sufficiently ahead of *Timemaster*, HRH decelerated the ship. He then deployed one mouth of a pair of artificial wormhole mouths and left it floating in space, while he took the other mouth off a distance and brought it back. One mouth of the wormhole was now 1.6 seconds younger than the other mouth. He placed the 2 mouths about 120,000 kilometers (0.4 seconds light-travel time) apart, and set his ship robots to the months-long task of expanding the timegate mouths until they were 2000 kilometers across. The two wormhole mouths now constituted a timegate barrier, or "timetrap," that would automatically repel any high-speed object that attempted to enter the region between the two mouths. The two HRHs watched as Barkham made his last attack at point **E** and was defeated by the timetrap.

The oldest HRH then dilated the ship-Sol warpgate in *Timemaster* and went from point **E** along the track of *Timemaster* to point **M** on Sol at a Sol rest time of 2054.3. The oldest HRH then lived on Earth from 2054.3 Sol rest time to 2056.1 Sol rest time, during which period he closed out his affairs and turned the presidency of his company over to his 18-year-old son, Harold Randolph Hunter, Junior.

The oldest HRH was waiting at point **H** on Sol when the timegate from the future was first dilated. The oldest HRH greeted the younger HRH as he stepped through to the past. The oldest HRH then stepped through the timegate to make the first of his many 24-year-jumps into the future. At the end of the first jump, in the year 2079.7 Sol rest frame time, HRH met this Trust Officer for the last time, and stepped off through the timegate into the future.

APPENDIX — TIMETRAPS

An example of a timegate barrier or timetrap is shown in the following diagram. Two mouths of a Morris-Thorne Wormhole are spaced 0.4 light-seconds (120,000 kilometers distance) apart. One mouth of the wormhole is 1.6 seconds older than the other mouth and rotated 180 degrees about the line between the 2 mouths. This creates a "barrier" around the region between the 2 mouths. Any object with a sufficiently high velocity attempting to enter the barrier region will interact with itself in such a way that—in effect—it is sent back the way it came.

In the diagram, an object moving at 4.3% c approaches the timetrap. At time 0.2 seconds, an older version of the object appears out of the younger wormhole mouth traveling at 5% c. At time 1.0 seconds, the incoming object experiences a collision with the older version of itself, causing the incoming object to be deflected into the older mouth with velocity of 5% c. It enters the older mouth at time 1.8 seconds, travels through the wormhole to the other mouth, and emerges from the younger mouth at time $1.8 - 1.6 = 0.2$ seconds. The object is now moving at just the right velocity and direction to collide with the incoming version of itself in just the right way to deflect the incoming version into the older mouth, while the older version proceeds away from the timegate barrier in the opposite direction to the incoming object at 4.3% c, the speed of the incoming object. The net effect is equivalent to having the incoming object repelled by the timegate barrier region.

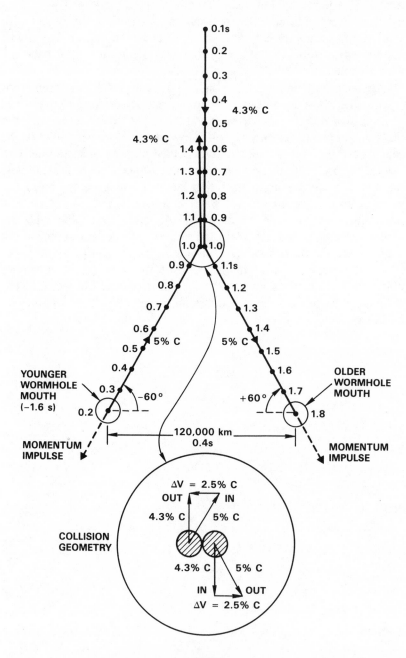

Timetrap

BIBLIOGRAPHY

Echeverria, Fernando, Gunnar Klinkhammer, and Kip S. Thorne. "Billiard Balls in Wormhole Spacetimes with Closed Timelike Curves: Classical Theory." *Physical Review* D44 (15 August 1991): 1077–1099.

Forward, Robert L. *Future Magic*. New York: Avon Books, 1988.

————"Space Warps: A Review of One Form of Propulsionless Transport." *Journal of the British Interplanetary Society* 42 (November 1989): 533–542.

————. "Negative Matter Propulsion." *Journal of Propulsion and Power* 5, no. 1 (January–February 1990): 28–37.

————. "Cable Catapult." AIAA Paper 90-2108, presented at the AIAA/ASME/SAE/ASEE 26th Joint Propulsion Conference, Orlando, Florida, 16–18 July 1990.

Friedman, John, Michael S. Morris, Igor D. Novikov, Fernando Echeverria, Gunnar Klinkhammer, Kip S. Thorne, and Ulvi Yurtsever. "Cauchy Problem in Spacetimes with Closed Timelike Curves." *Physical Review* D42 (1990): 1915–1930.

Garfinkle, David, and Andrew Strominger. "Semiclassical Wheeler Wormhole Production." Physics Letters B256, No.2 (7 March 1991).

Heinlein, Robert A. "All You Zombies." *Magazine of Fantasy and Science Fiction* (March 1959).

Mallove, Eugene F., and Gregory L. Matloff. *The Starflight Handbook*. New York: John Wiley & Sons, 1989.

Moravec, Hans. "A Non-Synchronous Orbital Skyhook." *Journal of the Astronautical Sciences* 25, no. 4 (October–December 1977): 307–322.

————. "Time Travel and Computing." Preprint. Robotics Institute, Carnegie Mellon University, Pittsburgh, May 1991.

Morris, Michael S., and Kip S. Thorne. "Wormholes in Spacetime and Their Use for Interstellar Travel: A Tool for Teaching General Relativity." *American Journal of Physics* 56 (May 1988): 395–412.

Morris, Michael S., Kip S. Thorne, and Ulvi Yurtsever. "Wormholes, Time Machines, and the Weak Energy Condition." *Physical Review Letters* 61 (26 September 1988): 1446–1449.

Novikov, I.D. "An Analysis of the Operation of a Time Machine" (English translation). *Soviet Physics JETP* 68 (March 1989): 439–443.

————. "The Time Machine and Self-Consistent Evolutions in Problems with Self-Interaction." Preprint NORDITA-90/38A. Nordisk Institut for Teoretisk Fysik, Copenhagen, and P.N. Lebedev Physical Institute, Moscow, February 1990.

Penzo, Paul A., and Paul W. Ammann. *Tethers in Space Handbook.* 2d ed. Washington, DC: NASA Office of Space Flight, 1989.

Pomeranz, Kalman B. "The Relativistic Rocket." *American Journal of Physics* (1965): 565–566.

Visser, Matt. "Traversable Wormholes: Some Simple Examples." *Physical Review* D39 (15 May 1989): 3182–3184.

ABOUT THE AUTHOR

Dr. Robert L. Forward writes science fiction novels and short stories as well as science fact books and magazine articles. Through his scientific consulting company, Forward Unlimited, he also engages in contracted research on the topics of advanced space propulsion and exotic physical phenomena.

Dr. Forward obtained his Ph.D. in Gravitational Physics from the University of Maryland. For his thesis he constructed and operated the world's first bar antenna for the detection of gravitational radiation. The antenna is now at the Smithsonian Museum.

For thirty-one years, from 1956 to 1987, when he left in order to spend more time writing, Dr. Forward worked at the Hughes Aircraft Company Corporate Research Laboratories in Malibu, California, in positions of increasing responsibility, culminating with the position of Senior Scientist on the staff of the Director of the Laboratories. During that time he constructed and operated the world's first laser gravitational radiation detector, invented the rotating gravitational mass sensor, published over sixty-five technical publications, and was awarded eighteen patents.

From 1983 to the present, Dr. Forward has had a series of contracts from the Phillips Laboratory of the U.S. Air Force Systems Command (formerly the Air Force Rocket Propulsion Laboratory) to explore the forefront of physics and engineering in order to find new energy sources that will produce breakthroughs in space power and propulsion. He has published journal papers and contract reports on antiproton annihilation propulsion, laser beam and microwave beam interstellar propulsion, negative-matter propulsion, light-levitated perforated-sail communication satellites, space warps, and a method for extracting electrical energy from vacuum fluctuations.

In addition to his professional publications, Dr. Forward has written over eighty popular-science articles for publications such as the

Encyclopaedia Britannica Yearbook, *Omni*, *New Scientist*, *Aerospace America*, *Science Digest*, *Science 80*, *Analog*, and *Galaxy*. His most recent science fact books are *FUTURE MAGIC* and *MIRROR MATTER: PIONEERING ANTIMATTER PHYSICS* (with Joel Davis). His science fiction novels are *DRAGON'S EGG* and its sequel *STARQUAKE, THE FLIGHT OF THE DRAGONFLY* (also published in a longer version as *ROCHEWORLD*), *MARTIAN RAINBOW*, and now *TIMEMASTER*. The novels are of the "hard" science fiction category, where the science is as accurate as possible.

Dr. Forward is a Fellow of the British Interplanetary Society and Editor of the "Interstellar Studies" issues of its *Journal*, Associate Fellow of the American Institute of Aeronautics and Astronautics, Senior Member of the American Astronautical Society, and a member of the American Physical Society, Sigma Xi, Sigma Pi Sigma, National Space Society, and the Science Fiction Writers of America.